The Price Of Passion

Finally, Rachel and John were alone together. And, sensing an opportunity for her love to triumph over John's stubborn principles, Rachel wrapped her arms around him. Even through his heavy uniform, she could feel his firm muscles tense at her touch. But she persisted, lifting her head to press her lips to his.

Still, John did not respond. Could it be that he did not love her? Rachel pulled away, at a loss for words. Then, when she'd given up hope, she found herself in John's strong embrace. His large, powerful arms held her so tightly that she could feel the beat of his heart against her breasts.

"Rachel," he whispered, almost painfully. "You have no idea of the high price we will pay for this night. . . ."

BESTSELLING ROMANCES BY JANELLE TAYLOR

SAVAGE ECSTASY (824, $3.50)

It was like lightning striking, the first time the Indian brave Gray Eagle looked into the eyes of the beautiful young settler Alisha. And from the moment he saw her, he knew that he must possess her—and make her his slave!

DEFIANT ECSTASY (931, $3.50)

When Gray Eagle returned to Fort Pierre's gates with his hundred warriors behind him, Alisha's heart skipped a beat; would Gray Eagle destroy her—or make his destiny her own?

FORBIDDEN ECSTASY (1014, $3.50)

Gray Eagle had promised Alisha his heart forever—nothing could keep him from her. But when Alisha woke to find her red-skinned lover gone, she felt abandoned and alone. Lost between two worlds, desperate and fearful of betrayal, Alisha hungered for the return of her FORBIDDEN ECSTASY.

BRAZEN ECSTASY (1133, $3.50)

When Alisha is swept down a raging river and out of her savage brave's life, Gray Eagle must rescue his love again. But Alisha has no memory of him at all. And as she fights to recall a past love, another white slave woman in their camp is fighting for Gray Eagle!

Available wherever paperbacks are sold, or order direct from the Publisher. Send cover price plus 50¢ per copy for mailing and handling to Zebra Books, 475 Park Avenue South, New York, N.Y. 10016. DO NOT SEND CASH.

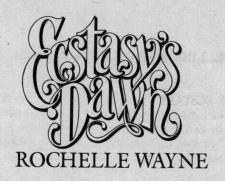

Ecstasy's Dawn

ROCHELLE WAYNE

ZEBRA BOOKS

KENSINGTON PUBLISHING CORP.

To my mother and father, with all my love

ZEBRA BOOKS

are published by

KENSINGTON PUBLISHING CORP.
475 Park Avenue South
New York, N.Y. 10016

Printed in the United States of America

PART ONE

Chapter One

Rachel O'Brian sat at the hotel window looking down on the activity in the dusty street below. Because she had lived her entire life in the quiet of the Knolls, her family plantation in Mississippi, the clamor and commotion of St. Joe caused her heart to race with expectations.

In the two weeks since Rachel and her family had arrived in St. Joseph, Missouri, she and her sister had been confined to the hotel. At the young age of sixteen, Rachel's spirit longed to be free of this restriction. She hoped the chance would come tonight. There would be a meeting of all the families going west. Word had spread that the wagon master had arrived and would meet with them at the church that evening. Afterwards, there would be music and dancing to celebrate.

Rachel wanted to attend the dance so desperately that she could barely control her impatience while she awaited her father's return. Being such a strong-willed young lady, Rachel fully believed that she'd be able to convince her father to let them go. As her father had often told her, "The Irish are a stubborn and hard-headed lot", and she had inherited both of these traits, handed down to her from Irish ancestors.

Absentmindedly she pushed her auburn hair away from her face as she wished restlessly that her father would hurry. Rachel was more enticing than she was beautiful because the expression in her eyes was usually obstinate and unyielding; but few men would ever find her less than beautiful when they became captivated by her natural and unsophisticated charms.

Leaning her head against the window she sighed in exasperation, "Please, Papa, let Deb and me have just one night of fun before our long journey begins."

Abruptly she sat upright as she saw her father crossing the street. He had gone to check on the wagon and the supplies, as they would be leaving sometime the next day. She noticed how he walked briskly and carried his tall but lean frame proudly. Her father refused to let the war destroy his will as it had destroyed the wills of others. Thomas O'Brian wouldn't give in and become beaten, because he was a survivor— another trait Rachel had unknowingly inherited.

She rose from the window seat and hurried across the bare floor to the door of the adjoining room which her parents shared. As she entered, her mother and sister looked up from their sewing.

Full of the enthusiasm only the young can possess, Rachel hastened over to her mother. "Papa's coming. Please Mama, ask him to let us go to the meeting tonight."

Her mother put down the shirt she had been mending. "Honey, don't get your hopes up too high. I don't think your father will let you and your sister go."

"But why, Mama!" she pleaded.

"You know your father's concern that you will come

8

into contact with the wrong kind of people.''

"I know, Mama, but these are the people we will be living with for the entire trip!"

Her mother started to reply but as she did her husband entered the room. Strolling over to his wife, he kissed her lightly on the cheek. "Everything is ready, dear. We will be pulling out sometime tomorrow."

Thomas O'Brian had at one time been a refined aristocratic planter. He'd ruled over his kingdom of cotton, land and slaves with a firm but honest hand. Never, in his wildest dreams, did he imagine that someday he'd lose it all. After the war his plantation had gone for taxes. He sold what he'd been able to hide of their silver and jewelry, but it hadn't been nearly adequate to pay the back taxes he owed.

He'd heard some of the men around town talking about California, where the soil was rich and fertile and the climate good all year round. It seemed there were people who had already gotten through to this miracle land. They'd mostly been trappers and mountain men, but a few families, he'd heard, had journeyed to California on wagon trains.

Thomas O'Brian knew there was nothing left for him in Mississippi. All he had to his name was his small hoard of money, with a wife and two daughters wholly dependent on him. As a plan began to form in his mind, he had asked himself, why not go to California and make a new start for himself and his family? He had no more and no less than his grandfather had when he first came to Mississippi from Ireland. From his grandfather's determination, skill, and, he always suspected, a little luck with the cards, he had built the magnificent plantation called "The Knolls".

9

Knowing he'd never be able to build another plantation in California, he hoped to start a small farm and perhaps in time it would prosper and grow. With thoughts of a new life he had decided to get all the information he would need about wagons heading west.

A few short hectic weeks later he had packed up his family and their possessions, left their homeland, and headed for St. Joseph, Missouri. There they would meet up with other families and form a wagon train, and then leave for California.

He looked over at his youngest daughter and smiled when he saw that she was watching him. He loved both of his daughters dearly, but he had a special feeling for Deborah. She resembled her mother, as he remembered her when they were young and falling in love.

Numerous times, he had asked himself if taking his family westward was a wise decision, and now with Deborah looking at him with such trusting eyes, he found himself asking the question again; but, he always came back with the same answer. What other choices do I have? The war took everything I owned. The Yankees have taken it all! Even my sons, and that, dear God, is what hurts the most!

He crossed over to Deborah and sat beside her on the threadbare couch. The hotel was old and it was cheap, but it was all he could afford. At least it was clean and respectable.

"What are you sewing, honey?" he asked.

"Just mending a dress, Papa." At fifteen, Deborah was beginning to blossom into the lovely woman she would someday become. He couldn't distinguish one feature and say it was her prettiest, because to him her beauty was flawless. Deborah was small, with hair as

black as a raven's and eyes so dark brown that sometimes they appeared to be the exact shade of her hair.

"Papa, are you going to the meeting tonight?"

He stopped thinking of Deborah and looked over at
the daughter that had spoken to him. "Yes, I'm going.
Why do you ask?"

Rachel took a deep breath, crossed her fingers behind her back for luck, and asked, "Are you taking
us?"

"Your mother and I are going, but you and Deborah
will stay here."

"But Papa, there's going to be a dance afterwards."

Anger flashed in his eyes as he replied, "We will not
be socializing with any Yankees!"

Rachel knew trying to persuade her father to change
his mind was futile, but she had to try! She just had to!
To miss this opportunity to attend a dance! Why she'd
never been to a dance in her entire life! Before the war
she had been too young, and during the war there had
been no opportunity. Oh, there had been a few parties
given at plantations nearby, but her oldest brother had
been killed early in the war. They were in mourning
and unable to accept social invitations. With the death
of her other brother her family remained in mourning,
but by that time the war was into its third year and no
one was giving parties anyway. The South and its people were too beaten, too poor, and too heartbroken.

"There will be Southerners there too, Papa!" Rachel insisted.

He raised his voice and answered sternly, "You'll
not be going and that's the end of it! There'll be no
more said on the subject!"

It took little to make her father's temper flare, but at

the moment Rachel didn't care. Her desire to go to the dance was stronger than the fear of her father's wrath.

"I've been cooped up in this hotel for two weeks, and tomorrow we are starting a trip that's going to take months and months. Is one evening of fun too much to ask?" Rachel demanded defiantly.

Angrily her father rose from the couch and trying to keep his temper in check answered, "I repeat: NO MORE will be said on the subject!" As he glared at her he recognized that familiar look in her eyes. Whereas his youngest daughter was just like her mother with her dark beauty and shyness, Rachel was her father all over again. Her height, her auburn hair, her green eyes, and her Irish temper had all been inherited from him.

"Rachel, you and Deborah go to your room. I want to talk to your mother alone."

Deborah moved instantly to obey him, but Rachel didn't budge. She was determined to stand her ground and convince her father to change his mind.

Reaching over and touching her arm, Deborah urged, "Please Rachel, do as Papa says."

She looked tenderly at her younger sister and saw the pleading in her eyes. She knew how Deborah hated scenes. Rachel lifted her chin rebelliously and glaring at her father once more, she left the room with her sister.

When they were gone he turned toward his wife. "Nadine, there will be Yankees there tonight. The thought of some Yankee talking to one of my daughters . . ."

Interrupting, she replied softly, "I understand, Tom. But Rachel is so young, and she only wants to have a little fun." Pausing, she added with a sigh, "There's been no fun in her life for a long time.''

Sitting beside her on the edge of the bed, he remarked, ''She'll have her fun later, after we are settled in California.''

''Tom, let them go to the dance tonight. Rachel wants to go so badly.''

Looking at his wife he spoke firmly. ''This afternoon Major Reynolds came into town with four ex-Union soldiers. Young soldiers, Nadine! They'll be at the dance tonight. Do you think four young bucks like that would stay away from our daughters?''

''I didn't know Tom. Of course you're right. They'll have to stay here.''

She shuddered at the mere thought of a Yankee soldier dancing with one of her daughters. She was a very gentle woman and before the war she'd never had ill feelings toward anyone; but now, every time she saw a blue uniform, she'd remember her sons had been killed by the same kind. She could feel nothing but hatred for whoever happened to be wearing it.

''Nadine, when I learned that Reynolds was going to be our wagon master, I almost called off this whole trip. Having to trust a Union officer to take us to California was hard for me to swallow. I'll have to force myself not to shoot him for the damned bastard he is!''

''Tom, such language.'' She reproached him gently, for she understood his anger.

''Sorry hon, but why does a man like this Reynolds want to work as a wagon master? He sure doesn't need the money. Word has it that he's a wealthy man, owns a big ranch somewhere in Texas.''

''A few of the wives that I've met on the wagon train say that he used to be quite an adventurer, and when the war broke out he went back East and joined up with the Union. He has quite a reputation, I understand. Have you seen him?"

"Yes, I saw him from a distance when he rode into town."

"Then you didn't see his face? You couldn't tell if he's handsome?" she questioned, not believing her own boldness.

He stared at his wife with astonishment. "Honestly Nadine! Such questions! Is he handsome? What the hell does it matter!"

"Of course it doesn't matter, but I've heard so much about the man that I was curious."

While her parents were discussing Major Reynolds, Rachel, still fuming with anger, was pacing back and forth in her room. Sitting on the side of the bed Deborah watched her with growing apprehension. She was worried that her sister would storm back into her parents' room and take up where she had left off a few minutes before.

Abruptly Rachel ceased her pacing and, looking squarely at Deborah, she stated, "I'm going to that dance tonight!"

"But Rachel, you heard what Papa said. He absolutely refuses to let us go."

"I don't care! I'm going anyway," she answered with determination.

Deborah couldn't believe she was serious. Surely she wouldn't deliberately disobey their father. As Rachel crossed the room to stand in front of her, Deborah could see the excitement shining in her eyes, the stubbornness written all over her face.

"Tonight, while they're still at the meeting, I'm

14

going to sneak out of here. The dance is going to be held where the wagons are. I'll go to our wagon and hide in it until everyone is dancing, then no one will really take notice of me as I sort of just mingle with the others.''

Deborah was so astounded that she was unable to speak, causing Rachel to mistake her silence for approval. Continuing, she said, ''When Mama and Papa return, you be sure to be in bed with all the lights out. Stick some pillows or something on my side and make it appear as though it's me. In the darkness they won't be able to tell, and if they think we're asleep they'll only glance in anyway.''

Finding her voice at last, Deborah protested breathlessly, ''Rachel! No! It's too dangerous for you to go out alone! If Papa were to find out . . . what would he do to you . . . and what would he do to me for helping you?''

Using her favorite expression, Rachel said irritably, ''Great guns and little switches! Are you going to spend your whole life being scared of Papa?''

Rachel knew the question was unfair because she herself had a certain fear of their father. He was a strict man and could be very stern in his punishments, but at this moment in her life the upcoming dance was more important than any punishment her father could possibly administer.

Sounding quite hurt, Deborah answered, ''Of course I'm scared of Papa, and if you had any sense, you'd be scared too.''

Rachel smiled mischievously. ''Well, we both know I've always lacked discipline, and that lack has gotten me into trouble with Papa before.''

"But they've always been small matters, of only minor importance. What you intend to do tonight isn't minor!" Deborah reasoned.

Rachel put her hands on her hips, tapping her foot impatiently. "I'm going whether you help me or not! If you don't want to see me get into trouble, then you'll help. If you absolutely refuse, then I'll just have to face the consequences."

"If you're bound and determined to go, then all right, I'll help you," Deborah said, knowing she really shouldn't be giving in to her sister in this willful disobedience of their father's wishes. After all, he was only trying to protect them.

Vigorously Rachel gave her a quick hug, then danced gracefully across the room with an imaginary partner. She danced herself and her handsome cavalier over to the window and, as she had done earlier, she looked down on the activity in the dusty street.

He was tying up his horse in front of the hotel when she saw him for the first time. The sight of him took her breath away and she completely forgot her imagined cavalier. She even forgot her so very important dance.

Rachel saw that he wore the blue uniform of a Union officer. Never before in her young life had she ever seen a man so masculine. Even from her second story window she could tell that he was very tall. She wished that she could see his face, but it was hidden by the shadow of his hat. Then, as if to grant her wish, he looked up and gazed in her direction. For an instant she froze as she met two very dominating eyes that seemed to paralyze her with their intenseness. Vaguely she knew that she should be embarrassed at being caught staring so brazenly out of her hotel window at a stranger, but she seemed to have lost all mobility. She couldn't have moved away from the window even if she had wanted to.

Rachel had never been guilty of conceit, so she had absolutely no idea what a charming picture she made, but Major John Reynolds found her not only charming but very exquisite in her rare and appealing beauty. He was fascinated by her youthful but very feminine qualities, and absentmindedly wished himself twenty years younger.

Smiling, he nodded his head slightly to acknowledge her presence. His smile, which was visibly crooked, held a boyish quality that the years had never erased. Her charm was not wasted on him, and his definitely had not been wasted on her.

She returned his nod with one of her own, and her lips curved with only the beginning of a smile that quickly disappeared as he brusquely turned away. She saw that a man had called to him. While starting a conversation, they walked out of her sight and into the hotel.

Rachel eased herself down upon the window seat and let out the breath she had unknowingly been holding. I wonder who he is, she thought. Lord, I've never seen such a man! Then, with angry disappointment in her voice, she muttered, "Too bad he has to be a damned Yankee!"

John Reynolds, dressed in buckskins, looked out among the crowd of people sitting on the hard wooden benches in the one-room church. He appeared to be entirely at ease with himself and his surroundings. As the families watched the man they had heard so much

17

about, they thought him relaxed and free of concern. His worries and his doubts were hidden from all by his calm and easy-going presence.

John Reynolds was two days away from his fortieth birthday. His maturity made him more handsome than he'd been in his youth. He was built strongly and powerfully, with wide shoulders, slim waist, and long muscular legs. Because of his strong aura of masculinity and his height, he seemed to dominate an entire room merely by entering it. Most men admired and respected him, and many a woman found him irresistible. He had only to look at her with his dominating eyes, smile his boyish grin, and she would become fascinated.

Standing before the emigrants, he caused much concern and skepticism. They didn't know what to expect from this man who had been a major in the Union army. He was not only educated, but rumor had it he was also wealthy. Could a man like that possess the knowledge to lead them safely across the wilderness to California?

When at last he spoke, his voice held such strong authority that he immediately got everyone's attention, down to the youngest child.

"Ladies and gentlemen, I'm sure all of you are aware that my name is John Reynolds, and I'm your wagon master. Most of you are probably asking yourselves why I agreed to take on such a position." He could hear stirring beginning in the crowd and a few whispers. "You have already met Zeke, who will be your scout."

Everyone glanced at the man standing a few feet away from the major. Zeke appeared to be the typical

18

mountaineer. He had a full long beard that was as red as his scraggly hair. His age was uncertain. He could've easily been anywhere from sixty to eighty.

"I was stationed in Independence waiting for my discharge from the army when Zeke came to see me." As he spoke everyone's attention reverted to him. "Zeke and I have known each other for a long time. Back before the war we had quite a few adventures together, one of those adventures being a trip from Missouri to California."

The people once more began stirring and whispering excitedly among themselves. The Major had actually been in California! He and Zeke had seen the land they all longed to reach!

"That's why Zeke came to me with the proposition to guide you folks across the plains, through the desert, over the mountains, and into California."

Those hoping to have more information about why he'd made the decision to become a wagon master were disappointed. He had no intentions of telling them any more of what he considered to be his own business.

"I will expect my orders to be obeyed at all times and under all circumstances." To add emphasis to his statement he gingerly placed his hand on the butt of the pistol strapped to his hip. "Gentlemen, I will not hesitate to use this if I feel it is warranted!"

The room became so motionless and silent they could hear nothing except the various sounds drifting in from the outside. From a distance came the barking of a dog; a piano could be heard playing in the saloon down the street, and the creaking of carriage wheels as they rolled down the dusty road.

Judiciously John's eyes scanned the group of people

sitting before him. He found it easy to separate the farmers from the small businessmen. The majority were from places such as Ohio, Illinois, or Indiana, but a few, he figured, came from the Southern states. Most of them poor before the war, but now even more so.

His eyes came to rest on a middle-aged man sitting in the third row. He distinctly clashed with the men around him. He sat too erect and proper for a coarse farmer. He looked too distinguished to be a small merchant. Although his suit of clothes was old and mended, it was evident that at one time they had been expensive and tailor-made.

The man was staring straight ahead, apparently at nothing in particular. Then he seemed to sense that he was being watched. He glanced up and John was met by two cold eyes full of open contempt and pure hatred. Suddenly he realized why the man was different from the others. He was a damned aristocratic southerner! He'd seen that look too many times during the war not to recognize it for what it was, and the type of person it came from.

John looked away from the man's unmistakably hostile stare and faced the others who had been waiting for him to continue. "I hope all of you have stored in your wagons the supplies you were told to purchase. I will read the list for you once more. If you don't have all the following items, you will have ample time in the morning to buy what you may need. We won't be leaving until around noon. Zeke or I will stop by to check out each wagon personally."

He reached into his shirt pocket, pulled out a piece of paper, unfolded it and read, "Supplies needed—coffee, tea, sugar, flour, pilot bread, dried beans, dried fruit, bacon, salt, cornmeal, rice, and a small keg of vinegar. For cooking you will need a cast-metal skillet, a sheet iron stove, and a dutch oven. Use plates, cups and saucers made of tin. Bring two churns, one for sweet milk and one for sour milk, and a keg for water. In every wagon there should be an axe, shovel, rope, rifle, and a shotgun.''

John put the slip of paper back into his pocket as he said, ''I repeat, if you don't have all the needed supplies, see to it that you do have them by noon tomorrow.''

His eyes seemed to survey everyone in the room. ''We will go by way of the Oregon Trail until we reach Utah. From there we will take the Hastings Cutoff. We will travel from Missouri into Kansas, up through Nebraska, cross over to Wyoming, down to Utah, then into Nevada, and over the mountains to Sacramento, California.'' He paused and watching the faces before him, he added with compassion, ''May God be with us.''

The room fell silent as everyone in his own way shared his solemn thoughts and hopeful prayers with his God.

Breaking the moment of silence he spoke again. ''If you have questions you'd like to ask, please feel free to do so.''

Immediately a huge bulk of a man dressed in overalls and a faded shirt stood and asked, ''What about the Indians? Are they all hostile?''

''Your name, sir?'' John inquired.

''My name is Jacob McAllister. I had a farm up in Springfield, Illinois. I could barely scrape a living out of it so I decided to take my wife and two sons and move

21

to California. And there, the good Lord willing, we'll start another farm; but one a damned site better than the one we had, if some heathen don't scalp us before we get there, that is!''

Some of the men murmured their agreement, as fear of the Indians began to materialize in their minds.

''Mr. McAllister,'' John began as the room became silent once again. ''You asked if all Indians are hostile. Let me assure you, there are no friendly Indians on the Plains.''

The people moved around uneasily on the benches and whispered among themselves. Having very little knowledge of the western Indian, they believed him the biggest danger on the trail to California. Little did they know that their greatest hazard would be the trail itself. The vast lonely plains, the dry hot desert, and the steep threatening mountains.

As John began speaking, they stopped their fidgeting to listen. ''None of the hostile tribes have confederated to make war until lately. Their war isn't so much with pioneers passing through, as it is with the cavalry and the trappers killing off their buffalo. If we do come into contact with Indians and they should appear friendly, make no mistake, there is not one nomadic tribe that is friendly with the whites. If he has the opportunity, he will steal, and murder, if necessary. But contrary to what you believe, wagon trains have been known to reach Oregon or California without once being attacked by Indians. Let us hope we can be as fortunate.''

As Jacob McAllister took his seat beside his plain and exhausted-looking wife, another man stood and questioned, ''Why are we leaving so early in April? The new grass hasn't even started growing yet. We've all been ordered to bring along grain for our oxen, cattle and horses. Why not wait a few weeks, and our livestock can graze off the land.''

John looked closely at the man who had spoken. He was a little man with a thick mustache that almost covered his upper lip. "Your name, sir?" he asked once again.

"Joseph Heiskill," the man replied.

"Mr. Heiskill, in a few weeks the spring rains will be upon us. The roads we must travel early on will become muddy and heavy, causing the wagons to bog down. We can avoid that nuisance by leaving early. Also, when the grass does start growing on the barren localities we will be first to take advantage of the scarce grazing land. Those who pass late in the season are likely to suffer greatly and much of their livestock will die from starvation.''

Joseph Heiskill had no sooner taken his seat when another man stood and asked, "Why were we ordered to use oxen? I'd rather use mules." He started to sit down, but changing his mind, he added, "My name is Seth Palmer.''

John figured the young man was a farmer and the lovely girl beside him was his wife. "Mr. Palmer, oxen can and will endure much better than mules. If properly taken care of, they will keep in better condition. Also, in an emergency, an ox can be made to proceed at a quicker pace than you may realize. We all know you can't make a stubborn mule hurry if he doesn't want to.''

Before anyone had the chance to question him further he told them, "If you need any more information, ask Zeke. He's well qualified to tell you anything you want to know."

Beginning to walk down the aisle between the benches he added, "If you'll excuse me, I have matters I must attend to."

John had no intention of passing up the man who had glared at him with such hostility. When he reached the third row he stopped, and looking at the man he demanded, "It's a hell of a long way from here to California, and sir, if you have anything you want to say to me, you say it now!"

The people in the room had begun to converse among themselves, and were not aware of what was being said between the two men.

"You are the wagon master on this train and I will try to carry out your orders, but I will under no circumstances be on friendly terms with you or pretend to like you! And before you ask, my name is Thomas O'Brian."

With a mock grin on his face, John replied, "Friends I don't need, and I don't give a damn whether a man likes me or not; but I do demand that my orders be obeyed!" Nodding at Mrs. O'Brian, he said politely, "Excuse me, ma'am."

Without waiting for a reply, he turned and continued to walk swiftly down the aisle and out of the church. Standing on the church steps, he wondered if the emigrants had any conception of what was in store for them. All the hardships they would be forced to endure, the dangers they would confront, and the deaths they would be compelled to face.

Slowly he strolled away from the church and towards the saloon. His thoughts were on the Oregon Trail, the pioneers and the Indians. He knew thousands more would migrate to the west. The Indian would lose his hunting grounds and be forced to move into remote lands, but the white man would eventually besiege him no matter where he settled. Civilization would wipe out the Indian. Towns would be constructed where now there was nothing but open and empty plain. The railroad would someday link the East to the West and the wild frontier would vanish entirely. He and the pioneers back in the church were only the beginning of what was to come.

The dangers of the upcoming journey were definitely not on Rachel's mind as she quietly slipped into the back of the covered wagon. The importance of what was going on around her had little meaning. In her still-immature mind, a dance was the only thing of any significance.

Sitting on the floor of the wagon, she tried to quiet her labored breathing. She had run most of the way from the hotel and felt close to exhaustion. Thank goodness the moon had been full, giving her the light she needed to find her way.

Rachel wondered if the men at the party would find her attractive. Critically she glanced down at her faded yellow gown. It was old and had been mended many times, but it was the best she owned. She wished it had been cut lower on top to expose a little more of her cleavage. She was thankful she'd never have to sew extra ruffles on her dresses to make herself look fuller.

She slid her hand down the dress, caressing the soft voluminous folds. Originally it had been made to be worn with many crinolines, but she had only one petticoat to her name, so one petticoat would have to suffice.

Rachel dismissed the thought of her improper manner of dress with a simple shrug of her shoulders. She knew she would be as well dressed as any of the other young ladies at the dance. After all, the other families on the wagon train were just as destitute, if not more, than hers.

Rachel tried desperately not to think about the consequences of her actions, should her father catch her. But the fear of being caught kept creeping into her consciousness. I must stop wondering if Papa will find out, she thought. If I don't quit this worrying, I won't have a bit of fun tonight!

Trying to relax, she leaned her head against the side of the wagon, looking up toward the evening sky. Oh, how I want to have fun. I want to dance and have beaux. I want to do all the wonderful thrilling things I've never done before! If it hadn't been for the war, I could've had all sorts of beaux by now. There would be dozens and dozens of parties to attend, elegant parties with dancing in a ballroom and hundreds of candles blazing from crystal chandeliers.

She brought her knees up in a very unladylike position, and with her elbows on her knees and her chin in the palms of her hands, she whispered sullenly, ''If only there had never been a war. Why couldn't the Yankees have minded their own business and left us alone?''

Tears welled up in her eyes as she thought of their home. The Yankees had burned it to the ground, causing her family to evacuate their magnificent house and reside in one of the slave cabins. How humiliating it had been, especially for Papa. Oh, Papa, she thought, losing your home, your land, and your sons almost destroyed you. The Yankees tried to rob you of everything. They even tried to rob you of your pride, but they didn't, did they Papa? You'll always have your pride.

The thoughts about her father caused Rachel to start feeling guilty and she had the impulse to terminate her secret adventure and hurry back to the hotel, but the impulse was forgotten when she heard voices coming close to the wagon. Peeking outside cautiously, she saw two men, one carrying a fiddle and the other a banjo. Stealthily she crept further back into the confines of the wagon and waited.

The music was playing strikingly loud and the dancing was in full swing when Rachel decided to venture out of the wagon. Her pulse began to race with excitement as she mingled with the crowd.

The space that had been cleared for dancing was now fully occupied by women and men of different ages dancing happily to a reel. All of them seemed to be trying desperately to have one last night of fun and enjoyment before they had to embark on their long and perilous journey.

Beginning to feel a little ill at ease about being seen alone, Rachel moved to a secluded spot a short way from all the activity. I'll just stay here and watch for awhile until . . . until I can get up the nerve to be seen, she told herself.

A cool breeze blew soothingly across her brow, ruffling the smoothness of her hair. Absentmindedly she brushed a stray lock back to its rightful place. What will I do if no one asks me to dance? What if I'm left just standing here like . . . like some kind of a wallflower?

If I'm not asked to dance, I'll die! I'll just die! The solemnity of her thoughts was written all over her youthful face.

Completely unaware that she was being observed, she did nothing to conceal the torment in her eyes. Although she was a distance away from him, her observer had no difficulty in studying her. The moonlight shining down on Rachel illuminated every feature of her face.

Leaning his tall frame against the wagon wheel, John Reynolds concentrated on the lovely girl standing apart from the others, when it was so obvious that she would rather have been dancing.

He found it quite easy to read what was on her mind and he also knew that her fear of not being asked to dance would be short-lived. She was too attractive to go unnoticed for very long.

Not taking his eyes from her, he reached into his pocket, removing a cigar and match. As he struck the match across the wagon wheel it flared into life.

The sudden glow from the match startled Rachel, and she whirled quickly in his direction. She recognized him to be the same man she had seen from her hotel window, only now he had exchanged his Yankee uniform for buckskins. Dressed this way, in the frontier tradition, she found him even more attractive than before.

Rachel knew that his eyes had been watching her over the glow of the match before he extinguished it. Now in the darkness, she couldn't tell for sure if he was still watching. During those few seconds when she had seen him so distinctly, his face seemed to become implanted in her mind. If she were never to see him again, she felt she would forever remember his face.

Rachel had no way of explaining to herself the effect his presence had on her. If she had been more of a woman and less of a child she might have been able to understand her emotions, but at her young age her sexuality had not yet been awakened. Those moments when she had looked into the eyes of a stranger were the only time she'd felt any kind of desire for a man; but because of her innocence she had absolutely no way of knowing why he made her feel differently.

"Good evening, Miss."

The voice coming from behind her startled Rachel, and she turned swiftly to see who had so quietly walked over to her. She was happy to see that it was a young man who had spoken—and a handsome one, she quickly noted. He was tall and slim, with chestnut brown hair and eyes of the same color. Neatly dressed in his black pants and pale blue shirt, she found him quite dashing.

"I'm sorry if I scared you, I didn't mean to," he apologized.

Rachel could literally feel her spirits begin to tumble and fall, because she could tell by his accent that he was a Yankee. Lifting her defiant chin she told herself, I don't care! I want to dance and I don't care if it is with a damned Yankee! Loyalty to the Confederacy, though, caused her to make a quick promise to herself that she wouldn't dance with any Yankees once she'd met some of the Southern men.

"That's all right. You didn't scare me. I was only a little startled," she replied.

"My name is Josh Kendall. May I ask yours?" He wondered if he was making a fool of himself. He had always found it difficult to start a conversation with a lady, especially Southern ladies, and he knew she was from the South by her soft way of speaking.

"I'm Rachel O'Brian," she answered, flashing one of her best flirtatious smiles. She knew it was good because she had practiced it so many times in front of her mirror, but until now she had never had anyone to use it on.

"Are you and your family members of the wagon train?" he inquired.

"Yes, we are . . . and you?" Rachel was hoping that he'd be on the train, even though she realized her father would never allow her to associate with a Yankee.

"Yes, ma'am. Three of my friends and I are going to California to try our luck in the gold fields. Although I understand most of it is gone. We really don't have anything better to do, though. We just got here today. We rode in with Major Reynolds. He was the commanding officer in our regiment in the army."

Rachel didn't know who Major Reynolds was, but Josh spoke his name as though she were somehow aware of this man's existence. "Major Reynolds, is he going to California too?"

"Don't you know?" he asked.

Rachel stared at him with a bafflement that was changing rapidly into boredom. She certainly didn't want to waste precious time standing here discussing some Union Major, when she could be dancing!

"Know what?" she asked trying very hard to keep her patience intact.

"The Major is the wagon master," he explained.

"Oh, dear!" she gasped. "You mean Papa has to go

30

all the way from here to California obeying orders from a Union officer? From a damned Yankee!''

Due to her astonishment, she had fully forgotten that she was speaking with a Yankee. Noticing the sudden blush in her cheeks, Josh fought the impulse to smile with amusement.

"I'm sorry, but I seem to have this terrible habit of speaking without thinking first," she told him. "Mama has always warned me that someday I'd embarrass myself."

He was only half-consciously listening to her apology because he was too absorbed in her loveliness. In the moonlight he could see that her eyes were the green of emeralds, but it wasn't their color that attracted him. He was intrigued by the spirit reflected within her bewitching eyes.

"Please don't be embarrassed. But ma'am the war is over and now we must all learn to live together in peace."

Rachel spoke so softly that he had to strain to hear her words. "The war will never be over for Papa."

"I'm afraid that's true for a lot of people," Josh replied.

For a moment they retreated into their own private memories. The loud music, all the different sounds of voices, and the happy ringing of laughter was lost to them. He was painfully remembering all the men he had been forced to kill. Their deaths would be there to haunt him all the days of his life. My God, he thought, it was brother killing brother. How do we ever live with what we did?

In Rachel's mind she was seeing again the two young and handsome men she remembered so well. They had

31

possessed such a great zest for life and that life had been taken from them, in a war they had never asked for and never wanted. A sharp pain tore at her young heart as she thought, I'll never see my brothers again.

Josh was the first to come back to reality and gently he touched her elbow. "Would you like to dance?"

She pushed the thoughts of her brothers from her mind. "Yes, I'd love to."

As she turned to walk away with him she glanced over to where the stranger had been standing. She was surprised to see that he was still there. Not taking her eyes from the tall man in buckskins, she asked, "Who is he? Do you know?"

Josh followed her gaze to see whom she was speaking of. Then realizing who she meant, he answered, "That's him! Major Reynolds."

Noticing her apparent amazement he asked, "Is anything wrong?"

Not knowing how to answer him, she only shook her head and started walking in the direction of the dancers. Proudly, because he considered her quite a find, he fell into stride beside her. If at that moment he could have seen her eyes, he'd have found them gleaming with aroused curiosity and excitement. Her mind was running over the weeks and months to come. All those days and all those nights, she thought, to spend in the presence of that man. It'll be just awful for Papa . . . but I . . . I find the prospect most thrilling! . . . I wonder . . . I wonder if he'll ever speak to me . . . Surely he will . . . after all . . . it's going to be a very long trip!

Then she easily dismissed him from her thoughts because she was more interested in dancing. Smiling with youthful enthusiasm, she told herself, I can't believe I'm actually going to dance and have fun! With a cross of her fingers she added, Oh, please God, don't let Papa find out!

A smile curved the major's lips as he watched them walking away. He raised his eyebrows slightly and there was a twinkle in his eyes as he silently wished his second lieutenant good luck.

Rachel quickly and easily became the most popular girl at the dance. Some women are naturally born with the gift to attract the opposite sex, and this gift had been born into Rachel. By the time the party was half over she surprisingly, but happily, realized that she held a certain power over men. She had absolutely no indication as to what that power was and she didn't care. She was just glad that she had it.

Most young men in that period of time pictured their "ideal woman" very differently from Rachel. Their "ideal woman" would be shy and gentle with soft loving eyes. Rachel had none of these qualities. She was too bold to be shy and too stubborn to be gentle. Her eyes, although they were her best feature, could never be described as soft. They were too mischievous, too excitable, and too quick to flare into anger.

In the years to come, many a young man would find himself captivated by Rachel's charms. The vision of his "ideal woman" would rapidly change and materialize into the shape and form of Rachel. Forgotten would be his shy and gentle woman. His entire life, but without his knowledge of course, he had really been searching for a woman just like Rachel; spirited and a challenge. A woman so spirited that she must be tamed by him, and such a challenge that she must be conquered by him . . . and therein lay Rachel's power!

The festivities came to an end too soon for Rachel's satisfaction. Just because they all had to head out the next day to face a long and tiresome journey meant absolutely nothing to her. She was so elated, she felt as if she could dance all night and still be able to walk all the following day. Some of the families began strolling toward their wagons, while others headed for their hotels.

Touching her lightly on the arm, Josh inquired, "Miss O'Brian, may I escort you back to your hotel?"

Looking up into his face she considered the possibilities. This time of night she would be much safer walking with a man beside her, and she did so enjoy his company, but if her father was to catch them she'd be in twice as much trouble for associating with a Yankee. The fear of her father unquestionably made the decision for her.

"Thank you, Mr. Kendall, but I must go alone," she answered.

"But I insist. It's too dangerous for a young lady to walk the streets at this time of night."

"Mr. Kendall, there's something I must tell you," she said with excitement.

Rachel glanced cautiously around them as though to make sure they weren't being overheard. She appeared very mysterious to him, and he was pleasantly intrigued by her mystifying anxiety.

"I slipped out of my room tonight and Papa doesn't know I'm here. I can't take the chance that he could find us together. If you see me tomorrow you must pretend you don't know me . . . because you see . . . Mr. Kendall . . . my father hates any man who was in the

Union army.''

Without waiting for a reply, she gathered up her long skirt and ran gracefully off into the night. At a distance he began to follow her. He trailed her past the covered wagons and into the almost deserted town.

Not looking anywhere but straight ahead Rachel fled down the sidewalk of wooden planks. As she passed the saloon she could hear the laughter from within and a piano playing. She wished she possessed the nerve to take a quick peek inside. The laughter had been that of a woman and she'd never seen one of those kind of women before, but this was not the time to satisfy her curiosity.

Rachel continued her flight, without slowing her pace, past the saloon and then past the bank. She paused in front of the general store for a moment to catch her breath, then made her way across the street heading toward the hotel. Standing back in the dark shadows, Josh watched her until she had safely entered the lobby, then turning he walked away.

Rapidly she ran up the flight of stairs to the second floor. The hallway was always kept lit, so she had no difficulty in finding her way. Rachel knew her disobedience had gone undetected, because if her father had found out he would have been at the dance searching for her.

Walking further down the narrow hall, she turned the corridor, but as she made the turn, the door to her parents' room opened. Her heart seemed to lurch into her throat when she caught sight of her father.

Whirling, she dashed silently around the corner. Thank God he hadn't seen her! What do I do now, she wondered. She had to get out of sight because she could

35

hear his footsteps approaching.

Suddenly Rachel realized that she was leaning against a door. On impulse she reached for the knob, praying it would be unlocked. As it turned in her hand she rushed into the room.

There was a lantern burning next to the bed and she could see that she was in a room similar to the one she shared with her sister. She was grateful that, at the moment, it was unoccupied.

Leaning against the door, she listened closely so that she'd hear her father when he passed by the room. All at once she heard another sound. More footsteps coming down the hall, but from the other direction.

"Evening, O'Brian," she heard a male voice say. "I'd like to talk to you for a moment. Why don't you come in and we'll have a drink."

Rachel almost cried out in alarm. As she began to panic her eyes explored the room for a place to hide. She spied a tall wardrobe against the far wall. With her heart pounding, she darted toward it and, opening the door, she was relieved to find it empty. Swiftly crawling inside, she sat down, pulling the door shut behind her. The interior of the wardrobe was narrow and she had to pull up her knees in order to fit. She felt as though she couldn't breathe, but it wasn't from lack of oxygen, it was from fear.

Through the door of the wardrobe she could hear someone enter the room. She was sure it was the man she heard talking to her father. Oh let him be alone, she thought. Please God, let him be alone!

When Rachel didn't hear any conversation, and heard only one person moving about, she let out a sigh of relief. Now that the worst of her fear was over, which of course was her father's anger, a new kind of fear suddenly arose. She was alone in a man's room! What would this man do to her if he was to find her? Maybe he won't stay, she hoped. Make him leave! Oh please . . . please God, make him leave!

Rachel was deeply engrossed in her prayer when the door to the wardrobe opened. Slowly she turned her head to look beside her. Because she was sitting and he was standing, all she saw was a pair of man's boots. Gradually her eyes moved upward over his large frame. The tight-fitting pants he wore made it quite apparent that his legs were hard and muscular. She saw that he wore a holster and gun strapped around his hips. Raising her gaze a little higher, her eyes widened with recognition as she observed the buckskin jacket fitting snugly across his powerful shoulders. With all the courage Rachel could muster, she tilted her face and looked him straight in the eyes.

From his expression she couldn't tell if he was angry or astonished by her unexpected presence. She could tell nothing from those piercing steel-gray eyes that were staring at her so intensely.

Rachel opened her mouth to speak but found herself unable to utter a sound. Swallowing very hard, she took a deep breath and tried again. This time she succeeded although her voice sounded terribly weak. "Major . . . I can explain . . . Honestly, I can."

While still looking at her he leaned his arm across the front of the wardrobe and raised his eyebrows questioningly.

"Well . . . you see . . . I am . . . Well . . . I'm hiding!"

It baffled Rachel when, for some reason unknown to

her, he roared with laughter. She could find nothing humorous in what she had said, and she resented his mirth. Perturbed at his reaction to her predicament she spat out at him, "It isn't funny!"

At that his laughter ceased, for which she was grateful, but she could see that he was still greatly amused. I wish . . . I wish, she thought, he'd stop looking at me as though I'm something . . . comical!

He spoke to her for the first time and his voice was so deep and full it seemed to surround her. "Do you plan to stay in there all night?"

Without answering, she attempted to stand but was halted abruptly. Sounding as if he was losing his patience, he said sternly, "Will you get out of there!"

"I can't," she whispered.

"What?" he snapped.

Because her chin was beginning to quiver she raised it ever so slightly as she replied, but clearly this time, "I can't."

Taking a step backwards so that he could see her better he asked with irritation, "What do you mean, you can't?"

I won't cry, she thought. I won't let this man see me break down and cry like some . . . some foolish child! Trying very hard to compose herself she replied, "My dress is caught on something. I think it's stuck on a nail."

Kneeling, he slowly but deliberately bent over her and Rachel found herself in such close contact with him that his chest was actually touching her breasts.

Unknowingly she let out a soft moan causing him to look into her face. His lips were so close to hers that for an instant she thought he was going to kiss her. I want him to, she thought surprisingly. I really want him to!

But instead of kissing her, he chuckled slyly as though he could read her thoughts. Reaching behind her, he loosened the dress from the nail. Standing, he grabbed her hand, and effortlessly pulled her to her feet.

"I'm waiting for your explanation," he said, once again penetrating her with his eyes.

"I slipped out of my room tonight so that I could go to the dance. You see . . . Papa refused to take me . . . and I wanted to go so badly!" She lowered her eyes so that she wouldn't have to look into his. They had such a strange effect on her. "I was on my way back to my room when I saw Papa. I couldn't let him see me so I came in here. And then I heard you speaking to him and I was afraid he'd find me . . . so I hid in the wardrobe."

Disregarding her explanation entirely he stated, "It's hard to believe that you're Tom O'Brian's daughter."

She forced herself to look at him again as she asked, "Why?"

"You obviously don't share your father's hatred of Yankees," he said teasingly.

Hoping she sounded nonchalant, she asked, "Oh, and why should you think that?"

"Don't tell me you didn't know Lieutenant Kendall was in the Union army. And from what I could see tonight, you danced with more than just one Yankee."

With a small amount of guilt she remembered her promise not to dance with any Yankees once she had met some of the southerners. Well, she thought as she lifted her chin defiantly, it's not my fault there weren't any good-looking southern men at the dance!

Sharply she cut her eyes at the major. As before, he seemed to be reading her thoughts and finding them humorous. Forcing as much contempt as she could in her voice she remarked, "If a girl wants to dance badly enough she'll dance with most anything . . . even a low-down . . . yellow-bellied Yankee!"

Whirling arrogantly she began heading toward the door, but in two easy strides he caught her. Grasping her roughly by the shoulders he jerked her to where she was facing him. The fury and rage in his eyes were frightening. "Listen to me, you little hypocrite, pretend you hate Yankees all you wish but don't ever in my presence, call them low-down or yellow-bellied! Because if you do, I'll take you over my knee and spank your bottom so hard you won't be able to sit down for a week!" He released her so suddenly that she almost lost her balance.

But being her father's daughter, her Irish temper exploded and she blurted out the first words that came to her mind. "If you ever lay a hand on me . . . I'll kill you . . . you damned bastard!"

Her hand flew to her mouth, her eyes opened wide with astonishment, and she caught her breath deeply. I've never said that word before in my life, she thought. I've heard Papa and my brothers say it many times, but it certainly isn't a word a lady would ever use. If Mama had heard, she surely would've swooned!

Rachel knew she was blushing shamefully, but she had never before been so embarrassed. She could tell by the large grin on his face that he was enjoying her discomfort immensely.

He strode over to the door and started to open it, but

changing his mind, he asked, "By the way, my little hypocrite, do you have a name?"

Oh Lord, she prayed, just let me get out of here safely and I promise I'll never again get myself into such a predicament.

"Rachel," she answered.

With relief she watched him open the door and glance down the corridor both ways. Seeing that it was empty, he opened the door wide enough for her to leave. "Meeting you, Rachel, has been charming, to say the least."

Perturbed, she noticed he still had that annoying grin on his face. Trying to act as though she didn't care, she haughtily lifted her head and walked straight out of his room without so much as a backward glance. When she heard the door close behind her, she quietly but speedily headed for her room.

Chapter Two

Rachel stood beside her father's wagon viewing the activity going on around her with mild indifference. The wagon train would be pulling out in a couple of hours, and everyone was busy with their final packing, minor repairs, and purchases. Ignoring the preparations, she kept hoping she'd catch a glimpse of Josh. Her mother and sister were at the general store, and her father had gone into town. If only she could find Josh, she'd be free to speak with him.

Suddenly, Rachel caught sight of the wagon master approaching. Remembering her brazen behavior of the night before, she blushed with embarrassment. She noticed he once again had that annoying grin on his face. As before, his imposing masculinity made her feel helplessly flustered. Rachel wondered if she'd ever be capable of being in his presence without experiencing awe and confusion.

As he drew nearer, she subconsciously took a few steps backward until she was blocked by the side of the wagon. Bracing herself flatly against the wood, Rachel watched him with increasing apprehension.

Pausing in front of her, he moved intimately closer.

Rachel couldn't believe that he could be so bold as to make such personal contact with her. He was so near she could smell the odors of brandy and tobacco.

Still smiling as though he found her amusing, he said, "Good morning, my little hypocrite."

"Don't call me that!" she snapped with quickly aroused anger.

Raising his eyebrows in his usual fashion, he answered, "We both know what you are, don't we? So why not call the kettle black, my beautiful little hypocrite."

Knowing he would only laugh at her were she to try and deny his accusations, she replied ill-temperedly, "Even if I were a . . . a hypocrite . . . I wouldn't be yours! Also, if you were any kind of a gentleman you wouldn't be so rude and insulting!"

Placing his hands on the wagon, one on each side of her, he leaned over her, looking deeply into her eyes. "But I'm not a gentleman. Don't ever mistake me for one of your southern gentlemen, and don't expect me to act like one. And if you were a few years older I'd show you why a man would be a fool to stand on formalities with you, but then, you aren't a woman yet." With all traces of humor erased, he continued, "Someday though, my enticing little hypocrite, you're going to become a very desirable woman. It's a pity I'm too old for you."

Rachel was barely paying any mind to what he was saying, because of the fear that her father might return. What would he say, or do, if he were to find her in such a compromising situation? The man was intentionally standing as close to her as he dared.

"Will you please leave before Papa returns!" she

urged fretfully.

"Did he learn of your daring escapade last night?"

"Of course not, and will you stop hovering over me!"

"No one has told him that his charming daughter was the most popular and most sought-after girl at the dance?"

Noting her shocked expression, he began smiling again. "You haven't considered the possibility that someone might mention it to him?"

"No . . . I . . . I simply didn't think about it. How could I have been so foolish?"

"Rachel, you're the first female I've ever met whose stupidity I not only find delightful, but also fascinating."

"Oh will you shut up!" she demanded irritably. "And will you please move away from me! If Papa finds out about last night I'm going to be in enough trouble without him seeing you . . . and . . . and . . ."

"And what?" he encouraged, obviously enjoying her discomfort.

"Well you are too close for decency!" she huffed.

"Decency? Is that what you call it," John chuckled, as he finally stood erect and stopped leaning over her so brazenly. Instead of moving away, he placed one hand under her chin tilting her face upward. "Rachel, I envy the man who will someday take your innocence. I wish I could be that lucky man, but too many years stand between us."

Rachel was astounded when she realized he was actually speaking to her with unmistakable desire. She wasn't able to fully comprehend exactly what he meant, but she was enjoying his words and closeness. Completely forgotten was the fear of her father's return.

I wonder if he'll kiss me, she thought. Surely this time he will! Should I allow him to take such liberties with me? . . . I don't care! I want him to kiss me!

Reading her thoughts was no mystery to him, and what she wanted was reflected openly in the eyes he found not only enchanting, but very inviting. He appeared to be seriously studying her features, but unexpectedly a smile curled the corners of his mouth. ''It takes about six months to reach California, and you won't become a woman in that short period of time. I'll never have the pleasure of knowing you as the sensual woman you'll someday be. Instead of taking you in my arms and kissing you, I'll have to be satisfied with only knowing you platonically and seeing you as you are now. A tempting, charming, bewitching, and hypocritical brat.''

''Brat!'' she yelled as she roughly pushed him away. ''How dare you call me a brat!''

Angrily she stalked a short distance, then turned back in his direction. Placing her hands firmly on her hips she said with unhidden rage, ''Major Reynolds, I hate you! You are the most impudent . . . insulting . . . impolite and discourteous man I've ever had the misfortune of meeting. Not only do I hate you, but I find you obnoxious, annoying, and offensive!''

Trying not to laugh, he replied, ''You forgot impertinent and detestable, but never mind my love, I got the message anyway.''

''If you had one shred of chivalry, you'd go away and not return. I hope I never see you again!''

''But you will. It seems we are destined to travel thousands of miles together. But to prove I can be amiable and obliging, I will leave as soon as I check out your father's wagon."

"Just keep away from his wagon and leave now!" she ordered.

"Sorry, but I can't do that. Have you forgotten, I am the wagon master and it's my job and duty to personally examine the wagons," he answered, not sounding the least serious.

"Then get on with it, but you'll do it alone because if you won't leave . . . I will!"

"Sorry to disappoint you again, Rachel, but a member of the wagon must be present at all times. A little assurance against being accused of taking some article that could turn up missing."

Crossing over to her and placing his hand on her arm he asked, "Shall we check the supplies inside, my love?"

Glaring at him with contempt, she pulled away from his touch and walked briskly to the back of the wagon. She was lifting her skirt to step up into the bed of the wagon when effortlessly he picked her up in his arms and easily placed her inside.

Climbing in behind her, he said, "There's only a few supplies I want to be sure your father has . . . his rifle, shotgun, axe, shovel, and a rope. I'll take it for granted that he was smart enough to purchase enough food."

Grudgingly she showed him where everything was located. When he had finished his inventory, she asked brusquely, "Now are you leaving?"

"Not until I check the exterior of the wagon," he answered as he stepped down to the ground. Turning, he placed his hands on her waist lifting her from the wagon. Slowly he lowered her to the ground. For a woman Rachel was considered tall, but she had to look up to see into his face. He was staring at her with those dominating eyes that she found so mystifying. She wished she could somehow understand her emotions. Only a moment before she had been so angry with him, but now she was only aware of his masculine aggressiveness, and it caused her pulse to race.

Looking at her with tenderness, he asked, "How old are you, Rachel?"

"I'll be seventeen next month, and you had no right to call me a brat!"

"But I also said you were tempting, charming, and bewitching," he reminded teasingly.

"And hypocritical, if my memory is correct," she remarked indignantly.

He grinned good-humoredly. "I'd better check the wagon before that Irish temper get's you all riled up again."

Rachel wanted to inform him how much she resented his insolence, but before she had the opportunity, he turned away brusquely and walked to her father's wagon.

Following him, she asked, "Exactly what can you examine on a wagon? I should think a wagon is just . . . a wagon."

He was busy moving his hands expertly over the wheels. She felt her eyes being drawn to those hands. They appeared so tough and powerful, yet somehow she instinctively knew they could also be gentle and tender. Unexpectedly, she found herself imagining how it would feel to have his hands caressing her with passion and love.

Suddenly becoming aware that he was watching her,

she visibly blushed as if he had in some way read her thoughts.

Noting her discomfort, he chuckled slyly as he inquired, "Are you all right, Miss O'Brian?"

Wanting to change the subject, she answered briskly, "I'm fine." Trying to sound nonchalant, she asked, "Why were you examining the wheels?"

"Wagons used on a long trip should be of the simplest possible construction. They should be strong, yet light in weight, and made of well-seasoned timber, especially the wheels because the atmosphere in the elevated and arid regions over which we will travel is exceedingly dry. Unless the woodwork is thoroughly seasoned, during the summer months they will require constant repairs to prevent them from falling to pieces."

"And my father's wagon?" she asked.

Reaching into his shirt pocket under the buckskin jacket, he brought out a pouch of tobacco and paper. He completed the task of rolling the cigarette before he answered. "It's a good solid wagon. He shouldn't have any problems with it." He placed the cigarette between his lips, then put the pouch of tobacco back into his pocket. Drawing out a match, he struck it rapidly across the wagon wheel.

Watching him closely, Rachel was reminded of the night before when she had seen his face over the flare of a lighted match. She recalled the emotions he had stirred within her. He makes me feel like a woman, she thought, and most of all, he makes me want to be a woman!

"Speaking with you again has been charming," he said as he turned to walk away.

49

"Please don't leave!" she called, not caring how forward it sounded.

The boyish crooked grin appeared on his face. "Will you never learn to practice what you preach?"

Raising her chin in her usual defiant fashion, she answered, "I don't know what you could possibly mean."

"Then allow me to enlighten you, Rachel. First you claim to detest low-down yellow-bellied Yankees, but you enjoy dancing and flirting with them. We both know that you don't hate Yankees, you only like to pretend you do, when it's to your advantage. Very hypocritical of you, my love. You informed me in no uncertain terms just how abundantly you despise me and how much you want me to leave. Now, you ask me to stay. It would seem you also hate me with the same hypocrisy you hate all Yankees. And by the way, Rachel, begging me not to leave really wasn't very tactful."

Feeling uncontrollable anger consuming her, she shouted, "I didn't beg you! Damn you, Major Reynolds! I do hate you! And I do want you to leave! NOW!"

Touching the brim of his hat, he bowed slightly. "Never let it be said that I couldn't take such a subtle hint. Good day, Miss O'Brian."

Packing clothes in the narrow confines of the wagon, Deborah said anxiously, "I wonder what's keeping Papa. We'll be leaving within the hour and the oxen haven't even been harnessed yet."

"I'm sure he'll be here any minute," her mother reassured her as she put away the supplies they had purchased.

Glancing over at her oldest daughter who was sitting solemnly in the rear of the wagon, she asked, "Did your father come by while we were at the store?"

Rachel didn't respond to her question because she was not even aware of the discussion between her mother and sister. Her thoughts were in a turmoil; she was trying to understand her feelings for John Reynolds. I don't understand, she was thinking, sometimes he'll look at me and speak to me as if I'm a woman. Then for no reason he'll rudely change and tease me like a child. When he's treating me like a woman though, why does it make me feel so strange?

"Rachel! Rachel, did you hear me?"

Startled out of her secret thoughts she turned to her mother. "Were you talking to me, Mama?"

"Since Deborah and I returned from shopping your mind has been up in the clouds somewhere. Come back to earth dear, there's work to be done. We have been doing it all, while you sit there daydreaming."

"I'm sorry, Mama. What do you want me to do?"

She started to answer when all at once she heard her husband calling out to them. "Nadine! Girls! Come here! I want you to meet someone!"

The three of them climbed hastily down to the ground, just as Tom O'Brian and another man were walking around the corner of the wagon.

Staring at the stranger standing beside her father, Rachel thought him to be the most perfectly handsome man she had ever seen. He was young, tall, and well built. His hair, which was noticeably thick, was black and curly. His eyes, framed by full arched eyebrows, were dark brown with long lashes. His lips were sensual

51

and pouting.

Looking first at his wife, and then at his daughters, Tom O'Brian introduced the young man. "I'd like you to meet Edward Phillips."

"I'm happy to make your acquaintance, Mr. Phillips," his wife responded politely.

"How do you do, ma'am," he answered in a voice that was strong, deep and distinctly southern.

"Nadine," her husband began, "Mr. Phillips has agreed to travel with us to California. With him to help, it'll take a lot of the workload off me. Besides, you know I was worried about how you and the girls would manage if I were to become sick or injured."

"But Tom, I don't understand. How did this arrangement come about?"

"While I was in town, I stopped to have a drink at the saloon, and Mr. Phillips was standing at the bar next to me. We just happened to strike up a conversation. He told me he wanted to go to California, but had arrived here too late to sign up or buy the wagon and oxen. That's when I offered him a deal. He can have the use of our wagon and supplies, and in return he'll do his share of the work. God only knows, Nadine, we need him!"

"But isn't it too late for you to register on this train, Mr. Phillips?" she questioned.

"No, ma'am. We found Mr. Reynolds before we came here and he gave his permission. The wagon master has that authority," he explained.

"I'm so thankful you're going to be traveling with us."

"Not nearly as thankful as I am to you and your husband for your hospitality. If you'll excuse me, Mrs.

O'Brian, I need to go to the hotel and pick up my belongings and then to the livery stable for my horse." Glancing at her husband, he added, "I'll return as quickly as I can."

"We'll be leaving very soon so you'd best hurry."

"Yes sir, I will," he answered.

The O'Brians watched quietly as he headed briskly for town, each thinking about the young man who would become a part of their lives. Tom O'Brian's thoughts were those of relief because he had found a man to share his heavy load. His wife was grateful because he'd be with them on the long and tiresome journey to help her husband. His oldest daughter wondered if he would bring romance and excitement into her life; but his youngest daughter watched him walk away with the very beginnings of love growing deeply in her young heart.

"Well, I must hitch up the oxen. Have you finished with the packing, dear?"

"Yes, everything is packed. I'll help you with the team."

"That's no kind of work for you, Nadine. But come along anyway and give me the pleasure of your company."

As they strolled toward the waiting oxen, Deborah turned to her sister. "Have you ever seen such a handsome man?"

Rachel looked at her with surprise. "Why, Deb, I didn't know you even noticed men."

Blushing, she answered, "How could a girl help but notice Edward Phillips?"

Rachel offered no comment because she had at last caught a glimpse of Josh. He was three wagons down from them, standing next to his team of oxen.

"Deb, I'll be right back. If Mama or Papa asks about me, tell them you don't know where I am."

"Where are you going?"

"There's someone I must see," she answered, hurrying away.

Josh noticed Rachel before she could reach him and, smiling broadly, he hastily walked over to meet her. Dressed in a plain brown dress with her long auburn hair pulled back into a bun, she still appeared extremely lovely to him.

"Miss O'Brian, it's so nice to see you again."

Glancing back in her father's direction, she said excitedly, "I don't want Papa to see us. Let's go behind your wagon where we can't be seen."

Josh found her boldness and her directness not only refreshing, but irresistible. Taking her hand, he led her quickly to the back of his wagon. He was relieved that his companions hadn't returned from town. He had no wish to share Rachel with anyone.

"Mr. Kendall, did you by any chance warn your friends that I danced with last night not to speak to me in Papa's presence?"

"Don't worry, they know not to say anything, and call me Josh, please."

"You must start calling me Rachel . . . that is if we ever get the chance to talk to each other again."

"I hope we will," he answered.

Watching him closely, she realized how nice he was, and how much she liked him. Why does Papa have to hate *all* Yankees, she wondered.

"Josh, where are you from? Do you have any family?"

"I came from a small town in Pennsylvania. I was an only child. My parents were already getting on in years before I was born. I'm sure I came as quite a shock to them. They were wonderful people and very loving parents. I lost my mother when I was sixteen and my father passed away right before the war started, so you see, I had no one to return home to."

"I'm sorry, it must be terrible to lose both your parents."

"I still miss them. I guess I always will. But tell me about yourself, Rachel. What part of the South are you and your family from?"

She leaned back against the wagon as she allowed her thoughts to drift back through the years. She could once again see their magnificent home, the fields after fields of budding cotton, the hundred slaves her father had owned, and the two brothers she had so dearly loved. Rachel began telling Josh about life on a Mississippi plantation and how her father had ruled over his kingdom. With pain and heartache, she also told him about her brothers.

Josh was genuinely interested in all she was saying and they lost track of time as she talked to him about her life as the daughter of a wealthy aristocratic planter. She was deeply engaged in her conversation with Josh, when her father found them.

"Rachel! What in the hell are you doing here?" he demanded.

"Papa!" she gasped.

"Mr. O'Brian," Josh tried to explain, "this is all my fault."

"Who are you and how do you know my daughter?"

"My name is Josh Kendall. I just happened to run

into Rachel and we started talking to each other."

"You have not been given permission to call my daughter by her Christian name!" he bellowed.

Josh started to reply but at that moment Edward Phillips walked up to them, leading his horse. "Is something wrong, sir?"

"You're damned right something is wrong! This young buck had my daughter all alone behind his wagon!"

"I'm not one of your black slaves, Mr. O'Brian, and I don't take kindly to being called a young buck!" Josh told him, trying to keep his anger under control.

"You listen to me, Kendall, if I ever find you alone with my daughter again, I'll kill you!"

"Papa, please! It wasn't like that. We weren't exactly secluded. There are people all around."

"You stay out of this, young lady! How dare you shame this family by associating with the Yankees who murdered your brothers! Get back to our wagon! I'll tend to you later!"

"I won't leave, Papa, until you let me explain." Rachel knew how angry it made her father when she openly defied him, but she couldn't leave Josh to face her father's wrath alone.

"Mr. O'Brian," Edward suggested, "why don't you take her back to the wagon and I'll handle this Yankee!"

Angrily Josh strode closer to him. "I don't know who you are mister, but if you think you can handle me, then come on!"

Dropping the reins to his horse, Edward answered lazily, "Where I come from sir, satisfaction is demanded, when a lady's honor has been jeapordized."

Making a move toward him, Josh was stopped abruptly by a strong voice of authority. "Lieutenant Kendall, the war is over!"

None of them had heard the man ride up on his horse. All, except Rachel, looked up at him with surprise. Rachel found the scene already embarrassing without him becoming a part of it. She had a sickening feeling the situation was going to now become worse.

"What is going on?" John Reynolds asked the group of people standing before him.

"I'll tell you," Rachel's father began. "I found Kendall and my daughter together!"

John raised his eyebrows questioningly. "Together, Mr. O'Brian? Together, how?"

"Here! Hidden behind his wagon!" he raged.

"We were only talking," Josh explained.

With the barest trace of a smile on his face, John glanced at Rachel. "Miss O'Brian, did Mr. Kendall insult you in any way?"

Still refusing to look at him she snapped, "No, of course not!"

"Mr. O'Brian, I don't see where you have any argument with this man. I suggest all of you return to your wagon."

Edward reached down, picking up his horse's reins. "Come on, sir, let's go."

Glaring once more at Josh, Tom O'Brian ordered, "Stay away from my daughter!" Grabbing Rachel by the arm roughly, he started back to his wagon with Edward following.

"Mr. O'Brian," John called as he rode his horse over to them. "I'd like a word with your daughter."

"Why?" he asked suspiciously.

57

"I need to talk to her. It'll only take a minute, I assure you."

Thinking he was going to warn her to stay away from the likes of Kendall, he answered, "All right, but make it fast." Leaving them alone, he and Edward headed for the wagon.

Sitting on his horse, and leaning his arm across the saddle horn, he grinned down at Rachel. "This wagon train hasn't even pulled out yet and you've got men fighting over you. I hate to think what a chaos you'll have caused by the time we reach California."

"Oh go away!" she replied angrily. She stared up at him, knowing full well he'd be watching her with that annoying grin on his face.

"You really must try to control your flirtations, Rachel. I'd hate to see some poor fool get hurt because of you."

"Are you insinuating a man would be a fool to care for me?"

He studied her seriously for a moment. "He'd be a fool to ever take you for granted."

"I'm not sure if you meant that as a compliment or not."

"Take is as a compliment, my beautiful hypocrite."

Stomping her foot angrily, she replied, "Will you stop calling me that?"

"What? . . . Calling you beautiful?" he asked.

"Damn you, Major Reynolds! You know what I mean!"

Laughing at her, he remarked, "That's twice today that you have damned me. I thought gentle southern ladies didn't use such coarse language. But, if I remember correctly, it seems last night you were very fond of another word that a lady would never use . . . Could it possibly be, Rachel, that you are no lady?''

Letting her Irish temper run amuck, she yelled, ''I wish I could call you every vile name there is . . . and if I ever learn what they are, I'll use them all on you!''

''Would you like me to teach you a few?'' he chuckled.

''No! I don't want you to teach me anything. I want you to go away and leave me alone!''

''I'll leave, my love, but I'll not stay gone, because I find you too entertaining.'' Without waiting for an answer, he turned his horse and rode away.

Sitting on his horse, John stared gravely at the twenty-five wagons lined up before him. Speaking to the man beside him he inquired, ''Zeke, did you find out if there's a doctor on the train?''

''Nope, no doctor. It seems we ain't that lucky,'' Zeke drawled while spitting a straight stream of tobacco juice down to the ground.

''Too bad. A doctor on the trail can save a lot of lives.''

''Don't ya think we oughta be leavin'?'' Glancing up at the sun, Zeke judged, ''It's already past noon.''

John took one final look at the wagon train, which would be wholly his responsibility, before answering. ''Move 'em out.''

Galloping his horse over to the lead wagon and raising his arm, Zeke yelled, ''Wagons ho!''

John watched as the oxen strained against their harnesses and the wagons slowly but steadily started to roll. He estimated they would cover quite a few miles before sunset, as the day was sunny and clear. First they would need to cross the river, but he could foresee no difficulty. Ferries would be there to move them all safely across.

John's intuition proved to be correct as his wagon train easily and with no major problems crossed the river into Kansas, leaving Missouri behind. Steadily the oxen's hooves plodded over the trail as the wagon wheels turned away the long miles.

The emigrants were surprised to find the land alive with doves, whippoorwills, and meadow larks. Also grouse, better known as prairie chickens, ran abundantly wild. In the spots where water lay, the fields were ripening with early stalks of corn.

John and Zeke were riding at the front of the wagons, when, turning his horse, John said, "Zeke, I'm going to check on the wagons."

"I'll go with ya," he replied, following the wagon master back toward the train of wagons.

The first in line was the McAllister family. Jacob McAllister was walking alongside his oxen shouting to them, "Giddup there you ornery critters. Haw!" He carried a long lashed whip and was threatening them with it, but when he noticed the two men riding in his direction he stopped yelling at his beasts and called, "Howdy Major . . . Zeke."

"Mr. McAllister, I'm no longer a major," John corrected. Slowing their horses to a walking pace they pulled up beside the huge man.

"I hope I didn't offend you," Mr. McAllister apologized.

"No, of course not, but the name is Reynolds." Glancing up he smiled at the woman and two young boys riding in front of the wagon. She quickly returned his smile. She thought him very attractive and excitingly commanding. She wondered if he had a wife or a sweetheart, or was he the type of man that would never settle down with one woman?

Her two sons were also fascinated by him. They had heard so much about his frontier adventures and his courageous war record that he had become their hero.

"We'll be making camp in a couple hours," John informed the large man. "If you need me for anything just let me know." Touching the brim of his hat, he nodded to the woman. "Mrs. McAllister."

She turned and watched him as he and Zeke rode down past the wagons, but when she noted her husband's stare, she immediately looked straight ahead.

When they approached the O'Brian wagon, John didn't pull up his horse but rode on past. Tom O'Brian was walking beside his oxen with a whip held securely in his hand. As they passed by him Zeke caught a quick glance at the man and he detected the glare in his eyes.

He brought his horse up alongside John's. "If looks could kill, you'd be a dead sonofabitch."

Grinning, John pulled his horse to a stop and looked over at his friend. "He hates every man who was in the Union army."

"A stuck-up southerner, huh?"

"Worse than that. An aristocratic southerner."

"Don't he realize he ain't gonna have no slaves to do his work fur 'im, and his woman ain't' gonna have no house-slaves to do her cookin' and empty her chamber pots?" Zeke chuckled.

"I'm sure he's fully aware of his circumstances," John replied.

"By the time he reaches California he's gonna know

he ain't no better than nobody else, and his dainty wife is gonna dirty her lily white hands a-pickin' up them buffalo chips. Yep, they'll learn them a thing or two!"

Observing the wagons passing slowly, John answered, "I doubt if any of them know what's in store. The dangers, the hardships, the suffering, and the deaths."

Chewing loudly on his wad of tobacco, Zeke speculated, "Well if'n they don't they soon enuf will."

By the time they set up camp, Rachel was bone tired from being jolted around in the back of the wagon for what seemed like endless hours. When her mother asked her to fetch some water from a nearby stream, she thankfully accepted the chore. It would give her a welcome chance to stretch her legs and move about.

Dusk had fallen when Rachel reached the stream with her empty keg. She knelt and awkwardly filled the container. Then she set it beside her and splashed the cool refreshing water on her face. Knowing her mother would be expecting her to return promptly, she stood bending over to lift the keg, but suddenly a hand appeared reaching toward it.

"I'll carry that for you."

Startled, she took a step backwards and then with relief registering on her face, she saw Edward Phillips.

"Thank you," she replied. Rachel turned to walk back to camp but he quickly stopped her.

"Wait! Let's talk for a moment."

"I can't. My mother is waiting for the water." Flashing him an enticing and teasing smile she added, "But I see no reason why we can't walk to our wagon, very slowly."

He fell into stride beside her. "I know it's none of my business, but is there something going on between you and Kendall?"

"Whatever do you mean?" she asked, sounding nonchalant.

"You know exactly what I mean. Don't act coy with me, sweetheart."

"Mr. Phillips, there is nothing going on between Josh and me, and I am not your sweetheart."

"The name is Edward, and you definitely are a sweetheart."

She ceased walking to turn and look at him. "Are you always so forward?"

He placed the water keg on the ground, then smoothly pulled her into his arms pressing her body close to his. "Yes, I am."

Rachel put her hands against his chest to push him away, but it only caused him to hold her tighter. She quit fighting him and looked up into his handsome face.

Is he going to kiss me, she wondered. Her aroused curiosity made her stop trying to squirm out of his embrace.

Expertly he pressed his lips to hers, crushing her body to his so tightly she could feel his male hardness through her petticoat and skirt. He roughly forced her mouth open beneath his, and kissed her with such passion she felt as though she would faint if he didn't stop.

The man's approach was totally soundless and neither of them was aware of his closeness until he spoke. "Nice weather we're having isn't it? A little hot maybe, especially in certain places."

Abruptly Edward removed his arms from Rachel.

"You move as quietly as a damned Indian!"

Rachel's cheeks were flaming red with embarrassment, but somehow she found the courage to look unwaveringly at John Reynolds. The tension she sensed in his eyes confused her. Although he appeared completely casual and relaxed, she instinctively knew that barely under the surface, he was more dangerous than a coiled rattlesnake; ready to strike with the slightest provocation. Even Rachel with her inexperience was able to analyze the strain between the two men.

"If you hadn't been so occupied, you'd have seen me coming."

"Next time make some noise!" Edward answered angrily.

Raising his eyebrows, John glanced at Rachel and smiled slyly. "Next time?"

Finding her voice, she said, "Edward, will you please take the keg of water to the wagon. I'll be along in a moment." Rachel honestly didn't understand why she wanted to stay and talk alone with John Reynolds. For some reason that she couldn't even begin to comprehend, she wanted to be near him.

Edward looked at her with annoyance as the truth of the situation became apparent. Not only would he have to go through Josh Kendall to reach Rachel, but he'd also have to go through John Reynolds. He could foresee no problems with Kendall, but he knew Reynolds would be an entirely different story. He reached down and picked up the keg of water. "She's all yours, Major, for now!" Briskly he walked away.

The evening shadows were becoming heavy and Rachel was beginning to find it difficult to see John's face clearly. The tall trees surrounding them cast even more darkness over the spot where they stood.

Suddenly, with no forewarning, he reached out grabbing her by the shoulders pulling her close.

"Listen to me, my ignorant little hypocrite, because I'm going to give you some advice you damned well need! Don't tease a man like Edward Phillips!"

Trying to push away from him she answered with resentment, "What could you possibly know about a man like Edward? He's not only a southerner but he's also a gentleman!"

"A southerner he may very well be, but he's no gentleman," he commented as he turned her loose.

"Of course he's a gentleman. If he hadn't been, Papa would never have hired him."

"Rachel, your father places all men into three categories: Yankees, poor white trash, and southern gentlemen. Phillips is no Yankee and he's too polished to be white trash, so your father automatically figures he must be a gentleman. And if you don't watch yourself around your father's so-called gentleman, you're going to lose your virginity."

Seeing her expression of shock, he asked teasingly, "You are still a virgin, aren't you?"

Her temper flaring, she replied in rage. "How dare you speak to me as though I'm a . . . a . . . loose woman!"

Uncontrollable laughter consumed him as she angrily placed her hands on her hips and continued, "You are the most rude . . . insulting . . . discourteous . . ."

With all traces of laughter abruptly erased, he interrupted, "Please Rachel, don't bore me again with your list of insults.'' Placing his hand under her chin, he tilted her face up to his. ''But always remember, my love, *you* don't bore me, only your unlimited list of adjectives concerning my character.''

She smiled at the man she found so complex. ''But, of course! How can I possibly bore you when you find me so entertaining,'' she replied flirtatiously.

''Another piece of advice, my love, don't be so foolish as to tease me either.''

He started to walk away from her, but she quickly asked, ''Where are you going?''

''A little further downstream, the water branches out and becomes deeper. I was on my way to take a bath when I accidently came across you and your southern gentleman; so if you'll excuse me, I shall proceed with my previous intentions.'' He smiled shrewdly. ''Unless you'd care to join me?''

Instead of becoming perturbed by his rudeness, she answered flippantly, ''My mother is expecting me, but perhaps next time, Mr. Reynolds.''

Proud of herself for having learned how to hold her own with him, she whirled smugly and began walking back toward camp.

The night air was unusually humid and warm for early spring. The heat inside the narrow enclosure of the wagon was making sleep impossible for Rachel. She could tell by their even breathing that her parents and sister were all asleep.

Quietly gathering up two blankets and her pillow, Rachel crept silently from the wagon. She peered across the campground, searching for a place to try and get some sleep. She'd have liked to have made her bed under the wagon, but that was where Edward was spending the night.

As the refreshing evening air blew across her shoulders, Rachel remembered she was dressed only in a thin petticoat. Hastily she wrapped one of the blankets around her. Without making a sound, she passed fleetingly by the burned-out campfire, hurrying over to a secluded area under a large tree.

Spreading out the other blanket and the pillow, she lay down. Surprisingly, she found she felt not only cool but also comfortable. Glancing upward, she watched the thousands of stars twinkling brightly in the dark Kansas sky. Staring at the glittering stars her eyelids became heavy and finally she fell asleep.

Rachel was soon to experience the frightening nightmare, that mysteriously would periodically recur and haunt her through the years to come.

John was making his nightly rounds when he heard a soft moan in the distance. Looking in the direction from which the sound came, he could see someone sleeping underneath a tree a short way from camp.

Soundlessly, but rapidly, he walked over and with surprise saw that it was Rachel. Obviously she was having a nightmare because although she was asleep, she was thrashing and moaning.

Kneeling beside her, he couldn't help but notice how she had restlessly pushed off her blanket. He found his eyes being drawn toward the soft tempting breasts exposed under the thin petticoat, and instantly he felt himself becoming sexually aroused; but when a frightful moan escaped from deep in her throat he turned his head, gazing down into her troubled face.

Gently he took her into his arms. "Rachel, honey, wake up."

Startled, her eyes flew open and she looked up at him terrified. She began trembling, and he pulled her tightly into his strong embrace. Putting her head on his shoulder, she slipped her arms around his neck, holding on to him securely.

"Baby . . . baby . . . it's all over now. It was only a bad dream," he told her soothingly.

Snuggling closer to him she whispered, "It was so horrible."

"Would you like to tell me about it?" he asked, while very conscious of her breasts, rubbing seductively against him.

Rachel raised her head from his shoulder, and blushing, she suddenly became aware that she was intimately in his arms. Moving away, she gathered her blanket, wrapping it about her. Although she didn't return to his embrace, she remained very close to him.

"Do you want to talk about it?" he asked again. He saw she was still trembling and as he reached for her, she gratefully went back into his comforting arms.

"It wasn't a nightmare. I think . . . I think it was a premonition . . . and if it was a premonition . . . someday I will be forced to endure a fate worse than . . . than. . . ."

"Than what?" he encouraged.

He could feel her stiffen in his arms as she answered dramatically. "A fate worse than my own death!"

Studying her closely, he noticed she was genuinely frightened and seriously believed what she had told him. Trying not to be amused by her childish fear, he suggested, "Why don't you start at the beginning and

68

explain exactly what happened.''

Holding herself rigid she began nervously, ''In the dream . . . there was a thick heavy fog . . . but suddenly the fog lifted and everything was clear. I saw myself riding a horse but I'm riding without a saddle. I could sense that my mind was in some kind of frightening turmoil. . . . Then the fog returned and I couldn't see anything, but I could actually feel a terrible . . . piercing pain! A pain of anguish and heartbreak! The fog lifted again and I was standing someplace but I couldn't tell where it was because everything around me was blurred and hazy . . . I barely recognized my own face because it looked so . . . so tormented! . . . And then . . . I raised my fist toward the sky. . . . The fog enveloped me again and I no longer saw myself, but I could still feel that terrible pain! The fog lifted once more and I saw myself lying face down on the grass with my head resting on my arms . . . and I was sobbing. The fog covered me again and even though I couldn't see anything I still . . .'' Raising her voice she continued, ''Oh God, I still felt that horrible terrifying pain!''

She placed her head on his shoulder, wrapped her arms tightly around his neck, and cried.

John allowed her to cry for a moment, but then he gently moved away from her and stood. The torture of holding her in his arms to comfort her, when he felt more like seducing her, had become unbearable to him.

He reached down and grasped her hand, pulling her to her feet. ''Rachel, I'm sure it was no premonition. It was nothing more than a bad dream.''

''Do you really think so?'' she asked.

Looking down into her tear-stained face he became

acutely aware of her virginal innocence and simple immaturity. "I can assure you of one thing, my love, if you don't go back to your wagon to sleep, something worse than a nightmare may decide to visit you."

Noticing her baffled expression he said ill-temperedly, "Damn Rachel! Don't you realize that you could be attacked out here alone!" Then his anger mysteriously vanished as he teased, "I knew you were a hypocrite, but I didn't know you were also a fool."

"I'm not fool enough to stand here and be insulted! Goodnight, Mr. Reynolds!"

She picked up the blanket and pillow, but instead of leaving she surprised him by saying sweetly, "Thank you for being kind to me when I needed you."

Not waiting for a reply, she turned and ran quietly toward her father's wagon. He remained to watch until she had safely climbed inside.

During the long tiresome weeks that passed, Rachel was never again alone with John Reynolds. She saw him often, but only from a distance. Although he visited the other wagons, he refused to stop by at theirs. Instead he'd send Zeke to check on them.

There had been no more romantic encounters with Edward Phillips, but she would often find him watching her with open desire. She noted he was shrewd enough not to look at her that way when her father was near.

She only caught a glimpse of Josh a few times. She wondered if she'd ever have the opportunity to speak with him again.

Rachel found the tedious journey not only terribly boring, but extremely tiring. Sometimes she didn't know which was worse, being roughly tossed about in a wagon, or wearily placing one foot in front of the other and trying to walk the dreary miles.

The wagon train crossed into Nebraska at Cottonwood Creek and then headed northwest to the Platte River. The green fields of Kansas were gone, replaced by the sandy hills of Nebraska.

Rachel was walking beside the wagon when she caught her first sight of the Platte River. She was astonished to find it was so unbelievably flat. It also appeared eerie to her because nothing seemed to be moving, or to be alive, over the vast landscape close to the river. Then with repulsion, she saw there was life on the banks of the Platte. Lizards were busily squirming over the sand and darting through the tall grass. At the sight of the disgusting creatures, she hurridly climbed into the wagon, deciding it was better to ride than to walk.

Rachel forgot her disappointment over the Platte River when she was astounded by her first glimpse of the natural landmark called Courthouse Rock. Its summit, resembling a castle, towered four hundred feet above the plains. Even though the wagon train made twenty-five miles a day along the Platte, for two days and nights the colossal Courthouse Rock remained in view.

The next landmark, Scotts Bluff, materialized as a blue mound on the horizon. It became larger as the wagon train traveled along the Platte. As they drew steadily nearer, it looked to Rachel like a huge fortress overlooking the vast plains. She was relieved when at last they reached it, because they would camp there for the night.

* * *

After supper, Rachel's parents left to visit with neighbors. Edward and Deborah were sitting beside the fire, and Edward was entertaining her with card tricks. Bored with having nothing to do, Rachel decided to take a stroll.

She headed leisurely toward the river bank hoping she wouldn't run across any lizards on the way. As she was nearing the bank she spotted John Reynolds and Zeke standing by the edge of the Platte, talking. Their trained, experienced sense of hearing detected her before she reached them. When they turned in her direction, she halted shortly, but noticing their smiles, she hurried over to them.

"Evenin', Miss O'Brian," Zeke said cheerfully.

"Good evening, Zeke."

He spat out a stream of tobacco juice before asking. "What do ya think of the journey so far?"

"I think it's as boring and as tiresome as that dreary river," she answered sullenly, pointing at the flat body of water.

Chuckling, Zeke agreed, "Yep, it's drury, but don't forget little gal, that river thar is gonna be our life line fur some time yet."

"How did it get its name? Do you know?" she asked.

Casually John moved toward her, and standing very near he answered, "The Omaha Indians and their cousins, the Otoes, named the river "Ni bthaska", which means flat water. That name appeared on some of the early maps, but eventually it was given to the territory of Nebraska."

Rachel tried to concentrate on what he was saying but she was too aware of his nearness. Will I never be able to be in his presence without being totally awed by him?, she wondered.

"Back in 1739, I think it was, two French brothers traveled up the river and named it 'LaRiviere Plate', which is French for the 'Flat River', so Platte River it finally became."

Moving away from him because his nearness was too confusing, she asked, "Do you also know how Scotts Bluff got its name?"

"It was named for Hiram Scott. He was a mountain man, who presumably died at the foot of the bluff; but, there's many different stories as to how it actually happened."

"I know what really happened," Zeke began. "It was back in the autumn of 1828, Scott was returnin' with some other fur trappers. They'd been in St. Louis but they had an accident with the canoe and it drownded their gunpowder, which was real bad cause they didn't have no way to hunt. Then Scott, he come down sick. The others searched fur food, wild fruit, and roots that were fittin' to eat. One day whilst they was searchin' fur some kind of food, they come across a fresh trail belongin' to white men. Now, these guys, they asked theirselves . . . what should we do? If'n they was to hurry, they could catch up to them white men and be able to reach a settlement, but they couldn't take Scott with 'em cause he was too sick to be moved, and they was too weak to carry 'im. So they just abandoned 'im to his fate . . . and off they took. When they found the white men they told 'em that Scott had died of his illness. Well, the next summer, when them same fur traders took the trail back up the Platte into the mountains, they come on Scott's remains sixty miles from where they had left 'im. At the foot of the highest bluff they found his bones and his grinnin' skull, a lookin' straight up at 'em. The poor devil had drug hisself sixty miles 'fore he finally died.'' Looking over toward the bluff he continued, ''Right over thar, little gal, is where they found 'im.''

Rachel followed his gaze and vividly she imagined the man still lying there abandoned and left alone to face a terrifying death. As Zeke walked away she was still staring at the bottom of the bluff.

Suddenly hearing John's laughter, she whirled and looked at him. ''What's so funny?'' she asked, instantly on the defensive.

''You, my gullible little hypocrite. Hell, Rachel, do you really believe a dying man could crawl sixty miles?''

Realizing the humor of the situation she laughingly replied, ''Well at least you've been entertained.''

''You've never failed me yet, my love.''

''John,'' she began, using his Christian name for the first time, ''why haven't you come to see me?''

''Rachel, don't you know a lady should never ask such a forward question of a gentleman?''

''As you have already informed me, I am no lady and you are no gentleman, so what you ask is immaterial . . . my love!''

Smiling cheerfully, he took her hand into his and led her to the river bank. ''If I remember correctly you are usually ordering me to go away and leave you alone. Can't you make up your mind, my little hypocrite?''

''Will you stop teasing! I'm serious. I want to know why you never come to our wagon.''

John continued to hold her hand, and it gave her a

feeling of comfort and contentment. Mysteriously, she somehow sensed that when she was with him, she was where she belonged.

"I've stayed away because I have no desire to maintain the damned war. Men like your father, will never stop fighting it. I'm surprised he doesn't have a Confederate flag waving over the top of his wagon."

"Then you've stayed away because of him and not because of me?"

He studied her face for a sign of coyness but decided she was sincere. "Didn't I once tell you, that I wouldn't stay away from you?"

"But only because you find me entertaining," she pouted.

"Entertaining, yes, but also beautiful, charming, and . . ." Abruptly he stopped speaking as he glanced back over his shoulder. Quickly looking in the same direction, she saw her father coming toward them.

"Oh no!" she gasped.

Instantly she pulled her hand away from his. Staring up into John's face, she thought to find him upset, but instead he was grinning down at her with amusement.

She also expected to hear her father holler with rage, but he said to her calmly, "Rachel go to the wagon. Don't talk back to me, just go."

She noticed that he was perspiring heavily, and his shoulders were slightly slumped. "Papa, are you all right?"

"I find you alone in the night with a man who is not only too damned old for you, but also a Yankee, and you ask me if I'm all right! Go to the wagon, Rachel! Get out of my sight before I do something that I may later regret."

"Do as he says," John advised, giving her a gentle push.

Taking one last worried look at the two men, she ran back toward camp leaving them alone.

Losing his composure, Tom O'Brian ranted, "Reynolds, my daughter is not yet seventeen!"

"I'm very aware of Rachel's age, Mr. O'Brian, and her innocence," he replied unruffled.

"I'm going to believe you because even though I don't like you, I do consider you an honest man," he answered, wiping perspiration from his brow. "But I'm warning you to stay away from her!"

John appeared to be relaxed, but a glint of anger flickered in his eyes. "Don't warn me to do anything. I'll do as I damned please."

"Not with my daughter you won't!" he demanded in a voice that was becoming weak. "My God, I'd rather see her dead, than to see her with Yankee scum!"

"Because of the circumstances, I'm going to forget what you said. But I advise you to get the hell away from me, just in case I can't forget."

With hate in his eyes, Rachel's father doubled his fist and stepped forward, but his steps came to a sudden stop as dizziness overtook him. Stumbling, he tried to retain his balance, but as John moved to help him, his body grew limp and, falling, he passed out.

Cholera! In a matter of minutes the word spread panic through the entire camp. Most of the emigrants had very little knowledge of the disease, but they all knew it was highly contagious and in most cases fatal!

Unknown to John, one of the McAllister boys already had the illness. His mother, believing it was only a stomach ache, had mentioned nothing of her son's nausea. When she heard of Zeke and the wagon master's prognosis concerning Mr. O'Brian's illness, she immediately informed them of her son's condition.

John was then reasonably sure he knew how the cholera had started. A few days before, a group of fur trappers had visited the wagon train. One of the men had struck up a friendship with Jacob McAllister and had been invited to their wagon for supper. He now remembered the man had appeared to be ill the following morning when the trappers and the wagon train had left in their separate directions.

John's first order was to have the McAllister wagon and the O'Brian wagon moved away from the others. Hereafter they would be forced to trail them from a reasonable distance.

John and Zeke were fully aware there would soon be more wagons joining the two that were now isolated. Cholera had been known to easily wipe out half the population on a wagon train. Both men had witnessed cholera before, and knew there was little known treatment for the disease. Even with a doctor's care most victims didn't survive. The epidemic would soon be in full force!

Within the short span of twenty-four hours, the number of wagons isolated due to the cholera had increased to six.

As the sounds of the pioneers setting up camp for the night drifted around him, John stood alone, watching the desolate wagons that had been banished from the rest. Even across the vast darkening plains, he could distinguish the O'Brian wagon. The last he had heard, Tom O'Brian and the McAllister boy were still alive.

The Palmer wagon was now out there with the Heiskills', the Wilsons', and the Donaldsons'. Seth Palmer's wife had taken ill early that morning. Joseph Heiskill's daughter and Jesse Wilson's aging mother came down with cholera that afternoon. Only a couple of hours before, Mace Donaldson had had to remove his wagon from the other nineteen as his son and daughter had been suddenly stricken.

John could see a figure approaching him from the direction of the isolated wagons. As the boy drew nearer he recognized him as Wilson's son, Daniel.

When he came within hearing distance, the boy halted and called, "Mr. Reynolds, is that you?"

"Yeah, what's the latest?" he asked, though dreading the answer.

"My grandmother died a few minutes ago, sir," he replied with a sob in his throat. Then he proceeded, "Mr. Palmer's wife is getting worse, but the Heiskill girl is holding her own. It's too early yet to know about the Donaldson kids."

"And Tom O'Brian?" he inquired.

"He's still alive, but two other members of his family have come down sick."

The quiet of the still night seemed to be smothering him as he waited for Daniel to continue. Rachel's face flashed vividly across his mind, and losing his usual composure he demanded, "Who are they?"

"Mrs. O'Brian and one of the daughters," he answered.

The darkness of the night concealed his face from the boy's vision, so he wasn't aware of the tension in the man's eyes and was startled when the wagon master said angrily, "Damn it kid, which daughter?"

Afraid of the man's sudden anger, he replied meekly, "I don't know, sir."

Hearing the fear in the boy's voice, John apologized. "I'm sorry, son. I shouldn't have yelled at you, but I want you to go back and find out which daughter. I'll wait here for you."

"Yes, sir. Right away, sir," he answered.

The boy dashed off into the night. While watching him leave, John figured Daniel to be around twelve and at once felt a strong surge of compassion for the child. Chances were the boy would be forced to face a death worse than that of his grandmother or any member of his family. It could be his own. Cholera took no pity on the young.

Strolling over to be with his friend, Zeke asked, "Heard anythin' yet?"

"The Wilson boy, Daniel, was just here," he replied.

"How close did he come to ya?" Zeke asked.

"No closer than hearing distance," John answered as he began rolling a cigarette.

"What'd he say?"

"His grandmother died and Palmer's wife is getting worse. The rest are still alive. Mrs. O'Brian and one of her daughters have taken ill."

"Which one?" Zeke promptly asked.

Lighting his cigarette he replied, "The kid didn't know, but he's returning to tell me."

"Hope it ain't Miss Rachel, don't you?"

"Hell, I wish it didn't have to be either one," he answered irritably.

"I ain't got nothin' against Miss Deborah. She's such a shy little lady, that I ain't never paid her no mind, but Miss Rachel, why when I'd ride by her wagon to check up on 'em she'd be kind of sweet and nice to me. Flashing that pretty smile of hers, always tellin me somethin' cute or funny. Yep, thar's somethin' 'bout that little gal that a man finds downright appealin'." Watching him out of the corner of his eye, he asked again, "Sure hope it ain't Miss Rachel, don't you?"

Angrily John threw down his unfinished cigarette. "All right, damn it! I hope it isn't her!"

"Too bad you ain't younger, or she ain't a little older, don't ya reckon?" he asked slyly.

Losing his patience with Zeke's questions, John replied ill-temperedly, "No, I don't! I think things are best the way they are!"

Nodding his head, Zeke agreed, "Yep, yur right. Considerin' how it is with you and yur life, cause she ain't the type of gal a man could find easy to furgit."

As they waited for Daniel's return, Zeke remembered the way John had looked at Rachel the night before down on the river bank. Yep, he thought, he's got a thing fur her. Cain't say that I blame 'im none.

After a few moments had passed, John mumbled impatiently, "What's keeping the kid! This waiting! Damn this waiting!"

Zeke looked at him with surprise. "That gal has really gotten to ya, ain't she?"

Nervously John walked a few paces before swerving back to face him. "Not in the way you mean. But yeah, she's gotten to me."

"Well, maybe it won't be her."

"So what if it isn't her?" he asked loudly. "Hell, what chance does she have out there with cholera all around her?"

"Ya know just as well as I do how some people don't seem to catch it. Someone's a comin', maybe it's the boy."

Instantly, John peered in the direction of the wagons. Due to the darkness that had fallen, he barely made out the small figure coming toward them.

"Daniel, is that you?" he asked.

"Yes sir, Mr. Reynolds," he answered sounding exhausted.

"Son, are you all right?"

"No, sir. I feel sort of sick," he replied weakly. "I've been feeling bad since we stopped to make camp. Mr. Reynolds, I'm scared! Will I die too . . . like grandma?"

"Dear God," he whispered, and then he called out to the child, "Can you make it back to your wagon?"

"I'll try," he answered.

Daniel turned to leave when suddenly a profuse spell of vomiting overtook him. Both men watched helplessly as the boy doubled over, retching violently. Then his small body grew limp as he collapsed to the ground.

John made a move toward the sick child, but swiftly Zeke grabbed him by the arm. "Ya cain't go out thar!"

"What do you expect me to do? Stand here and watch that kid strangle to death on his own vomit?"

"Damn it, John! If ya go to 'im, ya cain't come back!"

"Zeke, you're perfectly capable of leading this wagon train. If something happens to me, you can see them safely to California."

"Yur place ain't out thar with them folks whats a dyin'. It's here with the livin' who are dependin' on ya! I'll carry the boy to his wagon."

Roughly John pushed the man's hand off his arm. "No! I'll take him!"

Zeke watched as he ran to the child. Gathering Daniel into his arms, he began carrying him toward the silent wagons standing eerily alone on the dark horizon.

When his friend had disappeared into the darkness of the night, Zeke muttered under his breath, "It's not only the boy. It's that gal. She's the reason yur a-headin' fur them wagons."

Nora Wilson never wanted to leave their small farm in Illinois. She had been happy and perfectly content with her home and taking care of her family and elderly mother-in-law; but her restless, ambitious husband could not be satisfied with what the Lord had given them, and he had insisted they move to California.

With tears in her eyes, she now watched as he walked away from their wagon with shoulders bent in grief and carrying a shovel loosely in his hands. Somehow she knew he would find the strength to go out there on the barren God forsaken plains to dig his mother's grave.

Startled when her son's dog suddenly barked, she turned and saw the wagon master approaching with her child held securely in his arms.

"Dear God! No!" she screamed as she began running toward them.

The dog easily reached the man first, but as he detected the familiar scent of his young master he wagged his tail and whined.

With the woman crying hysterically beside him,

82

John climbed inside the wagon and placed the boy on a bed of blankets. Glancing beside him he noticed the covered body of the elderly Mrs. Wilson.

"Where's your husband?" he asked.

Between broken sobs, she answered, "He's gone . . . to dig a . . . a grave for his mother." Kneeling beside her son, she rubbed her hand across his feverish brow.

"Mama . . . Mama . . ." the child murmured. "Where's Skipper? . . . where is he?"

Looking up into the questioning eyes of the man, she explained, "The dog. He's always been so fond of that dog. Mr. Reynolds, what should I do for him?"

"Try to keep his fever down by bathing him with cool water and get as much liquid down him as you can. And let his dog come in. Maybe its presence will give him some kind of comfort."

"Is there anything else I can do?"

"Pray, Mrs. Wilson. . . . Tell your husband when he returns to come find me, and I'll help him move his mother's body to the grave."

"Thank you, Mr. Reynolds," she replied, as she moved to the opening at the rear of the wagon.

"Skipper! Come on boy, come on!" she called.

Swiftly the dog leaped into the wagon and went directly to his young master. Lying beside him, he whined softly as he licked the boy's flushed cheek.

During his lifetime, John had often been forced to witness grief and sorrow, but nothing had ever touched him so acutely as the sight of the small blondheaded boy with his faithful little dog.

"I'll be back, Mrs. Wilson, but if you need me don't hesitate to send for me." Taking one last glance at the child, he left the confines of the stuffy wagon.

With grief and concern weighing heavily on his shoulders, he walked away from the Wilson's wagon. He stopped to see about Seth Palmer's wife, but when he looked down into her pinched, drawn face, he knew she would soon die. With sympathy he watched her weeping husband beg God to have mercy. As he regarded the young pretty woman so near death, Rachel's face once again flashed across his mind.

John checked on the Heiskills, Donaldsons, and the McAllisters, but it was too soon yet to know if the cholera victims would miraculously survive. As he neared the O'Brian wagon, he fought back from his tortured mind the image of Rachel lying seriously ill.

When he saw her step down from the wagon and walk wearily to the small glowing fire, he felt such relief that he unconsciously groaned aloud, "Thank God!"

At the sound of his voice, she dropped the empty basin she'd been holding and quickly ran over to him. In one swift movement he pulled her into his arms and held her close.

"Rachel," he whispered. "I've been so worried about you."

Slowly Rachel stepped back from him, looking thoughtfully up into his face. He cares! He really cares!

"You've been worried about me?" she asked, finding it hard to believe that a man like John Reynolds could be so concerned about her.

Smiling at the childish bewilderment on her face, he replied, "Of course, I've been worried. If I were to lose you, my beautiful hypocrite, who would I have to tease between here and California?" As her puzzled expression began to fade, he became aware of how tired and worn out she appeared.

Glancing toward the wagon, he asked, "How are they?"

Tears filled her eyes, as she answered, "I don't know!"

"What have you been doing for them?"

"Edward and I . . . we've been trying to keep them clean . . . comfortable. . . ." Raising her voice she cried, "When they become sick . . . we hold them so they won't . . . strangle." Coming very close to hysteria she sobbed, "I don't know what to do! I know nothing about cholera . . . or death! God help me! I don't know what to do!"

Drawing her into his arms, he kissed the top of her bowed head. "You've done just fine, Baby. Just fine."

Crying heavily against his chest she begged, "Help me! Please John! Tell me what to do!"

Placing his hands on the upper portion of Rachel's arms he moved her so that he could see into her face. "I want you to go down to the river and fill a bucket of water. When you return save part of the water for bathing purposes, but boil the rest. We will have to force them to drink the boiled water. The liquids they are losing must be replenished. And Rachel, I want you to stop by the wagons and tell the others to do the same."

When she made no response, he ordered, "Go on! Do it!"

John watched as she moved to the wagon picking up the empty keg. With her head bowed and shoulders bent she walked away. Keeping his eyes on her, he saw how she pitifully dragged one foot behind the other, carrying the container loosely by her side. But his heart filled with admiration and respect as the young woman suddenly, and bravely, lifted her head, straightened her narrow shoulders and stood erect. Holding the keg tightly in her hand, Rachel walked boldly and courageously to accept whatever might lay ahead. The gallantry of her Irish ancestors flowed proudly through her veins as she moved through the quiet and tranquil night.

Entering the restricted enclosure of the O'Brian wagon, John could see Rachel's parents and sister lying on the wooden floor that had been padded with heavy blankets. Edward Phillips was kneeling beside the ailing Deborah, bathing her face with a damp cloth. The glow of the flickering lantern cast dark shadows on the rounded canvas walls.

"Reynolds! What in the hell are you doing here?" Edward demanded.

"It's a long story. How are they?"

Moving away from Deborah, he threw the cloth into a nearby basin. "Damn it man! Don't you realize your place is with the other people on this wagon train. Why are you here in the midst of cholera? If you die, what happens to all those families? They paid you hard-earned money to guide them to California. Not to play angel of mercy!"

The two men silently stared into one another's eyes and the tension hung heavily in the air. Detecting Edward's compassion, John realized that he been mistaken about the young man's character. The suspense was suddenly broken when a choking sound escaped from Nadine O'Brian's parched throat. Alertly both men hurried to her side. Kneeling, John lifted the woman's head, helping her bend over as, coughing weakly, she cleared her throat. Carefully, he helped her back on the pallet and closing her eyes she drifted into sleep.

"She isn't going to make it, is she?" Edward asked.

Looking over at the worried man kneeling beside him, John answered, "I doubt if she makes it through the night. How bad are the other two?"

He rubbed his hands anxiously through his thick hair as he answered, "Hell, I don't know. I don't know a damned thing about cholera."

Noticing the strain on Edward's face, John suggested, "Why don't you go outside and get some fresh air. You look as though you could use a break."

"Yeah, I'm beat. Rachel or I, neither one, have had any rest since this started."

As Edward climbed down from the wagon, John checked on the sleeping Deborah, and from the feel of her brow, he judged her fever to be moderate. Moving around Deborah, he knelt beside Tom O'Brian. Instantly he became concerned over the man's blanched and pallid complexion. Feeling compassion for Rachel, he realized that she would inevitably lose both parents.

A strangling gasp for air came once again from Mrs. O'Brian. Moving to her, he tried desperately to help the enfeebled woman to breathe. When the long and futile moments had passed, the gentle southern-bred Nadine O'Brian died in the arms of a Yankee.

John was standing beside the campfire talking with Edward when he spotted Rachel coming toward them carrying the heavy keg of water.

Glancing in the same direction, Edward asked, "Do you want me to tell her?"

Instead of giving the younger man a reply, he only

shook his head, and with dread left to meet Rachel. When she saw him approaching she hurried her footsteps.

As Rachel neared him she asked, "How are they?"

He remained silent for a moment before taking the full keg from her hand placing it on the ground. "Unless Deborah takes a turn for the worse, she'll pull through. Your father is very ill."

With fear materializing rapidly on her strained face, she pleaded, "And my mother?"

Looking tenderly into her frightened eyes, he replied, "She died a few minutes ago."

He caught her in his arms as she fainted.

Early the next morning, while conversing with a safe distance between them, Zeke and John decided not to move the wagon train for the next few days. There had been no new cases of cholera; it was beginning to appear as if the epidemic had been contained.

Holding a shovel in his hand, John stood near the fresh grave that Jesse Wilson had dug the night before. With his muscles flexing under his buckskin jacket, he pushed the blade of the shovel into the hard dirt and proceeded to dig. When he saw Jacob McAllister approaching, he stopped and waited. He noticed that the man also carried a shovel by his side.

"Thought you could use some help," Mr. McAllister offered.

"How's your son?" he inquired.

"Seems to be a little better."

"Maybe he'll make it."

"Do you want us to dig Mrs. O'Brian's grave, or do

you want me to start on the other one?''

"Other one? What do you mean?'' John asked.

"Haven't you heard? The Wilson boy died.''

The concern Jacob McAllister felt didn't show on his face, as he witnessed the wagon master's reaction. He stood silently and watched, as the man jerked his shovel out of the solid ground, held it high over his head and then brought it crashing down to earth. He reached down, picked up the partially broken shovel and sent it flying through the air as he yelled, "Damn! . . . Damn it, not the boy!''

The huge man walked over to John and, placing his callused hand on the wagon master's broad shoulder, he sympathized, "It's always hardest to lose the young-uns. I'll go fetch you another shovel.''

Rachel had also been a witness to John's display of grief. She had been on her way to find John when she saw him with Jacob McAllister. As the other man was leaving, she hurried over to John. He detected her approach and tried to compose himself, but his sorrow was still depicted vividly in his eyes.

"John what's wrong?'' she asked.

Rachel wanted desperately to hold him in her arms and try to give him comfort and take comfort from him. She remembered how kind he had been to her through the long heartbreaking night. The way he had held her so tenderly as she cried for her mother.

"The Wilson boy died,'' he uttered softly.

"Did you know the little boy?''

"No, not really, but there was something about the kid that got to me.''

Tears began streaming down her face as she asked, "When will it end? How many more will die before it's over?''

He reached over and put his hand gently on her cheek. She found the contact pleasing and wanted him to take her into his arms, but instead, removing his hand, he inquired, ''How are your father and sister?''

''Deborah isn't any worse, but I was searching for you to . . . to tell you . . . Papa died!''

Seven days later, the survivors of the cholera were getting well, and miraculously there had been no new cases. The epidemic was over, but it would leave behind six deserted graves in the desolate plains of Nebraska. The markers, which had been crudely and hurriedly made, were inscribed with a name and age carved into each wooden cross. The simple epitaphs would be read by emigrants passing through for years to come: Thomas O'Brian—Age 52; Nadine O'Brian—Age 43; Mary Wilson—Age 71; Daniel Wilson—Age 12; Edith Palmer—Age 20; Margaret Donaldson—Age 6.

Deborah was resting comfortably in the back of the wagon, and Edward was busy hitching up the oxen, when Rachel decided to slip away and say goodbye to her parents for the last time. Walking despondently toward her parents' graves, she wondered what would become of Deborah and herself. She knew Edward would take care of them until they safely reached California. But what then? Tears filled her eyes as she strolled nearer to where her parents and the others were buried.

When she spied the little dog lying pathetically over the small mound that covered his young master, it caused a sob to break from deep in her throat. The dog lifted his head and alertly raised his ears.

Walking over and kneeling beside him, she petted his trembling body. "You poor little dog, what will become of you, and what will become of me? But you still have a family, don't you! They'll love you and take care of you, but I have no one to take care of me."

Standing and staring forlornly at her parents' graves, Rachel cried, "I love you! And I feel so lost without you! Oh Papa! Mama!"

Her shoulders shook and for a moment she wept uncontrollably. Then, following a period of silence, she glanced down to where the dog lay and spoke with intrepid courage. "But I will survive! Somehow . . . somehow I will learn to accept what has happened!"

Moving with the silence of an experienced adventurer, John said, "It'll take time, Rachel."

Startled, she turned swiftly and looked warmly into the eyes of the man she had come to know so well.

"We'll be leaving in a few minutes. Why don't you go on back to your wagon," he suggested.

"I hate to leave them . . . out here . . . so far away!"

He took her hand tenderly into his. "It'll be all right, Baby. Believe me, in time it'll be all right."

Before releasing her hand, he gave it a reassuring squeeze and instantly she missed the comfort of his touch.

"What in the hell?" he questioned looking away from her.

Quickly she swerved and saw Jesse Wilson strolling rapidly in their direction toting a rifle. Without looking at either of them, he went to his son's grave where the dog lay and aimed his gun.

Frantically clutching John's arm, Rachel cried, "Stop him!"

"Wilson! Put the rifle down!" he ordered.

At the sound of his voice, the man turned abruptly and only then did he seem to become aware of their presence. Slowly he lowered the rifle to his side.

"Why are you going to shoot that poor dog?" Rachel asked.

"Miss O'Brian, ma'am, if you don't want to watch, then you'd best leave."

"No! I won't let you kill him!" she insisted angrily.

"It ain't your dog. You got no right to stop me," he sneered.

Looking at John with pleading eyes, she begged, "Don't let him shoot the dog, please!"

"Wilson," John began, "why do you want to kill him?"

"I don't, not really. I ain't got nothin' against the mutt, but it's my wife. She wants me to get rid of it."

"But why?" Rachel cried.

"The dog reminds her of the boy. My wife, she ain't been thinkin' right since Daniel died. The damn dog wouldn't stay away from his grave, so I tried tying him up but he whined the whole time. And, my wife, she just couldn't take it."

"Return to your wagon, Mr. Wilson, because I'm not going to let you shoot the dog," John stated.

"You ain't got no right to stop me!" he bellowed. "The dog belongs to me and it's none of your goddamn business what I do with him!"

"You're right, but I'm making it my business."

"Why do you give a damn whether or not the mutt

lives?'' he asked angrily.

As the memory of a small blond-headed boy with his dog lying beside him crossed his mind, John answered, "I have my reasons."

Jesse Wilson's thoughts went no further than aiming the rifle at the man, but the instant his grip on the weapon tightened, John had his pistol out of its holster. "Don't try it," he warned.

Staring at the pistol pointing at him, Jesse Wilson asked cautiously, "You wouldn't shoot a man over a dog, would you?"

"Wilson, don't ever be fool enough to even think about pointing a gun at me," he answered in a voice that left absolutely no doubt in the other man's mind.

Returning his pistol to the holster, he ordered severely, "Go back to your wagon!"

"What about the dog?" he asked.

"I'll take care of him," Rachel offered.

"Just keep him away from my wife," he demanded gruffly before walking away.

Rachel hastened to the dog and kneeling beside him, she picked him up, hugging him protectively close. With the small black-and-white dog held lovingly in her arms, she strolled over to John. "You saved the dog because he loved the little boy, didn't you?"

Reaching over and patting the dog affectionately, he disregarded Rachel's question. "His name is Skipper and tie him to your wagon because if he gets loose he'll come right back here. And Rachel, you've got to keep him tied until he accepts you." With a changed expression in his eyes, he added "And learns to love you."

The strange way he was watching her confused Rachel. She wished she could understand why he was staring at her with such intensity; but Rachel would always be plagued by a shallow depth of conception.

"I left my horse close to your wagon, so I'll walk part of the way with you."

Rachel turned and, looking at the two graves, she silently said goodbye. With John Reynolds by her side, she walked away from the parents that she had loved.

The warmth of the morning sun reminded her that the day would be clear and hot. She knew they would cover quite a few miles along the Platte before nightfall.

When they reached his horse, Rachel started to leave but curiosity caused her to change her mind. "How did you learn to draw a pistol so fast?"

Smiling at her with the grin she now found so familiar, he answered, "From a Mexican bandit."

"A bandit!" she exclaimed. Rachel was getting ready to ask him all sorts of questions when she detected a certain twinkle in his eyes.

"Oh no you don't, John Reynolds! I'm not going to entertain you by believing some incredible story about Mexican bandits!" Lifting her chin and cutting her eyes at him sharply, she stated smugly, "Besides a man drawing a pistol with your expertise is somehow . . . indecent!"

Hurrying toward the wagon, Rachel could still hear his robust laughter. Why is it, she wondered, even when I'm trying very hard not to entertain him, I get the feeling . . . I do anyhow!

With no parental guidance to curb her spirit, Rachel took full advantage of her new-found freedom. To Deborah's dismay and embarrassment, her first act of rebellion was to exchange her cumbersome dress for pants.

Remembering that her mother had kept some clothes belonging to her brothers, Rachel searched through the large chest until she found a pair of trousers that would fit with only slight alterations. Joyfully, she also discovered a couple of shirts and a pair of riding boots that her younger brother had worn in his youth.

Hurriedly she made the simple alterations. Quickly she pulled off the restricting dress and petticoat. Giving her sister a defiant glare of determination, she put on the clothes and then the boots.

Frowning with worry over what people would think, Deborah fretted, "Rachel, must you do this?"

Looking at her impatiently, she frowned, "Great guns and little switches, Deb! It's not that I don't want to wear dresses and be a lady, but just how do you suggest I dress to ride Edward's horse!"

Deborah's eyes widened with astonishment as she declared, "Rachel, you can't ride a horse astraddle!"

"And why not?" she smirked.

"The posture is very unbecoming to a lady," Deborah explained.

Chapter Three

Perturbed with her sister, Rachel told her, "You sound just like Mama." Carefully she jumped down from the wagon leaving Deborah shocked by her behavior.

The wagon train had stopped for their noon break, but was now preparing to pull out. Giving the tied dog a loving pat on his head, she hurried over to Edward. He was waiting for her with his horse saddled.

Enjoying how the tight pants outlined her full hips and slim legs, he smiled, "When you asked earlier if you could ride my horse, I wondered how you intended to go about it with any comfort." As his eyes raked her womanly curves, he cautioned, "I guess you know you're going to cause quite a scandal among all the ladies on the wagon train."

She raised her chin stubbornly. "I will not stay cooped up in that wagon or walk when I can ride! And if that means I'm not a lady, then I don't care!"

Amused, he laughed. "That's the spirit, sweetheart. Besides, Rachel, ladies never have any fun."

Edward helped her mount the horse. "He's easy to handle and you shouldn't have any trouble with him."

Picking up the reins, she told him, "Papa taught me to ride when I was only four."

She turned the horse's head. Riding away, she glanced back, yelling, "So you don't need to worry."

As Rachel expertly guided the horse through camp and around the covered wagons, the eyes of most men followed her with admiration and desire. The disapproving stares of their wives trailed her with jealousy and resentment.

She was glad to be on a horse after so many days in a wagon or walking tiresomely beside it. But most importantly, the horse gave her the opportunity to spend more time with John Reynolds. Now she could ride at the front of the wagon train beside him!

During the epidemic, she'd become accustomed to seeing him every day. In the three weeks they had been traveling since then, he had frequently found time to stop by the wagon, but those few minutes he shared with her were not enough. Besides, Deborah and Edward were always present, and she longed to be alone with him.

While nearing Josh's wagon, she caught a glimpse of him and abruptly pulled up her horse.

"Rachel!" he exclaimed. "What do you think you're doing?"

Looking down at him keenly, she responded, "I'm doing as I please."

Since her parents' death, Josh had visited her often. Rachel sincerely liked him and enjoyed his company, but she knew all she really wanted was simply to be with John.

"You shouldn't ride around dressed like that!" he objected sternly.

Indulging wickedly in her new rebellious attitude, she asked, "And how do you suggest I ride without a side-saddle? In bloomers?"

Seeing his startled expression, she laughed gaily. "Honestly, Josh, I never knew men could shock so easily."

Losing his anger, he laughed along with her. "We usually don't, but Rachel, you have a way of saying exactly what isn't expected."

He noticed how radiantly she appeared. "It's so good to see you smiling again. You suffered so much because of the cholera."

"Please, Josh, I don't want to talk about it."

"Of course, I'm sorry," he apologized.

"Have you seen John?" she asked.

"John?" he questioned, not realizing whom she meant.

"Major Reynolds. Have you seen him?"

Josh was surprised to hear she was on a first name basis with his ex-major. He wondered if Major Reynolds were in some way responsible for the glow in her cheeks and the merriment in her eyes.

"I haven't seen him since this morning. I didn't realize you and he were friends."

Josh had always hoped that Rachel would give him some kind of romantic encouragement, but as she spoke to him, he could only conceal his disappointment.

"We became very close during the epidemic. If it hadn't been for John, I don't know how I could've gotten through those terrible days. I needed him so desperately!"

The expression of adoration in her eyes was a declaration in itself. Disheartened, he realized she was falling in love with John Reynolds.

"Do you know him very well?" she asked.

In spite of his disappointment over Rachel's obvious infatuation, he found himself smiling. "I know him about as well as a Second Lieutenant ever knows a Major. It just so happens he's the main reason I decided to go to California. When I learned he was going, I figured what the hell, it's as good a place as any. The guys traveling with me felt the same way, I guess. We got used to following him while in the army and old habits are hard to break."

Observing the wagons preparing to leave, she said, "I'm sure I'll find him. See you later."

Josh watched as she rode off in search of John Reynolds. He wondered how much the major had told her. He was sure it hadn't been much, because if she knew, she wouldn't be so happy!

Riding beside John Reynolds, at the head of the wagon train, Rachel was happier than she'd ever been in her seventeen years of life. She felt too contented and satisfied to question her undeniable obsession with him. Rachel accepted her need for John Reynolds as naturally as she accepted the soft breezes blowing gently through the trees, the falling raindrops replenishing the earth, and the splendid sunrise she viewed each morning.

The sweetness of first love was growing rapidly in Rachel's naive and innocent heart, but her virginal and simple thoughts never went further than the hope of a kiss. She was fully aware that more went on between a husband and wife. Rachel's mother had tried to prepare her daughter for womanhood and marriage, so she understood a wife had "certain unpleasant duties" to her husband, but that part of life seemed unreal somehow. Reality was the comfort of being held in John's arms, the charm in his boyish grin, the thrill when he looked at her with those dominating eyes, and the prospect of the so long awaited kiss!

Rachel had very little knowledge of his personal life, and she often wondered about his past. John had never freely offered any information concerning himself. Regarding him inquisitively while he rode quietly beside her, she decided to try a probe into his personal life.

"John," she began curiously, "I remember Papa once saying that you are wealthy. Are you?"

With his usual grin and a slight raise of his eyebrows he answered, "And here all along, my tactless little hypocrite, I thought you liked me for myself when you were really interested in my money."

Trying very hard not to lose her patience with his teasing, she remarked, "If a man is wealthy, I see no reason why he should deny it."

"Neither do I, so I admit it."

"Then why are you working as a wagon master?" she pried.

"Obviously not for the pay."

He glanced over toward her and Rachel detected no mischievousness in his eyes. Gratefully, she realized he was going to be honest with her.

"My father owned a shipping line in Boston, which had been his father's before him. Being born into wealth, I had all money could buy and my father never once doubted I would someday take my rightful place in the company. When my education had been completed to his satisfaction, my uncle was ordered to undertake the unpleasant chore of teaching me the business. Charles was related to the family by marriage. Being that he wasn't a Reynolds, he became the hired help. Hell, he knew the shipping line as well as my father, but only a Reynolds deserved the honor and privilege of operating the 'Reynolds Shipping Line.' ''

"You sound bitter. Didn't you like your father?"

John remained silent for so long she began to doubt that he was going to answer. With the sounds of plodding oxen, the cracks of whips, men shouting, and the voices of children drifting over the plains, Rachel waited patiently for him to continue.

"I loved my father, Rachel, but I didn't like him. He was usually selfish, cruel, and overbearing. He died when I was twenty-one. I promptly handed half-interest in the company and operating procedures over to Charles and left. I had no intentions of living my father's kind of life. I remained in touch with my uncle, but I never once returned to Boston. Charles had no wife or children, so when he died six years ago I had the business sold."

"But why?" she asked.

"After the way I had lived for thirteen years, I could never have stayed in Boston or behind a desk."

"When you left home, where did you go?" Rachel questioned.

While rolling a cigarette, he recalled, "I went to St. Louis looking for adventure. That's where I met Zeke. He was a fur trapper back then. I can still remember how shocked I was by his manner and appearance. I'd never met a man like him in civilized Boston. He took a liking to me and took me under his wing, so to speak. I

102

definitely needed someone to look out for me. Hell, I was as green as the day is long. When he left St. Louis to return to the mountains, he invited me to tag along, and I left with him. I was so damned ignorant, I actually thought I was going to find adventures worth writing home about.''

''Did you?'' she asked.

Smiling reminiscently he lit his cigarette. ''Hardship is what I found, to put it mildly. For twenty-one years I'd had life served to me on a silver platter, and then in a matter of a few short weeks, I was served Zeke and his God-forsaken wilderness. But he was a patient man and eventually he taught me everything I needed to know about trapping, and how to stay alive in the mountains. Four years we wintered and trapped in those mountains, and traveled to St. Louis during the spring. By the end of those four long years, Ashley Jonathan Reynolds III, heir to Reynolds Shipping Line of Boston, Massachusetts, had perished forever. There was no trace of him left in the man known only as John Reynolds.''

When he didn't say any more, she encouraged, ''Go on, what then?''

He smiled at her as though he were amused by his own thoughts. ''Let's just say, I went on to bigger and better things.''

Returning his smile, she commented. ''I'm sure you did. But you aren't going to tell me what they were, are you?''

''You know, honey, when you smile the way you are now, how much you mean to me strikes me like a bolt of lightning.''

Not anticipating such a confession, Rachel was too

astounded to speak and responded by staring at him in amazement.

"Now that your parents are gone, have you given any thought as to what you'll do when you reach California?"

"Of course, I've given it a lot of thought but . . . but I don't know what I'll do or what will happen to me."

"You can stop worrying, Baby, because with your permission, I'll take care of you."

My Lord, she thought, he's proposing to me! I can't believe it! What should I say? Say yes, you silly fool! No! . . . No, I mustn't appear too anxious. I'll be coy. But only for a few minutes!

Trying to appear quite reserved and mature she replied, "I want you to know how flattered I am by your marriage proposal. But, sir, you've taken me completely by surprise."

Rachel's self-restraint turned quickly into bafflement when suddenly he roared with laughter.

"Will you stop laughing!" she snapped irritably. Entertainment, she bristled, that's all I am to him!

"Rachel, my love," he began while trying to keep a straight face, "I wasn't proposing holy matrimony to you. I was offering you and your sister my financial resources."

Struggling to salvage her pride she answered smugly, "For your information, Mr. Reynolds, I was planning to refuse your proposal, but instead I will refuse your finances! I don't want any help from you!"

With the boyish grin on his face, which even in Rachel's anger tore at her heart, he teased, "I'd adopt you, my lying little hypocrite, before I'd marry you."

John touched the brim of his hat, nodded to her

slightly, and before riding away he chuckled, "As always, my love, talking with you has been charming."

Early the following morning, John stopped by Rachel's wagon and invited her to ride with him. The anger and hurt she felt upon seeing him again lasted no longer than the time it took her to gladly accept his offer.

As the strenuous and tiresome days stretched endlessly onward, the wagon master and Rachel O'Brian, riding together in front of the wagon train, became a familiar and controversial sight to the emigrants. Most of the women thought Rachel's conduct disgraceful and scandalous, but a few, with more charitable hearts, found her obvious infatuation with the attractive Union major exciting and romantic. And John Reynolds carried the envy of many a man, especially Josh Kendall's.

Josh sadly realized that he had lost the spirited girl of his dreams to the major. Surprisingly, he found the best way to ease his broken heart was to talk quietly with the gentle Deborah. He never confessed to her that he was in love with Rachel; Josh possessed too much male pride to admit he wasn't man enough to win Rachel's challenging heart.

Edward Phillips felt no envy over John Reynolds' relationship with Rachel. He understood men with scruples, like the major, and he fully realized Reynolds would leave her when they reached California. And he'd leave her still an innocent virgin. All he had to do was bide his time and be there to help Rachel recover from her first heartbreak.

Deborah didn't find Rachel's fascination with the wagon master exciting or romantic. She regarded Mr.

Reynolds as entirely too old for her sister, but she did recognize why Rachel was attracted to the man. Even Deborah found the major quite good looking and very masculine. Perhaps in time she could've accepted him being a Yankee, but never would she be able to accept him being old enough to be their father. Considering the difference in their ages, she couldn't help but question the man's motives.

As the wagon train moved steadily over the plains of Wyoming, the people looked forward with expectation to reaching Fort Laramie, located at the junction of Laramie Creek and the Platte River. The pioneer women didn't want the officers' wives to look down on them, so they found their best dresses and neatly pinned up their hair. The few who actually owned a pair of white gloves wore them to conceal their red and callused hands.

Rachel, riding beside John Reynolds as they neared the fort, didn't give a "hoot" about good dresses and white gloves. As far as she was concerned, if the wives or soldiers found her apparel disgraceful, then that was their problem. Because Rachel lacked conceit or experience, she was too modest and naive to realize how sensual and enticing the soldiers would find her. Women were so scarce on military forts that even the homely ones became immediately popular. But the spectacular vision of the beautiful young woman riding into the fort, wearing tight pants that outlined the shape of her long slim legs and feminine full hips, would curse many a soldier with sleepless nights on his lonely bunk.

As John Reynolds and Rachel rode into Fort Laramie, the settlers on the wagon train began to set up camp nearby. The women excitedly left their wagons to hurry inside and shop at the trader's store. The men headed straight for the enlisted men's bar, where wine and beer could be bought.

They had stopped at other forts along the Oregon Trail but none of them had been as large as the well-known Fort Laramie. It was built resembling a hollow square, with adobe walls fifteen feet thick. Heavily fortified blockhouses stood at each corner, and inside was a vast courtyard. A large number of trappers and trading Indians visited the fort, and traveling wagon trains always camped and remained for a few days.

Rachel was finding the fort stimulating after the lonely barren plains. Then, suddenly, she became conscious of the admiring stares she was receiving from the soldiers and the fur trappers. She wondered if John had noticed how the men were following her with their eyes. Glancing over toward him, Rachel was surprised to find that he was watching her. When he smiled at her, and winked knowingly, she completely forgot the soldiers and the trappers. During that moment, she lovingly believed there was only one man for her on the face of the earth.

"I'm going to the Officer's Club where ladies aren't allowed, so why don't you pay a visit to the trader's store? Perhaps you can find something pretty to wear for the dance tonight," John suggested, as they pulled up their horses.

"What dance?" she asked with sudden enthusiasm.

"There's always a dance on the first night a wagon train comes through. And just think of all the soldiers you'll have to dance with this time."

"This time?" she inquired trying to sound casual as she remembered with embarrassment the dance that led up to the events in his hotel room.

"And by the way, my love, tonight please try to refrain from hiding in some man's room."

Cutting her eyes at him sharply, she asked cunningly, "Why? Would it make you jealous, my love?"

He dismounted, then, glancing up toward her, he smiled cheerfully. "I'll come by at eight and escort you to the dance, and I will also walk you back to your wagon."

"Haven't you ever heard of asking a lady, instead of ordering her?"

"Those trappers coming in from the mountains have been months without a woman, and they are a hell of a long ways from being one of your southern gentlemen. I don't intend to let you go anywhere alone after dark. As for asking a lady, I thought we already agreed that you are no lady."

He started to walk away but then turned, and with a grin, he added, "And Rachel, see if you can manage to wear a dress."

Colonel Douglas Werlin was walking out of the billiard room as John Reynolds entered the bar in the Officer's Club. The colonel hadn't seen or heard from the major in over two years, and he was astounded to see him dressed in buckskins instead of an army uniform.

Swiftly approaching him, the colonel exclaimed, "John! I can't believe my eyes! Is it really you?"

Smiling with pleasant surprise as they shook hands, he answered, "It's me all right. It's good to see you again."

"What in the hell are you doing here in Fort Laramie? And more importantly, why aren't you in uniform?''

Laughing lightly at the older man, he explained, "I'm not in the army anymore."

Colonel Werlin was in his early fifties and had spent over thirty of those years in the service of the United States Army. Why any officer would ever want to resign was beyond his comprehension. "I'm hoping you're going to tell me you came here to reenlist. We need men like you!"

"Sorry to disappoint you, but I came in with the wagon train, and I'll be leaving with it."

Glancing at the man behind the bar, the colonel ordered, "Bring us two brandies." Looking back toward his friend he inquired, "You still drink brandy, don't you?"

As he followed Colonel Werlin over to a table, John replied, "Whenever I can find it." While pulling out a chair to sit down, he quickly surveyed the room. "Nice place you have here."

"Better than most forts. We even have a billiard room and a card room."

"How long have you been here?"

"Only six months, but let's get back to you. Why are you traveling on a wagon train?"

"I'm not exactly traveling on it. You see, I'm the wagon master."

"You're what!" His bellow was so loud that it startled the man carrying their drinks to the table nearly causing him to drop the serving tray. The room, which contained eight tables, was empty at the moment, so no one else became a witness to the colonel's outburst.

After they had been served, John smiled good-humoredly as he repeated, "You heard me right. I'm the wagon master.''

The colonel took a large drink of his brandy before asking, ''Why in the hell did you take on such a position?''

''I was seriously thinking of going to California anyway, and when Zeke came to me with the offer I figured, why not? Besides, as Zeke explained, they were having a hard time finding someone to take the job. There's only twenty-five wagons and most experienced wagon masters wait for larger trains. They make a lot more money that way.''

''So you had to be a good samaritan and take on the job, right?''

He started to deny the accusation but Colonel Werlin stopped him by saying, ''I know you too well, John, so don't bother to contradict me. But tell me, how is Zeke?''

''He's the same as always. Zeke never changes and never seems to get any older either.''

''Tell him I'd like to see him. He is with you, isn't he?''

''He's our scout.''

''I should've known. Hell, you can't find a better one than Zeke.'' Chuckling to himself, he recollected, ''I remember the first time I saw Zeke. It was right towards the beginning of the war and he wanted to sign on as a scout for your regiment. When you told me his qualifications, I was damned glad to get him. If he could sneak up on an Indian camp, I figured he could sure as hell sneak up on some damned Rebs. But I'd never seen a mountaineer before, and I must admit I was fascinated by him. At the time I had this second lieutenant working for me, a fresh snob right out of

110

West Point. I sent Zeke over to him to sign up and be sworn in. Well, the first thing this lieutenant did was to hold a handkerchief over his nose.'' Chuckling even louder he remembered, ''Hell, Zeke did smell like a damned buffalo! Does that man ever take a bath?''

Laughing, John answered, ''He's been known to, on special occasions.''

''Well, this lieutenant, he asked Zeke his name, and of course, he told him, 'Zeke'. The lieutenant explained, ''I need your full name, to which Zeke replied, 'Ain't Zeke full enough fur ya?' They bantered back and forth for a while about last names and a small crowd of soldiers gathered to listen. It became a battle of wits between the sophisticated and polished lieutenant and the uncultured and rugged mountaineer. The lieutenant kept insisting that Zeke must tell him his last name. Well finally, he told the lieutenant, 'Ya tell me yur last name and then by God, I'll tell ya mine.' The lieutenant, while disgustingly waving away odor with his handkerchief, replied, 'My name, if it's any of your business, is Godwin.' Zeke leaned across the lieutenant's desk and looked him square in the eyes and said, 'Now ain't that a coincidence. Godwin just happens to be my last name. Reckon we could be kinfolk.' The soldiers never let the lieutenant forget that one.''

''Zeke Godwin, huh? I'll have to remember to address him as Mr. Godwin when I see him. What's the situation with the Sioux?''

''You shouldn't have any problems with them. Next on the Oregon Trail is Fort Fetterman and then Fort Casper. With these three forts on the trail, the Sioux have pretty much left wagon trains alone. But being that you have only twenty-five wagons, it might be best to give you a military escort from here to Fort Fetterman, and then they can give you one on to Fort Casper.''

"Thanks, Doug. I'll rest easier with a military escort.''

"Don't thank me. That's one of the reasons the army is here. The forts protect trails, and defend miners, settlers, and cattlemen. Soon we'll also survey the railroad lines and guard construction crews. Civilization is coming to the West and the railroad is going to hasten it.''

"You forgot to mention engaging the enemy in battle. Hell, Doug, civilization is going to exterminate the Indian!''

"And would that be so bad? After all, they are nothing but damned savages!'' he replied.

"They are human beings who happen to have a different culture from ours.''

"You could almost say the same for the Rebs, couldn't you? But we fought them just the same and came pretty damn close to exterminating them! And you were there, John!''

"At least I believed I was fighting on the side that was in the right. With the Indians, I wouldn't be so damned sure.''

"But your loyalty would lie with your own kind. How about it John? Come on back in the army. I know it's in your blood and we need men like you desperately. I don't expect you to give me an answer right now, but think about it while you're here. I happen to know that Fort Craig on the Rio Grande in New Mexico is losing their commanding officer. Now, before you say anything, I realize you have an obligation to the people on the wagon train, but is there any reason why you can't take them on to California and then go to Fort Craig?"

"Hold on a minute, Doug. You've already got me traveling to Fort Craig and I haven't said one damn thing about reenlisting."

The Colonel smiled shrewdly. "But you'll think about it, won't you? And John, tell Zeke Fort Craig can always use an experienced scout."

John slowly took a drink of his brandy, then looking thoughtfully at the colonel he said, "I'll think about it."

Rachel wished she owned a full-length mirror, instead of the small one her mother had packed. She would like to have seen her appearance in the pale green gown. Sighing with disappointment, she put down the hand mirror. At least she had been lucky enough to find hair ribbons at the trader's store that were the exact shade of her dress.

I wonder if John will think I'm pretty, she thought. But of course he will! My goodness, how many times has he called me his beautiful little hypocrite.

A smile curved her lips slightly as she dreamed about the man that she was learning to care for so deeply. She wondered if he would kiss her tonight. Perhaps when he walked her back to the wagon!

"Rachel," Deborah called to her from outside.

Reluctantly she stopped thinking about John Reynolds and climbed down from the wagon to see what her sister wanted.

"Where is Skipper?" Deborah asked.

Promptly Rachel glanced toward the spot where the

dog had been tied and was alarmed to find him gone. "Oh no!" she gasped.

Deborah was fully aware how much her sister had grown to love the dog, and trying to give her some reassurance she said, "Maybe he'll come back."

"I must go look for him! If John comes before I return, tell him to wait for me."

"Rachel! No! You can't run off by yourself at night. Wait for Mr. Reynolds and let him go with you."

"I can't wait! By then Skipper could be too far away!"

"Let's see if we can't locate Edward or Josh, and ask one of them to look for the dog," Deborah pleaded.

"You go find them, but I'm not wasting any more time," Rachel called as she began running from the wagon.

Desperately worried about her sister's welfare, Deborah left to search for someone who could help. She was hurrying toward the fort when she glimpsed John, Zeke, and Edward walking in her direction. Thankfully, she ran over to them.

Noticing the look of concern on her face, Edward inquired, "Is anything wrong?"

"It's Rachel! She's gone off to look for that dog," she answered breathlessly.

"Where did she go?" John asked.

Deborah looked at the wagon master, and though he appeared calm she could sense his concern and uneasiness. "I don't know. She just ran off into the night. But she was heading out of the camp."

"Toward the fort, or away from it?" Zeke questioned.

"Away from it," she replied.

"Miss O'Brian, go back to your wagon and stay there," John ordered.

Reaching out and touching her arm, Edward reassured her, "Don't worry, we'll find your sister."

Due to her concern over the dog, Rachel was aware that she had wandered so far away from camp until she decided to turn around and go back. She was astounded to find that she had walked such a far distance. In the dark she could barely distinguish the campfires burning near the wagons.

Wearily Rachel paused for a moment to catch her breath, when suddenly she heard footsteps approaching from behind her. With mounting anxiety she carefully turned. Her heart raced with fear when she spotted two men walking toward her so fast that they were upon her before she had a chance to flee. By their clothes and appearance, they were obviously mountain men. One was tall and heavyset with a full black beard. The other was much shorter and also had a beard.

The larger of the two scanned Rachel with his beady eyes as he said, "Just look at what we got here, Luke. A pretty little gal. And all by herself."

"Ain't she somethin'. Hey Judd, let's get us some of that before we leave."

Eagerly the huge man rubbed his hand up and down over the front of his pants. Breathing heavily, he uttered, "This is gonna be the best lookin' piece I ever had."

Rachel tried to scream in terror, but already the big man had his large callused hand over her mouth and was roughly pulling her toward him. Turning her brutally he thrust her back against his broad chest pressing

115

his aroused manhood forcefully against her.

Rachel's eyes widened with fright as the other man walked over to her. With one downward sweep he ripped the bodice of her dress and petticoat to the waist. Hungrily he stared at her naked and firm breasts.

"Judd, let's take her over yonder to them bushes," Luke suggested.

When Judd spoke, the odor from his foul breath, so disgustingly close, made Rachel feel faint with nausea. "Listen to me, girlie, and listen good. You can walk over to them bushes or I can drag you." Removing his hand from her mouth he asked, "Which one will it be?"

"I'll . . . I'll walk," she managed to say. Desperately she breathed in the much-needed air his large hand had been blocking from her lungs.

Carelessly he loosened his hold, and with instant alertness Rachel frantically attempted to escape. Grabbing her long hair, Judd pulled her painfully toward the bushes.

"Can I have her first, Judd?" Luke asked, following along beside them.

"Hell no, you ain't gonna use her first. But shit, as hot as I am fer her, you ain't gonna have to wait fer long."

Rachel knew her only hope to be rescued was to scream, even though she realized the huge man would ruthlessly punish her. But there was no way she could elude the two men, and if by some miracle she did, she'd never outrun them. Finding the bravery that had been born and bred into her, Rachel screamed!

Tightening his grip on her hair, he jerked Rachel toward him, striking her across the face with the back of his other hand. "Shut up, you damned bitch! Scream again and I'll kill you!" Using the strength in his powerful arms, he shoved her violently to the ground behind the low bushes, as a deep blackness overcame her.

Coming slowly out of that peaceful state of unconsciousness, she was horrified to see Judd kneeling between her legs lifting her skirt. Rachel tried in vain to move her arms to push him away, but became terrifyingly aware that they were being held forcibly over her head by Luke.

Noticing she was again conscious, Judd grinned down at her hideously as he moved his tongue back and forth across his saliva-covered lips. When he placed his large hand over her breast, Rachel tried desperately to scream, but alertly Luke put one of his hands over her face as he whispered hoarsely, "Does that feel good, bitch? Ya just wait, ole Luke is gonna kiss on 'em."

The man became uncontrollably aroused from watching Judd caressing the beautiful young breasts and unconsciously he removed his hand from Rachel's mouth. Courageously Rachel took a deep breath, and once again her agonized scream carried piercingly through the quiet night.

Drawing back his arm, Judd slapped her across the face so that her lip began to bleed. Then with his other hand, he hit her so hard that her cheek began immediately to swell.

"Do ya reckon anyone heard her?" Luke asked.

"Naw, there ain't no one out here," he answered.

"Let's hurry up and take her, then get the hell out of here!"

As Judd reached up under the full skirt to remove her underclothing, Rachel prayed she would mercifully

117

die. Hysterically she tossed her head from side to side and moaned, "No! Please no! . . . No! . . . No!"

It was then she saw Luke's rifle lying close beside her, and gallantly saving her sanity with a stability ironical in the situation, she thought, if I live through this, I'll find a way to get that gun and kill both of them! Dear God, I swear it!

Because Luke and Rachel were facing the same direction, they saw the three men as they swiftly and soundlessly approached. But Judd was so engrossed with trying to pull down Rachel's undergarments, that he wasn't aware of the fear rapidly registering on his companion's face. As the cold steel touched his temple, he froze and the hardness inside his pants shriveled instantly.

"I ought to shoot your goddamn brains out!" John said, holding the pistol to the man's head.

"What do ya mean, you oughta?" Zeke roared. "Hell, in my day if I catched a weasel like him rapin' a lady, I'd shot him dead first. And then give the sonofabitch a chance to speak!"

Nudging the man with his pistol, John ordered, "Get up and move slowly away from her. Make one fast move and you're dead!"

As Judd began carefully to stand, Rachel suddenly felt ashamed and crossed her arms over her chest to hide her exposed breasts. The dress was still pushed up around her waist, and without taking his eyes off Judd, John bent over slightly and pulled down the skirt.

Luke, standing behind Rachel, quickly noted that the man holding his pistol on Judd and the old man were the only two with guns. The other one didn't appear to be armed. If he could just reach his rifle and grab the woman at the same time, then he would tell them to drop their guns or he'd kill the girl.

It all happened so fast that it was over in a matter of seconds, but to Rachel it seemed an eternity. She started to rise at the exact instant Luke lurched for his rifle. The deadly buckshot from Zeke's shotgun hit Luke with such force, it knocked him completely off his feet and back over the surrounding bushes.

The thundering explosion from the gun caused Rachel to scream. Fearfully she drew up her knees and leaned over them, sobbing hysterically. Even in her mad frenzy, she vaguely wondered why it was raining when the night had been clear. Unable to reason, she glanced up into the dark sky and was puzzled to find stars twinkling and a full moon shining. Strangely she could feel fresh dampness on her shoulders and arms. Rachel looked to see what it was and frantically she saw it wasn't rain but splotches of Luke's blood running down her arms.

Raving deliriously, she shouted, "God no! . . . No! . . . Get it off! . . . Please . . . get it off!"

As John turned from Judd to look at Rachel, the huge man instantly reached for the knife hanging on his belt. He knew this would be his only chance to escape because the old man's shotgun was empty and the other man wasn't armed. Judd was an expert with a knife and he figured sending it through the air directly into the man's back would be simple.

Immediately he had the knife grasped in his large hand, but he fatally underestimated his opponents' keen instinct for survival. Drawing back his arm to throw the deadly knife was the last thing Judd ever did in his worthless life. With the alertness and speed of a rattlesnake, John pivoted toward the man and shot him straight through the heart.

Edward hurried over to Rachel, and kneeling beside her, he took off his jacket, wrapping it around her shoulders. Crying wretchedly, she thankfully gathered the coat, using it to shield her nakedness.

"It's all right, sweetheart. It's all over." Trying to console her, Edward made an attempt to draw Rachel into his arms but she stiffened her body, pulling away from his touch.

With tears streaming from her eyes, Rachel could only stare blankly at the ground. Vaguely she became aware of a movement close by and through the blur of tears she could see someone standing directly in front of her. Focusing her eyes, she insensibly glanced up and saw John Reynolds watching her with concern.

Without saying a word, he lifted her effortlessly in his strong arms and the comfort of his loving touch caused Rachel's stability to incredibly return to her. When Rachel looked deeply into his eyes, she mysteriously sensed her own destiny, and miraculously it changed her from a girl into a woman. She loved John Reynolds and she was destined to always love him.

Following a hot bath, Rachel felt a lot better, although her body still ached from the brutal treatment and there was an ugly bruise on her cheek.

Quietly she sat in the back of her wagon and wondered if John would return. After bringing her to Deborah, he had left immediately to report the incident to the authorities.

Feeling Deborah's eyes on her, she turned and looked at her sister. With her usual impatience, she said irritably, "Great guns and little switches, Deb! Go ahead and say it and get it over with!"

"All right, I will!" Deborah scolded. At that moment Deborah's resemblance to their mother was uncanny. Not only does she look like her, Rachel thought, but she also sounds like her. And now she's going to give me the same lecture Mama would.

"You are so hard-headed and so stubborn that you never listen to anyone . . ." Suddenly she was interrupted by a voice from outside the wagon.

"Miss Rachel, can I speak with you for a moment? It's Jesse Wilson."

Startled, Rachel whispered, "I can't see anyone! Not the way I look!"

"I'll see what he wants," Deborah answered.

She stepped down from the wagon. "I'm sorry, Mr. Wilson, but my sister is ill. May I help you?"

"Yes'm, I guess you can. It's about the dog."

"Skipper?" she asked.

"I reckon somehow he got loose and he come to our wagon."

"I see, and where is Skipper now?"

"He's still at my wagon, ma'am. When my wife seen the dog, why Miss Deborah, she actually hugged the little mutt and for the first time since Daniel died, she broke down and cried. Thank the good Lord, I think she's going to be all right. And now she don't want to part with the dog. He still makes her think of the boy, but in a good way, if you know what I mean."

"You want my sister to give him back, is that correct?"

"Mr. Wilson," Rachel called from inside the wagon. "You can have Skipper. I'm sure the dog will be happier with you and your wife.''

"Thank you, Miss Rachel," he replied. Hastily he walked away to tell the good news to his wife.

Rachel decided to lie down and rest, when all at once, she heard the familiar voice that she loved so much.

"Good evening, Miss O'Brian."

"Mr. Reynolds," Deborah replied curtly.

"How is Rachel?" he asked.

"She's doing all right, considering the ordeal she suffered," Deborah answered with cold politeness.

Her formality didn't go unnoticed and John studied her face closely as he questioned, "Ma'am, do you detest me because I was in the Union army, or do you just flatly dislike me?"

"I do not dislike you, Mr. Reynolds, and I'll always be very grateful to you for saving Rachel." Deborah didn't tell him her reserved manner was caused by the distrust she felt over his relationship with her sister.

"I'd like to see her for a monent," he said.

"She's resting, and I think it's best not to disturb her.''

Rachel, feeling very perturbed with her sister, started to climb out of the wagon when John spoke again. "I don't intend to disturb her, Miss O'Brian, but I do intend to talk to her. If you'll excuse me ma'am, I'll go see how she is."

Observing Rachel waiting for him, John stepped up into the narrow wagon. The small enclosure under the white canvas caused his large frame to appear even larger than it was.

Sitting beside her, he tenderly touched her bruised cheek as he asked, "Are you all right?"

She smiled adoringly at the man she loved and needed so desperately. "Yes now that you're here. John, I think I'd have gone out of my mind tonight if it hadn't been for you." Detecting the troubled expression appearing on his face, Rachel wondered if what she had said could somehow be the cause.

Looking intensely into her eyes, he replied, "Listen to me honey, and listen closely. I am not the reason you emotionally survived what happened to you. You're a survivor, Rachel. A trait you probably inherited from your father. And you always will be a survivor, because you have strength, character, and courage. Rachel, I am not your strength or your bravery. Baby, your strength and your bravery lie within yourself."

"No, I'm not brave! I was scared to death!"

"Even the brave are scared. Hell, that just means you have good sense. But you are brave, my love. I'm sure you were beaten both times you screamed, but it didn't stop you."

Taking her completely by surprise, John reached for her hand. His face revealed his true feelings, as he admitted. "Damn Rachel, when I heard your screams and I was still a distance from you, all sorts of thoughts went through my mind. I was afraid that I wouldn't get there in time. My God, if they'd hurt you or killed you, . . . I'd. . . ." Suddenly he seemed to become aware of what he was saying, and he abruptly stopped speaking.

Why, she wondered, why is he fighting what he feels? Doesn't he know I love him? . . . And he loves me! . . . I know he does!

For a moment he studied her lovely features with a torment in his eyes that Rachel found confusing, then leaning over he lightly kissed her swollen and bruised cheek.

"Goodnight, honey," he whispered. Swiftly he stepped down from the wagon and began walking toward the fort to inform Colonel Werlin that he'd reenlist and accept the position at Fort Craig. But John Reynolds would unwillingly take the memory of her green eyes, her enticing smile, and her alluring charm with him to Fort Craig.

As the lonely, tiresome days turned into lonelier, weary weeks, Rachel endured John Reynolds' sudden indifference to her with anguished and suffering silence. She saw him occasionally, but he seemed to go out of his way to make sure they were never alone. She longed to saddle Edward's horse and ride with him again, but his attitude toward her left no doubt that he opposed it. Rachel couldn't understand why he was avoiding her and her pride prevented her from asking him.

At the end of each long and dreary day, Rachel was too fatigued to solve the perplexing situation with John Reynolds. Following one endless night after another she'd awaken the next morning to face a hot, exhausting day on the Oregon Trail. But her young heart never stopped aching for the man she loved.

John Reynolds didn't avoid Rachel entirely. Often during the long journey to California, he and Zeke would stop by her wagon to visit, but always John had an aloofness about him that she couldn't understand. For some reason, the man she loved had made himself a stranger to her. Zeke, sensing Rachel's loneliness and love for John Reynolds, charitably gave Rachel most of his time. The moments they shared soon developed into a deep friendship.

Following long weary weeks of traveling, the wagon train finally reached Hasting's Cutoff which led to the California Trail. From the northwest tip of Utah they moved southwest across Nevada to the sluggish Humboldt River, which was inseparable from the California Trail for two hundred miles. The Humboldt offered needed water and green intermittent meadows for the oxen and livestock. Along the river could be seen the shallow graves where emigrants before them had buried their dead. Also there were the skeletons of oxen and mules, that had perished because their owners had left too late to take advantage of the scarce grazing land in the barren localities. The crumbling wood and rotting canvas from abandoned wagons would remain beside the river for years to come.

Diggers, the tribe of Indians along the Humboldt, were unfriendly. Often they could be seen hiding behind the tall grass, peering at the passing train. They would silently wait for their prey, then discharge their arrows into the oxen. A dead or injured ox would have to be left behind, supplying the Indians with fresh meat.

A few of the emigrants on the wagon train never survived to reach the Forty-Mile desert, but considering the dangers of the perilous journey, the loss of lives had been minimal.

Before crossing the desert, the pioneers rested and camped for two days. They cooked meals over sagebrush fires, cared for the sick, fixed their wagons, and cut loads of grass for the desert passage.

The wagon train crossed the barren desert in two

nights traveling, and came out at the Truckee River. Further south, it changed course and turned westward. Along the river they ploddingly journeyed toward the Sierra Nevadas. Here the pioneers rested before attempting to climb the high pass, that after the year 1846 carried the fateful name of "Donner".

Their prairie-fed beasts climbed a trail which led along sheer cliffs. The route still led up the Truckee, which guided them through gorges, blind canyons, and twisting ridges, which were the barrier along the eastern border of California. The wagons then arrived at Truckee Lake, but the wagon train still had to climb through the pass and track its way down steep slopes to the Sacramento Valley.

Six months, two weeks, and three days out of St. Joseph, Missouri, they finally reached the end of the trail. The lonely plains, the hot desert, the steep mountains, the suffering, and the deaths, now lay behind them.

John Reynolds stood beside Zeke as dusk settled peacefully across the far horizon, and watched the pioneers set up camp for the last time. Tomorrow everyone would be heading for their different destinations.

"We done real good," Zeke began. "We got 'em here, and didn't lose many a doin' it neither."

With a sigh, John turned to his horse and started unsaddling it, as he remarked, "I'm glad the trip is over. Remind me to never again let you talk me into taking such a damned job."

"Me?" Zeke bellowed. "Hell, cain't no one talk you into nothin' ya don't want to do! Yur as bull-headed as an old mule when ya git yur mind set against somethin'."

Glancing over at his friend, he asked, "Zeke, are you trying to tell me something?"

He shrugged his bony shoulders. "I might be, but it ain't none of my business. Besides, everytime I bring her up, ya git so dadblasted mad that ya become meaner than a damned polecat."

Placing the saddle on the ground, John suggested, "Why don't you quit running off at the mouth and just tell me what you're obviously dying to say."

"It ain't so much somethin' I wanna say, as somethin' I wanna ask ya."

Grinning cheerfully at the man he loved more than he had loved his own father, he prompted, "Go ahead and ask."

Zeke studied John out of the corner of his eye. "Ya won't git all riled up?"

"No, I won't, but I will if you don't hurry up and ask whatever the hell it is!"

Zeke remained silent for a moment, then inquired, "What do ya plan to do 'bout that little gal?"

"I presume you mean Rachel."

Not trying to hide his agitation, he replied irritably, "Well I'd . . . presume . . . you'd have to be blind as a damned hoot-owl not to know she done went and fell in love with ya."

"Surely you don't think I'd let Rachel and her sister go to San Francisco without making sure they'll be taken care of."

"San Francisco? Is that whar they're a headin' fur?"

"Well, that's were Phillips is going and I'm quite certain they'll go with him."

"But what ya gonna do 'bout the love that gal's got fur ya?"

"Time and absence, I'm sure, will quickly mend her young heart. Now if you'll excuse me, Mr. Godwin, I need to see Edward Phillips."

Zeke watched him walk away. Taking a large bite from a hunk of chewing tobacco, he mumbled, "Time and absence, huh? Is that gonna make you furgit?"

When John neared the O'Brian wagon, he could see Edward and Josh sitting by the campfire drinking coffee. Hearing his approach they glanced up toward him.

"Evening Reynolds," Edward called. "Would you like a cup of coffee?"

"Thanks," he replied.

Edward poured the coffee, then pointed to an empty space by the fire and said, "Sit down and join us."

Accepting the mug of hot coffee, he sat beside him as he asked, "Where are Rachel and Deborah?"

"They're off saying goodbye to some of the women because we'll be leaving early in the morning. Josh told me he's going with you and Zeke to Fort Craig." Glancing at the other man, Edward continued, "I can't understand why you'd pass up life in California for life in the U.S. Cavalry."

Josh smiled good-humoredly. "The Army gets into your blood."

"Spills your blood is more like it!" Edward mocked.

Letting his remark pass, Josh began, "We've been discussing Rachel and Deborah. We're wondering how they'll manage in San Francisco."

"That's why I came to see you, Phillips," John stated.

Looking at him with bafflement, Edward replied, "I can take them to San Francisco with me, but after we get there, I don't know how I can help them. Hell, I wish I could, but to put it bluntly, I'm practically broke!"

Reaching into his shirt pocket, John removed an envelope. "This is a letter to a Mr. Carlson at the bank in San Francisco. I'm well acquainted with the man and the information in this letter will leave no doubt that it's from me."

"What's in it?" Edward asked.

"Permission to give you free reign on a substantial sum of my money."

"Well, I'll be damned!" he exclaimed. "Why?"

"I want you to use the money to buy the girls a small business of some kind, perhaps a dress shop or something akin to that."

"They won't accept your charity, Reynolds. Where money is concerned some people have a foolish virtue called pride."

"I know they have a little money their father was going to use when he reached California. From what Rachel has told me, it isn't nearly enough to set them up in a business, but the girls aren't aware of that."

"I understand," Edward began. "You want me to find that dress shop, tell them they have enough to buy it, and make up the difference with your finances."

"I'm sure you can manage it, Phillips," he said handing him the envelope.

Accepting the envelope, Edward studied it a moment before asking, "How can you be sure I won't help myself to your funds, then skip out?"

Staring him straight in the eyes, John answered, "It'll be tempting to a man of your trade."

"So you know I'm a gambler, huh?"

"It's fairly easy to spot a professional gambler, Phillips, but the way you handle a deck of cards is a damned give-away."

"What's to prevent me from taking your money and leaving town?"

"Because eventually I'd be told, and someday I'd find you."

"Maybe you couldn't."

"Don't bet on it, Phillips."

Putting the envelope into his shirt pocket, Edward grinned. "I try to make it a point to never bet against the odds. I'll do as you ask, Reynolds. I care about the ladies myself."

John stood up to leave, but looked back at Edward and informed him, "When you finish the job, Mr. Carlson has been instructed to pay you five thousand dollars for your trouble. It should be an adequate amount to stake you in your next poker game." Not waiting for a reply, he left and had walked a short distance before Josh caught up to him.

"Major, I need to talk to you," Josh called.

Turning toward the younger man, he stopped and asked, "What about?"

"Well sir, considering what you are doing for the girls, it's quite apparent that Rachel means a great deal to you."

"What are you trying to say, Kendall?"

"None of this is any of my business, but. . . ."

"If it's none of your business, Lieutenant, then don't say it!"

He started to walk away but Josh remarked, "Rachel's in love with you!"

Angrily, John shouted, "Damn it, Kendall, stay out

of it!"

"I can't, sir. You don't know how hard it's been for Rachel since you became so indifferent to her. Deborah told me that at night, she often hears Rachel crying herself to sleep."

"Listen to me, Lieutenant. Your concern for Rachel is admirable, but the girl is young and barely more than a child. She's too damned immature and inexperienced to be in love with me or anyone else!"

Gathering his courage, Josh implied, "Major, if you were to tell her about Carmelita, I think it'd help her get over you sooner than anything else."

Josh could see the fury in the steel gray eyes, that stared at him with open hostility. "How in the hell do you know about Carmelita?"

"It was that time you were wounded and Zeke and I were carrying you off the battlefield to find the doctor. You were delirious, Major, and you said a lot of things about Carmelita and Mexico. Because I knew so many bits and pieces, Zeke explained what happened."

"Have you told anyone?"

"No, of course not. Hell, I'd never do that."

The fury slowly went out of his eyes, as he answered, "See that you never do!"

"Don't you think it'd be best to at least tell Rachel part of it?"

"Part of it! Good God man, you know what happened. How in the hell do you tell someone part of it!"

Observing the distress on John's face, Josh realized even after all this time, the grief was still there and that the major would carry the memory of that day with him for the rest of his life.

"You're right, sir. You'd have to explain every-

131

thing."

"If you think it'll help Rachel get over the infatuation she feels for me, I'll tell her what I should've told her from the beginning."

"Well, at least it'll end any dreams she may have concerning the two of you."

Smiling, John replied, "Kendall, a young girl's heart mends very quickly. When she gets settled in San Francisco and all the young men come calling, she'll forget she once thought herself in love with an older man."

Nodding his head in agreement, Josh answered, "You're probably right."

"What about you, Lieutenant? I thought you were interested in Rachel?"

"I was, at one time. But now I . . . I sort of like her sister. Deborah has promised to write me. Who knows, maybe in time something will come of it."

"When Rachel returns, tell her I'm down by the creek and I want to see her."

Josh almost asked him to be gentle with her, but he caught himself in time. John Reynolds would be kind, but even his kindness would break Rachel's heart.

Night had fallen, but the full October moon cast ample light and Rachel could distinctly see him as he waited patiently. Leaning one arm across the trunk of a tree, John smoked a cigarette while staring down at the shallow stream flowing placidly before him.

He'll tell me goodbye, she thought, and there's nothing I can say or do to keep him from leaving. Slowly she began walking in his direction. Before she could reach him, John heard her and instantly he turned.

If I never see him again, for as long as I live, I'll still remember how his eyes light up when he looks at me. The way he wrinkles his brow when he's questioning something I've said or done, and the smile that is so damned attractively crooked. Oh John, she cried silently, I love you! I love you!

"Josh said you wanted to see me." Rachel found it hard to believe that she could actually be talking simple formalities, when she really wanted to fling herself into his arms and beg him not to leave her.

Tossing away his cigarette, he advanced toward her and taking her hands into his, he said, "I'll be leaving at dawn, and I wanted to say goodbye before I left."

Pulling her hands away from his, she solemnly walked over to the creek and stood beside it. "Will I ever see you again?"

"I don't know, Baby," he answered.

On impulse, because it was tearing her to pieces to hear him call her Baby, she whirled and cried out, "Don't call me that! Don't call me Baby or Honey . . . or . . . or anything but Rachel!"

"All right, if that's what you want."

The hurt and pain she was feeling changed into anger. "What I want! Damn you, John Reynolds, you know that isn't what I want!"

Raising his eyebrows questioningly, he asked, "Would you mind explaining that to me?"

"And don't do that!" she snapped. Rachel realized his familiar expression that she held so precious would soon become only a memory.

"Do what?" he asked.

"Raise your eyebrows!" she answered sternly.

With the barest trace of a smile on his face, John

133

walked toward her and as he came closer she unconsciously stepped away from him, but was halted when she felt the trunk of the tree against her back.

Placing his hands on the tree, one on each side of her, he leaned his tall frame over hers. "If I were younger, and things were different in my life, I'd be taking you to Fort Craig with me even if I had to kidnap you to get you there."

"Younger! You talk like you're an old man!"

"I'm twenty-three years older than you, and those years have placed a whole lifetime between us."

Heedlessly throwing away her pride, Rachel looked him in the eyes and with anguish she cried, "But I love you!"

He smiled the boyish grin Rachel found so appealing. "What could you possibly know about love? In so many ways, you're still a child."

"But someday I'll be a woman, John Reynolds, and I swear to you that somehow I will find you and then you can't use my youth for an excuse. And that's all it is, an excuse! For some reason you're afraid to tell me you love me!" Raising her voice she continued willfully, "But I know you do! Do you hear me, John Reynolds? I know you love me! It's in your eyes every time you look at me! And I love you!"

He spoke to her tenderly, "You aren't in love with me, Rachel. You only think you are. When you do fall in love, it'll be with a man closer to your own age and a man who will want to marry you."

Resigning herself to the inevitable, she sighed, "And you don't."

"I couldn't if I wanted to. I'm already married."

Rachel's first reaction was unreasoning anger, and

drawing back her arm she slapped him across the cheek. Wanting somehow to insult him she yelled, "You bastard!"

Gently he took her hand and placed a kiss on her palm. "I'm sorry, Rachel." Releasing her hand, he started to leave.

"Wait!" she cried.

John turned to face her again and in spite of her anger and hurt, she could see the torment in his eyes.

"Why didn't you tell me? Why did you lead me on and give me hope where there was none?"

"You aren't being fair, Rachel. I never allowed our relationship to advance any further than friendship. If there was any romance, it existed only in your imagination. But I should've told you I was married."

"Why didn't you?" she pleaded.

"It's something I usually don't discuss. My marriage is a part of my past I wish to hell I could forget!"

Moving closer, John put his hand under her chin. Tilting up her face, he studied her features as if he were trying to memorize them. Then stepping back from her, he explained, "Her name is Carmelita and I met her when I was in Mexico. I was twenty-eight and she was only seventeen when we married. I bought a ranch in southern Texas and we lived there for a couple years, until she returned to her father in Mexico. I placed the running of the ranch into the hands of a reliable friend and I left that part of my life behind me."

"Have you seen her since then?" she asked.

"I haven't seen Carmelita in over ten years, and I hope to God I never see her!" The cruelty in his eyes was frightening. "After all this time, I'd still be tempted to kill her!"

"Why? What happened?"

Suppressing the rage he still felt for his wife, he answered, "It's over, Rachel. It doesn't matter anymore."

"You're not going to tell me, are you? You insist on treating me like I'm a child!"

"I don't talk about that time in my life to anyone, regardless of their age. I'll walk you back to your wagon."

"No! I want to stay here for a few minutes . . . alone."

"All right," he replied. With a slight raise of his eyebrows and a crooked grin, he asked, "Will you tell me goodbye without calling me insulting names?"

Rachel managed a feeble smile, although her heart felt like it was breaking. With her pride under control but her love for him written all over her face, she held her head high and told him, "Goodbye, John."

John Reynolds had never found her sweeter or more vulnerable than he did at that moment. Fighting the urge to take her into his arms, he turned away and replied, "Goodbye."

Rachel leaned against the tree for needed support as she watched him walk out of her life. Releasing the flood of tears she'd been forcibly holding inside, she placed her arm across the trunk of the tree, leaned her head over her arm and cried, "I love you! Though you never once held me in your arms with passion, and never kissed me, I still love you with all my heart and soul!"

With tears in her eyes, she looked in the direction in

which he had disappeared. Barely above a whisper, she said, "I love you, John Reynolds, and I will always love you!"

Chapter Four

San Francisco! Rachel found the town fascinating, and the most magnificent sight she'd ever seen in her whole seventeen years of life. After the secluded, peaceful days on a southern plantation, she thought San Francisco a setting for reckless and exciting adventure. When she saw the bustling city for the first time, Edward informed her that San Francisco was a lot like himself. . . . It played for high stakes and took its losses with a simple shrug. . . .

Rachel was fascinated to learn that she and the city were approximately the same age. Gold was discovered in 1849 and the city suddenly sprang into life. That such a place could be put together in so short a time, seemed incredible to her. In only seventeen years, with the mad gold rush behind it, San Francisco extraordinarily became a city populated by over 100,000 people. It had a stock exchange, theaters, churches, gambling casinos, and many expensive, magnificent homes.

A city sitting on the shimmering beauty of the Bay, it was cut off from the westward expansion by a thousand miles of empty plains and towering mountains. Facing towards the blue Pacific, it was young America's primary contact with the Far East.

For years, San Francisco would remain wholly dependent on imports from the outside world. Lumber came from Maine, agricultural products from Latin America, oranges from Tahiti, prefabricated houses from Chicago, ice and apples from Boston, silk from China, and coffee from Java.

Most of San Francisco's immigrants were Chinese and Australians. They provided the much needed labor in the growing urban economy. Rachel's first sight of an oriental, with his black pigtail hanging down his back, caused her eyes to widen with astonishment. Deborah finally had to reproach her and tell her to stop staring because it was not only "unladylike", but also quite rude!

Neither of the O'Brian girls possessed enough business knowledge to question how their small sum of money had purchased a prosperous dress shop in the respectable area of town. They unquestioningly allowed Edward to handle the whole unfamiliar transaction. The two present employees, worried they would lose their jobs when the store was sold, happily agreed to stay on. The girls foolishly believed that the former owner came to the shop every day to teach them the operating procedures strictly out of the kindness of her charitable heart.

The furnished living quarters above the shop were small, but adequate for their needs. It had a comfortable sitting room, a modern kitchen, and two separate bedrooms. It wouldn't have filled up a fourth of the space in their former beautiful mansion at the Knolls, but after six months of living out of a covered wagon, the tiny rooms looked like a heavenly refuge to them.

Quickly and with comparative ease, Edward managed to see that the girls were properly taken care of. Convincing the owner to sell the shop was very simple. He generously, with John Reynolds' money, offered her twice what the place was worth, and she gladly agreed to teach the young ladies the business when he charmingly informed her of how much he would pay her for the inconvience.

It was Deborah who willingly learned about the business and how to profitably operate it. Rachel half-heartedly tried a few times to concentrate and take an interest in the dress shop, but it bored her immensely. Her social life was so full and so exciting, that she excused her indifference to their livelihood by telling herself she didn't have the time to learn. . . . After all, Deborah very seldom went anywhere unless Edward was taking them out; otherwise, she seemed to be perfectly contented ordering fabrics, sewing dresses, and being proud of herself when the profits started to steadily grow. Secretly Deborah began to wonder why they had bought the shop for such a small amount, when it obviously was a very prospering business.

Edward escorted Rachel to dinner and to the finest most substantial gambling houses only a few times before she had more male admirers than she ever dreamed possible. In the "gilded palaces of chance," her cavaliers argued openly with one another for the honor of teaching the enticing and lovely Miss O'Brian the games of faro, roulette, monte, and rondo. She received more invitations to dinner, dances, and the theatre than she could possibly accept. The young girl, who once sat hidden in the back of her father's wagon and dreamed about beaux and dancing under crystal chandeliers, never imagined her dream would come true six months later in San Francisco.

Many a young man became captivated by Rachel's desirable charms, and fell helplessly in love. To their great disappointment, she never allowed more than a goodnight kiss, and if they should become serious, she quickly found a way to be sweetly but mysteriously evasive.

As the busy and exciting days turned into weeks, and then to months, Rachel flirted shamelessly, danced for hours on end, and laughed charmingly. Her most ardent admirers were each determined that he alone would become the one who would miraculously tame and conquer her challenging spirit . . . but Rachel's young heart still longed for only one man.

The fog was so thick and dense that Rachel could see nothing but the swirling gray mist surrounding her. Suddenly she heard the distant sound of thundering hoofbeats steadily approaching. Unexpectedly the fog lifted, and Rachel strangely felt as though she were looking down on the earth from somewhere remote and far above. For a fleeting moment she could clearly see herself riding a horse bareback across the plains. Desperately Rachel tried to locate the area she was in, but the fog swiftly settled thickly over the scene. It was then she felt the pain . . . Rachel sensed it wasn't physical. If it had been, she could've borne it, but the pain came profoundly from her heart and from deep in her soul.

The dense fog again mysteriously dissolved and Rachel could see herself once more. She was now standing with one fist raised toward the sky. Rachel could not recognize her surroundings as everything close appeared only as a dim blur. The one lucid view she had was the vision of herself and the look of agony that showed vividly on her tormented face. The heavy recurring fog drifted down from the heavens . . . the pain returned. . . . Her anguish and suffering were so unbearably painful, that shockingly Rachel realized, she had been begging God for her own death.

The fog disappeared and she was now lying face down on the grass with her head cradled in her arms. Rachel could tell by the uncontrollable shaking of her body that she was weeping. Then the fog obscured her vision. . . . Panic-stricken by the horrifying and endless pain, Rachel fought her way back to wakefulness.

Rachel's eyes flew open, and she bolted upright in the bed. The dream. . . . Oh God, she'd had the dream again! . . . Shivering from the unknown fear, she pulled the covers tightly around her and feeling the dampness of tears on her face she realized she'd actually been crying in her sleep. Achingly, Rachel longed to be comforted again by the strong arms that had held her so tenderly that warm night under the darkened Kansas sky.

Forcing his memory from her tormented mind, she threw off the covers and walked restlessly across the bare floor. She moved over to the window and stared up at the glittering stars shining brightly in the late night sky. "Dear God," she whispered, "if my dream is a premonition, what will I do that's so terrible I'll wish myself dead?"

She continued to feel the overpowering need for love, and to be held securely in the strong embrace of a man. Suddenly she thought . . . Edward! He would care.

Hadn't he always been there when she needed him? After the death of her parents, it was Edward who safely saw them to San Francisco, and Edward who found the dress shop. It had always been Edward! . . . Not John Reynolds! . . . He had carelessly abandoned her in the Sacramento Valley to face alone whatever should lie ahead!

She knew it could prove dangerous to venture out alone at this hour of the night, but Rachel quickly decided she needed Edward too desperately not to throw caution to the wind and take her chances. Swiftly removing her gown, she frantically hoped he would be in his hotel room and not off somewhere playing cards. Hastily, she grabbed her favorite powder blue dress from the wardrobe and wasted no time questioning her sudden and overwhelming need for Edward. Rachel was only aware that she needed someone to hold her lovingly in his comforting arms . . . and maybe then the terrifying impact of her dream would fade into oblivion.

Quickly she put on her undergarments, slipped into the dress, and fastened all the tiny buttons. Peering into the mirror, she pinched her cheeks to make them rosy, then carelessly drew the brush through her long auburn hair. Taking a shawl and wrapping it around her shoulders, she slipped quietly from her room, creeped soundlessly down the stairs, and hurried out into the refreshing night air.

Edward's hotel was located a short distance from the dress shop, and hoping she wouldn't pass anyone on the way, Rachel began walking briskly in that direction.

* * *

When the cork from the iced bottle of champagne popped toward the ceiling in Edward's hotel room, Sarah laughed gaily. Holding the two glasses in her hands, she tried to steady them as Edward filled the glasses with the bubbling liquid.

"Eddie, my love, this is our second bottle already." Handing him one of the glasses she looked at him seductively and added, "It's not as if you had to get me drunk in order to get me in your bed."

Raising his glass slightly as a tribute, he replied, "Sarah, my desirable whore, I never knew you to be sober." He leaned over and kissed her painted lips passionately. "I won so much money last night, that I bought the champagne for celebration and bought you to celebrate with me. . . . So let's take the bottle into my bedroom and . . . celebrate."

The knock on his door was timid, and Edward almost didn't hear it. "Who in the hell could that be?" he mumbled.

"Whoever it is love, get rid of 'em," Sarah said.

Quickly he walked over to the door and opened it. He was astounded to see Rachel standing in the hall. Due to the quantity of champagne he had consumed, he found it a little difficult to focus her but she still appeared to be as beautiful as always . . . and so damnably innocent!

"Edward, may I come in?" she asked.

Smiling amusingly over the interesting prospect of the two women meeting in his room, he bowed to the waist and stepped aside. "Miss O'Brian, ma'am, welcome to my simple abode."

Rachel saw the woman the moment she entered the room, and her astonishment could clearly be seen on

145

her youthful face.

Edward closed the door and placing his arm over Rachel's shoulders, led her into the room. "Miss O'Brian, may I introduce Sarah, a most charming and obliging prostitute, from San Francisco's renowned red light district. And Sarah, may I introduce Miss O'Brian, a true aristocratic southern lady, from the renowned Knolls Plantation in the fair state of Mississippi."

Cutting her eyes sharply at him, Rachel said angrily, "Edward Phillips, you're drunk!"

He took a large drink of his champagne, then answered, "Only slightly inebriated, sweetheart. My original plan though, was to become delightfully intoxicated with my lady friend, until you knocked so gently and sweetly at my door."

"What he says is true, dearie, so why don't you return to your nursery before your Ma and Pa come a lookin' for you!" Sarah added brazenly.

Since Rachel's arrival in San Francisco, she had seen many harlots on the street, but not once did she imagine she'd ever meet one of them. Staring openly at the woman before her, she was fascinated. Rachel had never seen hair as red as Sarah's, and she wondered if the woman actually had the bad taste to dye it! Glancing away from the woman she looked toward Edward and said, "I'm sorry I disturbed you."

Rachel turned to leave, but instantly Edward reached out and grabbed her by the arm. Moving in front of her so that he could see her face, he asked, "Why did you come here? And just what in the hell are you doing out alone this time of night?"

"I had this terrible dream and it frightened me . . .

146

and I wanted someone to hold me. No, not just some-one . . . I wanted you!''

The sweetness and trust in the green eyes looking up at him were a renewed reminder to him of how much he cared about her. Seeing the seriousness on Rachel's face, he told her soothingly, "It's all right, sweetheart. I'll always be here when you need me."

He reached into his pocket and brought out a wad of bills and strode over to Sarah. Sticking the money snugly down the bosom of her dress, he said, "This should more than cover any inconvenience I may have caused you."

"I don't believe you!" she shouted. "This child comes here and cries about some bad dream and you want me to leave! What in the hell's going on around here! What are you? Her nursemaid?"

"She isn't quite that young. In fact, she's a very de-sirable young lady, don't you think?" he asked.

Angrily, Sarah walked swiftly to the door and opened it, but before closing it behind her, she said, "I won't stay mad at you, Love! When you get to needin' some good lovin', you know how to find me."

When they were alone, Edward turned to Rachel and asked, "Would you like to celebrate with me, and have a glass of champagne?"

"I've never had any before," she answered.

"But you've had wine, and that's all champagne is, only it bubbles," he told her as he poured her a glass.

"What are we celebrating?" Rachel asked, accept-ing the glass he offered.

"My luck with the cards. Not to mention my great skill."

Giving him the smile that men found to enticing, she

147

replied, "To you, Edward." Rachel took a sip of the champagne, then giggled happily as she said, "The bubbles tickle my nose."

Laughing with her, he answered, "Ah Rachel, I wonder if you have any idea what a sensual and captivating female you are." Seeing her look of bafflement, he continued, "Of course, you don't, my naive little temptress. But your aura of innocence only adds to your charm."

She glanced away from the unmistakable desire in his dreamy eyes and took another drink of the champagne.

"Sweetheart, you've never been alone in a man's hotel room before, so you probably have no conception of how compromising it could appear." He continued talking to her, but she wasn't listening anymore . . . she was lost in her memories. Rachel was remembering the other time she was alone in a man's room . . . the way his gray eyes had stared at her with such intensity. The sound of his laughter, when she explained her presence by childishly stating the obvious. The bewildering thrill of his close masculine contact when he loosened her dress from the nail. The anger and rage in his dominating eyes when she purposely insulted the Union soldiers. The boyish grin she had found annoying, but which later became so familiar and dear to her! Oh, John, I miss you! And I still love you!

Touching her arm firmly, Edward said, "Rachel . . . you aren't listening to me."

"I'm sorry, Edward. What were you saying?"

"It wasn't important. Obviously you're very disturbed over something. Why don't you tell me about it, Baby?"

"Please don't call me that!" she yelled. Grasping the glass securely, she put it to her lips and emptied it, then picked up the bottle and refilled her glass. Raising her chin in defiance, she glared at him and quickly finished the second glass as well.

"Rachel, you aren't accustomed to drinking, and in a few minutes you're going to become . . . well to put it bluntly, you're going to be drunk!"

"I don't care," she replied stubbornly. Rachel noticed how the room was beginning to strangely rock back and forth.

"Why don't you tell me about this bad dream you had."

Refilling her glass, she answered, "It isn't a dream. It's a premonition and this is the second time it's happened to me." Her hand started to shake as she took a large drink from the glass. "Oh, Edward, it's terrifying!"

Swiftly, he moved over to her and took the glass from her trembling hand and placed it next to the champagne bucket. The terror and fear in her eyes worried him, and with concern he pulled her tenderly into his arms. She surprised him when, suddenly, she clung to him tightly. Gently he moved her so he could see into her face. "Listen to me, sweetheart, I wish I could hold you and comfort you . . . but I can't."

"Why?" she asked.

"Damn it, Rachel! I find you so damned desirable, that it's impossible for me to hold you like this and not want to make love to you."

The champagne was causing her head to spin and her thoughts to become incoherent. Losing sensibility and awareness of reality, she felt as if she were gliding

149

serenely into a far-away dream, and toward her awaiting destiny.

"Make me yours!" she pleaded to the man in her dreams. "Please make me yours!"

Slowly he met his lips to hers. At first he kissed her gently, but as his passion began to build he forced her mouth open and under his. "Rachel . . . Rachel. . . ." he whispered into her ear. "I've wanted this from the moment I first laid eyes on you. I knew you had been made for love, and to pleasure a man." Picking her up into his arms, he continued, "And I'm going to please myself with you tonight. I'll be damned if I'll wait for you any longer!"

Anxiously, he carried her across the carpeted floor and into his spacious bedchamber which was lit only by the moon shining romantically through the open window. Pausing next to the large bed, he placed her on her feet. "Tell me you want me!" he ordered with passion and desire heavy in his voice.

Still drifting dreamily and irrationally in her fantasy, she answered, "Surely you must know . . . I've always wanted you."

Roughly he gathered her into his strong embrace and ravished her moist lips with his own. He moved his hand caressingly across her back and down over the fullness of her hips. Moving away from her, he expertly unfastened the tiny buttons in front of her dress. He slipped it off her shoulders, but then, impatient, she took the initiative and pushed the dress past her petticoat, easily stepping out of it.

Eagerly he pulled her back into his arms, and fleetingly ran light kisses over her neck to her shoulders, then down to the softness of her breast. Smoothly Edward picked her up in his arms and lifted her onto the bed. Lying down beside her, he whispered, "I want you, Rachel! I've wanted you for so damned long." He covered her mouth passionately with his own as his hand fondled her firm young breast.

Responding to the fiery passion of his kiss, Rachel drifted into blissful ecstasy. As his warm lips once again traveled teasingly down to her breast, she moaned with pleasure and instinctively arched her body toward his. With her virginal sexuality aroused for the first time, she cried yearningly, "John . . . oh John. . . ."

Rachel didn't understand why, all at once, Edward stiffened and moved away from her. Puzzled, she watched him rise from the bed and walk over to the dresser. He opened a square box, removed a small cigar and taking a match he angrily struck it across the top of the dresser. As he held the flaming match to light his cigar, she was bewildered to see the rage and fury on his face.

Sitting up on the bed, she asked, "Edward, what's wrong?"

"You don't even know, do you?" he replied angrily.

"Know what?" she asked.

"Rachel, when I make love to a woman, I want her to be making love to me! Not to someone else!"

"I don't understand," she replied, still confused.

Startling her, he yelled furiously, "You called for Reynolds, damn you!"

"Oh no!" she gasped.

"In the other room, when you said seductively . . . Make me yours . . . you wanted Reynolds to be the man taking your virginity. When you said you wanted me, it was really Reynolds you wanted!" With his voice shouting at her in rage, he continued, "It wasn't me you were kissing so damned passionately and your moan of pleasure wasn't for me! . . . It was for him!" Before Rachel had a chance to attempt an apology, he suddenly threw his cigar out the open window, moved swiftly toward her and grabbed her painfully by the arms. Shaking her violently, he ordered, "Admit it, damn you! Admit it was Reynolds!"

"Yes, it was him," she cried. "I'm sorry, but I couldn't stop myself! I love him so much!"

When he released her, she fell back across the bed and began to sob heavily as she pleaded, "Forgive me, Edward. . . . Please!"

Standing over the bed, and watching the young woman cry pathetically, Edward suppressed his anger. "Rachel, it's been six months since you've seen him. How long is it going to take you to get over your childish hero worship?"

"It isn't hero worship. I love him, Edward. I'll always love him!" she answered.

"How old are you?" he asked.

"I'll be eighteen in a few weeks," she replied.

"At eighteen, Rachel, always is a hell of a long time!"

Looking up at him through tear-blurred eyes, she said, "You sound as though you were years and years older than I am."

"Nine years to be exact, but decades wiser. I've been on my own since I was fourteen and believe me, Rachel, I had to grow up and grow up fast."

She quickly sat erect on the bed, and looked at him stunned. "Fourteen! Did you run away from home? What did your parents do? Didn't they search for you?''

Smiling at her youthful and unenlightened concept of life, he replied, ''Do you think all children had your upbringing, Rachel? Can you really be so ignorant of life?''

''I guess I never thought about it,'' she answered honestly.

Edward slowly walked to the window and looked out. He stood staring thoughtfully for a moment, then said to her, ''I didn't run away from home, Rachel. I was sold away from home along with my mother.''

''What?'' she cried with astonishment.

Glancing towards her, he replied calmly, ''My mother was a mulatto slave and I came from the loins of Master Ashbury. My mother was his bed wench. He owned a large and prosperous plantation in Louisiana, and he also owned us.''

Rapidly he moved to her, and the expression in his eyes was wild as he spoke in a husky and frightening tone, ''Do you find me offensive and repulsive, Rachel? Now that you know I'm a nigger? Did you know your refined aristocratic father would have me castrated for being in bed with you?''

''Stop it, Edward!'' she pleaded. ''Don't say these things to me! Please!''

''Why?'' he asked cruelly. ''Is the thought of a black buck touching you more than a gentle and southern-bred lady can stomach? Do you feel faint, Miss O'Brian? Shall I find your Negro maid and see if she has some smelling salts for you?''

Furious with him, she stood and yelled angrily, ''Shut up, Edward! Will you please stop it! I don't feel any of those things!'' Seeing the look of torment on his

153

handsome face, Rachel sensed the pain and hurt he had been forced to endure. Compassionately she took him into her arms and said softly, "Your heritage makes no difference to me, Edward. I still care very much for you, and I always will."

Holding her closely, he replied, "I'm sorry, Rachel. I had no right to strike out at you the way I did. You can't help being the daughter of a plantation owner, any more than I can help being the bastard son of a slave woman."

She moved out of his embrace and holding his hand in hers, they sat beside each other on the edge of the bed. "Tell me about your life, Edward."

"My mother's name was Louise, and a more gentle and loving woman has never been born. It was her curse to be not only black, but also beautiful. She never wanted to be Ashbury's bed wench, but when she turned sixteen she was ordered to move out of the slave cabin and up to the big house. Two years later, I was born. My . . . father . . . didn't send me out to the fields. You see," he said sarcastically, "my father was such a kind and generous master that he allowed his wench to keep her pickaninny, because it was conceived by him. When I was eight, Ashbury decided to get married. Well, he couldn't allow his young bride to be embarrassed by our presence in the house . . . so he sold my mother and his own son to a house of prostitution in New Orleans. May God damn his rotten soul to eternal Hell!"

"Oh, Edward, no!" she cried sympathetically. "How could he do such a cruel thing?"

"For him it was easy. We were nothing but a couple niggers he needed to get rid of. The Madam he sold us to put my mother to whoring and put me to mopping floors, cleaning rooms, and emptying chamber pots. My God, Rachel, what Mama was being forced to do was destroying her! She was so tiny and fragile, but it wasn't so much what the men did to her body, as what they did to her gentle soul. . . . The others would sleep in late every day, but Mama would rise early and help me with my chores. I was only eight, and I had more work on me that an adult could've finished in one day.'' With a break in his voice and his shoulders shaking slightly, he said, ''But Mama was always there to help me, and she did most of the damned work. . . . Rachel, I loved her so much!''

She reached for him, and he pulled her roughly into his arms. He held her so tight that it was painful. Rachel could feel the moisture from his tears on her cheek. ''One night, after we'd been there about a year, this huge sonofabitch wasn't satisfied with Mama's performance in bed. So he beat her unmercifully, and then he stabbed her over and over with his knife! In the legs, the arms and everywhere he could that wouldn't kill her instantly. He wanted her to die slowly . . . and God . . . she did! I've never stopped looking for the bastard, and if I ever see him again . . . I'll kill him!''

He moved out of her arms and with the moonlight shining through the open window, she could see him clearly. Lovingly, she reached over and wiped a stray tear from his troubled face. Rachel's compassion for Edward Phillips, combined with her love for John Reynolds, was the birth of her maturity.

''There was a gambler,'' he continued, ''who came to see my mother whenever he was in town. Frank worked on a riverboat. Well, that night the boat docked in New Orleans and he came to the house to spend the night with his favorite prostitute . . . I don't mean to sound bitter. He was a man with compassion, and actually cared about my mother as a person instead of an object. When Frank got there she was still alive, and I was kneeling beside her on the floor pleading with God not to let her die. He walked over to us, lifted my mother from the floor and carried her to the bed. Before she died, she begged him to buy me from the Madam, and to give me my freedom."

"Did he buy you?" she asked.

"He not only bought me, but on the same day he gave me my freedom papers. He took me to the riverboat with him, and got me a job as a cleaning boy. We lived on the boat for a year and he taught me some math, history, and how not to speak like a nigger. Then he moved us to St. Louis, where no one knew me. He enrolled me in a white school as his nephew, and Frank, being a professional gambler, made a living for us with a deck of cards. . . . I don't guess I have to tell you, I learned how to gamble from him. When I was fourteen, he was killed one night during a poker game, so I was suddenly on my own. Taking odd jobs, I was able to support myself. After a few years I became as good a gambler as my teacher. Eventually I started traveling, and I was in Atlanta when the war started. I went up North and joined the Union army."

"The Union!" Rachel exclaimed. "But Papa thought. . . ."

"I know what your father thought. But I needed a way to California. And besides, a nigger passing for white learns how to lie very easily."

"But the way you talked to Josh that day in St. Joe!"

"I only said what your father wanted to hear. After he died, it didn't take me long to make friends with Josh, did it?"

He walked over and picked her dress up from the floor, and handed it to her. "Here, put this on and I'll take you home." Watching her slip into the dress, he said, "Tomorrow I'll probably hate myself for letting the champagne and my frustration over you cause me to tell you my life story."

"There will be no reason for you to hate yourself, Edward. I promise you, your secret is safe with me."

Rachel and Deborah were closing the dress shop for the day when they heard an insistent and demanding knock on the front door. Rachel put down the fabric she'd been folding. She walked over and said impatiently through the bolted door, "I'm sorry, but we're closed!"

"That don't matter none, I didn't come to buy no dresses. Ain't never had a hankerin' to wear one!"

Hearing the familiar voice she remembered with affection and fondness, Rachel hurriedly removed the heavy bolt and opened the door. "Zeke! Oh, it's so good to see you again!" She totally astounded him when she joyfully flung herself into his arms and hugged him vigorously. Never in his life had the old mountaineer been so warmly and enthusiastically welcomed. The devotion and adoration he felt for the young woman grew stronger than ever when she embarrassingly flattered him with her open display of affection.

Removing herself from his arms, she grabbed his hand and pulled him inside the shop. Closing the door behind them, she exclaimed happily, "Deb, look who's here!"

"Zeke, how are you?" she asked politely, but distantly. She couldn't possibly understand how Rachel could actually hug the uncouth and foul old man.

"Just fine, ma'am. I brung ya a letter from Lieutenant Kendall. By the way, he done got hisself promoted to first lieutenant. He was gonna mail it to ya til he found out I was a comin' here."

He handed her the sealed envelope and taking it from him, she replied, "Thank you, Zeke."

"Yur welcome, Miss Deborah. You and Lieutenant Kendall been writin' each other a lot, ain't ya? I know he sure talks 'bout ya a powerful lot. Thinks a lot of ya, he does."

"If you'll excuse me, I shall go upstairs," she replied.

"Ma'am, he asked me to bring 'im a reply to that thar letter."

"I see. How long to you plan to be in town?" she asked.

"A few days, so ya got plenty of time to writ yur answer."

"If you will be so kind as to return before you leave, I shall have a letter for you to take back to Lieutenant Kendall. Good night, sir."

Zeke watched her as she walked quietly out of the room. Turning toward Rachel, he said, "Fur sisters, you two sure ain't nothin' alike."

Laughing gaily, she replied, "Zeke, you'll have to overlook Deborah's manners. She thinks she's a refined southern lady."

"And I'm poor white trash, I reckon," he answered.

"I'm sure she doesn't feel that way."

"Maybe so, but yur sister's turnin' into a cold woman. That's what most times happen to a female when she don't get the man she's a wantin'."

"Deborah's not in love with anyone. Why she never even goes anywhere, unless Edward invites us." As the truth ultimately registered in Rachel's mind, she looked at Zeke with pure astonishment. "Do you think Deborah is in love with Edward?"

"Miss Rachel, you was with yur sister them whole six months it took ya to git here. Ya done lived here in this shop with her fur another six months . . . and ya stand thar and tell me in all that thar time ya never knew she was pinin' away fur Phillips?"

"No, but I never thought about it. Not really," she replied.

"I reckon I think more of ya than I ever did any lady, but Miss Rachel, ya cain't see no further than the end of yur purty little nose."

"How long have you known?" she asked.

"I figgered that one out way back yonder on the Oregon Trail. Ain't you ever seen the way she looks at 'im? With all that thar love a shinin' in them eyes of hers?"

"I wonder if Edward is aware of how Deborah feels."

"Don't know nothin' 'bout that. But it wouldn't make no never mind if'n he did. He ain't the marryin' kind, and if fur some reason he did decide to tie the knot, it wouldn't be with a lady like that thar sister of yurs. It'd be with a spirited gal like yourself. Cain't blame him none fur that. Talkin' 'bout Phillips, just where could I find 'im? I need to do some talkin' with

159

'im.''

"He's staying at the Washington Hotel, a few blocks west from here."

"Have ya seen 'im lately?" Zeke noticed the blush that suddenly appeared in her cheeks.

"I haven't seen him for a few days," she answered, remembering vividly the night in his hotel room.

"Reckon I'll go see 'im. I'll be back tomorrow, Miss Rachel."

She watched him as he strode over to the door with his old tattered hat pulled low on his head and the fringe hanging from his buckskin jacket flapping freely. The buckskins were just too much of a reminder, and forgetting about her pride she called out to him, "Zeke . . ."

He halted his steps and turned back toward her. "Yes'm, Miss Rachel?"

Taking a deep breath, she asked, "How . . . how is Major Reynolds?" She hoped she sounded nonchalant, but Rachel suspected that he not only knew about Deborah, but about her, as well.

"He ain't no major no more. He done got a promotion, too. Now he's a Lieutenant Colonel. Colonel Reynolds . . . sound purty good, don't it?" Understanding the undisguised disappointment on her face, he realized that what she wanted to hear about Reynolds was not his rank. Slowly he walked over and looked at her tenderly. "He's doin' all right, Miss Rachel." He yearned to tell her the truth, how John Reynolds had sent him to San Francisco to check on her welfare and make sure Phillips had successfully accomplished his task. Proving beyond a doubt that Rachel was still very much in the man's thoughts.

With hope and anticipation, she asked, "Does he ever . . . ?" Deciding not to finish the question because she was afraid of the answer, she glanced away from him.

"Does he ever . . . what? Ya can go ahead and ask me, little gal. I understand how ya feel 'bout 'im."

So he does know, she thought. By now I should've realized, nothing much ever passes by Zeke's incredible insight where people are concerned. Turning back toward him, she asked, "Does he ever say anything about me?"

"The Colonel and me . . . we don't most times set around discussin' ladies, but yep, he's mentioned ya a couple times."

"What did he say?" she asked curiously.

Zeke, becoming bored and uncomfortable answering what he considered a young woman's foolish questions, replied, "I don't rightly recollet, Miss Rachel. I got to be a goin'. By the way, ma'am, where is a good place fur me to stable my horse?"

"We have a small stable behind the store, and you're welcome to use it. The stable was already here when we purchased the shop." Smiling at him, she continued, "One afternoon, a few weeks after we moved in, Edward drove up in a fine carriage drawn by two grand looking horses. Deb and I were shocked, to say the least, when he informed us that the carriage and horses belonged to us. He never would tell us how he managed to get the money to buy them. We've always suspected that he won the money in a card game and is so kind and generous, he spent his winnings on us so we'd have our own transportation."

Grinning slyly to himself Zeke thought, it ain't

161

Phillips' kindness and generosity little gal, it's John Reynolds'!

"I'll walk around back with you and help you get your horse settled." Rachel started to lead him across the room but, changing her mind, she asked, "Zeke, why did you come to San Francisco?"

Feeling anger towards John Reynolds for forcing him into a lie, he looked away as he answered, "I just wanted to git away from army life fur awhile, and I figgered I could find me some good times here in San Francisco."

"Zeke, you are a very poor liar." Fondly taking his large hand into hers, she said, "You wonderful, sweet, and dear friend. You came all the way to San Francisco to make sure my sister and I were all right. My goodness, couldn't you tell we were fine by Deborah's letters to Josh?"

Yep, he thought to himself, it were fairly plain by them letters but not plain enuf to satisfy that stubborn hard-headed man who's too damned ornery to admit he loves ya. . . . But instead of saying what she would've been thrilled to hear, he replied, "Miss Rachel, I just got an over-powerin' hankerin' to see them thar purty green eyes."

Deborah sat on the side of her bed and held the letter from Josh loosely in her hand. With tears in her eyes, she stared down forlornly at the opened envelope on her lap. Abruptly she stood, and the envelope slid lightly and soundlessly to the floor. Grasping the letter tightly in her hand, she paced back and forth for a moment before she resentfully, and furiously, tore the paper into pieces. Dropping the shredded remains of Josh's letter, she cried, "Why must he be the one who loves me?" As heartbreaking sobs tore from deep in her throat, she ran across the room and fell on the bed. "Oh Edward! Why can't it be you? It's your proposal I want . . . not his!"

Hearing Rachel's knock on her bedroom door, Deborah quickly regained control of her emotions. "Just a minute," she called. Hurriedly she gathered all the torn pieces of the letter and shoved them into a dresser drawer. "Come in."

Entering the room, Rachel asked inquisitively, "What was so important that Josh wanted you to send back a reply?"

"He asked me to marry him. If I say yes, he'll take furlough and come to San Francisco. He wants us to be married here, and then return to Fort Craig."

When she didn't say anymore, Rachel said impatiently, "Well? What is your answer? Are you going to marry him?"

"No, of course not," Deborah replied, walking over and looking into the mirror hanging above the dresser. Slowly she began removing the pins from her hair.

Hoping to trick her sister into confessing the truth, she said, "If you're worried about what will become of me, I can manage alone."

"You couldn't correctly run this shop for one day, Rachel O'Brian, and you know it. But you aren't the reason I'm refusing his proposal. Besides, he generously offered you a home with us. He wouldn't dream of leaving you alone in San Francisco, but it's all immaterial anyway. I'm not going to marry the man."

Disappointed, because she realized Deborah wasn't going to honestly reveal her feelings for Edward, Rachel started to leave the room, when suddenly what Deborah had been saying struck her profoundly! "Josh invited me to live with you . . . at Fort Craig?"

"Where else would we live? That's where he's stationed."

To think she could actually be at the same fort with John Reynolds, and see him everyday! If only . . . if only Deborah wasn't foolishly in love with Edward.

"Deb, maybe you shouldn't be so hasty in making your decision. After all, Josh is very attractive and also a very nice person."

"And also a Yankee!" she replied angrily as she briskly brushed her long hair.

"What has that got to do with it?"

Banging the brush down on the dresser, she turned and faced her sister. "Maybe you have forgotten how Papa felt about Yankees, but I haven't! Being friends with one, I can understand, and in time, so would our father have understood. I agree Josh is a very likable person, but I absolutely refuse to marry a man who fought for the Union! My Lord, what would Papa have said about his daughter marrying a Yankee!"

Irritably Rachel thought, Yankee indeed! What would Papa have said if he knew you were in love with a man who was once a black slave! "You're a fool, Deborah! And so was Papa!"

"What!" she exclaimed, unable to believe that Rachel actually had the audacity to call their father a fool!

"The whole Confederacy were fools. They never should have started that stupid war."

"Rachel, how can you say such things! Our own beloved brothers died for the Cause."

Angrily, and with disgust, Rachel walked to the door, opened it, and with a wisdom beyond her years, she said, "The Cause! There never was a cause worth fighting and dying over!"

"I bet you don't speak this way in front of Edward. What do you think he would do if he could hear you saying those awful things about the Confederacy? He believed in and loved the great Confederacy, same as Papa!"

Bewildered, Deborah wondered why Rachel was laughing when she slammed the door shut behind her.

Rachel was abruptly awakened during the middle of the night by a loud and continued banging on the door at the rear of the dress shop. Quickly she leaped out of bed, reached for her dressing gown, and slipped it on as she hurried from her room. As she awkwardly collided with her sister in the dark hallway, Deborah excitedly grabbed hold of her arm and asked, "Who do you suppose it could be?"

"I don't know," Rachel answered as the thundering knock continued. Sounding more courageous than she actually felt, she added, "But there's only one way to find out."

With Deborah following cautiously, Rachel swiftly descended the stairs and walked quickly through the storage room located in the back of the shop. "Who's there?" she called.

"It's me, Miss Rachel, with Edward Phillips," Zeke replied from the other side of the closed door. Hastily she unlocked it, and the two men rudely pushed their way in and shut the door promptly behind them. At once Rachel and Deborah realized something was amiss.

"What's happened?" Deborah asked looking anxiously at Edward.

Glancing toward her, he answered gravely, "I don't know how to tell you girls this . . . but. . . ."

Finishing his explanation Zeke said brusquely, "He done went and killed a man."

"What?" Deborah cried in astonishment. "No, I don't believe it!"

"I'm afraid it's true," Edward began. "I have to get out of town and fast. Zeke said I could have his horse because it's too dangerous for me to go to the livery stable for mine. There's probably a posse already out searching for me."

"But why must you run away? Surely you killed in self-defense," Deborah replied.

When he made no comment, Zeke told her, "He killed 'im in cold blooded murder . . . anyways that's how the law will look at it."

Suddenly, Rachel felt a strange sensation and intuitively she knew exactly whom Edward had murdered. She went to him, and placed her hand on his arm. "You found him at last, didn't you? The man you told me about."

"Yes, I found him," he answered, so quietly she barely heard his reply.

"I'm glad you killed him!" she stated with approval. "He deserved to die after what he did!"

While trying to conceal her jealousy, Deborah stared at Rachel with envy. The man she loved obviously was so close to her sister, that he confided in her.

"Zeke and I were having a drink together when he walked into the barroom. God, Rachel, the instant I saw him I stopped thinking rationally and went crazy! I got up from the table, walked over to the bastard and told him who I was and why I planned to kill him!''

"Oh, Edward, no! Did he say anything about your mother?''

He put his hands on Rachel's shoulders and roughly jerked her closer to him. With anguish and hatred in his voice, he continued, "The sonofabitch told everyone in the bar that my mother had been a dirty nigger whore and I was her bastard son . . . I can't even remember pulling my gun from the holster. I shot him right in his horrified and ugly face. Before anyone recovered their senses and tried to stop me, I ran outside. Zeke caught up to me before I got here.''

Only Zeke noticed the look of horror on Deborah's face, as she covered her mouth with her hand and pulled in her breath with astonishment. . . . Oh God, she thought, the man I loved is a Negro! . . . With repulsion she abhorrently fled from the room and ran wildly up the stairs. . . . How dare he pass himself off as a white man! A Negro! I desired a Negro! And Rachel knew! Why didn't she tell me! Why?

Becoming aware of Deborah's departure, Rachel whispered, "Oh no!'' Looking at Edward, she explained, "Deborah's in love with you.''

"In love with . . . me?'' he asked, showing apparent surprise. Then suddenly his expression changed, and sarcastically he said, "Yeah, she loves me so much she couldn't stand being in the same room with me.'' Compassionately he drew her into his arms. "You didn't run from me when you heard the truth.'' Holding her tightly, he confessed, "If I could ever love a woman enough to marry her, it would be you.''

Gruffly Zeke muttered, "You ain't got time fur that mushy stuff. You gotta git goin'. I'll go saddle up the horse fur ya." Before walking out the back door, he added, "Make yur goodbyes quick, Phillips, or ya'll find yurself a hangin' from a rope."

"He's right, Edward. You must hurry," Rachel said moving out of his arms.

"There's something I want to tell you first. It's about Reynolds."

"John?" she asked.

"Just listen, Rachel, and don't interrupt. I don't have time for your questions. It was Reynolds' money that bought this dress shop. The little dab of savings you and Deborah had wouldn't have been enough to buy a corner of this place. And Reynolds, though he doesn't know it, bought the buggy and horses. He also paid that old Biddy to teach you two the business. . . . The last night on the wagon train when we were camped a couple miles out of Sacramento, he gave me a letter addressed to a Mr. Carlson at the bank here in San Francisco. It gave me permission to use his money to make sure you and your sister were taken care of financially. It seems Reynolds has quite a large amount of money in the bank here. And Rachel, he also paid me five thousand dollars for my trouble. If you should need it, Mr. Carlson is holding the deed to this shop. . . . Sweetheart, I'm telling you all this because I know how much you love him." Smiling at her stunned expression, he said, "Find a way to get to Fort Craig, Rachel, even if you have to con Zeke into taking you. A man doesn't spend the kind of money on a woman that Reynolds spent on you, unless he loves her."

"Then he does love me! I was always so sure he did, until he left without caring what happened to me." Looking up at him with joy, she exclaimed, "But he did care!"

Gently, Edward took her into his arms. "Kiss me goodbye, Rachel. And for once kiss me and not John Reynolds."

She reached up and wrapped her arms around his neck, and touched her lips to his. She could feel tears stinging her eyes as she kissed him farewell with all her heart.

"I love you, Rachel," he said before hurrying from the room and out into the darkness of night.

Leaning against the wall, Rachel broke into sobs as she heard the horse galloping away from the back of the store. When Zeke came through the door, he saw her distress and to comfort her, he said, "He'll git away, Miss Rachel. Thar ain't no faster horse than that one he's a-ridin'."

Looking at the old man with affection, she replied, "It was so kind of you to give him your horse."

Embarrassed by her flattery, he muttered, "Weren't really mine, no how. It belonged to the U. S. Cavalry."

"Is he gone?" Deborah asked.

Startled, because she hadn't heard her sister enter the room, Rachel whirled swiftly in her direction. Wiping away her tears, she answered, "Yes, he's gone, and we'll probably never see him again."

Angrily, Deborah shouted, "Why didn't you tell me he was a Negro? All this time you knew and you kept it to yourself!"

"I've only known for a few days. I couldn't tell you

because I promised Edward his secret was safe with me."

Zeke studied Rachel with admiration and wished John Reynolds could see her now. He'd be as proud of their little gal, as he was himself! But Deborah studied her with contempt. "You are a traitor to this family, and most of all, to the memory of our father!"

Trying to compose herself, Deborah continued, "I didn't come down here to argue with you. What you did is done and over with. I wanted to tell you . . . I have decided to mary Josh, and you are welcome to live with us." Glancing toward Zeke, she said, "I don't want to wait for Lieutentant Kendall to take a furlough, and I was wondering if you'd be so kind to escort me to Fort Craig. I understand there is a small town close to the fort. There should be a reverend there to marry us."

"But what about the shop?" Rachel asked.

"I have decided, with your permission, to offer the former owner the shop for the same price we paid for it. I'm hoping she will accept my proposal."

"I know she will!" Rachel exclaimed. "This place is worth a lot more than we think it . . ."

Realizing Edward had told her the truth, Zeke reached over and grabbed her arm as he interrupted, "Let her do as she pleases, Miss Rachel. The sooner you two sell this here store, the sooner you get to Fort Craig. Are you understandin' me, little gal?" Chuckling to himself, Zeke could hardly wait to see the expression on the colonel's face when he informed him the ladies sold the shop for a fraction of what he paid for it!

"When I was unsaddlin' my horse," Zeke said, "I

seen you two kept yur Paw's wagon. When ya git all yur business taken care of, pack up what you wanna take with ya in the wagon. Sell that thar fancy buggy, but don't sell them horses. We'll need 'em to pull the wagon. When we know fur sure what day we'll be a leavin', I'll send a wire to the fort." Looking tenderly at Rachel, he added, "The colonel will not only send out a military escort fur us, but I bet he'll be a leadin' it . . . when he knows this here little gal is a comin' too."

PART TWO

Chapter Five

Rachel felt as if she were once again back on the wagon train traveling the long, tiresome journey toward California. Except this time, there was only the single wagon rolling endlessly over the empty plains. She missed the sound of whips cracking through the air to encourage the oxen to continue plodding steadily onward. Rachel wished she could hear the constant comforting voices of the other emigrants talking and yelling to one another, as their wagons covered the long, fatiguing miles.

Zeke guided them down through California and into the hot territory of Arizona. Even in late spring, the sun was unmerciful and unyielding as it shone down on the weary travelers.

Although the trip was tiresome and exhausting, Rachel was glad to be away from life in the city. She had found San Francisco exciting and exhilarating, but surprisingly Rachel now realized that nothing stimulated her senses more than the wide-open plains. She could understand why men like John Reynolds and Zeke loved their untamed wilderness with a passion, and finally she understood what John had meant that day when he told her he could never have stayed in Boston or behind a desk.

The vast plains of Arizona, however, weren't in the least stimulating to Deborah. She was too deeply engrossed in bitterness. She despised and hated herself for still being in love with Edward Phillips. All her life she had heard that it was terribly wrong and sinful for a white woman to desire a man with Negro blood. Deborah believed that she was not only sinning against God, but also against the memory of her parents. Appalled, she knew during the rare moments when she'd forget her parents and God, that if only Edward had loved her, she'd have willingly married a Negro. With determination and constant effort, Deborah finally learned to bury those thoughts so far back in her mind that they no longer surfaced; but losing the one man she had so desperately loved, and the shocking discovery of his heritage had turned Deborah into a hard and cold woman at the tender age of seventeen.

Rachel was aware of the change in her sister, but she was truly convinced that it was only temporary and that soon Deborah would return to her former self. She believed that marriage to a good man like Josh was all that Deborah needed to completely heal her emotional wounds.

By Zeke's reckoning they should have rendezvoused with the military escort from Fort Craig about two hours out of Tuscon. They had already traveled six hours from the town, and Zeke was becoming worried. He was fully aware that a man traveling with two lone women could be extremely dangerous in this part of the territory. If they were to come upon a band of Apaches, the Indians would more than likely try to take the fine looking pair of horses. But what Zeke feared was a band of warriors consisting entirely of young braves. Rachel and Deborah were beautiful women, and the Apache braves would most assuredly capture them. Zeke knew when the Apaches finished raping the girls, they would give what was left of them to the squaws for torture and finally when their death came, it would be mercifully welcome. His hands tightened on the reins he held, and nervously, he chewed loudly on a wad of tobacco. Glancing over at Rachel, he realized how much he had grown to love and respect the young woman sitting beside him. Silently he promised himself. . . . Nope, they ain't gonna git her nor Miss Deborah. I'll kill 'em myself first, 'fore I let them savages git ahold of 'em . . . Zeke was liked by many tribes of Indians and they held him in high esteem, but the Apache weren't among them. There had been a time when Zeke was on friendly terms with some of the Apache, but they were now at war and the Apache had proudly proclaimed themselves the enemy of all white men. . . . Cain't rightly blame them none, Zeke thought, but that ain't here nor thar no more. When it's kill or be killed, I ain't gonna stop first to wonder who's right or wrong.

"Zeke," Rachel began, "what do you suppose is keeping the soldiers?"

"I reckon we made better time than I figgered we would. Don't worry none, we'll run into 'em 'fore nightfall."

"Is there any chance they could've been attacked by Indians?" she asked.

Seeing the fear on her face, he half-truthfully answered, "Slim chance of that." Though Zeke doubted the Apache would attack the military escort, it wasn't as unlikely as he wanted her to believe.

"Yer worried 'bout the colonel, ain't ya?"

"The colonel? Oh, you mean John." He noticed how her eyes softened when she spoke his name. "I keep forgetting he isn't a major any more. Yes, Zeke, I'm terribly afraid and worried about him."

He started to try to reassure her, but was suddenly startled by Deborah's piercing screams coming from the back of the wagon. "Indians!" she shouted.

Zeke looked back and saw seven Apache warriors following their wagon from a distance. Handing the reins to Rachel, he ordered, "See them boulders over yonder? Head fur 'em as fast as you can git them horses to run. When ya git thar, you and Miss Deborah jump out and hide behind 'em!" Grabbing his shotgun he moved swiftly to the rear of the covered wagon as Rachel guided the horses toward the shelter of the massive rocks. Aiming his weapon at the approaching Indians, he realized they were shrewd enough to keep safely out of his shooting range. Quickly he picked up the extra two rifles he had brought along, plus the ammunition. Throwing the boxes of ammunition to Deborah, he said, "Take these behind them rocks with ya." He leaned across the enclosure of the wagon and placed the rifles beside Rachel and told her, "Don't furgit to take them when ya run fur cover."

The wagon jolted to an abrupt stop and the girls hurriedly climbed down. While clutching the ammunition and guns, they ran for the rocks. Zeke jumped out of the back and moved quickly to the horses and led them to the boulders. Then he joined Rachel and Deborah crouching behind the rocks.

With her heart pounding in fear, Rachel asked, "Are

178

they going to attack?''

"I don't rightly know, ma'am. They might just want them horses.''

"Then let's offer the horses to them," Deborah said.

"Cain't do that," he replied.

Irritated with the old man, she asked, "And, why not?''

"What if fur some reason that escort ain't a comin'? We'd die out here in the middle of nowhar without no horses to pull that thar wagon.''

"Nonsense, we're only about six hours out of Tuscon," Deborah answered, but then added, "so why don't you tell us what they really want?''

Running his eyes over her feminine curves, he spat out a stream of brown tobacco juice, then said, "Now just what in the hell do ya think they're a wantin'? And as fur them horses, we'd be helpless without 'em. They many be our only chance out of here . . . so just shet yur mouth 'bout them thar horses, besides, they are a wantin' more than just them horses, and I reckon you're a understandin' what I mean.''

"Oh, my God," she whispered as the truth dawned on her.

"They ain't gonna git you or Miss Rachel. I guarantee it," he said not forgetting the promise he'd made to himself.

"But how can you possibly fight them all alone?'' Deborah asked, peering over the edge of the rock. She caught her breath in terror when she saw the Indians were steadly advancing.

"I don't reckon either one of you ladies know how to shoot.''

"I do," Rachel answered. "My brothers taught me

179

how.''

Finding another reason to admire his "little gal," he asked, "Have ya ever shot at a livin' target?"

"No, of course not! I never wanted to kill anything."

Placing a loaded rifle into her hands, he questioned, "Think ya could kill a man?"

Remembering vividly the two men who had ruthlessly attacked her, she answered with a hatred in her eyes Zeke had never seen in them before, "Yes, I could!"

"Them Indians ain't dumb, so they ain't gonna ride up to us right out in the open. Nope! Some of 'em will climb up thar in them rocks behind us so they got them some kind of cover. The others will stay out yonder so we cain't make a run fur it with the wagon and horses. When them up in the rocks start a shootin' the ones down here will come at us. They'll attack from both sides.''

"Dear God," Deborah sobbed. "We don't stand a chance.''

"Not much of one," Zeke replied bluntly.

Looking in the direction of the Apaches, Rachel observed, "That's exactly what they're doing. Four of them are heading for the rocks, but three are staying down here." They watched as the muscular young braves skillfully climbed up the huge boulders that circled over and behind them. Breaking the eerie silence, Deborah shrilled hysterically, "Why don't you shoot them?''

"They ain't in shootin' range," Zeke muttered. Thar ain't nothin' more aggravatin' than a dumb female, he thought. But noticing the trace of tears in Rachel's eyes, his heart softened. "Are you afraid of dyin', little gal?''

Rachel reached over and placed her hand on his arm, and as she spoke her fingers unintentionally dug into his flesh. "Oh Zeke, I've never even kissed him . . . I've never heard him say that he loves me!"

While awkwardly trying to console her, Zeke patted her hand and answered, "It's goin' to take them Apaches a while to climb up and cross over behind us, so bein's we have some time, I'm goin' to tell ya somethin', little gal. I know John Reynolds better than anyone on this here earth, and you can believe me when I tell ya, he loves ya, Miss Rachel. But he done set a high standard of life fur hisself and he don't ever go against what he firmly believes in, and he don't believe in takin' advantage of a young innocent gal like yurself and ruinin' her. He ain't got nothin' to offer ya, and even if he could offer ya marriage, he might never be able to settle down."

"But once he did! Zeke, please tell me what happened!" she pleaded.

"Ain't got the right to tell ya that," he answered.

"Why? We both know we're not going to come out of this alive."

"He wouldn't want me to be a talkin' 'bout it."

"But why?" she insisted.

"Rachel, I can't believe what I'm hearing," Deborah began crossly. "In a few minutes we are probably going to be murdered, or else be inhumanely tortured, and you sit there discussing John Reynolds."

"What do you suggest we do?" Rachel asked sharply.

"If you two sisters don't wanna die a feudin', you'd best be fur makin' up, cause them Apaches are purttin' near behind us.''

Quickly Rachel gathered Deborah into her arms and hugged her tightly. ''He's right. We shouldn't be arguing. Oh Deb, I do love you!''

Gruffly Zeke ordered, ''Git down and find the best cover you can, and Miss Rachel, you watch them down thar. When they git in your shootin' range aim fur their chest and fire. Don't aim fur the head, makes too small a target.''

Wedging herself between two narrow rocks, Rachel stared toward the three Apaches waiting patiently on their horses. When she heard the first shot ring out, it ricochetted against the tall boulder beside her. Simultaneously she heard Deborah's shrieking scream. At the same instant, the three warriors charged forward. Rachel carefully aimed her gun at the Apache riding in the lead, but her finger froze on the trigger and she couldn't force herself to shoot. Nervous perspiration accumulated heavily on her brow and she had to wipe away the wetness dripping into her eyes. I must kill him, she thought. I must! Oh God, forgive me! Gently she squeezed the trigger, bracing herself for the recoil as the rifle discharged the fatal bullet into the approaching Indian. With horror, she watched as his body fell lifelessly from his speeding horse.

Zeke also fired his rifle, and seconds later another Apache fell from the high rocks, landing on the ground directly in front of Deborah. In a mad frenzy she started screaming, and swiftly Zeke moved toward her, slapping her severely across the face. ''Shet up, goddamn it, and listen!''

In the quietness, the sound was still faint, but Zeke and the Indians easily recognized the bugler blowing

"Charge" as the U. S. Cavalry raised a storm of dust across the horizon. Zeke realized they had sent a scout ahead, who had seen the trouble, and rode hastily back to the troops to report the incident. The sound of the bugle sent the remaining Apaches fleeing for their lives.

While walking away from his rifle, Zeke had his back turned to the Indian he mistakenly thought to be dead, and he did not see the slight movement the injured brave made. The girls, overjoyed at the arrival of the soldiers, were happily hugging one another. The wounded Apache soundlessly pulled out his knife and leaped towards Zeke. With the alertness and instinct of a mountain lion, Zeke pivoted away from the deadly blade in the warrior's hand. The Apache was young and strong. He knew, even wounded, that killing the old man would be easy. Sneering at him, he raised the knife once more with intentions of ramming it into the white man's heart.

Rachel had moved away from her rifle, and she realized the closest weapon to her was Zeke's old shotgun. With a speed she never knew she possessed, she reached for the gun. Rachel lifted the heavy weapon and aware of its wide pattern she didn't waste precious time aiming but fired in the direction of the Apache. As the deadly buckshot tore parts of the Indian's body into bloody pieces, the fierce kick from the huge gun sent Rachel sprawling backwards. Violently she hit the ground, the side of her head striking a protruding rock. The last she heard was Deborah's ghastly scream as blackness engulfed her, and she fell into the depths of unconsciousness.

* * *

As Rachel slowly regained consciousness, she became aware of being gently lifted into strong, comforting arms. Forcing her heavy eyelids open, she could see the outline of John Reynolds' worried face as he carried her towards the wagon. She lingeringly regarded the man she had missed so desperately. The setting sun casting its peaceful glow made his thick brown hair appear almost golden. Free from the usual restricting hat, it fell carelessly over his forehead. She longed to tenderly brush the stray locks back into place. With adoration, she noticed how his dark eyebrows were perfectly arched over those steel gray eyes that could look at her with such intensity.

Sensing he was being observed, John Reynolds glanced down into her face and instantly smiled the boyish crooked grin she hadn't seen for over six months. Feeling perfectly content just being near him, Rachel easily slipped her arms around his neck and held him tightly. He stopped walking and stared lovingly into her spirited green eyes. "Hello, my beautiful little hypocrite."

Smiling happily, Rachel remembered how angry she used to become when he called her a hypocrite, but the way he now caressed the word made it sound more like an endearment. When she moved slightly to speak to him, her head began to throb, and painfully she asked, "What happened? The last I remember . . . I grabbed the shotgun and . . . oh my God, is Zeke all right?"

"Why don't you see for yourself," he answered, as he turned around and placed her on her feet. Thankfully, she saw Zeke standing in front of her.

"The Apache! I didn't miss him, did I?" she asked.

"No, ma'am. It's nigh on impossible to miss with

that thar shotgun of mine." Chuckling, he continued, "But Miss Rachel, that Apache was standin' mighty close to me. If ya'd had that gun pointed just a couple more inches in the other direction, ya'd have blowed us both away."

Although the movement caused her head to ache, she walked over to him and placed a kiss on his bearded cheek. "I'm so glad you're alive." Looking Zeke squarely in the eyes, she told him in all sincerity, "I love you, you dear sweet friend."

Flustered and embarrassed by her display of affection for him, the old mountain man blushed under his red scraggly beard, as he answered, "I owe my life to ya, Miss Rachel, and I'll always be beholdin' to ya." Lowering his voice so John Reynolds couldn't hear his confession, he added, "Ma'am . . . I . . . I, oh hell and damnation! What I'm tryin' to tell ya is . . . I think a lot of ya, little gal!"

Walking over and touching her arm gently, John said, "Deborah has fixed you a bed in the back of the wagon. I think you should rest for a while." Placing his arm around her shoulders, and with Zeke following, they walked to where Josh and Deborah stood waiting for them.

"Are you all right?" Deborah asked.

"Yes, I'm fine, except for a dreadful headache." Turning to Josh she smiled, "It's so good to see you again."

"Hello, Rachel. I understand you're quite a heroine."

"You mustn't believe all my sister has told you," she answered modestly.

"It isn't Deborah who's been bragging on you, it's

Zeke," he replied.

"Didn't say nary a thing 'bout ya that weren't true neither. Yur 'bout the bravest female I done ever had the pleasure of knowin'."

Rachel was climbing into the rear of the wagon, when she became aware of all the soldiers a short distance from them. There appeared to be about thirty men busily unloading their gear or moving around setting up camp.

"All those blue uniforms," she began, "I can remember how I used to hate the sight of them and the men who wore them."

Glancing at the man standing beside her, she noticed he was questioningly raising his eyebrows. "I know what you're thinking, John Reynolds!" Lifting her chin in defiance, she added, "Well I used to hate them, until that night in St. Joe!"

Laughing cheerfully, he picked her up in his powerful arms and easily placed her inside the wagon. "Get some rest, Baby. I'll be back later." He started to walk away with Zeke, but added before he left, "I haven't been entertained in a hell of a long time."

As he headed in the direction of his horse with the old mountaineer strolling along beside him, Zeke said, "I sure am proud of that thar little gal of ours."

"Ours?" John questioned. "I wasn't aware she belonged to us."

"Bein' that she's an orphan, I reckon I kinda adopted her as the granddaughter I ain't never had." Watching his friend out of the corner of his eye, he proceeded, "Since you're so fond of her too, I reckon you could sorta adopt her as a daughter."

John threw back his head and laughed so uproariously loud that the nearby soldiers stared at their commanding officer with confusion and astonishment.

Laughing along with him, and feeling encouraged, Zeke asked, "What ya gonna do 'bout that hankerin' ya got fur her?"

He looked at the old man seriously for a moment, then answered, "Not one damn thing!"

Zeke abruptly halted his steps, and as John continued walking away from him, he shouted loud enough for all the surrounding men to hear. "You ornery stubborn jackass!"

The nights were considerably cooler in the open plains of Arizona, in contrast to the scorching heat of the day, and Rachel wrapped her shawl tightly around her shoulders. She slipped her hand into John's hand and walked leisurely beside him. The refreshing evening breezes whispered through the darkness of the night as he led her a short distance from the camp. One of the soldiers began strumming his guitar, and in a clear tenor he began singing the Irish ballad "Kathleen." Hearing the familiar beloved melody caused tears to sting Rachel's eyes.

Noticing her distress, he asked, "Does the song remind you of your father?"

Nodding her head, she answered, "He loved that song so much." Laughing lightly but sadly, she continued, "He used to sing it all the time, but always off key. Papa loved music, but he couldn't carry a tune."

Gently he put his arm around her and drew her into his embrace. While studying Rachel thoughtfully, he put his hand under her chin to tilt her face upward. When he didn't say anything, she asked, "What are you thinking about?''

"About a sixteen year old girl standing off by herself while everyone else danced, and she was so obviously worried she wouldn't be asked. Ah, Rachel, my love, you've come a long way since that night. In a little over a year you've seen both your parents die of cholera, you've been brutally attacked and almost raped. Then today you very courageously fought the Apaches.''

Stepping away from him she walked slowly towards a large rock and sat on the edge. "I killed two men today, John!'' Her shoulders began to shake as she cried, "Oh God . . . I killed them!''

Hastening to her side, he drew her into his arms, "Baby, you had no choice.''

Trying to control her sorrow, she replied, "We could have surrendered. Perhaps then no one would've been killed.''

"My God, Rachel, surely you don't believe that! Eventually they'd have murdered all three of you.''

"Eventually?'' she asked.

"After they finished torturing you, but there's no way in hell Zeke would've let them take you and Deborah alive.'' As her eyes grew wide in astonishment, he told her the truth. "Rachel, he'd have killed both of you himself before letting the Apaches capture you!''

Rising, she walked a short way from him and stood quietly for a moment watching the flickering glow of the campfires. Then she remarked, "I don't want to talk about it anymore! It's too horrifying.''

He changed the subject. "Zeke told me about Phillips. I don't blame him for killing the man, but it's too bad he had to leave San Francisco. The city is a gambler's paradise.''

Turning around to face him, she replied with sudden enthusiasm, "San Francisco was so exciting and so much fun! I was continuously invited to the theater, dances, dinners, and even the casinos."

Watching her closely with an intensity she didn't understand, he asked, "How many men fell in love with you?"

Smiling at him coquettishly, and hoping to make him jealous, she answered, "Quite a few, Mr. Reynolds. Apparently not all men agree with you."

"About what?" he asked.

"That I'm too young and immature for love," she replied.

"How did Edward Phillips feel about you?"

With embarrassment she remembered the night in Edward's hotel room and how close she had come to making love to him, while dreaming it was really John Reynolds. The flush in her cheeks caused her to look away from him. "In a very special way, we loved each other."

If Rachel had maintained eye contact with him, she'd have recognized the brief but unmistakable glint of angry suspicion; but as she faced him again, he mastered full command of his emotions and the moment of his exposed reaction passed unnoticed.

Standing and walking toward her, he asked, "Is Phillips the reason you decided to move to Fort Craig with your sister?"

"What could Edward possibly have to do with my moving to Fort Craig?" Rachel inquired.

"He had to leave town, didn't he? I'm sure you didn't want to stay in San Francisco without him." The sudden hardness in his eyes confused her as he added, "Since you're in love with him!"

Hastily, she tried to explain, "You don't understand! It's true that I love Edward but not in the way . . ."

Interrupting, he said, "Rachel, you'll probably fall in love a dozen times before you ever take it seriously."

Furious, she placed her hands on her hips, and said the first words that came into her mind. "I'll never love any man but you!"

Laughing sarcastically, he replied, "Didn't you just tell me you're in love with Phillips?" With all signs of humor erased from his face, he moved so close to her that his masculine nearness caused her heart to pound. He stared deeply into her eyes. "Very fickle of you, my little hypocrite."

Throwing pride and caution to the wind, she wrapped her arms around his neck, pressed her slim body against his large frame and not caring how forward it sounded, she whispered, "Kiss me, John!"

He tightened his arm around her waist and forced her so intimately close to him that she could feel his maleness aroused. Rachel closed her eyes as rapture filled her senses. For once she was actually being held passionately in the powerful embrace of the man she loved. When he suddenly released her with no warning, she stared up into his face with confusion and the fury she saw there was frightening. "I told you once before Rachel, don't be so foolish as to tease me! I'm not one of your southern gentlemen or some love-struck fool you can add to your list of admirers. And if you want to save your virginity for your husband, don't throw yourself at me again! Not even you, Rachel, could be so naive as to believe I would stop with a kiss!"

With her Irish temper exploding, she yelled at him, "A list of admirers! Is that all you think I want? Well you haven't seen anything yet, John Reynolds. Watch closely and you shall see my list grow even longer!" Fighting back tears, she hurried away from him.

As Rachel neared one of the campfires surrounded by a group of young soldiers, they eagerly stood at her approach. It was very easy for Rachel to achieve her goal. All she had to do was flash her enticing smile, laugh gaily, and tease with her dancing green eyes and within minutes the cavalrymen were added to her list of male admirers.

John remained by the large boulders and watched intensely as Rachel laughed and flirted with the soldiers. Feeling a growing tension building in his nerves that he hadn't felt in years, he awkwardly attempted to roll a cigarette, and after the third try, he finally accomplished the simple task. Angrily, he struck a match across the rough surface of a nearby rock and lit the carelessly rolled cigarette.

Moving with the silence of an experienced, aged hunter, Zeke noiselessly walked up to his friend, saying gruffly, "Well, I see you went and done it."

Startled by his unexpected arrival, John answered, "Damn it, Zeke! Don't sneak up on me like that! And just what in the hell have I done?"

"Just what ya said ya was gonna do . . . not one damn thing. . . . That is what ya said, ain't it?" Nodding his head in Rachel's direction, he tried to explain, "Don't matter none how it looks with all them thar men 'round her, she ain't like Carmelita." When John glared at him with open hostility, Zeke realized he'd gone too far and quickly he added, "No sense in ya gittin' all riled up. Didn't come a lookin' fur ya to talk 'bout that little gal.''

"You sure could've fooled me!" he replied angrily.

Zeke waited quietly for a moment until the colonel's temper cooled, and then said, "I was just wonderin' how things are at the fort."

Taking a drag off his cigarette while still staring toward Rachel, he replied, "Everything's just fine."

"Well, we both know how highly unusual it is fur a commandin' officer to leave the fort on just an ordinary military escort, when the lieutenant could've handled it alone. But we know why ya did, don't we? Of course that ain't here nor thar, I was just wonderin' who you left in charge."

Smiling slyly at the old man, he replied, "Correct me if I'm wrong, but if my memory is right, he's a distant relative of yours. Captain Godwin?"

"Godwin!" Zeke exclaimed. "You mean to tell me that thar weasel done went and made captain?"

"He showed up a week or so after you left. We needed a second in command, and he's what the army sent us."

"The army must be gittin' hard up fur men," Zeke muttered.

Laughing good-humoredly, John placed his arm over the bony shoulders of his old friend and together they headed for camp.

Fort Craig appeared to Rachel like all the other forts she'd seen on the Oregon Trail. Like Fort Laramie, it was built in the shape of a hollow square, only on a smaller scale. Most of the buildings inside the fort were made of stone, but a few were still log or adobe structures.

The particular house that had been assigned to Lieutenant Kendall, and his future bride, was depressing. The four rooms were extremely small, and the few furnishings were shabby and badly worn. It did have two bedrooms, but the extra one could easily have fit into Rachel's closet at the Knolls with space to spare. Rachel accepted the tiny room with no complaints, as she was more than willing to put up with discomfort to be near John Reynolds.

The Reverend from the nearby town of El Rio was summoned to perform the marriage ceremony for Deborah and Josh. The simple wedding took place in the mess hall because it was the only building large enough to accomodate the troops and the few families residing at the fort.

To Rachel's disappointment, marriage to Josh did nothing to improve her sister's bitter disposition. Deborah found no happiness in her marriage, and the sexual duty she was forced to endure, was not only disgusting but also degrading. Night after night she lay rigid and unresponsive beneath her husband until finally he'd shudder in a climactic spasm. As soon as he'd roll his sweaty, naked body off her, she'd quickly pull down her gown to cover herself from his view. Certain the frigidity in his young bride was only temporary, Josh would fall asleep feeling sure she'd soon respond to him. While her husband slept peacefully beside her, Deborah would sob quietly into her pillow and tell herself that with Edward it would have been different somehow.

Rachel found life at the fort stimulating. Not even the unreasonable heat could put a damper on her spirits, and she was happier than she'd ever been in her life. Each day John Reynolds spent part of his time with her, and happiness to Rachel was simply being close to him.

Every morning she was awakened by the bugler blowing reveille at 5:30. Quickly she would hop out of bed, hastily eat her breakfast, and hurry outside to watch the first drill at 6:15. With pride, because the man she loved was their commanding officer, she would observe the soldiers as they marched and handled their rifles with expertise during the gun drill. Fallout for fatigue duty was signaled at 7:30. Then Rachel would return to the house and impatiently try not to lose her temper with Deborah's new and unbecoming personality.

All the different bugle calls became familiar to Rachel: guard mount took place at 8:30 A.M., afternoon fatigue commenced at 1:00, drill again at 4:30 and taps always sounded at 8:15 in the evening. Rachel felt that she lived, ate, and slept by the bugle calls. But the dreaded call-to-arms sent fear racing through her pulse, when every soldier grabbed his rifle and every officer buckled on his sword. From the moment Colonel Reynolds and his troops rode hastily out of the fort, until the moment they returned, Rachel felt as though her heart stood still!

Rachel had been living at the fort for a little over a month, when one evening, she decided impulsively to ask John if he wanted to take a cool walk around the fort with her. While joyfully anticipating spending the evening with him, she slipped into one of her prettiest summer dresses. It was white, trimmed with narrow red

194

ribbons circling the low neckline and the short puffed sleeves. It had a wide red band to fit snugly around her small waist. Vigorously she brushed her long hair and let it hang loose, framing her face with its auburn beauty. Looking into the mirror, she knew she was pretty, but she innocently had no conception of the sensuality she projected. Hurriedly she left the stuffy hot confines of the small rooms that made up what was supposed to be a home.

As she neared the building where the colonel had his office and living quarters, she noticed Zeke sitting alone on the wooden steps. Smiling at him, she said pleasantly, "Hello, Zeke."

"Howdy, Miss Rachel . . . ma'am, if ya was plannin' on visitin' the colonel, you'd best furgit 'bout if fur tonight."

"But why?" she asked.

"The colonel, he ain't in a very good mood tonight. He's got a bottle of whiskey in thar and if I know John like I reckon I do, he's done drunk 'bout half of it already." Anxiously Zeke glanced behind him at the closed door to the colonel's office, then looked back at Rachel. "Ain't the first time he got hisself liquored up on this here date. It's July second, ain't it?"

Nodding, she answered, "Yes, I think so. Why does he get drunk on this date?"

"Don't always. Sometimes he ain't no whar 'round no liquor, but most times he is. Been that way fur years now."

"What happened to cause him to act this way?"

"His son would been eleven today, if'n he hadn't died."

With her knees weakening from shock, she moved

swiftly to the steps and sat beside him. "His son! Did he die when he was a baby?"

"Miss Rachel, I ain't got the right to tell ya what happened. If'n he wants ya to know, he'll tell ya. I'm sorry, ma'am."

She reached over and touched his arm. "Zeke, tell me about Carmelita."

"What do ya 'wanna' know 'bout her?" he asked.

"Anything you feel free to tell me without betraying any confidences. How did he meet her, do you know?"

"Yep, I know." He leaned against the post next to the steps, and settled himself comfortably as he continued. "John and me was in Mexico. Just ramblin' 'round like we done a lot back in them days. I reckon John was 'round twenty-eight or so. . . . Well, we stopped in this here little Mexican town and John got hisself in a poker game with some mean lookin' hombres. He's a damned good poker player, and he won a lot of their money. Later on him and me got to drinkin', and like fools we got purty drunk and headed out of that town still all liquored up. A few miles on down the road we got bushwacked by them same hombres that was in that thar poker game, only they had some of their friends with 'em. Thar was 'bout eight of 'em and only two of us, so we didn't have nary a chance and right off John got shot in the shoulder. I figgered we were both gonna be dead fur sure when here come a bunch of Mexicans ridin' in to help us out. I reckon them Mexicans were one of the purtiest sights I done ever seen." Grinning largely at the young woman, he added, " 'Cept fur them thar green eyes of yurs."

Smiling affectionately, she replied in a heavy southern accent, "Zeke, 'dahlin', you flatter me 'suh' with your fancy compliments.''

"Ain't never gave you one that weren't true neither. . . . Well to git back to what I was a-tellin' ya. When them Mexicans showed up, them other hombres high-tailed it out of thar. The leader of these here Mexicans was a big ornery lookin' cuss and I started wonderin' if they done saved us so they could kill us theirselves. Don't reckon I'll ever know fur sure what they'd done to us if this big hombre's daughter hadn't been a ridin' with 'em that day. When her Paw rode in to help us, he'd left her off a ways with a couple of his men. I was on the ground a kneelin' beside John tryin' to stop the bleedin' when she rode up to whar we was. She jumped off her horse and run over to us . . . and I swear to ya, Miss Rachel, she took one look at John and decided right then and thar that she wanted 'im fur herself.''

"Carmelita?'' she asked.

"Yep, it was her. . . . They had a buckboard with 'em cause they'd been in town buyin' supplies. Carmelita ordered some of the men to lift John into it. She argued a couple minutes with her Paw 'bout takin' us with 'em, but she won and got her own way. I got back on my horse and she climbed into the buckboard to tend to John. He'd lost a lot of blood, but he was still conscious. Well, we'd only ridden 'bout a mile when the big hombre ordered a couple of his men to blindfold me and John. He didn't want us to see whar they was a-takin' us.''

"Bandits!'' Rachel exclaimed. "They were bandits, weren't they?''

"Yep, I reckon you could call 'em that, but how did you know?''

"Just something John told me once. Go on . . . what happened then?"

"When we reached their hideout, they took off them blindfolds. Miss Rachel, it was like bein' in a small village hidden from the outside world by surroundin' steep cliffs towerin' on all sides of it. Carmelita took John into her own home, and with the help of the house servant, Rosa, they patched 'im up. . . . Well, Manuel Villano, her Paw, he took a likin' to John. While he was healin' hisself, Manuel spent a lot of time with 'im."

"Did he teach John how to draw a pistol?" she asked.

"Now Miss Rachel, how in tarnation did you know that?"

"One day I asked John how he learned to draw a gun so fast, and he told me from a Mexican bandit. I didn't believe him at the time."

"Ya can believe anythin' he tells ya, ma'am. He may tease ya a lot, but he won't never lie to ya. . . . Well, to git back to my story. Manuel, he knew John was smitten with his daughter, and he whole-heartedly approved of the match."

Incapable of suppressing her female curiosity, Rachel asked, "Zeke, was Carmelita pretty?"

"She was more than purty. Carmelita was beautiful. Yep, she was a Mexican beauty with that long shiny black hair and them dark brown eyes. Had a figger that even an old man like myself kept a lookin' at. . . . To git back to what I was sayin'. John had told Manuel 'bout bein' a wealthy man. Somethin' he don't most times tell anyone. Well this Manuel, he asked John to marry his daughter knowin' he could take good care o her and all. Manuel wanted Carmelita out of the kind of life she was bein' forced to live. As John's wife she could have not only respectability, but also wealth. Well, John bein' so takin' by Carmelita, he told her Paw he'd marry her. I tried my best to talk 'im out of it. He weren't in love with her, I knew he weren't! He was just blinded by her beauty . . . and Miss Rachel, she weren't what he thought she was. She acted different with 'im cause she wanted to catch 'im fur a husband. He would be her way out of that thar secluded place. That's what she knew from the moment she first set eyes on 'im, and that's why she wanted 'im fur herself. Him havin' money only made it that much better fur her. . . . What I'm tryin' to tell ya, Miss Rachel, is that she had . . . uh . . . already had herself lots of men, if you know what I mean.''

"Yes, Zeke, I understand," she answered.

"But John, he didn't know this 'bout her and once I tried to tell 'im and got the hell knocked out of me fur tryin'!''

"Oh, no! You mean he actually hit you?'' she asked.

"He was crazy whar she was concerned, Miss Rachel. But a woman like Carmelita can do that to a man. . . . Well, he sent me on to southern Texas to see 'bout buyin' some land fur 'im. He wanted to build 'em a ranch. We planned to meet later in El Paso. While I was gone, he married up with her. Well, I ran into some luck fur 'im. Thar was this widow woman who was a-wantin' to sell her ranch. Real nice place it was with a fine lookin' house a-settin' on it. She was askin' a high price fur it, but John's got plenty of money. The cowhands workin' fur her wanted to stay on and keep their jobs. . . . To make a long story a little shorter, they moved into that thar ranch. Fur a while everythin' seemed to be all right between 'em. But Carmelita, she weren't happy with livin' way out on that ranch. She thought marryin' a rich man would mean parties, travelin' and livin' a busy social life. John, he started feelin' sorry fur her and promised her a trip to San Francisco, but then he found out she was expectin'. In her condition he didn't want her to endanger herself or the baby by takin' such a long trip. Carmelita got mad as all hell when he cancelled that thar trip. She didn't want to have a kid no how, and she hated it fur what it had done to her. She asked the housekeeper if she knew how she could git rid of it. When John found out what she was a-plannin' on doin', he hardly ever let her out of his sight. They had some powerful arguments and I think they started hatin' one another, but John never stopped wantin' the child she was a-carryin'. On July second his son was born, and Miss Rachel, John loved that thar little baby with all his heart. Carmelita showed no love fur her son, and never even held him, unless it was feedin' time.''

When Zeke looked deeply into her eyes, she could see a trace of tears. ''Miss Rachel, that baby was John's whole life. He gave his son all the love he had inside of 'im that he'd never been able to give to anyone before . . . I used to hold that baby a lot myself and he'd wrap his little hand around my finger while grinnin' up at me. He sure was a purty baby. Had hair as black as his Mama's, but his eyes were gonna be just like his Pappy's.''

''Zeke, you loved the child, didn't you?'' she asked softly.

"Yes'm, I did. Never had nothin' to do with babies 'fore he come along. I couldn't have loved 'im no more if'n he'd been my own grandchild."

"That's because you love John as a son," she replied as she fondly placed her small hand on his wrinkled and callused one.

"Well . . . one day when the baby was 'bout five months old, John had to go into town on business and I rode along with 'im. 'Bout halfway to El Paso he done realized he'd left some important papers at the house and he needed 'em fur the business he was a tendin' to, so we turned 'round and headed back fur the ranch. . . . Naturally Carmelita weren't expectin' us back so soon."

When he became silent, she coaxed, "Go on. Please tell me what happened."

"Miss Rachel, that was the day the baby died, and the reason John's in thar drinkin' that whiskey."

Suddenly she rose from the steps, but Zeke reached and grabbed her hand. "Whar ya goin', Miss Rachel?"

"To see John, of course," she replied.

"You ain't got no idea what he's like when he's in one of them moods, and a-drinkin'. I learnt a long time ago it's best just to leave 'im alone."

"When a man is drinking, he usually says things he otherwise wouldn't say. If I'm ever going to know why he hates Carmelita and why he's afraid to love again, then tonight may be my only chance." Rachel knelt in front of the old man, and with tears glistening in her eyes, she said passionately, "I love him so much, Zeke! Maybe somehow I can help him, if only he'll let me."

Looking tenderly at the young woman, he answered,

"If anyone could help 'im furget, Miss Rachel, it'd be you . . . I just ain't sure you should go in thar. When a man's drinkin' he don't only say things he wouldn't otherwise be sayin', but sometimes he does things he shouldn't oughta do. But I know thar ain't nothin' I can say to keep ya from goin' to 'im, so I ain't gonna try no more."

Feeling certain that he'd only order her to go away, Rachel decided not to knock. Boldly she opened the door, walked into the room and quickly shut it behind her.

The colonel's office was the largest on the fort. In one corner stood a huge wood-burning stove used for heat during the winter months. Next to the far wall was a long table, and extra chairs to dine with other officers in the privacy of the colonel's quarters. The door at the back led to a small adjoining bedroom. On one wall hung a map of the territory of New Mexico and Arizona.

When Rachel entered the dimly lit room she saw John Reynolds sitting on a chair behind his desk with a partially empty bottle of whiskey held loosely in his hand. When he looked up at her, the kerosene lamp burning on his desk shone on his face, and the hard glare reflected in his eyes was so severe that she felt shocked by its cold intensity. While still staring at her, he took a drink from the bottle, and then said angrily, "Get out!"

Though her heart was beating rapidly in fear of what he might say to her, she answered, "I'm staying!"

As usual his mood changed abruptly toward her, and rising from his chair he replied pleasantly, "If you insist on staying ma'am, then I'll get you a chair." Placing the bottle on his desk he started walking across the room. Impulsively Rachel hurried over to him and lovingly looked up into his eyes. She could once more detect their familiar warmth. She noticed his hair was again tousled, but this time she reached up and ran her fingers through the unruly locks. Her loving and tender gesture went to his heart more than any words.

Gently he took her hand into his, and raising it to his lips, he kissed the palm. Then he turned brusquely, walked back to his desk and took another drink. "Go home, Rachel!"

Gathering all her reserved courage, she said, "Zeke told me about Carmelita."

Swiftly he spun away from the desk, and in two easy strides he reached her. Putting his hands on her shoulders, he jerked her roughly toward him and asked, "What did he tell you?"

"How you met her, your life on the ranch and that you had a son. How did he die, John? What happened that day?"

She was confused by the urgency in his voice. "Why, Rachel? Why in the hell do you want to know?"

"Because I love you!" she cried.

Slowly he released the tight hold on her shoulders and turned away as he moved back to his desk. Rachel wondered if he was feeling his liquor. If he was, it wasn't apparent in the way he spoke or in the straightness of his walk. He sat on the edge of his desk and seemed to be completely at ease. "What was the last thing Zeke told you?"

"You were on the way to El Paso, but had forgotten some papers, so you rode back to the ranch." She

203

yearned to move nearer to him, but was afraid to stir or do anything that could alter the course of their conversation.

Rachel watched him apprehensively as he placed his hand on the bottle of whiskey, but instead of picking it up, he said, "Zeke and I went into the house. The room I used for a study was located at the end of the hall. That's where the papers were and I had to pass Carmelita's bedroom on the way to it." She noticed how his hand tightened on the neck of the bottle. "I knew my son was in her room because earlier I had moved his crib in there. A few days before I had given Maria, our housekeeper, a couple of weeks off, and I knew there would be no one but Carmelita to take care of him while I was gone."

"Where was the crib usually kept?" she asked.

"In my room." Explaining to her, he added, "Carmelita said he disturbed her sleep, and I didn't think it was Maria's place to take care of him through the night." Smiling, he continued, "I didn't mind. I sort of enjoyed bunking in with him."

Suddenly his smile vanished, and this time he lifted the bottle and took a big drink. Instead of putting it back on the desk, he held the bottle firmly in his hand. "I opened the door to her room to check on the baby." Rachel could distinctly hear the anger increasing in his voice as he continued speaking. "She was in bed with a man who worked on our ranch. They were so busy lusting after one another, they didn't hear me enter. I can still see the picture in my mind as clearly as if it happened only yesterday . . . Carmelita was lying naked in his arms, and all I could think was how she didn't even have the decency to move our son's crib away from the bed.''

With the bottle held securely in his hand, he walked slowly to the window and stared silently at the darkness of night creeping over the fort. He remained quiet for so long Rachel had begun to fear he wouldn't say any more, when suddenly he looked towards her again. The vivid hurt and pain on his face caused her to instinctively take a deep breath. The light from the lamp flickering over his large frame made the gold buttons on his blue uniform flash brightly, reflecting a shining blaze into his angry eyes. Rachel had never been more awed by his powerful masculinity, or his towering height, than she was at that moment.

"When I walked into her room, I slammed the door shut behind me. I remember Carmelita yelled . . . 'Oh God, no!' . . . but I didn't even glance at her. I headed straight for the child. All I could think was to get him out of that damned room and away from her!''

Rachel could feel her hands begin to tremble with fearful anticipation when she heard his strong voice break with agony. "I reached into the crib for my son . . . and I saw he had pulled the blanket over his head and it was tangled underneath his body. I jerked it off him . . . but dear God . . . I was too late!'' In one swift movement, he swerved, slammed his large fist against the solid wall and shouted with rage, "While his mother rutted in bed with her lover, our child helplessly wrapped himself in a blanket and smothered to death!''

The pain she felt for him made Rachel feel as though she were being torn apart inside, and heartbroken, she cried, "No! . . . Oh John! . . . No!''

He raised the bottle and took another drink before he

said, "I can't remember what happened after that. I only know what Zeke told me later. I went into a rage and hit the man who was with her, as he fell he struck his head and was knocked unconscious. Then I turned on Carmelita. By that time, her screams had brought Zeke into the room followed by some of the ranch hands. If they hadn't pulled me off . . . I'd have killed her. While Zeke and another man held me back, the others got the two of them out of the room. That same night Zeke found Carmelita a way to leave the ranch and go to her father. He knew if I saw her again, I'd kill her! We buried my son the next day on a small hill behind the ranch. Charles James Reynolds, born July 2nd, 1856, died December 8th, 1856."

Rachel sensed he wasn't telling her everything, and quickly she went over to him and jerked the bottle from his hand. Before he could stop her, she threw it across the room and as it hit the floor it shattered into pieces. Inwardly sensing the truth, she cried out to him, "The reason you keep punishing yourself is because you feel guilty! Why?" Raising her voice she yelled again, "Why? Tell me why, damn it?"

"All right!" he replied furiously. "Before I left that day I told Carmelita to be sure and cover the baby when he fell asleep. I even got the blanket myself and handed it to her! My God, I gave her the blanket that killed my son!"

Rachel turned away to hide her heartrending tears, as he brusquely pushed past her and walked rapidly to his desk. Taking another bottle of whiskey out of the drawer he opened it and took a drink before he said fiercely, "It's my fault he died!" With a powerful sweep of his arm, he violently knocked everything from his desk, and shouted, "If I hadn't insisted on giving her the blanket . . . my son would be alive today!"

"If you hadn't given her the blanket, she still may have gotten it herself and covered him."

All his anger seemed to vanish as he answered calmly, "No, not Carmelita." Carefully he placed the bottle on his desk, and walked over to her. "Now that you know the truth, will you please go home?"

"Why do you keep insisting I leave?" she asked.

"Rachel you're such an innocent little fool. Don't you realize I've had too much to drink?" Startling her, he grabbed her roughly by the shoulders. "Do you have any idea how I feel at this moment or how damned much I want you?" Suddenly his grip on her tightened so severely she winced with pain. She tried to understand the expression on his face, and in his eyes, as they looked deeply into hers. Slowly his eyes traveled away from hers and down over the shape of her slim but feminine curves.

Rachel was confused when his obvious desire changed into anger, and he shouted, "If you won't leave, then by God I will!"

He started to move away from her, but desperately she reached out and clutched his arm. "Just once. . . ." she pleaded. "Just one time, please take me into your arms and kiss me! Please!"

Callously he shoved her hand off his arm and told her harshly, "I'm in no mood to play your childish games!"

Beseechingly she begged him, "Please let me help you!"

"How in the hell can you help?" he yelled. Suddenly observing the torment on her face he became aware of

207

his unjust anger towards her and gently he said, "Forgive me, Baby. I didn't mean to be cruel, but you have no business being with me when I'm like this." He started to turn away from her, but instinctively, Rachel sensed this was the opportunity for her love to triumph over his principles. Before he could stop her, she agilely wrapped her arms around his neck and pressed her lips to his.

When he didn't respond immediately to her kiss, she heartbrokenly thought it was because he didn't love her, and, devastated, she resigned herself to what she believed to be the inevitable. Rachel started to terminate the futile kiss, when unexpectedly, he vigorously pulled her into his strong embrace and eagerly forced her waiting lips open under his. She could feel her body tremble in ecstacy as his passionate kiss kindled a desire within her she never dreamed could exist. His powerful arms held her so tightly that Rachel could actually feel the beat of his heart against her breast. Putting one arm around her waist, he easily lifted her body into contact with his and pressed her thighs against his male hardness, causing her to moan with expectation and pleasure. She responded to his demanding kiss with a burning intensity, and her yearning sexual desire uncontrollably consumed her.

With no forewarning he quickly broke the embrace and stepped back. Having no inkling that he would release her so abruptly, Rachel almost lost her balance as she looked up at him with bewilderment. Fleetingly she glimpsed the unmistakable longing in his eyes before he hurriedly walked over to the door.

Roughly he swung it open, and desperate, she cried out to him, "John, I love you!"

When his steps came to an abrupt stop, her heart felt as if it had suddenly ceased beating. In the semi-darkness of the room she couldn't see his face, and wasn't aware of the flickering rage in his eyes. Stepping back into the room, he violently slammed the door shut, pushed in the bolt, and began walking steadily towards her. As John drew closer, she became frightened by the penetrating fury in his eyes.

Rachel longed for him to speak compassionate loving words to quiet her fears, but silently and swiftly he lifted her in his arms and carried her across the room. When he reached the closed door leading into his bedroom, he forcefully kicked it open. After entering the small room lit only by a low burning lamp, he kicked the door shut behind them and carried her straight to the bed. Placing her on her feet, he ordered harshly, "Take off your clothes, or by God, I'll take them off myself!"

Appalled, she felt as if she were staring into the eyes of a cold stranger, and she knew nothing about this cruel man who intended to take her so ruthlessly. Rachel tried to control her tears, but the hurt was too severe. Deep sobs broke from her throat and her shoulders began to shake. She brought her hands up and covered her face from his hostile stare as she started crying pathetically.

Hearing her heartbreaking sobs, he swiftly pulled her into his arms and whispered, "Rachel, I'm sorry . . . I shouldn't take my anger out on you." Putting his hand under her chin he gently tilted her face up, and looking tenderly into her eyes, he explained, "I'm angry at myself, Baby. Not at you."

"But why?" she questioned.

Wiping the tears from her troubled face, he replied, "You really don't know, do you?"

"No, I don't," Rachel answered, wishing she somehow understood what he was trying to say.

"My God, you have no idea what a high price we will pay for this night. Someday, Baby, it's going to cost us. . . . But I can't fight what I feel for you any longer." Lightly, with his hands placed gently on each side of her face, he kissed her forehead, then her cheeks, which were still moist from her tears. Before pressing his mouth possessively on hers, he whispered, "Rachel, I want you!"

Her lips were trembling from the effect of his overpowering and passionate kiss when she whispered shyly, "John, I'm afraid."

"Why, Baby?" he asked gently.

"I want to please you and I'm afraid I won't," she replied.

He smiled at the virginal sweetness in her fear. "Rachel, I want you more than I've ever wanted any woman. And don't worry, Baby, you will please me!"

Stepping behind her, he easily undid the buttons at the back of her dress and removing it, he placed it on a nearby chair. Putting his hands on her shoulders, he eased her to the bed. Lying beside her he leaned his large frame over her slim body, and his mouth once again found hers as his hand slowly caressed her breast.

Impatiently he began to remove the rest of her clothes, and feeling shame, she closed her eyes to blot out the embarrassing scene. When he finished undressing her, he said sternly, "Open your eyes, Rachel, and look at me!"

Obeying him, she did as he ordered and as she

looked deeply into his eyes, he whispered, "You're beautiful, Rachel!" Hungrily he brought his lips to hers, and soothingly his hand traveled down the length of her body leaving a tingling sensation wherever it touched. When he moved his hand to the place where no man had ever been, she stiffened in his embrace. She tried to cry out, but his mouth drowned her feeble protest with a passion that made her forget her apprehension and pull him into her arms.

Rising from the bed he quickly started removing his uniform. As he took off his shirt, Rachel watched the muscles rippling in his powerful arms and chest. When he unbuckled his belt she once again felt timid and closed her eyes.

Glancing over at her, he laughed lightly as he said teasingly, "I would turn off the lamp, my virginal little hypocrite, but I don't intend to miss watching your face when I make you a woman."

Rachel could feel the bed give under his weight, and opening her eyes, she saw him studying her face closely. Without looking away, he gently took her arm and placed it around his neck. His mouth came down passionately on hers. She felt her own passion building as she pressed herself against him and felt him move over her trembling body.

Tenderly he told her, "The first time will be painful for you, Baby, but the pain will be gone quickly, and then my love . . . I promise you . . . you shall know the ecstacy of becoming a woman."

"Your woman, John! I want to be yours now and always," she cried.

"Baby . . . Baby . . . I want you . . . now!" he replied before he greedily met his lips to hers. Forcefully he parted her thighs, then suddenly he penetrated and took her virginity as she cried out in pain. But as he had promised her the pain was gone quickly, followed by an ecstasy she never imagined she could feel. Freely and boldly she responded to his fiery kisses, his sensual touch and his powerful thrusting until they ecstatically climbed to the peak of their rapture together!

For as long as Rachel lived, she'd remember the night and the moment she first become one with the man she loved.

The first golden rays of the morning sun cast their warm glow over the flat New Mexico plains and the quiet fort. As the awakening dawn crept silently into the colonel's bedroom, its soft light fell upon John Reynolds and Rachel lying in each other's arms, serenely asleep.

He was the first to stir as the brightness of daylight persistently absorbed the remaining darkness in the small room. Lovingly, he glanced at the sleeping girl lying beside him, and gently kissed the top of the head nestled comfortably on his shoulder. When she opened her eyes and looked up at him, he said, "Good morning, my beautiful little hypocrite."

Smiling happily, she replied, "This is the most beautiful morning of my life!"

Laughing lightly, he asked, "Why is that?"

"Because I woke up next to you," she answered, snuggling closer to him.

Enjoying the feel of her body against his, he pulled her to him tightly. "It may not be such a beautiful morning when you explain to Deborah where you've been all night."

"I'm sure she already knows where I spent the night, and I honestly don't care if the whole fort knows. I love you, and I want to shout it to the world."

"Well do me a favor, my love, and don't. Officers are not allowed 'live in' ladies for their comfort and needs. We are supposed to set an example for the rest of the men and you, my sensual little hypocrite, are not a proper example to set before them."

Rising slightly, she leaned across his chest, unconsciously rubbing her bare breasts seductively against him. "John, do you still think I'm a hypocrite?"

Tenderly he moved his fingers back and forth across her soft shoulders as he answered, "No, Baby, I don't. But the name has become a habit and to me you'll always be my beautiful little hypocrite." Smiling the boyish grin she loved so much, he asked, "By the way, my love, do you have any idea what you're doing to me?"

"What do you mean?" she asked in bafflement.

"Baby, it seems you lost your virginity last night, but you still have a virginal mind. Rachel, you are pressing your delightful body next to mine but I must talk to you seriously for a moment before I help myself to your tempting charms."

Enjoying her new-found sexual power, she moved even closer while teasingly running light kisses over his face, and then passionately found his mouth with her own. Laughing at his surprised reaction to her boldness, she quickly rolled to the other side of the bed and said, "Very well, Colonel, I'm listening, so talk all you wish."

"What I have to say won't take very long and then, my love, you will pay for your wanton behavior."

213

Reaching over and taking her hand into his he continued, "For various reasons, we will have to be careful Rachel. As far as I'm concerned what I do with my personal life is my own damned business, but the Army doesn't see it that way. We also have your reputation to consider. The wives on this fort would feel it their Christian duty to have you tarred and feathered. I'm sure they believe fornication is the worst sin a woman can commit. Do you understand what I'm saying Rachel?"

Nodding, she answered solemnly, "Yes, of course, understand. But surely we'll find a way to be together."

"I have no intentions of living on the same fort with you and keeping our relationship platonic. But we'll have to use caution at all times, so Baby, see if you can manage to be discreet."

Cutting her eyes at him sharply, she replied, "Of course, I will! Damn you, John Reynolds, stop treating me like a silly child!"

Swiftly, with no warning, he threw off the covers and ran his eyes over her slim figure. "A child you most assuredly are not." Suddenly he pulled her roughly into his arms, and before kissing her, he added, "And now my wanton little hypocrite, you shall get what's coming to you."

He kissed her passionately, then curiously, he looked down into her face. He thought removing the cover might have embarrassed her, but stretching sensually Rachel murmured, "I'm more than ready, my darling."

John raised his eyebrows, his grin light-hearted "Have you no shame, my love?"

Wrapping her arms around his neck, she gleamed, "None whatsoever!"

Slowly, his mouth came down to meet hers. Teasingly, he ran his tongue lightly across her moist lips, sending a tingling sensation through Rachel's whole being. John's passion was building, and fervently he pried her mouth open under his. He was a little surprised when, all at once, Rachel returned his demanding kiss, her tongue entering his mouth, driving him crazy with desire.

She placed her lips against his ear, whispering exciting endearments, as her hand traveled intimately over his masculine frame, her touch arousing him more than any woman's had ever done before. Boldly, her fingers encircled his throbbing manhood, causing him to groan with pleasure.

John felt as if he would explode if he didn't hurry and take her. He moved over Rachel, and willingly she spread her legs, waiting for the man she loved to totally possess her.

"Rachel," John gasped, "you are driving me wild."

"Take me, John," she pleaded seductively.

"Believe me, my love, when I get through with you, you will know you have been taken."

As the sound of reveille loudly awakened the sleeping fort, Rachel was happily surrendering her body, heart, and soul to the man she loved.

Chapter Six

Rachel stood among the military dependents and watched the troops in dress uniform performing the afternoon drill in honor of Colonel Werlin's visit to the fort. Glancing away from the soldiers, she looked across the courtyard to study John Reynolds as he stood formally between Colonel Werlin and Captain Godwin. Proudly, she noticed how the man she loved overwhelmed both men with his height and masculinity.

Rachel wished she could turn to the wives standing beside her and proudly tell them that Colonel Reynolds belonged to her! Keeping her feelings a secret was almost impossible for Rachel. She was a young woman experiencing the joys of first love, and she longed to joyfully shout it to the world.

Once she attempted to discuss her love for John with her sister, but Deborah angrily told her exactly what she thought of Rachel's sinful and unforgivable behavior. This resulted in a violent argument, and even though the two women shared the same house, they seldom spoke a civil word to one another after that. Josh understood Rachel's and the colonel's love, and frequently envied the colonel his relationship with her. He wished Deborah would give him the same kind of warmth and passion he was sure Rachel gave to John Reynolds. For different reasons, their secret was perfectly safe with Deborah and Josh. Deborah kept quiet out of embarrassed shame for their disgraceful conduct, and Josh was silent out of his deep respect for both Rachel and the Colonel.

Slowly Rachel walked a short distance from the others, and with an expression of adoring love obvious on her pretty face, she ignored the marching drill as she stared openly at John Reynolds. She watched him standing at attention and saluting the American flag as her mind began to drift back over the past three months since they had become lovers.

Smiling to herself, she contentedly thought about the fulfilling nights they spent together in the privacy of his quarters and their long, quiet conversations which made her feel she could sit for hours just listening to his deep, clear voice.

To stop the others from hearing, she brought her hand to her mouth to smother an uncontrollable giggle, as she remembered her boldness on the afternoon the Colonel had ridden in with his troops after a three-day absence.

She had missed him so desperately, she had no intentions of waiting until evening before seeing him. Trying to appear casual, she had walked to his office and cautiously glanced around her to be sure no one was watching. Quickly she had opened the door and rushed into the room. By the splashing sounds coming from his bedroom, it had been apparent that he was in the process of taking a bath. Smiling slyly, as she remembered that night in Kansas when he had brazenly invited her to join him for a bath in the river, she had swiftly pushed in the bolt, securely locking the door. While unbuttoning her dress, she hurried across the office and into the adjoining room. The large bathing tub was facing in her direction. Speechlessly, he had looked up to see her standing in the doorway, and the shock on his face had caused her to laugh aloud.

"Rachel, what in the hell are you doing here?" he bellowed.

Removing her dress, she answered, "I'm going to take a bath."

Flustered by her audacious behavior, he demanded, "But you can't do that!"

"And why not?" she asked, stepping out of her petticoat.

"What if someone were to come in? Am I suppose to hide you by drowning you under the water?"

"The front door is locked, my love!" Laughing hilariously at the look on his face, she added, "Why, John Reynolds, you're actually shocked by my new and unvirginal personality. I would never have believed! . . . My goodness, haven't you ever bathed with a lady before?"

Gruffly, he replied, "Of course, I have! Hell, in my day, I had my good times just like anyone else."

Stepping into the tub, she easily slid her body close to his. "In your day! Great guns and little switches, you'd think you were over the hill! I'm going to show you, my darling, that your good times are only beginning!" Kissing him passionately, she moved her soft body over his. "Are you having a good time, my love?" she asked.

Pulling her into his embrace, he replied laughingly,

"You're damned right, I'm having a good time!"

Giggling, Rachel grabbed the bar of soap. "Relax, my darling, because I am going to bathe you. Every beautiful inch of you."

Offended, John grumbled, "Rachel, men are not beautiful."

"You are!" she argued. "You're as beautiful as a sleek, untamed stallion."

"Stallion?" he chuckled.

Lathering the soap, Rachel held it to her palm as she washed his manly form, allowing her fingers to curl around the thick hair that covered his chest, before tapering down to his stomach and beyond. Easily, she slid the bar of soap farther down his large frame, her eyes following the same path as her hand. Seeing his erect manhood, it was quite obvious that he was enjoying her ministrations, very much so!

She turned her eyes to his, smiling saucily. Raising his eyebrows, he laughed, "You are the only person on this fort who can make the commanding officer come to attention."

Tossing her head, Rachel giggled merrily, her laughter tinkling with joy.

Swiftly he reached out, grabbing her around the waist, causing water to splash out onto the floor. "You teasing little vixen," he uttered, sitting her slim frame on top of his. "Stallion, am I?" he reminded her. "Well, my love, it's about time you learned how to ride your stallion."

Rachel tilted her head, looking at him questioningly. Understanding her expression, he explained, "You only think you are a woman of the world. There is more than one way to make love."

Putting his hands on her waist, he raised her hips, positioning her. Smoothly, he eased her down to his awaiting erection, sliding into her easily.

Rachel's eyes widened with wonder and total delight. Oh, why hadn't he shown her this position before? She liked being on top, this way she could look into his face as they made love.

When she failed to move, John chuckled at her inexperience. Moving his hands to her hips, he lifted her up and down gently, sliding in and out of her teasingly. "Now do you get the idea, my innocent?"

Smiling sensually, Rachel had answered, "Ah yes, my darling, but someday I am going to tame my beautiful, wild stallion."

Her thoughts returning to the present, Rachel watched as the soldiers displayed their expertise during the gun drill. She tried to concentrate on the impressive show the troopers were performing, but wrapped up in her thoughts of John, Rachel's mind drifted back to the evening John found her alone with five of his soldiers.

She had gone alone to the stables to check on the two horses she and Deborah owned. When she neared the stables, she had heard the soldier with the tenor voice playing his guitar and singing a ballad. Noticing her approach, he had stopped abruptly, as he and the four troopers got to their feet.

"Don't stop singing on my account," she pleaded. "Please continue."

The young soldier was fascinated by Rachel's vivacious beauty, but he suspected the colonel was interested in the lovely young woman. Seeing his apparent confusion at her presence, she asked sweetly, "Will you please sing 'Kathleen' for me? You see, it was my father's favorite song, and you sing it so beautifully."

Unable to deny the irresistible pleading in the enchanting eyes looking up at him, he replied, "Thank you, ma'am." Strumming his guitar, he began singing the Irish ballad.

Hearing the familiar melody had sent Rachel's thoughts roaming back over the years and to the once magnificent plantation in Mississippi. She could again hear the robust laughter and the playful teasing of her brothers. Her mother's soft and gentle voice whispered fleetingly across Rachel's heartbreaking memories. Vividly, she could picture her father proudly residing over his family and majestically reigning over his kingdom of cotton and slaves.

When he finished the song, and the stable had become depressingly silent, Rachel had been afraid the hurting memories would cause her to cry for the loved ones that were gone forever. Determined to overcome her melancholy, she had requested that he play something happy and lively.

Wanting to please her, he started to sing a cheerful and brisk melody which led her to unconsciously tap her foot in time with the rhythm. Quickly one of the soldiers grabbed her arm, and gaily, she began to dance with him. The other three soldiers rowdily took turns cutting in so they could also have the pleasure of dancing with the beautiful young woman. As the song came to an end, the handsome trooper who held her placed his hands on her waist, twirling her around gracefully. Rachel threw back her head and laughed merrily; but the laughter suddenly vanished when she looked across the stable and was shocked to see John Reynolds' large frame blocking the darkened entrance.

Nervously dropping his treasured guitar, the young soldier shouted, "Attention!"

The trooper holding Rachel released her so abruptly that she almost lost her balance. Swiftly he turned from her, came stiffly to attention, and along with the others, saluted the colonel.

Returning their salute, he said in his powerful voice of authority, "At ease men!"

Rachel stepped farther back into the confines of the stable and wished she could somehow miraculously disappear.

At once he dismissed the troopers, and she was left alone with him. As he approached her, she mustered what courage she could and looked him straight in the eyes. Puzzled, she noticed there wasn't the slightest trace of anger on his face, and he was actually smiling the boyish grin that always melted her heart.

Understanding Rachel's apparent confusion, he raised his eyebrows as he asked, "Did you think I would beat you, my flirtatious little hypocrite? Not that you don't deserve a good spanking."

Forgetting her relief that he wasn't angry, she blurted out, "Aren't you even jealous?"

"Should I be?" he asked teasingly.

Placing her hands on her hips, she replied sternly, "You're too damned sure of yourself, John Reynolds!"

Surprising her, he turned brusquely and walked away. Apprehensively, she watched him as he strode across the enclosure of the stable and easily shoved the huge doors closed, locking them with the heavy bolt. As he walked toward her, his dominating eyes penetrated hers deeply. Effortlessly, he lifted Rachel in his arms and carrying her to a large stack of hay he said, "Dance and flirt all you wish, my love, but never forget . . . I don't share what is mine! And tonight, Rachel, you will be mine again and then again."

When he reached the haystack, John didn't lay her down gently, but unceremoniously dropped her on the pile of soft hay.

Surprised, Rachel looked up at him with confusion. Placing his hands on his hips, he eyed her sternly. His height and masculinity seemed overwhelming, and Rachel was struck anew with how dearly she worshipped him.

"Rachel," he began firmly, "if you weren't so damnably naive, you would know that it is unsafe for you to be alone with five sex-starved soldiers!"

Rachel had to suppress the urge to laugh. Oh, he was jealous! How marvelous! How extraordinarily marvelous!

He pushed his hat back from his brow, then flustered, he changed his mind, lowering it back to where it shadowed his face. Frowning, he fumed, "Rachel, when you dance with a man, you shouldn't let him put his hands on you so intimately!"

Finding his jealousy amusing, Rachel giggled, "Intimately? My goodness, John, he was only holding onto my waist."

"Well, if you ask me, he was getting a little too damned familiar!" he said, his jaws clenched tightly.

Holding her arms across her stomach, Rachel doubled over with laughter. Annoyed, John waved his arms, shouting, "You won't think it so humorous, if I ever again catch you alone, and at night no less, with five young sexually aroused soldiers!''

Between rippling giggles, she reminded him, ''I thought you weren't jealous.''

''Jealous?'' he repeated, as if he had never heard the word before. ''Don't be ridiculous. I'm only worried about your welfare.''

''Yes, you are, John Reynolds!'' she taunted. ''You're jealous! Admit it!''

Suddenly, he grinned, his expression cunning. Swiftly he removed his hat, flinging it to the side. Then he unstrapped his scabbard, placing the heavy sword on the floor. ''I will admit nothing, my scheming little hypocrite. Take off your clothes. I don't think I have ever wanted you as badly as I do at this moment.''

''No,'' she answered pertly.

Instantly, his eyebrows were raised, as he looked at her questionably. ''What did you say?''

''No, I will not take off my clothes. I am tired of you giving me orders.'' Gazing up at him invitingly, she murmured, ''If you want my clothes removed, you will have to do it yourself.''

He moved so quickly that she wasn't even aware of what had happened, until she found herself jerked to her feet. Turning her around, he began unfastening the tiny buttons at the back of her dress. Lifting her long hair, he kissed her neck, then as he slipped the garment downwards, his lips found her bared shoulders. He pulled her against him so tightly, that she could feel his male hardness thrust against her buttocks. ''Rachel, my love,'' he whispered hoarsely, ''you have the power to drive me wild with desire.''

Gently, he turned her to where she was facing him. ''I think I will remove your clothes slowly, so that I can take in your beauty at my leisure."

True to his word, John undressed Rachel unhurriedly, admiring her firm breasts, her feminine thighs, and her long, shapely legs. When, finally, he had her fully unclothed, he grew impatient, slipping hastily out of his own clothes.

Placing his hands on her shoulders, he eased her down on the large stack of hay. He kissed her with a deep passion, before moving his lips downward. Cupping her breasts in his hands, his tongue circled one nipple, and then the other, bringing Rachel to such heights of yearning that she moaned aloud.

Putting his strong hands on her waist, he moved her body upwards, so that his lips were at her stomach, kissing her warm flesh. Slowly, he moved his lips even farther down her slender frame, bringing Rachel such ecstatic pleasures that she writhed and moaned under his tantalizing touch.

"Oh John!" she cried. "Please, please take me!"

His powerful frame covered hers, and lifting her legs, Rachel accepted him, drawing him into her deeper and deeper.

That night, John's love-making had carried her higher and higher into blissful ecstasy.

Bringing herself out of her romantic reverie, Rachel looked across the distance of the courtyard, gazing lovingly at John Reynolds. Suddenly, he glanced over in her direction. He was too far away for Rachel to detect the exact expression in his eyes, but instinctively she knew he was looking at her with desire. She wished she could heedlessly throw propriety to the wind and run over to him, flinging herself into his comforting arms.

Watching him as he turned to speak with Colonel Werlin, she anxiously wondered why he had never said that he loved her.

Someday, she thought, surely someday, he will tell me how much he loves me!

Rachel had taken great care in dressing for the formal dinner to be held in Colonel Reynolds' quarters. As she walked gracefully into the room beside Josh and Deborah, her radiant beauty prompted the three officers standing with John to stare at her with obvious approval.

Her virginal innocence was now completely gone, and Rachel was fully aware of her sensual appearance. The royal blue gown she wore was cut so seductively low, it exposed the fullness of her breasts before snugly fitting her small waist and then flaring out into voluminous folds.

Josh led them over to Colonel Werlin. "Sir, I'd like you to meet my wife and my sister-in-law, Miss O'Brian."

The colonel took Deborah's hand into his, and bowed formally to her. Looking into the woman's face, he found it hard to believe that she could be sisters with the lovely girl standing beside her. Studying the Lieutenant's wife more closely, he was surprised to discover that the young woman was actually beautiful. He wondered why she insisted on camouflaging her beauty with an unbecoming hairdo, a drab high-necked dress, and an unmistakable coldness in the dark brown eyes, which otherwise would have been soft.

"Good evening, Mrs. Kendall," he said.

"Good evening, Colonel Werlin," she replied politely.

Turning his attention to the Lieutenant's sister-in-law, he was met by two sparkling green eyes and a smile so enticing that he was instantly enchanted by her alluring charm.

'Miss O'Brian, it's a pleasure to make your acquaintance, ma'am.''

Offering him her hand, she replied, ''It's an honor to meet you, Colonel Werlin.''

''May I introduce you and Mrs. Kendall to Major Hartly?'' the colonel asked, as he looked toward the man standing beside him.

Rachel smiled openly at the major, as he gently accepted her gloved hand. Colonel Werlin had arrived early that morning with the fort's new doctor, but she had only seen him from a distance, and had no idea Major Hartly was so attractive. She intuitively sensed that the major's friendly smile was genuine, and the tiny laugh wrinkles in the corner of his blue eyes proved the doctor was a man who obviously laughed often.

''Major Hartly, we are so happy to have you here, at last. Fort Craig was in desperate need of a doctor.''

''If I had known such a beautiful young lady was anticipating my arrival, I'd have ridden day and night to reach the fort.''

Laughing lightly, Colonel Werlin placed his hand on Rachel's arm. ''You'll have to watch our for Major Hartly, Miss O'Brian. He's a bachelor.''

The major looked away from Rachel to acknowledge Mrs. Kendall, and the colonel led her over to Captain Godwin and John Reynolds.

''Miss O'Brian, you are extremely lovely tonight,'' Captain Godwin said as his eyes traveled hungrily toward the exposed cleft above the bodice of her gown.

When Rachel first moved to the fort, Captain Godwin had clumsily made a few offensive passes at her, but she sternly repelled his detestable advances. She found the captain insufferable, and a cold chill ran through her as his beady eyes examined her intimately.

"Thank you," she replied curtly.

Brusquely, she turned her attention to Colonel Reynolds. Rachel thought that Josh, Major Hartly, and Colonel Werlin were all dashingly handsome in their dress uniforms, but none could compare with John Reynolds. His aura of masculinity dominated the entire room.

The moment their eyes met, the magnetism of passion between Rachel and Colonel Reynolds went unnoticed by everyone in the room, except for Captain Godwin. With spiteful jealousy, he wished he could prove his suspicion and report the colonel's improper conduct to their superior officer.

The swirling mist was so thick it was blinding her and frantically Rachel tried to find her way out of the heavy fog. Suddenly, the sound of a horses's hoofbeats hauntingly returned. As before, the fog mysteriously vanished. From somewhere that seemed far away, Rachel looked down and saw herself riding a horse across the plains. Then swiftly the dense fog fell over the scene. The piercing pain tore at her heart!

The fog dissolved again, and Rachel could see herself standing with one fist raised toward the sky. Everything around her was blurred and hazy, blocking from view all but the naked look of torment on her face. The heavy gray mist drifted down from the heavens. . . .

The aching pain was so severe, Rachel felt she was being driven out of her mind!

When the fog dissipated again, she was lying face down on the grass with her head resting across her arms, and she could hear her own anguished cry of heartbreak. The recurring fog crept silently over her. The pain became horrifying! She tried to waken, but the heavy fog held her in its eerie depths. Deliriously she fought her way out of the suffocating mist!

Bolting upright in her bed, she cried, "The pain! God help me, I can't stand the pain!" With trembling hands, she threw off the covers and leaped out of bed. She hurriedly slipped a robe over her nightgown and darted across the small room. Opening the door, she slipped quietly out into the darkness of night. Her heart was still beating rapidly from the horrifying impact of her dream as she began to run toward Colonel Reynolds' office. In the year and a half she had known John Reynolds, Rachel had never needed him so desperately as she did at that moment.

The cool evening breeze blew refreshingly across her flushed cheeks, and her lonely tears were swept away in the drifting wind. All at once, Rachel felt a strange sensation, and for an instant she halted her steps. Standing alone in the pitch darkness of night, Rachel mysteriously sensed an awaiting destiny with the whispering wind as it fleetingly passed by. Suddenly, the feeling was gone, and forgetting the mystical moment in time, she continued her flight across the silent courtyard.

As Rachel resumed her flight to John Reynolds' office, Captain Godwin silently stepped back into the dark shadows and secretly watched her.

When she reached to colonel's quarters, she noticed a lamp was still burning and she knocked softly on the door.

"Come in," he called.

Hastily she opened the door, and rushed into the room. Observing the troubled expression on her face, John rose from his chair and hurried over to her. A sob escaped from deep in her throat, and she flung herself into his strong arms. The comfort of being in his loving embrace let her fearful tears flow freely.

"Baby," he whispered, holding her tightly. "What's wrong, honey?"

"Oh, John, the dream! I had the dream again," she answered, sobbing heavily against his chest.

Stepping back so that he could see into her face, he asked, "What dream?"

"The same one I had that night in Kansas, and I had it again in San Francisco."

Detecting the fright in her eyes, he asked with concern, "Is the dream always the same?"

"Yes. The fog covers everything and suddenly it lifts and I can see myself. First I'm riding a horse, then standing somewhere with my fist raised toward the sky, and finally I'm lying in the grass crying. And, John, the crying is so terribly heartbreaking! But it's the pain that tears me to pieces!"

"A physical pain?" he asked.

"No, if it were physical, it could be borne! But the pain is emotional. Oh John, it's more than I can bear!"

He drew her back into his arms. "Rachel, you're trembling."

"Please hold me tightly! I'm so afraid! John, in the dream, I think I'm begging God for my own death!

231

What will I do that's so terrible, I'll want to die?''

"Baby, you can't be sure it's a premonition. Recurring dreams aren't necessarily a glimpse into the future."

Moving slightly, so she could look up into his face, she answered, "It is a premonition! And someday I'm going to wish I could die! Why? What will I do to cause myself such unbearable pain?"

"Maybe it's not something you've done, but something someone has done to you," he replied.

Placing her head on his shoulder, she sighed, "John, if ever I'm forced to face that terrible pain, I'm afraid I will go out of my mind."

"Can you see where you are in the dream?" he asked.

Looking up at him, she answered, "When I'm riding the horse, I can see it all clearly, but I feel as though I'm looking down on myself from far above. I don't recognize where I am, but I'm riding across the plains. I can't tell what I'm wearing, but I'm sure I have on trousers and I'm riding the horse bareback. I don't know the color of the horse. I can never remember if I see his color in my dream. When I'm raising my fist toward the sky, everything around me is blurred and I never remember what I'm wearing. Also, when I'm lying on the ground crying, I have no recollection of how I'm dressed. The most vivid part of the dream is when the fog closes in and I suffer that heartbreaking pain.

Tenderly, he wiped the tears from her face. "Maybe unconsciously you're forcing yourself to repeat the dream because you naturally have a fear of the future. Do you, Rachel?"

"I only fear a future without you," she replied.

"Baby, listen to me and listen closely. As I told you before, you are a survivor. You have the courage and the grit to withstand whatever the future may bring. And that goes for a future without me."

"Are you trying to comfort me, or warn me?" she asked anxiously.

Roughly, he jerked her to him, and said angrily, "Rachel, you little fool, don't you want a home, a husband, and children?"

"Of course I do, but I want you for my husband, and I want your children!"

She could hear the strain in his voice when he replied, "I had a wife once, and a child! And, by God, once was enough!"

"John, you're scared to love me, because you're afraid someday I'll hurt you the way Carmelita did. Oh darling, I could never hurt you! If I ever hurt you, I would want to die! And someday I want to have your child."

Rudely turning away from her, he walked over to his desk and violently slammed his fist on the desk top. "Our child would be branded a bastard!"

Hurrying to him and wrapping her arms around his neck, she cried, "Somehow, we'll find a way to stay together and someday, my darling, you won't be afraid to love me. It may take years before I can prove to you how much I love you, but when you finally believe . . . then you will. . . ."

As usual his mood changed abruptly, and interrupting her, he said teasingly, "Rachel, my romantic little hypocrite, did you know you talk too much? And I know the best way to silence you." Passionately his mouth covered hers, as smoothly he pulled her slim body close to his.

Surrendering to her own passion, Rachel tightened her hold about his neck, accepting his kiss fervently.

Breaking their embrace, John took her hand leading her into his bedroom, which was lit only by the soft glow from the kerosene lantern in his office. The moment they entered the room, he began helping her to remove her clothes. Quickly they had her undressed, and as Rachel hastened to the bed, John slipped out of his uniform, letting his clothes drop randomly to the floor.

Lying on the bed, Rachel watched him as he came to her, and holding her arms out to him, she murmured, "I love you, John Reynolds."

Instead of going into her embrace, he paused beside the bed, his eyes raking her sensual curves. Rachel could see passion in his eyes, as he studied every inch of her slender frame.

Then slowly, he looked down into her face, and his look of passion was suddenly supplanted by sadness. "John, what's wrong?" she cried anxiously.

John studied the lovely face looking up at his so trustingly. She was so sweet and so vulnerable. What was to become of this enticing little rebel who had so innocently found her way into his heart? There was no permanent place for Rachel in his life. He was already married, and even if he wasn't, he was too damned old for her. In a few years, when his age started catching up to him, she would realize she had never truly loved him. For his sake, as well as hers, this affair had to end. But as long as she was within his reach, he knew he could never stay away from her. She had become an obsession with him, manipulating him totally. Damn, he thought resentfully, I'm in love with her! Damn it, I loved her from the first moment I found her hiding in my wardrobe! As his true feelings became apparent, John was only more determined to find a way to end their relationship. He had to end it soon, while he still had the strength to let her go. She wasn't in love with him, she was only infatuated with him. How could she possibly love a man twenty-three years her senior?

"John?" Rachel pleaded, as he continued staring at her with an expression she couldn't even begin to understand.

Bringing himself out of his deep thoughts, John hid his true feelings behind a cheerful facade. Grinning, he replied, "I was only admiring your beauty, my love."

Worried, she insisted, "John, are you sure nothing is wrong?"

Lying beside her, he took her into his arms. "There is only one thing wrong, Rachel."

"What?" she asked seriously.

"You are talking too much," he whispered, before his lips found hers. Wanting him, she arched her thighs to his, feeling him grow even harder as she pressed herself firmly against him.

Covering her face and neck with kisses, John ran his hand over her body, his touch inciting her senses. As his lips possessed hers, he placed his hand between her legs, stimulating her female cravings and making her gasp with pleasure.

Gently, he pushed away from her, and rising from the bed, he said, "Hold that position, my love, I'll be right back."

"Where are you going?" she cried.

"To turn off the lantern, so we won't be disturbed."

Anxious, she replied, "Oh John, do hurry! I want you so desperately!"

Walking across the bedroom floor, John teased, "Rachel, didn't your mother ever teach you that a lady is supposed to endure sex, not relish it?"

"But John," she began pertly, "I thought I wasn't a lady!"

Chuckling, he replied, "Touché, my love!"

When John extinguished the lamp, and his office was in total darkness, Captain Godwin, still hidden outside in the shadows, smiled smugly. Quietly, he began walking towards his own quarters. Now that he had the proof he needed, first thing in the morning, he would talk to Colonel Werlin.

Colonel Werlin studied John Reynolds closely as he sat across the desk from him. He not only respected Colonel Reynolds, but also liked him personally, and he felt very uncomfortable about reproaching the man. Damn Godwin! Why couldn't he have minded his own business! If the situation had never been brought to his attention, he could've been spared this unpleasant scene.

"John," he began. "What I must discuss with you is very awkward and I wish I could ignore the whole matter; but damn it, John, there's a certain code all officers must live by."

"You know about Miss O'Brian, don't you?" he asked.

"Yes, I do and I wish to hell I didn't! My God man, what in the hell is wrong with you? A commanding officer doesn't sleep with his lieutenant's sister-in-law! What kind of an example are you setting for your men?

Maybe they aren't aware of what's going on, but it's only a matter of time until everyone on this fort knows! How long do you think you can keep something like this hidden!''

Rising from his chair, John walked over to the window and distractedly observed the activity of his soldiers busily performing their morning fatigue duty. Turning back toward the Colonel, he replied, ''What do you want me to say, Doug? I'm guilty as charged.''

''Miss O'Brian is young and vulnerable! I can't help but believe you have taken advantage of the girl. I don't have the authority to order you to marry her, but I'm advising it very strongly!''

''I can't marry her, because I'm already married,'' he answered.

''What?'' the Colonel bellowed.

Walking over to him, John explained, ''I haven't seen my wife in eleven years.'' Sitting on the edge of his desk, he added, ''As far as I know she's still in Mexico.''

''What happened in your marriage is none of my business, but your relationship with Miss O'Brian most assuredly is my business. John, if you'll give me your word that you'll end this affair, then no more will be said on the subject.''

''I'm sorry, Doug, but I can't. There's no way I could live on the same fort with Rachel and not be with her.''

Rising to his feet, he replied, ''Then I suggest you put in for a transfer immediately.''

John started to reply, but there was a sudden loud knock on the door, and it roughly swung open as Zeke rushed into the room.

"A man just now come into the fort," Zeke began breathlessly, "and he said the stagecoach he was a ridin' in done been attacked by the Apaches. He's wounded, but the Doc is patchin' him up now."

"Are there any other survivors?" Colonel Reynolds asked.

"Nope, he said all of 'em was killed 'cept fur him."

"How did he get away?" John asked.

"Well, he said them Apaches wounded 'im, then they just rode off and didn't seem to care that he was still alive. Hell, they didn't even take the horses, so he unhitched 'em and rode one of 'em to the fort."

"It doesn't make any sense," John began. "Why would they only wound him and then let him ride to the fort?"

"Of course it don't make no sense! Them Apaches would want them thar horses and also their scalps. They sure as hell wouldn't let one of them passengers come a-ridin' here to the fort."

"Did he say how many there were?"

"Fifty or sixty tharabouts is what he said," Zeke answered.

"John," Colonel Werlin began, "I want you to take a battalion and the soldiers who rode in with me and find those Apaches."

"And what do you suggest I do when I find them?" John asked sarcastically.

Ignoring his disrespect, Colonel Werlin replied, "If they refuse to give up peacefully, then start killing them until they either surrender or they're all dead!"

"They may have returned to their village," Colonel Reynolds replied.

"Try to catch up to them before they get away. If

238

you can't, then ride into their village and attack the whole damned village if necessary.''

"Colonel Werlin, need I remind you that I am the commanding officer on this fort?" John asked irritably. "Besides Doug," he tried to explain in a friendlier tone, "there's something going on here. The attack on that stagecoach doesn't sound right."

"It sounds to me like those Apaches came to their senses, and got scared of the consequences so they ran!"

"If I take a battalion with me there won't be enough soldiers left here to protect this fort from a full attack! If I ride out and leave the fort unprotected, I may be playing right into their hands."

"Damn it, John! The fort doesn't need protecting! The Apaches are running in the opposite direction."

"How can you be so sure?" John asked.

"The Apaches would never dream of attacking Fort Craig. They know the cavalry wouldn't rest until they had exterminated every last one of them. Take Captain Godwin with you, but leave Lieutenant Kendall here." When he made no move to obey his command, Colonel Werlin yelled severely, "If you don't apprehend those Apaches, I'll bring charges against you for negligence!"

"I hope to God you're right. There are women and children on this fort." Looking at Zeke, he ordered, "Tell the bugler to sound the call-to-arms!"

The call-to-arms always frightened Rachel, but she soon realized that this time was more critical than any of the others. Never before had John ridden out of the fort with a full battalion. She had heard about the attack on the stagecoach, and she knew the army was going after the Indians responsible. If the war party was a large as rumor had it, then John and his troops were in grave danger!

Leaning against the closed doors of the fort, she could barely hear the hoofbeats of the horses carrying the troopers further and further into the distance. "Dear God," she whispered, "please keep him safe!"

"Miss O'Brian?" Startled, because she hadn't heard anyone walking up to her, she swerved quickly and was pleasantly surprised to see Major Hartly.

"Major! I thought you left with the others," she replied.

"I was ordered to stay here. They took the medic with them instead. I suppose they figure he's better qualified in battle."

"Battle!" she exclaimed. "Do you think it will come to that?"

"I'm afraid it's a distinct possibility." Noticing the visible anxiety on her face, he asked gently, "Tell me, Miss O'Brian, which one of our knights in blue has captured your heart?"

Smiling timidly, she answered, "Are my feelings so obvious?"

Tenderly returning her smile, he replied, "You wear your heart on your sleeve."

Quickly changing the subject, Rachel glanced down toward the empty bucket he was holding in his hand, and asked, "Are you going to the river?"

"Yes, it seems I need some water. Due to all the excitement this morning, my water bucket was neglected. I'm ordering the infirmary floors scrubbed, and I don't want to use our drinking water from the well."

240

Laughing lightly, she replied, "My goodness, I didn't know officers fetched their own water."

"We don't, but there seems to be a great shortage of men. Besides, a walk by the river sounds pleasant. Especially if you were to join me."

"Thank you, Major Hartly. I'd love to," she answered.

Before he could order the trooper standing guard to open the fort gates, he spotted Colonel Werlin walking briskly over to them.

"Good morning, Miss O'Brian," the Colonel said pleasantly. Looking at the major, he asked, "How is the man from the stagecoach?"

"He'll be all right, but he's been taken to El Rio. Sir, how serious is the situation with the Apaches?"

"I don't know yet, but those savages will be taught a lesson! We can't just sit back and allow them to kill white people in cold-blooded murder!" Changing the subject, he asked, "Are you two going to the river?"

"Yes, we are," the major answered.

"Would you mind if I were to tag along? I'd like to discuss the infirmary with you. I noticed the facilities are extremely outdated. I'm planning to put in a request to Washington for needed funds to have the old infirmary torn down, and a new one built in its place."

Placing his hand under Rachel's elbow, the major ordered the soldier to open the gates. As they walked out of the fort, he replied, "I certainly hope your request is approved."

Leisurely they strolled to where the Rio Grande flowed placidly beside the quiet fort. Kneeling beside the rippling river, Rachel cupped the cool water into her hands and splashed the refreshing liquid on her face. She only listened half consciously as the colonel told the major about his plans for a new infirmary. Rachel was too worried about John's safety to concentrate on anything else for very long.

Rising slowly to her feet, she dreamily looked over and beyond the river, when mysteriously, she felt a cold chill running fleetingly through her very soul. Sensing impending danger, she impulsively grabbed for the colonel's arm, concurrent with the sound of the urgent and threatening call-to-arms within the fort walls.

Crying out in alarm, Rachel spied a large Apache war party riding straight for the fort. The colonel whirled, and glancing in the same direction he moaned, "My God!"

Both men grasped her by an arm and began to run for the safety of the fort. We'll never make it, Rachel thought frantically. We'll be killed! . . . John! Oh John!

As the Indians drew perilously nearer, Rachel felt her heart beating more rapidly than the thundering of the horses carrying the Apaches closer and closer to them. Before they could reach the shelter of the fort, she suddenly heard multiple rifle shots bursting forth from different directions.

From inside the fort, Josh saw a small group of Indians cut their horses away from the others and head for Rachel and the two men. Ordering a few of his men to follow, he hastened through the gates of the fort. In kneeling position, the soldiers fired at the Apaches riding toward the three people fleeing for their lives.

They had only a few more steps before reaching the sanctuary of the fort, when one of the Apaches rode his horse up to them. Aiming his rifle at the colonel, he fired. Before he had a change to shoot again, Josh pulled out his sword and thrust it upward into the young brave's side. His lifeless body fell from the horse and thumped to the ground.

Quickly, along with the major, Rachel knelt beside the colonel. He was lying face down, and swiftly she helped Major Hartly roll him over on his back, and then she screamed! Colonel Werlin was dead, with a gaping bullet hole where part of his face used to be!

Drawing Rachel to her feet, the major yelled strongly over the constant sounds of gunfire, "Come on, we have to get out of here! There's nothing we can do for him!"

Clutching her arm and turning to run, they saw Josh had been shot and was on the ground dragging himself toward the entrance of the fort. Rachel and the major ran over to the wounded man, and with one on each side, they lifted him to his feet. As the gates opened for them they hurried inside. The remaining soldiers hastily followed, and the heavy gates closed securely behind them.

Riding at the front of the battalion beside Colonel Reynolds, Zeke asked, "You're a-thinkin' what I'm thinkin', ain't ya?"

"Yeah, Zeke, I'm sure I am." Looking over at the old mountaineer, he continued, "When we reach that stagecoach, the Indian tracks we find will be nothing more than a decoy."

"Yep, that's what I was a-thinkin'," he answered, chewing loudly on a wad of tobacco.

Abruptly, John pulled up his horse as he called, "Company, halt!" Looking over at Zeke, he said angrily, "Damn it! We're going back!"

"John, if what we was a-thinkin' is wrong, Colonel Werlin will live up to his threat and bring charges against ya fur negligence."

Watching his old friend closely, he replied gravely, "I know, but it's a chance I have to take."

"Ya think them Apaches are goin' to attack the fort, don't ya?"

Before he had a chance to answer, Captain Godwin rode up to them. "Colonel," he asked, "why are we stopping?"

"We're returning to the fort," he said bluntly.

"What!" Captain Godwin exclaimed. "Colonel Reynolds, we have our orders! I for one, intend to carry them out!"

"Captain Godwin," John said furiously, "I am your commanding officer, and you'll do as I tell you!"

Saluting the colonel stiffly, he replied, "Yes, sir! May I say something off the record, sir?"

Returning the Captain's salute, he answered casually, but a glint of anger flickered in his eyes. "Go right ahead."

"During your court-martial, I'll testify willingly against you!"

"I'm sure you will, Captain Godwin. Now return to your men! We're going back!"

Watching Captain Godwin as he rode away from them, Zeke spat out a stream of tobacco juice and recollected, "He reminds me of an old mule I once had . . . they're both jackasses!"

Rachel O'Brian had been born on a wealthy southern plantation, and from the moment of her birth, she

244

had been spoiled by her parents, waited on hand and foot by slaves, and shielded from the unpleasant realities of life. She'd been raised to believe that she and her breed were superior to others, and unquestioningly she reigned supreme over her inferiors in what she believed was her father's indestructible kingdom. Then the war shockingly brought her father's majestic kingdom crumbling to the ground as the fiery flames cremated the three generation mansion and all it had arrogantly stood for. . . . But the courageous young woman working conscientiously beside Major Hartly had nothing left in common with Tom O'Brian's pampered and delicate daughter.

The sight of the ugly wound and all the blood from the unconscious soldier made Rachel's stomach feel weak, but she swallowed hard and determinedly fought her nausea. Obediently she did everything the major ordered, and together with the deafening sounds of cannons exploding and rifles firing outside the infirmary, they worked diligently to save Josh's life. The bullet had gone deeply into his leg, severing an artery, and it was imperative that they stop the bleeding.

As the major was applying direct pressure on the upper portion of Josh's leg, the door of the infirmary swung open and two soldiers came into the room carrying a wounded man.

"Put him on a cot," the major ordered. Glancing at Rachel, he said, "See what you can do for him. I can't tend to him until I finish here!"

Rachel rushed to the cot where the soldiers had placed the injured man. Kneeling beside the trooper, she could see that he had been shot in the chest, and that blood covered the front of his shirt. Grabbing a clean cloth, she pressed it tightly to his wound. Looking into his face, she recognized him as the soldier who had sung "Kathleen." Holding back a sob, she told him, "The doctor will be here in a minute."

"Miss O'Brian," he whispered weakly, "help me. . . ."

The cloth she was holding against him was already saturated with his blood, and frantically, she hurried to the major. "He's seriously wounded! Oh God, how much longer are you going to be?"

"Come here and hold the cloth over the wound, and don't let up on the pressure."

Instantly she obeyed him, and he hastened to examine the young soldier. Returning momentarily, the major gently pushed Rachel's hand aside and resumed the pressure himself.

"The soldier?" she asked.

"He's dead," he answered bluntly.

Loudly the door crashed open again, and in an effort to be heard over the sounds of battle, the sergeant called out to them, "Excuse me, sir . . . ma'am. For their safety, all the women and children are being moved to the mess hall. I've come to take you, Miss O'Brian."

"How much longer can we hold out?" Major Hartly asked.

Stepping further into the room, he glanced at Rachel then back to the major again. Hesitantly, he answered, "I . . . well, sir. . . ."

"There's no need to lie because of the lady, Sergeant. How long?"

"Soon they'll be climbing over the walls, major. We just don't have enough men to hold them back. It's getting so bad, we can't even spare men anymore to bring the wounded to the infirmary."

Touching Rachel's arm, the major urged, "Go with him. You'll be safer there."

"And Josh?" she asked.

She could see the strain on his face as he replied. "He'll have to stay here, but I must go out there and help the other men. I'll put a tourniquet on his leg. It'll save his life, but probably cost him a leg. I'm sorry, but I haven't time to sew the artery now. I have an obligation to all those wounded men out there."

Rachel began to move toward the door, but with anxiety she looked at Josh and halted her steps. Oh God, she thought, I can't leave him! I can't!

Decisively she returned to Josh's side, and placed her hand over the cloth Major Hartly had pressed against the wound. Firmly she stated, "I'll stay with him!"

"Very well, ma'am," the sergeant replied, admiring the young woman's courage and loyalty to her brother-in-law.

He started to leave, but Rachel stopped him by asking, "Do you know if Mrs. Kendall has been informed of her husband's injury?"

"I don't think anyone has told her yet. Do you want me to tell her?"

Shaking her head, she answered, "No, there's nothing she can do for him. Let her stay with the other women, she'll be safer there."

"Yes, ma'am." he replied.

"Sergeant," the major began, "can you get yourself another pistol?"

"Yes, sir. Do you want me to leave mine?"

Walking over to him, Major Hartly accepted the pistol. "I'll get my bag and see what I can do for the wounded." Moving swiftly to Rachel, he placed the gun on the table beside her. "Keep pressing that cloth just the way you are now."

"Why would he lose his leg if you used a tourniquet?" she asked.

"It would cut off the blood circulation through the rest of his leg. If I were going to operate immediately I could use a tourniquet, but I don't know how long it'll be before I can get back to him. Continue to keep the cloth pressed firmly over the wound, and you'll save his leg and his life."

Hearing the violent sounds of battle, she answered solemnly, "In a little while none of us may be alive."

He reached over and touched her cheek. "If by some miracle we do come out of this alive, I want to meet that soldier of yours so I can personally tell him what a lucky man he is." Grabbing his black medical bag he quickly left with the sergeant.

The passing minutes seemed like hours to Rachel as she stood beside John pressing firmly on the cloth that covered the severed artery in his leg. Her arms ached, and perspiration from the unaccustomed strain accumulated heavily on her brow, but she was afraid to remove either hand from the wound to wipe her face.

As she first sensed a change in the sounds of fighting, Rachel wondered if her fear had caused her to hallucinate. Over the thundering cannons and constant gunfire, she concentrated intensely, trying desperately to detect the sound again. It was still faint, but this time Rachel instantly recognized the bugler blowing "Charge." "John!" she cried. "Oh thank God, you've come back! Thank God!"

Sitting rigidly on her chair, Deborah stared across the desk at John Reynolds. The man's huge size and blatant masculinity always overwhelmed her, and being alone in his presence made her feel very uncomfortable.

Four weeks had passed since the attack on the fort, and Josh was almost well again, but for the remainder of his life he'd be forced to limp slightly on the leg that had been wounded. Major Hartly had insisted that he be given a medical discharge from the army, because of the permanent injury.

John studied the young woman sitting across from him. He knew that Deborah was only seventeen, but he had to look at her very closely to find that youth she tried to conceal. Deborah's deportment and dress were identical to that of a matronly woman.

"You wanted to see me?" she asked.

"Mrs. Kendall," he began, "I'd like to know your opinion of the arrangement I discussed with your husband last night."

"Colonel Reynolds, your offer is very generous and my husband and I are both very grateful to you," she answered politely, but without a trace of warmth.

"Did Josh explain everything to you?" he asked.

"Yes, I think so. The foreman who has been taking care of your ranch, wrote you that in a few months he'll be buying his own place and you want Josh to take over his job."

"Before the foreman leaves, he'll have ample time to teach Josh all he needs to learn. Naturally, you'll live in my home. The housekeeper, Maria, and her husband Pedro have been taking care of the house. I'm sure you'll find it quite comfortable and adequate. Is the salary I offered satisfactory with you?''

"It sounds very generous, Colonel Reynolds," she replied.

Deborah watched him as he leaned leisurely back into the large chair and expertly rolled a cigarette. She wished he would dismiss her. She found it very difficult to be polite, considering how he had taken advantage of her sister's youth and ruined her in the eyes of God and man!

"If you or Josh should need me for anything, you know how to get in touch. I won't see you again before you leave. I've been summoned to Fort Stanton on military business, and I'm leaving this afternoon. I'll be gone at least three months." Deborah knew she had been dismissed when he formally added, "I wish you luck, Mrs. Kendall, and I hope you and Josh enjoy living on the ranch."

Gratefully she started to rise, but against her own better judgement, she found herself asking, "What do you plan to do about Rachel?"

While noting the look of contempt on her face, he casually struck a match and lit his cigarette before he replied. "If you have something to say, Mrs. Kendall, why don't you just say it."

Clasping her hands tightly in her lap, she leaned forward in her chair and with her eyes blazing, she released her bitterness. "I think your conduct with my sister is horrid and disgraceful! What kind of man are you, to take such cruel advantage of a young and innocent woman?"

"I'm a man who happens to care very much for you sister," he replied.

"What do you intend to do, Colonel Reynolds? Show her how much you care by making her your mistress? Completely ruin any chance she may have to find herself a husband? If you were free to marry Rachel, would you?"

When he didn't reply instantly, she continued, "Of course you wouldn't! If only Papa or my brothers were still alive! But she has no one to protect her from a man like you! I shudder to think of the consequences, should she find herself with child. The poor innocent baby would . . . would be called. . . . Oh it's so horrible I can't even bring myself to say that ugly word."

Suddenly, Deborah caught her breath in fright, when she saw the rage in his piercing gray eyes. Savagely he roared, "Bastard, Mrs. Kendall! The word is bastard!"

Angrily he pushed back his chair and strode briskly around his desk, staring down at her harshly. "There will be no children from our union, Mrs. Kendall, because Rachel is leaving with you and Josh. I spoke to your husband about Rachel last night, and make no mistake madam, your sister will be welcomed in your home!"

"Of course, she'll be welcomed! I don't blame her for what happened! All the blame is placed on you!"

Deborah was puzzled by how quickly his anger seemed to vanish, and quietly he answered, "I take full responsibility for what has happened between Rachel and me. What you say is true, Mrs. Kendall. I took advantage of a young girl's innocence."

"Why?" she asked. "Why would a man your age allow himself to become involved with someone as young as Rachel?"

"I assure you, madam, it wasn't done deliberately," he answered. He turned away from her and walked around the desk. Returning to his chair, he continued, "I'll be leaving for Fort Stanton in a couple hours. By the time I return, Rachel will be in Texas. You can relax, Mrs. Kendall. It's all over between us."

"Does she know?" Deborah asked.

"Not yet, but she soon will," he answered.

Acutely recalling her love for Edward, Deborah said with a compassion she hadn't felt in months, "It'll break her heart."

"Perhaps, but in time she'll get over her infatuation with me. When the right man comes along, she'll wonder how she could have thought herself in love with someone my age."

"I'm sure you're right, Colonel Reynolds. She may think herself in love with you now, but in ten years or so . . . if she were to see you again. . ."

Finishing the statement for her, he said, "She'd see a fifty-one year old man but she would still be a young and beautiful woman. At twenty-eight she'll be more attractive than she is now."

Deborah startled him when she replied wisely, "If you were free, the difference in your ages would still caution you against marrying her. Even if you loved her!"

He took a drag off his cigarette, and remained quiet for a moment before he answered, "For various reasons, Mrs. Kendall, I wish to never remarry. Rachel is helping Major Hartly in the infirmary. Will you please tell her that I want to see her when she is finished?"

"Yes, of course," she replied. Not knowing what else to say to him, she promptly rose from the chair and walked rapidly across the room. As she opened the door, she glanced back and said gently, "Goodbye, Colonel Reynolds."

"Goodbye, Mrs. Kendall."

When the door closed behind her, John reached into his desk drawer and pulled out a bottle of whiskey. As he opened the bottle, Rachel's loving and trusting face flashed across his mind. Quickly he tilted it to his mouth and helped himself to a large and much needed drink.

John was still sitting behind his desk when Rachel buoyantly rushed into his office. Her smile faded instantly when she detected his somber expression, and the partially empty bottle he was carelessly holding in his hand. His eyes pierced hers with an electrifying intensity and sharply he set the bottle down on his desk. Rising from his chair, he crossed over to her and took her hand into his. Solemnly he said, "We need to talk."

Rachel could hear the seriousness in his voice and with growing anxiety, she asked, "Is something wrong?"

Disregarding her question, he led her to the chair by his desk. "Sit down, Rachel."

"No!" she answered angrily. "Something is wrong, and I want you to tell me what it is! Now!"

Smiling at her slightly, he replied, "Your temper flares as quickly as mine." Suddenly the small grin vanished as he severely ordered, "Sit down, damn it, and listen to what I have to say!" Irritably she obeyed him.

He leaned his tall frame against the side of his desk

253

and watched her face closely. "Has Josh told you he is moving to my ranch in Texas?"

"No," she answered, surprised. "I don't understand. Why is he moving to your ranch? Was he supposed to tell me about it?"

"I guess he decided it would be best to let me be the one to tell you. My foreman is quitting in a few months, and Josh is going to replace him."

Looking up at him with pleading eyes, she asked, "What will this mean to us?"

"You'll be leaving with Deborah and Josh," he replied, before averting his gaze from the obvious trust in her eyes.

"But John," she began, "if I'm living in Texas, we'll be lucky if we can see each other once a year. It's so difficult for you to take furlough. When we learned Josh was going to be discharged from the army, and I asked you what would become of us, you said you'd work something out!"

Slowly he moved away from her, and walked to the other side of his desk. "I have worked something out. You will move to Texas."

Fretfully she sat on the very edge of her chair, and though she feared his answer, she asked, "Are you planning to come see me?"

"I'm sending you to Texas to forget me!" he replied.

With unrestrained anger overpowering her, she rose from the chair and shouted, "How can you betray me like this? I believed in you!"

"Betray you in what way?" he said furiously. "By giving you a chance to make something out of your life? To find a man who will love you and want to marry you?''

"But you're the only man I want!" she cried.

"You may think that now, Rachel . . . but after some time has passed. . ."

Interrupting him, she said with conviction, "After time has passed, I'll still love you!"

Swiftly he moved around his desk and grabbed her securely by the shoulders. Shouting, he replied, "I'm twenty-three years older than you! My God, I'm old enough to be your father! Ten or fifteen years from now when you looked at me you'd see an old man, and then you'd wonder, how in the hell you could have thought yourself in love with me! You'd thank God you weren't trapped into spending the best years of your life with a man my age!"

With an expression of tender compassion on her youthful face, she looked up at him appealingly. "You'll never grow older to me. I'll always see you just as you are now."

Brusquely he turned away from her and walked a few steps before angrily pivoting back in her direction. "You sound like a romantic school girl living in a fantasy world!"

Unable to fully relinquish her hopes, she pleaded with him, "What must I do to prove to you that the difference in our ages will never stop me from loving you?"

Rejecting her question entirely, he replied, "Rachel, you aren't thinking rationally. What in the hell am I suppose to do with you? Make you my mistress? Set you up in a room somewhere in El Rio and use you as my whore?" She could see the rage shining in his eyes, as he said firmly and commandingly, "You will go to

255

Texas!"

Resenting the callousness in his attitude, she replied angrily, "You're sending me to your ranch to ease your guilty conscience! How simple and easy you have made it for yourself! You get rid of me and your guilt all at the same time! Did you pay Josh five thousand dollars to take care of me?" Noticing his look of surprise, she laughed bitterly. "I know you bought the dress shop in San Francisco! Edward explained everything to me the night that he left. Do you know why he told me? Because he thought I should be aware that you love me! . . . Love me! . . . You don't even understand the meaning of the word!"

Savagely, he yelled, "What in the hell can I do? Damn it, I can't keep you here and even I were free to marry you, I'm too damned old for you!"

With an abrupt change of mood, he walked over to her and gently placed his hands on her arms as he said, "Someday when you're happily married. . ."

Interrupting him, she yelled sharply as she pulled away from his touch, "Married! What man will want me? Doesn't a man expect his bride to be a virgin?" Rachel knew her remark hurt him, when she saw the way he involuntarily flinched.

Hiding his true feelings behind an aloofness he didn't actually feel, he replied, "A man usually hopes his bride will be a virgin, but he doesn't necessarily expect it."

Unable to accept the inevitable, she reached out and clutched his arm. "It'll be at least a month before Josh is well enough to travel. That means I still have time to make you change your mind, and I know I can! I know it!"

Brushing her hand from his arm, John whirled abruptly and walked over to the gun cabinet where he had placed his sword and scabbard. With his back toward her, she couldn't see the expression of pain he had turned away to conceal. Strapping the heavy sword around his waist, he took full control of his emotions, and said strongly, "There will be no time to make me change my mind. Within the hour I'm leaving for Fort Stanton on military business."

"How long will you be gone?" she asked.

"At least three months," he replied, finding himself unable to look into her eyes and observe the torment he was causing her.

Trying desperately to salvage what was left of her pride, Rachel constrained her tears of despair and exchanged her misery for anger. "I'm amazed, Colonel Reynolds, at how conveniently you have arranged everything. You not only found a way to get rid of me, but you also found a way to make yourself scarce until I'm well out of your life!"

Fighting the desire to be gentle, he glanced toward her and said with a casualness he was far from feeling, "You give me too much credit, Rachel. I didn't plan this trip. I was summoned to report to Fort Stanton for an important meeting."

"How long have you known?" she asked.

"A few days," he replied.

"And you didn't bother to tell me until it's time for you to leave?" Raising her voice, she shouted furiously, "You damned coward! You're running with your tail between your legs like some mangy dog! Oh God, how I wish I could hate you!"

Walking toward her, he said tenderly, "Someday,

Rachel, you'll realize I'm doing what is best for you."

"You're wrong! Oh God, how wrong you are!" she cried.

He took her hand into his. "In time you'll feel differently."

Angrily she jerked her hand free. "Damn you, don't tell me how I will feel someday! And don't look at me as though you're sorry for me! I never wanted anything from you except your love, and I surely don't want or need your pity!" Her anger flashed vividly in her eyes, as she continued, "Because I will get over you, John Reynolds! Somehow . . . I'll find a way to live without you! I swear it!" But with every ounce of strength she possessed, Rachel had to restrain herself from disputing her very words by begging him not to leave her.

When he smiled, his familiar grin tore painfully at her heart. "I'm sure you'll forget me much sooner than you realize."

Resigned, with her anger defeated, Rachel crossed over to the window. Watching the Colonel's troops preparing for their journey, she replied, "Please spare me your wisdom concerning my future." Glancing in his direction, she added, "I really don't think I can take any more of your damned predictions."

Swiftly Rachel walked back across the room, and stopping directly in front of him, she said firmly, "Besides, I never said I'd forget you. I said I'd get over you and learn to live without you. But forget you? Or stop loving you? Never!"

Taking her by surprise, he grabbed her shoulders and jerked her to him. His eyes burned into hers with intensity. "You're a romantic little fool! Of course you'll forget me, and you only think you're in love!"

"Why do you refuse to believe that I love you?"

"You couldn't possibly be in love with a man my age!"

With anguish, she cried out to him, "What has age got to do with it?"

"Everything!" he answered, tightening his grip on her shoulders.

"No, age has nothing to do with it! It's you! You're afraid of my love!"

"That's ridiculous, Rachel!" he answered sternly.

For a moment they stared silently into one another's eyes, and extreme tension grew between them. Then her eyes softened with love, and she pleaded, "Kiss me, John! Kiss me goodbye!"

Roughly he pulled her into his arms and his mouth violently bruised her lips as he painfully crushed her body to his. Suddenly she could feel his rage becoming passion and a moan of desire escaped from deep in his throat.

When he brusquely turned her loose, Rachel was startled by the torture and suffering she could see on his face. His anguish and pain could be heard in his powerful voice, when he yelled, "No! . . . Damn it, no!"

Turning away from her, he crossed over to his desk and picked up the whiskey bottle. He wrenched it open and as he took a large drink, his steel gray eyes pierced her with a hardness that was frightening.

At a loss for words, she watched silently as he angrily put the bottle back on his desk. Without looking at her, he walked briskly to the door and boisterously swung it open. "Corporal!" he yelled.

Immediately he was answered, "Yes, sir!"

"Are the troops ready?"

"Yes, sir!"

"Did you see that my belongings were put in the wagon?"

"Yes, sir, Colonel!" he answered.

"Tell the troops to mount up! We're pulling out!"

Determined to remain calm, Rachel walked over and removed his hat from the rack on the wall. Unconsciously caressing the hat between her fingers, she slowly moved toward him. Her heart seemed to break a little more with each step that brought her closer to him and closer to hearing him say goodbye.

"The first time I saw you," she began softly, "you were wearing the uniform of a Union officer, and I wished that I could see your face, but it was hidden by the shadow of your hat." Handing it to him, she continued, "Then you glanced up in my direction, and I think I have loved you from that very moment."

Placing the hat on his head, he pulled it low over his forehead in the way Rachel always remembered him wearing it. "That day . . . I wished myself twenty years younger. There's just too many years between us, Rachel!"

"Time isn't standing between us, John. . . . You are!"

His eyes revealed his sorrow as he said, "Goodbye, Rachel."

He didn't wait for an answer, but stormed out of the door, slamming it shut behind him.

She stood rigid for a moment, and stared pathetically at the closed door that represented the end of her dreams. Forlornly, with her shoulders slumped under the weight of her misery, Rachel walked across the room and over to the Colonel's desk.

I won't cry, she thought. If I start crying now, I won't be able to stop! I'll cry later when the shock has passed, and I'm able to bear it!

Hearing the door open, she whirled about. There had been no time to comprehend how much she'd been hoping it would be John until she felt the disappointment. Forcing herself to smile, she said, "Hello, Zeke. Aren't you leaving with John?"

Walking into the room, he answered, "Nope, I ain't a goin'. The Colonel done asked me to take you, Miss Deborah, and Lieutenant Kendall to the ranch."

"It seems he's always asking someone else to take care of me."

"He thinks a lot of ya, Miss Rachel!"

Smiling disagreeably, she replied, "Of course he does! I was a good bed partner for four months!"

"Miss Rachel, don't you go and say them kind of things! He don't feel that a way, and you shouldn't oughta talk 'bout yurself like that!"

"Oh, Zeke!" she cried angrily. "He doesn't care about me! He walked out on me as though what we shared meant nothing to him!"

"Ma'am," Zeke began awkwardly, "I'm really sorry 'bout what happened. I thought ya'd be able to make that ornery jackass do somethin' 'bout gittin' out of that thar marriage he's trapped in. With all that money he's got, he could find 'im a way out of it, if'n he really wanted to."

"But he doesn't want out of his marriage. He'd rather hide behind Carmelita's skirts."

"Part of what ya say may be true, but if you was a little older, I think it woulda' been different fur ya. . . . Ya see, Miss Rachel, John's Mama was only

261

sixteen when she married his Pappy. When John was ten years old, his Mama left 'im and his Pappy and run off with another man. From what he'd told me he thought an awful lot of his Mama, and it broke his heart with she up and left 'im that a way. He said he cain't understand how a mother could just run off and leave her own kid. He figgers it's because she was so young when she got herself married, and didn't know yet what she was a-wantin' out of life. And then Carmelita was just seventeen when he married her and . . . well ya know what happened thar.''

"It's not fair that he should judge me by his mother and Carmelita!" she yelled.

"Maybe not, but he ain't got nothin' else to judge by, 'cept what he learnt from the past.''

When suddenly she began to hear the unmistakable sounds of the troops riding out of the fort, Rachel tried to control her tears but her sorrow was too severe and hard sobs tore from deep in her heart.

Wishing he knew some way to console her, Zeke came closer to her and said gently, "Miss Rachel, it'll be all right.''

Taking him by surprise, she flung herself into his arms and with her head resting on his shoulder she humbly cried heartbreaking tears.

Clumsily trying to comfort her, Zeke awkwardly patted her on the back. "Thar now, Miss Rachel . . . don't cry little gal . . . it'll be all right . . . you'll see . . . someday you'll furget all 'bout that ornery cuss and find yurself a real fine young man. . . . Get yurself married, and have a bunch of younguns. . . . You'll see. . . .''

Stepping out of his embrace, she looked into his kind

bearded face and said firmly, "I'm going to learn how to live without him! Somehow I'll find a way to get over him and make a life for myself. I'm through chasing a hopeless dream. But Zeke, I'll always love him!"

She turned away and walked slowly to the window. She watched as the huge doors to the fort closed behind Colonel Reynolds and his troops. With tears glistening in her eyes, she said barely above a whisper, "I love you, John Reynolds, and I will always love you!"

Chapter Seven

The day Tom O'Brian purchased the strongly built covered wagon for his journey to California, he never dreamed it would travel over so many additional hard miles. The sturdy wagon had traveled to San Francisco and to Fort Craig with no difficulties, and now the stalwart and seemingly indestructible covered wagon was rolling steadily across the rocky plains of southern Texas.

When Zeke informed Rachel that they were on Reynolds' property, she expected at any moment to catch a glimpse of his home. She was shocked when he told her the house was still twenty miles ahead.

Deborah and Josh were resting in the back of the wagon, and Rachel was sitting up front beside Zeke, when impulsively she asked, "Exactly how rich is John?"

Laughing at her question, he answered, "Miss Rachel, I don't know just how rich he is, but a lot of ranches in Texas are big. But this here ranch is makin' 'im even richer. That much I know."

Looking across the empty plains, she asked, "Where are the cattle?"

"We'll most likely run across some of 'em 'fore we get to the house."

"Who buys them?" she inquired.

"Most times they're sold to the miners, railroad crews, army forts, and settlers travelin' further west. But I heard, cause of the Kansas Pacific Railroad, the town of Abilene is now a shippin' line fur Texas cattle."

"Zeke, does John ever come to the ranch?"

Perceiving the meaning behind her question, he answered, "Now, little gal, don't ya go gittin' yur hopes up that he'll come a-ridin' up to his ranch anytime soon. It's been nigh on seven years now since he's been back to check on this place. He's just lucky his foreman is an honest and hard workin' man, otherwise he'd a had to sell this here ranch a long time ago."

Sighing deeply, she asked, "Why must he be so complex?"

"I ain't never thought of 'im as bein' complex. I ain't never had no trouble a figgerin' out why he does what he does."

She smiled at the old mountaineer. "Why does a wealthy man become a wagon master, and why does he join the cavalry? If I didn't know better, I'd think he was a little touched in the head!"

Guffawing loudly, he said, "Titched in the head, huh? I gotta remember to tell John what ya said. He'll git 'im a big laugh out of it."

"I'm sure he will!" she answered, feeling perturbed. "He always finds me so entertaining!"

Trying to control her curiosity, Rachel fidgeted on the wagon seat and tried to think about anything except what really interested her. Finally, deciding she was incapable of suppressing her curiosity, she looked over at Zeke and asked, "If you know him so well, then why did he become a wagon master? And why did he join the cavalry?"

"Well, Miss Rachel," he began, "he was a plannin' on goin' to San Francisco anyways. You see, I heered 'bout these here wagons a needin' a scout and a wagon master. I was offered the job of bein' the scout, so I went to Independence where John was still a-waitin' fur his discharge from the Army. I told 'im how these settlers was havin' a hard time findin' theirselves a wagon master cause thar was only twenty-five wagons."

"You mean he decided to take that job because he wanted to help some strangers?"

"Like I done said, he was plannin' on goin' to San Francisco anyhow, but yes'm, I think he done it mostly out of the kindness of his heart."

She looked at him with puzzlement. "I don't understand. If he was planning on going to San Francisco, why did he join the cavalry instead?"

"Miss Rachel, are ya ever goin' to git to whar ya can see any further than the end of yur purty little nose? Now just why do ya reckon he joined up with the cavalry 'stead of goin' on to San Francisco?"

"Because of . . . me?" she asked, finding it hard to believe that she could've had anything to do with his decision.

Zeke remained silent for a moment, before answering, "He was a runnin' from you, little gal. Ma'am, that man ain't got a cowardly bone in his body when it comes to somethin' he can see, hear, or touch. But when it comes to love, he's scairt, so he runs."

"Why is he so afraid?"

"Why do ya reckon he's scairt? First his Mama run off and left 'im, and he loved her a powerful lot. Hurt 'im bad when she up and left 'im that a way. Then thar was Carmelita. I don't think he was ever really in love with her, but he wanted to be, and you know what she done to 'im. When he lost that thar baby . . . well ma'am, he don't ever want to feel that kind of pain again. Just seems like every time he loves someone, he ends up a gittin' hurt."

"But he loves you and you've never hurt him!"

"Now just how do ya know I ain't never done nothin' to hurt 'im?"

"Because you love him! Oh, don't you see. The reason his mother and Carmelita hurt him was because they didn't love him. But we do love him, and that's why we would never do anything to cause him any pain!"

Observing the glint of hope shining in her eyes, he said gently, "Now, Miss Rachel, didn't ya tell me ya was goin' to make a life fur yurself without 'im? Ya ain't gonna make it no easier fur yurself a thinkin' them kind of thoughts. Ya might as well start right now a-puttin' 'im out of yur mind. He's done gave ya a new chance to find a good life here in Texas. If'n yur smart, ya'll find yurself a rancher, fall in love with 'im, and have yurself some younguns."

"Great guns and little switches!" she began indignantly. "Does every man believe the answer to a woman's troubles is simply to have babies!"

Laughing loudly, he answered, "Well, ma'am, it keeps her so busy, she ain't got the time to think 'bout any of them thar troubles."

* * *

Living the peaceful and quiet days on the ranch agreed with Rachel's feeling of melancholy, but she was determined that somehow she would overcome her obsession with John Reynolds. Although she had submissively resigned herself to the inevitable separation, she knew she would always love him!

John Reynolds' home met with Rachel's approval, and she wished fervently that she could be its mistress. The house's elegance lay in its simplicity. It was white with a red tile roof. It sat on top of a small incline overlooking the horse corral and the bunkhouse. A long narrow drive led up to a hitching post in front of the veranda. The large double doors were constructed of dark heavy wood.

Rachel had decided her favorite room in the house was the study, especially after Maria had informed her that it had also been Señor Reynolds preference. She spent many tranquil hours sitting behind the massive desk reading books borrowed from one of the two built-in bookcases situated on the wall behind the desk. It was definitely a man's room, with rifles hanging above the fireplace and a huge gun chest located against the far wall. The couch and chairs were Spanish design, upholstered in crimson velvet. Floor length drapes covered the doors leading out onto the patio at the back of the house.

Before Zeke left on his return trip to the fort, Rachel asked him, "When John decided against San Francisco, why didn't he return to the ranch, instead of joining the cavalry?" She couldn't begin to understand why he chose life in the army over his ranch. Zeke had answered her with his usual simple, but correct diagnosis, "He ain't learnt to live with his memories of that thar little baby."

During the lonely weeks that followed, Rachel would often gather flowers from Pedro's splendid garden, and then walk to the small hill behind the house. Kneeling beside the solitary and simple tombstone, she would place the colorful bouquet on the small grave of John Reynolds' son.

It was still mid-morning, but the June sun was already promising an unusually warm day when Rachel walked languidly around the corner of the house. She had just returned from visiting the small grave, and her thoughts were sympathetically with John and his son. She wasn't aware of the stranger walking across the veranda until she was almost upon him.

Startled, she abruptly halted her steps. "Oh, I'm sorry. I didn't see you," she apologized.

Removing his hat, the stranger replied, "You must be Señora Kendall."

Rachel gazed upward into a pair of clear blue eyes framed by black eyebrows and dark thick lashes. Taken back by his attractiveness, she stared openly at him. His hair was black as coal, with curls falling haphazardly over his forehead. When he smiled at her, his dark mustache curled slightly at the corners of his mouth.

"Are you Señora Kendall?" he repeated.

"No . . . no, I'm her sister, Rachel O'Brian," she answered, flustered.

He was finding her even more attractive than she had found him, and while appraising her beauty, he asked, "Miss . . . O'Brian?"

When she displayed her enticing smile, he became totally captivated. "Yes, it's Miss O'Brian."

"I'm your neighbor, William Granger," he informed her.

"Neighbor?" she asked puzzled.

"My property borders with Reynolds," he explained.

"I'm very happy to meet you, Mr. Granger."

"Not nearly as happy as I am to meet you, Señorita."

She looked at him inquisitively. "Your name is American but you. . ."

Interrupting, he explained, "My father was an American, but my mother was Spanish."

"Have you met my brother-in-law?" she asked.

"I was just talking to him out on the range. He kindly offered me an 'invitacion' for lunch and a cool drink. He said he'd join me shortly." Noticing her confusion, he tried to clarify, "All my life, I've heard more Spanish than English, and I have this habit of combining the two. 'Peródaname,' Señorita, if I confuse you, but if you plan to make southern Texas your 'domicilio,' then you should learn to speak Spanish. You will hear it spoken as often as your own language."

"So I've noticed. The majority of the ranch hands are Mexicans, but lucky for Josh, most of them can speak English. If you'll excuse me, Mr. Granger, I'll tell Maria that there'll be one more for lunch."

Touching her arm, he said, "You have plenty of time to inform the 'criada.' Stay and talk with me a few moments."

Sensing the sound of authority in his voice, Rachel

felt he was a man accustomed to having his orders obeyed.

At twenty-nine, William Granger was a very wealthy man, and expertly ran a ranch twice the size of John Reynolds'. In southern Texas he was a powerful figure of authority, and his orders were always unquestioningly followed.

"Your brother-in-law told me he was recently discharged from the cavalry. Did you live with him and your sister at Fort Craig?"

"Yes, I did," she answered.

"Then you must know Señor Reynolds. I understand he is now a lieutenant colonel in the cavalry. Very foolish man, Señor Reynolds."

Immediately jumping to his defense, she exclaimed, "John Reynolds is not a fool!"

"I didn't mean to imply that he was a 'necio' . . . a fool . . . I only meant, in my opinion, he is very foolish not to live on his hacienda."

Thinking about the lonely little grave on the hillside behind the house, Rachel answered, "He has his reasons, but maybe someday he'll find his way back home."

"When Señor Reynolds lived on his ranch, I was only around eighteen, and I used to follow him like a lost 'cachorro' . . . a puppy . . . I made him into some kind of a 'heróe.' His old friend, Zeke, I think was his name. Well he used to tell me these stories about all the exciting adventures they had shared together. I often dreamed of doing with my life, what Señor Reynolds had done with his. Ride away from my home and find adventures in the wilderness. But they were only the fantasies of a foolish 'nino.' "

"Did you know Carmelita?" she asked.

"Yes, I knew her! And if she had been my wife, I'd have followed her to Mexico and killed her with my bare hands!"

Noticing the hard cruelty in his eyes, Rachel instinctively took a few steps backward. Observing her reaction to his words his cruelty suddenly vanished, as he explained, "What she did to Señor Reynolds was unforgivable, but then perhaps you aren't aware of what happened."

"I know what happened," she replied softly.

"Not only did she cause the death of his son, but she was unfaithful! Marriage vows should never be broken! Do you agree, Señorita?"

She started to reply, but the front door unexpectedly opened as Deborah stepped out onto the veranda. Deborah's intrusion prevented Rachel from answering his question, and in a matter of moments, she had completely forgotten that it had ever been asked.

Zeke knocked loudly on the colonel's door, but without waiting for a reply, he opened it and strode vigorously into the room.

"Ya wanted to see me?" he asked.

John was sitting behind his desk studying some papers, and glancing up at Zeke, he answered, "If you have the time I'd like to talk to you for a moment."

Pulling out the chair across from the colonel's desk, he inquired, "Anythin' wrong?"

"No, what I need to talk to you about has nothing to do with business."

Leaning back in the chair, Zeke questioned, "What's on yur mind, John?"

"Rachel," he answered simply.

Gruffly Zeke told him, "I ain't fur sure if we should discuss Miss Rachel."

With the barest trace of a smile on his face, John asked, "Why not?"

"I don't think you done right by that little gal!"

"And what do you think I should've done?"

"I don't think ya should've took advantage of her innocence, and her love fur ya!"

"Come on, Zeke," he began impatiently. "You're a man! You know how damned enticing she is. How much will-power do you think I have?"

"Well I reckon she did sorta throw herself at ya. But it was only cause she loved ya!"

"Loves me? I wonder, Zeke, if she really does."

Feeling a glint of hope for Rachel, Zeke replied promptly, "Of course she does!"

"But damn it, she's so young!"

"Hell, she's done turned nineteen. She's the right age fur marryin' and fur lovin'."

Sighing deeply, he answered, "And I'm forty-two."

"John," Zeke began, "ya set too great a store on the difference in your ages."

Rising from the chair, Zeke walked around the desk. Placing his hand on John's shoulder, he said, "Son, thar ain't no sure things in this here life."

When their eyes met, the love and affection between the two men was vividly apparent. "That's the first time you've ever called me son."

"Couldn't think no more of you if'n ya was my own son, and I'm goin' to tell ya what I'd tell my own son if'n I had one. Ya can spend the rest of yur days a-wonderin' if'n ya let yur chance fur some happiness go by, or ya can go after that little gal and enjoy what ever time ya got with her. Whether it be days or years, thar ain't noway of knowin' what tomorrow will bring. Ya gotta live fur today.''

He turned to go back to his chair, but glanced over at John as he added, ''I never did find a woman who would have an ornery cuss like myself, but now, in my old age, I kinda wish I had me a woman to share my last days with. And some grandkids to set on my lap and tell 'em some of my stories. Yep, I had my good times and I had my adventures, but now that I'm an old man, what do I have to show fur it? Nothin'! Not a damned thing!''

Returning to his chair and sitting back down, he continued, ''Ya can foller in my footsteps and someday find yurself a lonely old man, or ya can do somethin' 'bout gittin' out of that thar marriage yur in and marry up with Miss Rachel.'' Smiling paternally, he added, ''Sorta hope ya marry that little gal of ours. Maybe then I can git me them grandkids I'm a longin' fur.''

John was deeply and emotionally moved by what Zeke had said. He had never been more aware of how dearly he loved the old man, than he was at that moment. Smiling at him fondly, he replied, ''I promise you, Zeke, if Rachel and I get married, the very first thing we'll do is see about getting you that grandchild.''

''What happened to cause ya to change yur mind 'bout Miss Rachel?''

Slowly rolling himself a cigarette, he answered, ''I haven't changed my mind where our ages are concerned. My common sense tells me there's no way she can remain in love with a man twenty-three years older

275

than she . . . and she's also very young."

"That little gal loves ya, and I'd be willin' to bet my last hunk of chewin' tobaccy that she'll still be a lovin' ya twenty years from now."

After lighting his cigarette, John replied, "Hell, Zeke, I don't have any idea how long it'll take me to get out of my marriage to Carmelita. I'll have to contact a lawyer and start divorce proceedings, but first I'll have to go back to Mexico and see if I can find Carmelita. I don't even know if she's still alive. And with the Apache situation the way it is, I can't possibly leave the fort. Hell, I don't know how long it'll be before I can tend to any of this business. How can I ask Rachel to wait for me when it may be years before I'm free?"

"Don't ask her to wait. Let her make the decision fur herself. Just let her know yur goin' to git out of that thar marriage to Carmelita." Smiling cheerfully, he added, "And let her know ya love her, ya ornery jackass!"

John reached into the drawer in his desk and pulled out an envelope. Handing it to Zeke, he asked, "Will you take this to Rachel for me?"

"Ya mean to tell me ya done got a letter writ? If'n ya already knowed ya was goin' to send this here letter, why'd ya ask me fur my opinion?"

"Because I hadn't made up my mind whether to send it or not, and I value your opinion very highly."

"I'm gonna ask ya again, John. Why'd ya change yur mind 'bout Miss Rachel?"

"It's not a matter of changing my mind. I still have the same doubts and fears."

"Ya still ain't answered my question," Zeke insisted.

"All right!" he shouted severely. "I want her, damn

276

it! Maybe it's wrong, but that's how I feel! And I never knew how much I wanted her until I lost her."

"Ain't got no one to blame but yurself fur a-losin' her, but I can understand why ya done what ya did. Hell, in yur place, I reckon I'd done the same thing. I'll take this here letter to her, but I'm a-hopin' it ain't too late and she was smart enough not to take my advice."

"What was that?" he asked.

"I told her to git herself married up to someone else, and have some younguns."

Smiling bitterly, John answered, "That's the same advice I gave her."

William Granger governed his hacienda with a hard, firm hand, and his vaqueros regarded him with respect and loyalty. He was more a true aristocrat than Rachel's father could ever have been, and he ruled majestically over his kingdom. His word was law, and his orders were indisputable. That he could ever be denied anything he wanted was incomprehensible to him, and he wanted Rachel!

For years he'd been searching for the right woman to become his wife, the mother of his children, and the mistress of his home. Now he had firmly made up his mind that Rachel would become that woman. To William Granger, love was unimportant. He believed love would come slowly and gracefully after marriage. Importantly, she had all the qualities he demanded in a wife. She was beautiful, desirable, and a lady.

For two months, he assiduously and extravagantly courted Rachel. He lavished her with gifts and charming compliments. He was determined to marry Rachel, and to marry her soon! On the same evening Zeke was to leave Fort Craig, William Granger decided the time had come to propose holy matrimony to the beautiful Rachel O'Brian.

The night was exceedingly warm, but a pleasant breeze was blowing refreshingly across the patio. William and Rachel stood beside the wrought iron railing overlooking Pedro's colorful flower garden. William was finding Rachel extremely lovely and desirable. She was dressed in a simple cream-colored gown. Her long auburn hair was pulled back from her face by the two large pearl-adorned combs he had given her the day before.

Rachel instinctively knew he was going to propose, and she knew she would accept. She was determined to make a life for herself without John Reynolds. She couldn't wait forever for a man who would never come back to her, and she didn't want to persistently remain dependent on Josh's charity for her support. That she didn't love William Granger mattered none at all! She believed she'd never love any man but John Reynolds!

"Señorita," he began, "I realize we haven't known each other very long, but from the first day I met you, I think I knew this night was inevitable."

"Why is this night special, William?" she asked, although she already knew the reason.

Taking her hand into his, he replied, "Because tonight I have a question of great 'importancia' to ask. For years, Señorita, I have searched for a woman like you to share my life. A woman who is beautiful, and a true lady in every sense of the word. . . . Rachel, will you do me the honor of becoming my wife?"

Instead of giving him an answer, she pulled her hand away from his as she turned and stared vacantly into the surrounding darkness of the night. A true lady, he had said. What he really means, she thought, is a lady of virtue. I have to tell him the truth. I can't give him love, but I can give him honesty!

She turned to face him. He was smiling, and for a fleeting moment, she sensed a certain coldness in his eyes. "There's something I must tell you, William, and then if you still want me to marry you, I will."

"But I'm not a priest, Señorita. Perhaps it would be best not to tell me your 'confesíon.' "

"It isn't a confession, only the truth." Rachel wasn't ashamed of her relationship with John Reynolds, and if she had it to do again, she knew she'd happily live those few months with him all over again.

Rachel stood tall and raised her head majestically as she told him, "I was involved with another man." As she said the words, John Reynolds' face flashed vividly across her mind. She could clearly see his steel gray eyes, and his boyish crooked grin that always tore at her heart. She could almost hear once again his deep and strong voice. She achingly remembered the comfort of being held in his arms, and the wonderful passion he could so easily awaken within her.

"Are you telling me that you have been intimate with another man?" he asked.

Glancing away from him, she answered simply, "Yes."

William Granger demanded perfection! Not only from his vaqueros and his servants, but also from himself. Finding out his future bride would not be perfect was a bitter disappointment to him, but somehow he would learn to forgive her. The Señorita was a very beautiful woman, and her presence would not only grace his home, but she would give him many tall and handsome sons.

Rachel could hear no passion or warmth in his voice, as he spoke to her with demanding authority, "I will not lie to you and tell you it doesn't matter, because it does! All men want their wives to be a virgin on her wedding night, but what happened in your past is done and over with. We shall leave it where it belongs . . . in the past. The subject will not be brought up again!"

Slowly he moved toward her and drew her into his arms. When his lips came down on hers, she waited for a tingling sensation to arouse her senses, but she could feel nothing. As his arms tightened around her and he forced her body close to his, she realized even though the kiss had left her cold, it was arousing his desire and passion.

When he released her, he said briskly, "We will be married very soon, Señorita. I see no reason for us to wait. One week from tonight, you will become Señora Granger. We will be married in my home, and you shall wear my mother's wedding gown."

Rachel's Irish temper almost flared out of control. She had the impulse to tell him to take himself, and his arrogance, back to his hacienda and stay there, but quickly she suppressed her anger. Let him make the wedding plans! She didn't care! Besides, the sooner she was married, the sooner she could start a new life. . . . Maybe then she could somehow push John's memory so far back into the recesses of her mind, that he'd cease being the very center of her heart and soul!

The wedding took place in William Granger's hacienda. Similar to John Reynolds' home, it was white adobe with a red tile roof, but there the resemblance ended.

Rachel's new home was built like a fortress with a large fountain in the center of the courtyard. It was surrounded by a radiant flower garden of bright and multiple colors. The bedrooms situated upstairs were completely separated from the lower floor, accessible only by one of the flights of stairs located on the outside, one in each corner of the hacienda.

They were married in the spacious and beautiful parlor inside the Spanish hacienda. The room was so large, that in order to comfortably heat it, there was a fireplace at each end of the room. The furniture was covered in wine colored velvet, and the tables were all of a dark mahogany wood. An enormous crystal chandelier hung from the ceiling in the center of the room.

During the ceremony, the patio doors were left open and a constant breeze kept the lace curtains over the glass doors blowing gently back and forth. Rachel fixed her gaze on these curtains, and willed herself to become hypnotized by the swaying fabric. She refused to listen to the marriage ceremony, or to look at the man standing beside her. When it came time for her to speak the marriage vows, the priest had to ask her twice to please repeat them. She forced herself to look away from the hypnotic swaying of the curtains, and unconsciously, she spoke the words that made her Señora Granger.

There had been no guests invited to the wedding, except for Deborah and Josh. William Granger had a few friends he considered to be his equals, but they all lived too far away to attend his wedding on such short notice. The house servants were allowed to stand in the entrance to the parlor and watch the services. The vaqueros and their families, who lived in adobe huts outside the hacienda, were enjoying a lively celebration of their own in the large courtyard. The 'patron' had promised them that after the ceremony he would introduce them to his new bride.

When he proudly led Rachel through the doors leading out into the courtyard, the loud and happy celebration ceased abruptly. William Granger could hear the intakes of breath as his people looked upon his beautiful wife.

The wedding gown Rachel wore was made of Spanish lace. It fit high around her long slender neck, followed by a transparent bodice. Tiny pearls ran from the shoulders to the V-shape in the front of the white gown. It had long fitted sleeves with miniature pearl buttons at each wrist. Small pearls adorned the entire skirt. A flowing veil of lace cascaded down her back, held in place by a mantilla and two pearl combs.

"It is with great pride," William began, "that I present to you, Señora Granger."

As the crowd began to cheer loudly, he whispered to Rachel, "Smile for them. Brides are supposed to be happy."

Obeying him, she forced herself to smile at the people who were shouting praises of the 'patron's' lovely bride.

"And now, my darling," he said quietly but firmly, "you shall retire to our bedchamber and prepare to consummate our marriage."

Trying to keep her voice low, she replied angrily, "No! I haven't even had a glass of wine yet, or a chance to speak with my sister."

The eyes glaring at her were ice-cold. "My orders

are always obeyed! Do not cross me Señora! We will have wine together in the 'soledad' of our room. If you insist on speaking with your sister, then she can help you prepare for bed instead of your servant girl."

Using all the will-power she possessed, Rachel controlled her anger and moved over to Deborah. "Will you come to my room with me?" she asked.

"Yes, of course," Deborah answered.

Together the climbed the long flight of steps leading up to the bedchamber on the upper floor. Embarrassed, Rachel could hear the laughter and sly gestures of the vaqueros as she neared their 'patron's' bedchamber. Hastily she opened the door, and Deborah followed her inside, closing the door quickly behind them.

The spacious and elegant bedroom took Deborah's breath away. In the center of the room stood a huge four-poster bed sitting on a raised step. The royal blue spread perfectly matched the drapes. The middle of the highly polished floor was covered with a pale blue floral print rug. The furniture was massive and made in dark wood. In front of the fireplace were two chairs with a long table placed between them. A huge wardrobe ran the entire length of one wall. In one corner was a dressing table with a large gold-framed mirror.

"Oh, the room is beautiful!" Deborah exclaimed.

But Rachel was not impressed by the magnificent bedroom, her thoughts were on the tiny and plain bedroom in the back of Colonel Reynolds' office.

Walking toward her, Deborah asked, "Do you want me to help you undress?"

Removing the mantilla and combs from her hair, she answered bitterly, "Yes, you may as well, since I've been ordered to prepare myself to consummate our marriage."

Looking at her sister incredulously, Deborah replied, "Rachel, must you be so crude?"

"When are you going to stop being the perfect southern lady?" Rachel began impatiently. "Don't you realize our mother's world is dead? It died the day Lee surrendered to Grant!"

Nimbly unfastening the tiny buttons at the back of her dress, Deborah sighed, "Sometimes I can't understand you at all, Rachel. You are married to a wealthy and handsome man, who is also a true gentleman, and yet you have the audacity to sound so bitter."

Helping her to remove the gown, Rachel replied, "A gentleman indeed! Your husband is more a gentleman than mine could ever hope to be! You should've heard the way he talked to me! He ordered me to come up here and . . . and wait for him!"

Placing the gown carefully across one of the chairs, Deborah told her, "That, I'm afraid, is one of the unpleasant aspects of marriage. I'll never understand why men can find it so enjoyable."

"It's an act of commitment, and if two people really love each other, it is enjoyable!" Unable to suppress her tears any longer, Rachel dashed across the room and flung herself down on the bed. "I wish I didn't love him!" she sobbed.

Deborah hastened to the bed and sat beside Rachel. Patting her sister gently on the shoulder, she asked, "Why should loving your husband upset you?"

Deborah was immediately sympathetic to the pain in her sister's eyes as she raised up on the bed to look at her. "My husband! I don't love William! I'll never love him! I'll never love any man but John!"

"Oh Rachel," Deborah began reproachfully. "How can you still be in love with a man twenty-three years older than you, when you have someone like William Granger? Colonel Reynolds was never the right man for you. Not only was he too old for you, but he was also married! He only used you to satisfy his own lust!"

Noticing the quick anger flashing into Rachel's eyes, Deborah added, "Don't mistake what I am saying. I think the man actually cared about you, and he was deeply concerned about your future . . . but, Rachel, men have absolutely no conscience where. . ." Lowering her voice, she continued, "Where sex is concerned."

Rachel's lips curled very slightly with a smile. "You sound so much like Mama. If she were here, she'd probably have said the same thing and in the same way." Reaching for her sister's hand, she added, "Deb, do you think about Mama very often?"

"Yes, I do, and I think about Papa and our brothers."

"So do I. I miss them so much! I wonder how our lives would've been, if there had never been a war. I'd never have met John or William." Squeezing Deborah's hand affectionately, she added, "And you'd never have met Josh or Edward. . . . Are you still in love with Edward?"

Jerking her hand away, she stammered, "What . . . whatever do you mean?"

"Don't bother to deny it, Deb. I know how you felt about Edward, and I also know why you married Josh. You married him because you knew you could never have Edward. Do you still love him?"

"I don't know," she answered truthfully. "My

memories of him keep fading more and more with the passing of time."

"Do you love Josh?"

"I'm very fond of him and, Rachel, the same will be true for you. As time passes your memories of Colonel Reynolds will fade, and you will find yourself growing fonder of William."

"I hope you are right, and my memories will fade. Perhaps in time I can even learn to care for William. But Deborah, I'll love John Reynolds until the day I die!"

When the door suddenly swung open, Rachel looked up guiltily to see William glaring at her with ice-cold eyes. "The bedroom door is very thin, Señora, and conversations can easily be overheard."

Hastily Rachel reached for the dressing gown that had been placed on the bed. Slipping it on over her petticoat, she replied, "I very much resent your listening in on my private conversation."

Walking further into the room, he ignored Rachel entirely as he said stiffly, "Señora Kendall, your husband is waiting for you downstairs."

Feeling embarrassed by the unpleasant scene, Deborah rose from the bed. "Goodnight, Rachel." Swiftly she kissed her sister lightly on the cheek.

"Goodnight, Deb. I'll see you tomorrow when I come over to pick up the rest of my things."

Glancing timidly at William, Deborah said softly, "Goodnight, Mr. Granger."

With her cheeks still flushed, she hurried from the room and closed the door behind her.

"Do you still wish some wine, Señora?" he asked formally. "I will order a 'sìrviente' to bring a bottle of my finest wine up to the room."

"No, thank you," she answered, but unable to forget her anger, she asked him sternly, "why did you listen in on my conversation!"

"Señora, I do as I please in my own home!" he said harshly.

"Am I to have no privacy in this marriage?"

Slowly removing his jacket, he replied, "You can have all the privacy you wish . . . from anyone except me!"

"I'm not your slave! I am your wife!" she demanded.

"Slave?" he questioned. "But, of course, you must know all about slaves being that your father once owned over a hundred of them. No Señora, you are not my slave."

Placing his jacket on the chair, he moved toward her. "Do not mistake your place in my home. You are its mistress, and you will be treated with respect. But, I think it is time that we come to an understanding."

He stopped directly in front of her, and unwaveringly, she looked him in the eyes. She would not be cowed by this stranger, who ironically was also her husband.

"Because my father was an American, you are mistaking me for a 'gringo' and you expect me to act as one. I never will, Señora. I know very little of your culture. My mother's father raised my father as though he were his own son. When my father was seven years old his parents were killed by Mexican 'bandidos'. My grandfather brought him to this house. As time passed, and there were no sons of his own, my father became the son he never had."

Turning from her, he crossed over to the fireplace. He looked up at the two large portraits of his parents hanging above the mantle. "My father was never taught your American culture. He was raised to be Spanish, and to someday take his rightful place as the 'patron' of this ranch. It was always unquestioningly understood that he would marry my mother."

Looking back at her, he continued, "The house servants are yours to command as you wish. If they displease you, you have the right to question them or to reprimand them."

Swiftly he moved to her and put his hands firmly on her shoulders. "But never, Señora, do you demand anything from me or question what I do! Obey me, Rachel! Do not force me to punish you! My punishments can be very severe. Do not be foolish Señora, and try my patience!"

"Are you my husband, or my Lord and Master?" she asked with scorn.

Tightening his grip, he answered harshly, "I am all three, Señora."

Finding herself incapable of looking into those unfeeling eyes any longer, she lowered her gaze.

"Ah . . . I see you are learning very quickly, Señora. That is very fortunate for you."

Arrogantly, she raised her eyes and glared at him. Forcefully she pushed his hands away. "You will never intimidate me, William! I am as proud of my heritage, as you are of yours! I am Irish, and we do not frighten easily!" But then, impulsively, she cried out to him, "My God, have you no compassion? Are you incapable of human emotion?"

Instantly he reached out, jerking her to him. "Yes, I

288

have compassion and feelings, Señora! I want to be gentle with you, and if you give me what I demand, then I in turn will treat you with respect and kindness.''

"What exactly do you demand of me?'' she asked, trying to hide the pain she was suffering from his powerful grip.

"Obey me, and honor me! Then perhaps in time, we can learn to love one another.''

"You mean you want me to be humble and meek!''

"But to no one but me, Señora! You will never humble yourself before anyone else but your husband. You are Señora Granger. I demand that you live proudly and arrogantly! Is what I ask too much for a 'gringa'? Your American men spoil their wives. A woman should know her place, and keep it!''

As he relaxed his tight hold on her, she answered honestly, "I will try William, but I have a lot of pride and a terrible temper.''

"I do not want to take away your pride or your temper. I admire your Irish heritage. Just don't use it on me!''

Unexpectedly, he swerved, took a few steps then turned back to face her. "Now, Señora, we have another matter that we must discuss . . . Señor Reynolds!''

Hearing his name made Rachel instinctively catch her breath, as she looked apprehensively at her husband.

"Never again will you tell anyone that you love him! You are my wife, and your loyalties lie with me! The night I proposed, I told you that your past would remain where it belonged, but you have already brought it into our marriage! I want to trust you, Señora, but I find it difficult to trust a woman who speaks of loving another man on her wedding night. Señor Reynolds is a part of your past, and that part of your life is now over! If ever I hear you say again, that you love him. . ." His eyes shone with cruelty, as he shouted hoarsely, "I will remove my belt."

He removed the thick leather belt from around his waist, and holding it securely in his hand, he continued, "And I will beat you, Señora! You have been warned! No more will be said on the subject!" Abruptly he demanded, "Take off your clothes. I want to see if you're as beautiful as I have imagined you to be."

Shocked by all he had said, Rachel could only stand immobile and stare at him flabbergasted.

"Did you not hear me, Señora?" he asked.

Rachel wanted desperately to fall across the bed and cry, but she realized there was no longer a place left in her life for tears. The days of crying childishly, when she didn't get what she wanted, were now completely gone.

As he began walking steadily toward her, she had no idea what to expect from him, but bravely she held her head high and stared unflinchingly into his eyes.

Tenderly he pulled her into his arms pressing his lips to hers. Hesitantly, she wrapped her arms around his neck, relaxing her body as he drew her closer to him. Returning his kiss, she tried desperately, but unsuccessfully, to respond to him.

Releasing her, he began to remove her clothing. When she finally stood before him completely nude, he caught his breath with passion. "Si, Señora, you are as beautiful as I knew you would be."

His eyes traveled over her high firm breasts, her

small waist, and down her feminine hips. "You make me proud to have you for my 'esposa' . . . my wife," he whispered.

Impatiently, he began taking off his own clothes. Hastily Rachel climbed into the huge bed and pulled the sheet over her to hide her nakedness. She closed her eyes tightly, refusing to look at her husband. Resolutely she tried to push the image of John Reynolds from her mind. If she could somehow forget him, if only for one moment, then perhaps she could actually respond to her husband.

Lying beside her, William grabbed the edge of the sheet jerking it from her. "Do not hide yourself from me, Rachel!" Greedily, he covered her mouth with his as his hand began exploring her body intimately. Instinctively, Rachel did all the things she knew were expected of her. She returned his kisses, arched her body toward his, and moaned deeply in her throat, but not once did he spark even a small kindle of flame within her.

Rachel was relieved when he finally lowered his body over hers, because she knew soon it would thankfully be over. . . . Oh John, she thought, it should be you! My wedding night should've been with you. I love you, I'll always love you!

As William Granger was consummating their marriage, his young bride was already unfaithful to him, in her mind and in her heart!

Rachel was basically an enthusiastic and vibrant person. But she was feeling none of her usual fervor or eagerness as she walked languidly toward the buckboard in front of John Reynolds' home. After checking to see that all her belongings had been packed, she turned in the direction of the bunkhouse to inform the driver that she was ready to leave. Unexpectedly, she noticed a lone rider coming slowly up the narrow lane. Suddenly, she recognized the rider to be Zeke, and her enthusiasm quickly reappeared as she ran joyfully to greet him.

Smiling happily from ear to ear, Zeke hastily dismounted from his horse. Opening his arms, he vigorously gathered her into his warm embrace. Hugging her tightly, he said cheerfully, "Miss Rachel, I don't never realize how much I miss ya, 'til I set my old eyes on ya again."

Rachel tried not to cry, but being held in the arms of the old man that she loved so much, caused her tears to overflow. Resting her face next to the familiar feel of buckskin, she cried openly.

"Is somethin' wrong!" he asked. "Is it Miss Deborah, or Josh?"

Slowly and reluctantly, she stepped back from the comfort of his embrace, and wiping at her tears, she answered, "No, everyone is fine. There's nothing wrong." With determination she controlled her emotions. It was too late for tears.

"Then how come yur a-cryin'?" he questioned.

"Oh Zeke, I'm just happy to see you, that's all. You know how easily I cry."

"Ya had me worried thar fur a moment. Yur sure yur all right?" he asked.

"Of course, I'm just fine." Forcing happiness into her voice, she continued, "The most wonderful thing has happened."

Instantly sensing a feeling of foreboding, he inquired, "What's that, Miss Rachel?"

"I'm married, Zeke. William Granger and I were married last night," she answered, while compelling herself to smile.

Feebly, Zeke attempted to conceal the disappointment on his face as he mumbled, "I'm real happy fur ya."

"You don't look or sound very happy. Great guns and little switches! Isn't that what you wanted me to do?"

"Yes'm it was, and it is the best thing fur ya, if'n ya love yur husband. Do ya?"

Her first impulse was to lie to him, but she knew she'd never be able to fool the old mountaineer. Not with his extraordinary insight. Truthfully, she blurted out to him, "I'll never love any man but John!"

Angrily, he asked her, "Then why in the hell did ya marry up with William Granger?"

It was the first time the old man had ever raised his voice to her, and Rachel could only stare at him with astonishment.

"Answer me, gal!" he ordered furiously.

Placing her hands on her hips, she met his hostile stare with one of her own. "What was I supposed to do? Wait the rest of my life for a man who doesn't want me, and live off Josh's charity indefinitely?"

"Ya could've waited 'til ya fell in love!"

"Then I'd have been waiting forever! Because I'll never love any man but John!"

"I reckon I can understand why ya done what ya did, but Miss Rachel, I never meant fur ya to marry a man ya didn't love."

Smiling at him fondly, she replied, "Well, it's done and now I'm married. I intend to make the best of it.

Zeke, what do you think of William!"

"I don't rightly know, ma'am. I ain't seen 'im in a long time, but what I can remember of 'im, he was a likable sort, but a might uppity at times."

"He still is! He's the most arrogant man I've ever met." With her eyes flashing indignantly, she added, "Do you know what he expects from his wife? Complete obedience!"

Chuckling, Zeke answered, "That's what ya git fur marryin' up with a Mexican. He may have 'im an American name, but he's still a Mexican just the same. A little obedience won't do you no harm anyhow. You ain't had no discipline since yur Paw died, and just look what it got ya. Ya got yurself all involved with John, then ya come a-runnin' down here, and fur all the wrong reasons ya marry the first man who comes along. A female always gits herself in a mess if she ain't got a man to look out fur her."

"You men!" she began perturbed. "You always stick together!" Abruptly changing the subject, she asked, "Zeke, how is John?"

Unconsciously, he reached toward his horse, rubbing his hand across the saddlebag holding the letter that would now go unread. "He's just fine."

"Does he think about me at all?" she asked pleadingly.

"I'm sure he does, Miss Rachel," he replied, looking away from the obvious pain in her eyes.

Noticing the concern on the old man's face, she asked curiously, "Zeke, why did you come to the ranch?"

He removed his hand from the saddlebag that was destined to remain unopened, and he settled quickly on a story. "I was in Mexico a-visitin' some friends of mine, and I just figgered I'd stop by on my way back to the fort."

Zeke dreaded breaking the news about Rachel to John Reynolds. When he arrived at the fort, and was informed that the colonel was out on an expedition with his troops, Zeke was almost relieved that he could put off the inevitable.

Anxiously, he waited at the fort for two days, but the colonel still hadn't returned. Tired of lingering, Zeke decided to ride into the small nearby town of El Rio and have a few drinks at the saloon.

Zeke was on his third drink, when the double doors of the saloon swung open, and glancing up he saw John Reynolds striding vigorously into the room. Seeing Zeke sitting alone at the rear table, he smiled broadly and called out to the bartender for a bottle and a glass.

Eagerly he approached Zeke's table, and pulling out a chair, he said cheerfully, "Glad to see you made it back okay."

"How did you know whar to find me?" he drawled.

"Major Hartly said you came into town. I'm sorry I wasn't at the fort when you got back."

"Don't matter none," he muttered.

Pouring himself a drink, John asked expectantly, "Did she send back a letter?"

"Nope," Zeke answered bluntly.

"No? . . . Well did she send a message?"

Zeke took a large and much needed drink, before he replied, "John, thar's somethin' I gotta tell ya."

"Damn it, Zeke!" he said impatiently. "Didn't you give her the letter?"

"Nope, I never gave it to her. I got it right here in my pocket." Slowly he pulled out the unopened envelope and placed it on the table between them.

John's hand tightened on his glass as he asked fuming, "Why didn't you give her my letter, Zeke?"

"Thar just ain't no easy way to tell ya this."

"Just say it, for God's sake!" he ordered harshly.

Looking John straight in the eyes, he answered clearly, "Rachel is married to William Granger."

During the twenty-one years that Zeke had known John Reynolds, only twice had he been a witness to the man's pain and anguish, when he had lost his infant son . . . and now!

"My God!" he whispered hoarsely.

Mumbling, Zeke replied, "I'm sorry."

Quickly John raised his glass to his lips and emptied the contents. Lowering the glass to the table, he stared at it for a few moments with his head bowed and his shoulders slumped. Then raising his head, he looked across the table at Zeke. His pain and anguish had been supplanted by anger. "I was right all along! She's too damned young to know what in the hell she wants out of life!"

"She's too young to know how to handle her life, but she ain't too young to know what she wants out of life."

Refilling his glass, John answered, "Obviously she wants William Granger!"

"Nope, she ain't a-wantin' 'im."

"She married him, didn't she?" he asked harshly.

"Yep, but don't make no difference. She don't want 'im, and she don't love 'im."

"Then why in the hell did she marry him?"

"Why do you reckon?" Zeke asked irritably.

"A woman usually marries a man because she loves him!"

"Usually, but not always. Sometimes she marries 'im cause the man she loves done sent her away from 'im and she don't want to keep livin' off the charity of her relatives. And sometimes, I reckon she just marries fur spite. But don't matter none. She's married and that's the end of it. Ya lost her, and ya ain't got no one to blame but yurself."

"You're right about one thing, Zeke! That's the end of it!" Angrily, he picked up the envelope, tearing it and the unread letter into pieces.

"John, I know it ain't none of my business, and I wouldn't blame ya none fur not answerin' me, but just what did ya say in that letter?"

Bitterly, he answered, "As you would put it, Zeke, I spilled my guts out to her!" He took another drink, then leaned back in his chair and said calmly, "William Granger. Well, at least she married good. He's quite a powerful figure in southern Texas, and also in part of Mexico. Señora Granger . . . I'm sure she enjoys living the aristocratic life once again."

"Wouldn't know nothin' 'bout that, but she did tell me she was goin' to try and make the best of her marriage."

"Rachel is a survivor, Zeke. She'll do just fine, and in time, she'll probably even fall in love with her husband, if she isn't already."

As he rose abruptly from his chair, Zeke asked, "Whar ya goin'?"

Looking down at him, he replied, "Where do you think?"

"You're goin' to see that Mexican gal whose always

a-throwin' herself at ya whenever yur in town, ain't ya?"

"And just what in the hell is wrong with that? You're beginning to sound worse than a nagging old woman."

"Not nary a thing wrong with it. If'n I wasn't so old I'd be fur findin' me a gal myself. Only three things I know of that a man cain't do without. A stiff drink, a full belly, and a woman, but not necessarily in that thar order."

"Well, I'll have to skip part of it, because I'm not hungry."

Rising from his chair, Zeke answered, "Neither am I. So I reckon I'll just mosey on back to the fort. My old age is a-catchin' up with me. Reckon I'll just go on to bed, turn my toes up, and get me some good ole shut-eye."

As Zeke's sluggish steps took him nearer to the door, John could hear the old man muttering, "After all . . . tomorrow's another day."

Chapter Eight

Rachel's determination to somehow overcome the loss of John Reynolds was totally futile. As her marriage slowly grew into weeks, and then into months, she plunged steadily deeper and deeper into a bottomless pit of depression.

Lacking a normal and healthy appetite caused the slim woman to become pathetically thin. Her husband, seriously concerned over his wife's health, ordered all sorts of tempting dishes to be served, but Rachel could only pick at the delicious meals the cook had so meticulously prepared.

William Granger tried everything he could possibly think of to cheer up his despondent wife. He presented her with expensive jewelry, but she would only smile sadly and thank him politely. He bought her a beautiful palomino mare and a Spanish saddle. Though she rode the horse often, it did nothing to lift her spirits, much to his great disappointment.

Following a long, grave conversation with his sister-in-law, he sent Deborah to his wife with the hopes that she would have the capacity and the understanding to help his young bride with her severe melancholy.

But when Deborah brought up the subject to Rachel, all she could get out of her were seven simple words. "I don't want to live without him!" Realizing whom she meant, Deborah knew there was no way she could tell William the source of Rachel's depression. She wisely informed him that she was unable to find the reason for her sister's sorrow.

William Granger was not a patient man, and he finally became fed up with his wife's gloomy disposition. Completely at a loss as to what to do for her, he'd storm irritably around the house taking his frustrations out on the servants. Finally, in desperation, he sent for the doctor, deciding Rachel's condition was physical instead of emotional. When the doctor told him what Rachel had already suspected, that she was pregnant, he became more concerned than ever over his wife's poor condition.

Finding out for certain that she was going to have a child did nothing to lift Rachel's spirits. It wasn't so much that she didn't want a baby; she wanted it to be John Reynolds'.

Immediately after the doctor left the hacienda, William headed straight for his wife. Quietly he entered their bedchamber, closing the door behind him. Rachel lay across the huge bed, and cautiously he walked over to her.

Sitting on the edge of the bed, he said gently, "The doctor informed me of your condition. You have made me very happy."

Slowly she rolled over and looked up at her husband. The empty expression in her eyes disturbed him. "Surely now, Señora, you will start taking care of your health."

"And if I don't?" she rebelled. "Are you going to beat me with your belt?"

"I have never laid a hand on you!" he reminded angrily.

"No, but your threats continuously hang over me."

"The threat, Señora, still holds! You will not speak of loving another man!"

Suddenly he reached for her, pulling her to him roughly. "Is this why you are so 'pesarosa,' Señora? Are you grieving for Señor Reynolds? No, don't answer my question! I don't want to hear your answer! I may become so angry that I will forget you are carrying my son!"

Abruptly he released his hold and she fell limply back onto the bed. Impatiently, he pleaded, "For the child's sake, will you please take care of yourself?"

"I wish no harm to the child, William, and I'll try, but I feel as though I have lost all will to survive." For the first time in weeks, he saw a hopeful expression on her face as she cried, "Surely someday I'll find a reason to live again!"

Experiencing a compassion he rarely felt, William gathered the young woman into his arms and held her tenderly as she cried dramatically and childishly.

Rachel did try to improve her health, but it was all in vain; and as her pregnancy progressed, her will to survive continued to deteriorate. Once again William sent for Deborah.

Deborah hadn't seen Rachel for weeks, and when she caught her first glimpse of her sister, she was shocked. Rachel was sitting in a large overstuffed chair, staring silently into the fireplace. Deborah was immediately appalled by her loss of weight, but as Rachel glanced toward her, Deborah was more startled by the vacancy in her sister's expression.

Quickly she crossed over to Rachel, and knelt in front of the chair. Clutching the thin hands that were folded in her sister's lap, she cried, "Oh, honey. I was so wrong. I'm sorry!" Placing her head on Rachel's knees, she sobbed heavily.

Tenderly, Rachel smoothed Deborah's hair as she asked softly, "Why are you sorry, Deb? You've done nothing."

With tears streaming from her eyes, she looked up into Rachel's pale, drawn face. "I was so wrong! We were both wrong!"

"What are you talking about?" she questioned.

"Colonel Reynolds and I. We were wrong! We both thought you weren't really in love with him."

"It makes no difference," she sighed. "What you believed, what John believed, or even what I believed. It just isn't important anymore."

"But you're important! You can't give up like this!"

"Why not? Give me one reason why not."

"I can give you more than one reason. For your baby's sake, for my sake, and also for William's. We all need you!"

Deborah begged and pleaded with her sister, but her words fell uselessly on unhearing ears. Desperately Deborah was afraid that she would lose her sister if someone couldn't miraculously break through her malaise. She would have liked to send for John Reynolds, unaware that was Rachel's secret hope, but Deborah knew William would never agree. But there was someone else who could possibly help Rachel! Deborah hurried to find William. She would tell him that he must immediately send a wire to Fort Craig!

Neither Deborah nor William would ever learn what was said between Zeke and Rachel in the privacy of her room. Nervously they had both paced back and forth in the courtyard, periodically glancing up at the closed door to Rachel's bedchamber. A few times they'd heard Rachel's heartbreaking sobs. Hearing his wife's anguish, William had started to go up to them, but Deborah had stopped him by saying, "Before she can get well, she'll have to cry."

When at last the door was opened, they were suprised to look up and see Rachel coming out of the room with Zeke. Happily, they noticed, she was smiling.

For the first time in weeks, Rachel had dinner in the elegant dining room. When she stared down at her food, Zeke cleared his throat, and glancing up at him, she saw how he was glaring at her. Responding in kind, she started to eat her dinner, and didn't stop until she had determinedly eaten every last bite.

Rachel's encounter with Zeke had tired her, and when dinner was over, she excused herself to return to her bedchamber. The moment she left the dining room, Deborah turned to Zeke and inquired, "How in the world did you do it? The change in her is like a miracle."

"Weren't no miracle, ma'am. I just got her good and mad, that's all. Ain't nothin' that little gal enjoys better than a good fight. It'll put life into her everytime. I guarantee it!"

"Oh Zeke, there had to be more to it than that," Deborah insisted.

"Thar is more to it than that. When she's a-fightin' and a-flashin' that Irish temper 'a' hers, it's gotta be with someone she loves, who loves her. It don't matter none how mad she gets at me, she knows how much I care and sooner or later she's goin' to reach out fur me. And that's what she done. She was just needin' a life line and I throwed it out to her."

"I'm sure what you say is true, but there had to be something else. Why, she seems almost happy," Deborah replied.

"I wouldn't say she was happy, but she's got her spunk back, and her spirit."

"You did more than argue with her, didn't you? Somehow you gave her back the will to survive. You must've told her something!"

"Maybe so, ma'am, but I reckon that's somethin' no one will ever know, 'cept fur me and her. Besides, Miss Deborah, she never lost any will to survive. She was just mostly a-poutin'. What she really needed was a good whuppin', and if she weren't with child, that's what I'd have gave her."

"Zeke," William began, "I would like to show you my gratitude by paying you fully for your trouble."

Looking toward the man sitting at the head of the long formal dining table, Zeke stated, "I don't want no money fur what I done. Anytime Miss Rachel needs me, ya just send fur me and I'll be here!"

"For some reason, sir, you are obviously a good influence on my wife. Could I possibly persuade you to stay on until after the child is born?"

"Don't worry none, Mr. Granger. She's goin' to

304

take care of herself now, and have a fine healthy baby. Tomorrow I gotta be leavin' fur the fort. The Apache situation ain't too good right now. I reckon I shouldn't have left the fort as it was, but when I told the Colonel 'bout that thar message from ya, he sent me a packin' mighty quick.''

"Colonel Reynolds?" William questioned stiffly.

While belching rudely, Zeke confirmed, "Yep."

On the second of August 1869, William Granger's son, and heir, was born. He was a small but healthy baby, and he made his debut into the world screaming at the top of his lungs. Deborah, assisting the doctor with the delivery, cradled her nephew lovingly in her arms and laughingly told him, "You have inherited the O'Brian temper."

After the birth of her child, Rachel was exhausted and fell immediately into a blissful sleep. A few hours later when she awakened, it was to find Deborah sitting beside her bed.

"The baby?" Rachel asked.

"He's just fine! Oh Rachel, he's so beautiful! And you should see William." Laughing happily, she added, "Why he's strutting around like a rooster in a barnyard."

"If the baby had been a girl, he probably would've drowned it!" she replied bitterly.

"Rachel, you shouldn't say such horrid things! William is a fine man! And all men want their firstborn to be a son!"

Suddenly Deborah reached for her sister's hand, and her eyes were shining enviously as she cried, "Oh Rachel, you are so fortunate! What I wouldn't give to have a baby!''

"I never knew you wanted a child," Rachel answered, surprised.

"Rachel, I love you dearly, but all your life your thoughts have seldom been on anyone but yourself. Naturally, you have no idea how badly I want a baby. You've never asked me, and you've never given me a reason to discuss it with you. Honey, I know it's not that you lack compassion, because you don't.''

"I understand, Deb. As Zeke would say, I can't see no further than the end of my purty little nose.''

Deborah smiled. "That Zeke! He does have a way of saying it just like it is.''

Rachel studied her sister closely. "I haven't been so blind not to notice the change in you. You're becoming your old self again, and you're so much like Mama!''

"I wish she and Papa could've seen this day. Their first grandchild! They'd have been so proud! . . . I'll bring the baby to you.''

Deborah started to rise, but instantly Rachel reached for her arm. "No! I'll see him later.''

"Rachel! Don't you want to see your son?'' Deborah asked astoundedly.

"He's William's son, not mine,'' she replied glumly.

"Nonsense! He's yours as much as William's!'' Deborah declared. Then suddenly she pleaded, "Rachel, don't be such a ninny! Don't you realize God has given you a beautiful baby? You should be happy, darling, not depressed!''

Rising from the chair, Deborah hurried across the room, saying firmly, "You're going to see your son whether you want to or not!''

Rachel had endured the agonizing labor of childbirth, and she had painfully pushed her child into the world. She had heard his first cry before drifting into sleep, but she still found it difficult to think of herself as a mother.

Anxiously, she stared at the door Deborah had closed behind her. In a few moments, she knew that Deborah would enter the room with the child held in her arms. Rachel was petrified! Never in her life had she ever been so apprehensive and frightened. Dear God, what if I can't love my own son? I never wanted him! Not William's child!

When at last the door opened, Rachel caught her breath in astonishment. It wasn't Deborah, but William! Holding their son carefully in his arms, he walked into the room. "I'm glad you have finally awakened, Señora."

Rachel's eyes were immediately drawn to the small baby. She tried to catch a glimpse of him, but all she could see was a patch of black curly hair peeping over the blanket.

Slowly approaching her bed, William confessed humbly, " 'Gracias,' Señora. From the bottom of my heart, Rachel, I thank you for my son."

Glancing up into his eyes, she detected a compassion she had never before seen in them. She watched him as he bent over and gently placed their child in her arms.

Rachel's secret fears prevented her from relaxing, and she held her son rigidly in her arms. Thinking her stiffness was due to inexperience, William smiled as he sat on the bed beside her. "Don't be nervous, my darling. You are his mother. Just follow your natural instincts. They will lead you."

Carefully he peeled the blanket away from their son,

and for the first time Rachel looked down upon her child. Her fears instantly evaporated as they were replaced by a love so overpowering and so beautiful that she felt her heart would burst with it. Tenderly she kissed the small forehead, the pink cheeks, and then the puckered little mouth. Lovingly she caressed his tiny hand, and was astonished at how perfectly each little finger was formed.

"Oh, he's so beautiful!" she whispered.

"We have been blessed, Rachel," William replied softly.

Forcing herself to look away from the child, she turned her gaze to her husband, and with tears in her eyes, she exclaimed, "It's like a miracle!"

"The miracle of life," he answered, glancing down at the baby.

Hesitantly Rachel placed her hand over his. "You love him very much, don't you?"

"Of course, Señora. He is my son!"

"And mine!" she promptly informed him.

Smiling, he leaned over and kissed her lightly on the forehead. Rising from the bed, he compromised, "He is ours. I'll give you some time alone with him. I'll send your sister up for the baby in a few minutes. You need your rest, Señora."

Feeling bewildered, she watched him as he strode across the floor and quietly left the room. She found her husband to be a very strange man, and she was incapable of even beginning to understand him.

Dismissing him from her thoughts, she glanced back at her child. "Oh, Deb was right! I do have a reason to be happy! I have you, my beautiful, beautiful son!" With tears now flowing freely, she sobbed, "My little baby. . . . Oh John, I have my baby. . . . My precious baby!''

Rachel's child filled her secluded days with a happiness and a contentment she had never known before. Never had she dreamed that such a love could exist, as the love she had for her baby. The only flaw in her relationship with her son resulted from her inability to nurse him, which the doctor explained to her had probably been caused by her poor health through most of her pregnancy. So a wet nurse was promptly moved into the hacienda, and disappointedly, Rachel had no choice but to watch another woman feed her son.

When the child was four months old, William was away in Abilene on cattle business, and Rachel had been invited to Deborah and Josh's for dinner. Because the ride from the hacienda to the ranch was fairly long, Rachel informed the servants that she planned to spend the night with her sister.

Temporarily free of William's dictatorial restrictions, Rachel rebelliously unpacked a pair of pants and a shirt from the old cedar chest that had belonged to her mother. She ordered her palomino saddled, and enjoying her independence immensely, she galloped away from the hacienda.

Rachel paid very little attention to the horse that was tied to the hitching post in front of her sister's home. Easily she unmounted her own horse, and carelessly flung the reins over the post. She ran up the steps, hurried across the veranda, and swung open the door calling, ''Deb, I'm here!''

Not waiting for an answer, she strode into the parlor

and suddenly froze! She hadn't seen him in over a year, but the moment their eyes met, the months fell away as if time had never separated them. I love him, she thought, I still love him!

His eyes were exactly as she remembered them, and they were watching her with a deep intensity.

Finally Deborah broke the uncomfortable silence. "We didn't know Colonel Reynolds was going to pay us a visit. He just got here a few minutes ago."

Rachel was unable to tear her eyes from the man she so desperately loved, even to acknowledge her sister's presence. He was wearing buckskins, and Rachel once again found him more attractive in this frontier fashion, than in a uniform. When he smiled his crooked boyish grin, she had to force herself not to cry out to him that she still loved him.

"Hello, Rachel," he said.

Finding her voice at last, she answered shakily, "Hello, John."

Deborah crossed the room, and taking her husband's hand, she asked, "Josh, would you mind helping me with dinner for a moment?"

He looked at her with confusion. "Maria can manage just fine."

"Josh, please!" she told him firmly.

Finally understanding her motive, he stammered, "Oh! . . . Sure . . . sure Deb, I'll help you."

"Will you two please excuse us? Rachel, why don't you fix Colonel Reynolds a drink," Deborah suggested, as she and Josh left the room.

"Would you like a drink?" Rachel asked when they were alone.

"No, thank you," he replied.

Slowly Rachel unbuttoned her jacket as she inquired, "How is Zeke?"

"He's fine. He said if I were to see you to tell you 'hello' for him."

As she started to take off her jacket, he moved closer to assist her, but she stepped away from him. Removing the jacket herself, she placed it on a nearby chair. Walking over to the glowing fireplace, she asked, "How have you been, John?"

"All right, I guess. I understand you and William have a son."

Turning towards him, she exclaimed, "Oh John, you should see him. He's so beautiful."

"How could he be otherwise, having you for a mother. What did you name him?"

"He was named after his father."

"You did well for yourself, Rachel. Your husband is a powerful man in Texas, and highly respected. You must very happy with a husband like William and your son."

"Happy!" she blurted out impulsively. "Yes, my child brings me happiness, but he hasn't replaced what I lost!"

Puzzled, he questioned, "What do you mean?"

"What difference does it make? You don't care! You've never cared!"

In three quick strides he was beside her, and glaring down at her, he demanded, "What are you trying to say? What did you lose?"

"You!" she cried.

The anger in his eyes increased. "My God! You never quit, do you?"

"Quit? Yes, once I tried to quit, but Zeke wouldn't

allow it! But I'm sure he has told you all about it!''

"You know that old man better than that!" he chided.

At once she felt ashamed. "Of course, he didn't tell you. He'd never betray a confidence. Oh John, I didn't mean to do him an injustice.''

"Rachel, I find it hard to believe that you could ever have given up. Not with your spunk and grit.''

"You always thought I could withstand anything, didn't you? Well, obviously, I'm not the survivor you believed me to be.''

Determined, he insisted, "You are a survivor. Hell, just look at yourself, Rachel. You're absolutely beautiful, and the way you rushed into this room a few minutes ago, you were actually buoyant.''

"That's because my son has given me a reason to be happy again, and a reason to live!''

"Rachel, my love, that is exactly what makes you a survivor.''

"Yes, I can live without you! I know that now!" Incapable of suppressing her emotions, she confessed, "But John, you are still in my thoughts every waking hour, and you haunt my dreams at night.''

"Don't Rachel!" he shouted. "Don't say any more!''

"Why?" she exclaimed bitterly. "Are you afraid of the truth?" Sneering, she added, "You have no need to fear me any longer, John. I can do no more harm to your conscience, or your principles. I'm married to another man, and I'll never be free of him!''

"Why in the hell did you marry him?''

"Because you sent me away from you! What was I supposed to do? Live forever with Deborah and Josh?

Spend my life pining away for you?''

"Do you love him?''

"No!'' she yelled.

"Did you love him when you married him?''

"No! Of course not!'' she cried.

"My God, what kind of fool are you?''

"It's all your fault, damn you!''

"My fault? I didn't tell you to marry William Granger.''

"You never told me not to marry! Because you really hoped that I would. Then I'd free your conscience forever!''

"I was right about you all along! You're too damned immature to know what you want.''

"I'm twenty years old, John. How old must I be, before you consider me a woman? I've loved you since I was seventeen, and I will always love you!''

"Don't say any more, Rachel!'' he demanded harshly. He turned from her, but she quickly grasped his arm, jerking him back in her direction.

With her emotions under control, she gazed steadfastly into his steel gray eyes, and stated calmly, "I'm fully aware that there is no future for us. If this very moment you were to ask me to go away with you, I'd have to refuse. I could never willingly leave my baby. I'm his mother, and I'll never forsake him. But John, I love you. I know you don't believe me, but as God as my witness, I swear that I'll love you until the day I die!''

John could read the truth in her eyes, but before he had the chance to tell her so, she turned abruptly and fled from the room. Colliding with Deborah in the hallway, she retained her balance, opened the door and ran outside.

"Rachel!" Deborah yelled. "You can't leave by yourself! It's getting dark outside." Running onto the veranda, she warned, "It's too dangerous!"

Apprehensively, she watched as her sister swiftly mounted her horse and galloped away from the house.

Stepping out onto the veranda, John assured her, "I'll see that she gets home safely."

Turning to him, she noticed that he had Rachel's jacket. "Do hurry, Mr. Reynolds, it's getting chilly."

He strode to his horse and easily swung himself into the saddle. Gently tugging on the reins, he turned the horse toward the long driveway and began to pursue Rachel.

With unrestrained tears blinding her, Rachel raced her horse across the rocky plains. Having no mercy on the poor animal, she forced the horse to run faster and faster. The young mare, already tired from the long journey she'd traveled earlier, became exhausted and broke into a sweat as she began to foam at the mouth.

At last noting her horse's condition, Rachel slowed the animal down to a steady walk. Turning the horse to the right, she headed for a secluded valley she had often visited while out riding. When she reached the green fertile meadow, she quickly dismounted and hastily removed the heavy saddle from the tired horse. Grabbing the blanket, she began to vigorously rub down the sweaty, exhausted animal.

Rachel didn't hear the approaching rider until he was almost upon her, and with mounting fear, she whirled in his direction.

"You shouldn't ride your horse so hard, Rachel. She

isn't strong enough to take such brutal treatment.''

"You needn't concern yourself with my horse, Mr. Reynolds. She'll be just fine." Turning back to the mare, she continued to rub her down with the blanket. "Why did you follow me? What do you want?"

Slowly he got down from his horse, and walked towards her. Halting his steps he told her truthfully, "I believe you love me, Rachel. And I believe you love me more than any woman ever has, or ever will."

Dropping the blanket and leaning her head against the palomino, Rachel cried, "You believe me! Finally you believe me! Now that it's too late, you believe me! Damn you! Damn you!"

Deep heartrending sobs tore from Rachel's throat as she began to cry uncontrollably. Hurrying to her, he swiftly gathered her trembling body into his arms.

Holding her tightly, he pleaded, "Don't cry, Baby . . . please don't cry!" His deep voice broke with emotion, "I love you, Rachel . . . Baby, I love you! . . . Oh God, how much I love you!"

Gently cupping her face in his hands, he tenderly kissed her forehead. Softly he kissed her tear-filled eyes, and then his mouth came crushing down against hers. A moan escaped from deep in her throat, as she wrapped her arms around his neck and pressed her body close to his.

"Oh John, hold me! Please just hold me! I love you, darling . . . I love you!"

Enclosing the slim woman securely in his powerful embrace, he whispered, "I know you do, Baby . . . I know . . . and I love you, Rachel."

Resting her head against his shoulder, she asked, "Where do we go from here, John?"

Despondently he released her. "We have nowhere to go. As you said earlier, you can't leave your child. I honestly don't think I could take another man's wife and child from him anyway . . . my God, I once lost a son myself! I know the pain of losing a child!"

Looking up into his drawn face, she replied in despair, "There's no hope for us."

"Maybe there never was any hope for us, Rachel. It just wasn't meant to be. Perhaps if we'd been born at a different time . . . before so many years came between us."

"We could've crossed the barrier of time, John! We could have! If only . . ."

He interrupted, "If . . . if I hadn't been married . . . if I hadn't been so much older than you . . . if you weren't married . . . if you didn't have a child. . . . Hell, Rachel, what's the sense in discussing what could have been?"

"John," she began desperately, "we have tonight! Please don't leave me! Give us this one night. It may be all we'll ever have!"

Roughly he drew her back into his arms as he whispered hoarsely, "I won't leave you! I can't! My God, I want you, Rachel! I want you!"

Greedily his mouth came down on hers, and pulling her close, he kissed her with a deep passion.

Gently he released her and walked swiftly to his horse. Hastily he removed two blankets from his pack, and spread one of them over the soft grass, then placed the other one beside it. Without speaking, he moved towards her. Dusk had fallen and Rachel found it difficult to see his face clearly, but she instinctively knew he was looking at her with deep longing.

Easily he picked her up into his arms, carried her to the blankets, and kneeling, laid her down gently. With practiced hands, he unbuttoned her shirt and slipped it off. Next he pulled off her boots, and impatiently unbuckled her belt. He began to tug at her tight-fitting pants, and she lifted her hips to assist him. When he had her completely unclothed, and she lay revealed, he whispered, "You're so beautiful."

She didn't turn her gaze as he freed himself of his restricting clothes. She wanted to see him. She dearly loved every inch of his masculine physique.

Lying beside her, he pulled her into his arms, and before kissing her, he swore, "I'll always love you, Rachel!"

Ardently, his lips came down on hers, tasting the sweetness that had been denied him so long.

Rachel placed her hand to the back of his head, and entwining her fingers in his golden brown hair, she pressed her mouth even tighter to his. Oh, it felt so wonderful to have John kissing her again! How had she survived so long without experiencing this exciting ecstasy that only John had the power to awaken?

She had now been married to William Granger for fourteen months, but he had consistently failed to arouse her passion. But in the embrace of the man she loved, all her fiery desire returned.

With her lips still under his, Rachel whispered raspingly, "Hold me, John! . . . My darling, hold me tightly!"

His strong arms encircled her even more powerfully, and Rachel felt as if her body and his were one. This is how it should be, she thought. John and I together as one! Oh, how shall I go on living without him?

Hurting tears came to Rachel's eyes, and feeling her tears against his face, John kissed them away, as his hand cupped her breast. Moving his lips downward, he ran light kisses over her throat, across her bare shoulders, and then his lips were on her breast, causing Rachel to moan with desire.

"Oh John," she gasped. "Love me . . . please love me!"

"Rachel," he groaned thickly, as his lips traveled even farther downward, his warm mouth intensifying Rachel's yearning, until she was pleading with him, "Now, my darling . . . ! Take me now!"

Moving his masculine frame over her, he parted her legs with his knee. Entering her swiftly, he groaned, "I love you, Rachel!"

"Oh John!" she cried. "I love you too!"

Placing his hands under her hips, he thrust her thighs tightly against his. "Heaven, Rachel," he said hoarsely. "Making love to you is heaven!"

She wrapped her legs around his back firmly, and ecstatically, John carried her with him to their highest peak of rapture.

In the east, the sky was gradually turning lighter, and Rachel knew that soon the sun would peek over the horizon. Snuggling closer to John under the warm blanket, she wished desperately that she could hold back time. Soon he would leave her. She wondered if he'd ever come back.

Suddenly, with no warning, he leaned his large frame over her and fervently crushed his lips to hers. Without speaking a word, he penetrated her quickly. Driven by desperation, because he fully believed he would never again embrace the woman he loved, John thrust against her powerfully, entering her deeper and deeper.

Controlled by her own desperation, she met his demanding passion, her nails raking his back as she completely accepted his probing manhood.

Their climax came to them suddenly and violently, making Rachel bite into her bottom lip, as she locked her hips to his.

John didn't move to her side. Instead he remained inside her, relishing her warmth. He gazed down into her face, as he whispered tenderly, "I wonder if you have any conception of how deeply I love you."

"John, you are the one who doesn't realize how much he is loved."

He smiled, his crooked grin pulling at Rachel's heartstrings. "But how would you feel ten years from now, when my hair is gray and my face wrinkled?"

Rachel giggled. "You will not be gray and wrinkled in ten years! Besides, ten years from now I may be fat and homely, and then, how would you feel?"

"I would still love you, only I would have to call you my 'plump little hypocrite.' "

"John, I'm serious," she began soberly. "Would you continue to love me, even if my looks were to change?"

"Of course," he replied genuinely. "Surely you must know it's your inner beauty that makes me love you so deeply."

Looking him straight in the eyes, she arched her eyebrows, her expression shrewd. "Then why should my love for you be any less?"

He studied her thoughtfully for a moment, then

319

lightly he kissed her on the forehead, before answering, "You made your point, my love." Slowly, he moved to her side, and sighing he added, "But why in the hell are we even discussing it? It's a dead subject." Tenderly, he took her hand in his, and bringing it to his lips, he kissed her palm. "I love you, Rachel," he murmured.

She went into his arms, resting her head on his shoulder. "I have dreamed and waited for the moment when you would confess to me that you loved me," Rachel began. "I thought it would bring me so much happiness, but now that my dream has finally come true, instead of happiness, I feel so empty and lost."

"I know, Baby. Maybe I shouldn't have told you, but I needed to say the words."

"I always knew you loved me, John, but you were too stubborn to admit it."

His arms tightened around her. Smiling dreamily, he replied, "I fell in love with you that night when I opened the door to my wardrobe and there you were."

She laughed merrily. "I was so frightened. When you found me, I was deeply engrossed in prayer. I was praying that you would miraculously go away."

"Rachel, you had no idea how damned enticing you were. But so young. A girl on the bloom of womanhood."

"But I'm not a girl any longer," she answered seductively.

He laughed lightly. "You're definitely a woman! But there's a part of you, Rachel, that will always remain innocent."

"Zeke calls it, not being able to see any further than the end of my nose."

"That old man really thinks a lot of you."

"John," she began curiously, "why did you come to the ranch?"

"I had some business to take care of with Josh. I left so unexpectedly last night, that I never got the opportunity to discuss it with him. Before I leave, I'll ride back to the ranch and finish my errand."

"Are you leaving for the fort today?"

"I think the sooner the better, Rachel," he replied somberly.

"The business you have with Josh, is it very important?"

"I'm leaving the ranch to Josh and Deborah in the event of my death."

Her eyes opened wide with fright, as she leaned over him exclaiming, "Don't even think such a thing!"

Chuckling, he answered, "Sooner or later death comes to us all, Rachel. And I don't exactly have the safest job in the world."

"Is the Indian situation still bad?"

"Well, it isn't good. The Apache aren't going to give up without a fight. They're proud, Rachel, very proud."

"How long do you intend to stay in the cavalry?"

"I have about three more months before reenlistment."

"Oh John, please don't reenlist! Come back to your ranch."

"Baby, if I decided to leave the army, I wouldn't come back here."

"Why?" she asked.

"Why in the hell do you think?" he remarked irritably. "Loving you the way I do, I couldn't stand seeing you with another man. It would be pure hell for me,

Rachel!''

Sighing sadly, she rested her head on his shoulder. "It would be hell for me too. But John, where would you go?''

"I don't know. There's still a lot of places where Zeke and I have never been. I guess we'd just wander around for awhile.''

"Don't you plan to ever settle down?''

"I don't know, honey, but then I may just decide to reenlist.''

The darkness surrounding them began to slowly evaporate, and fearfully Rachel moved closer to him. "Oh John, how will I go on without you?''

"You'll go on, Baby, because you have no other choice.''

Though she was afraid to hear his answer, she found herself asking, "Will I ever see you again?''

Disregarding her question, he pushed off the blanket. "Get dressed, Baby. It's time to go.'' Quickly he rose and began putting on his clothes.

Fighting back tears, Rachel reluctantly started to dress also. Slipping on her boots, she inquired, "John, why didn't you answer me? Will I ever see you again?''

Kneeling beside her, he placed his hands on her slim shoulders drawing her into his arms. He held her securely for a moment, then as he released her, he admitted, "Probably not.''

"Oh, John . . . no!'' she cried. Frantically she grabbed for him and flung herself back into his embrace. "No! . . . No!''

Gently he shoved her away, and standing, he said firmly, "Don't live for our memories, Rachel. You have a husband and a child. Learn to live for them.''

Entirely ignoring his advice, she rose and looked up at him pleadingly. "John, please don't tell me I'll never see you again! It's more than I can bear."

Tenderly, he took her into his arms. "Promise me, Rachel, that you'll always keep that defiant chin of yours held high."

"I'll try," she sniffled. "But, I'm going to miss you so much! Oh John, I need you! Please don't tell me I'll never see you again! Please!"

Stepping away from her, he bent down to pick up the blankets, which he quickly rolled and tied behind the saddle on his horse. Silently, Rachel watched him, as he prepared to leave and to ride out of her life, perhaps forever!

Noticing that his hat was still on the grass, she knelt and picked it up. Walking over to him, she forced herself to smile as she handed it to him. She watched as he put on the hat and pulled it low over his forehead in the way she always remembered him wearing it.

Returning her vulnerable smile, he said lovingly, "Goodbye, my beautiful little hypocrite."

Struggling to be brave, she replied softly, "Goodbye, John."

Roughly he jerked her into his arms and passionately brought his lips to hers. Rachel returned his kiss with all her heart, as she wished this moment in time could last forever.

Unable to accept what she could not change, she pleaded willfully, "Will I ever see you again?"

Anger flashed in his eyes. "Baby, let's not make this harder for us than it already is. Damn it, there's no future for us! What the hell does it matter whether we see each other again?"

Abruptly he let her go, and hastily swung himself into the saddle. Picking up the reins, he looked down at her. "Try to find happiness with what you have, instead of grieving for what you can't have." Somberly, he told her, "I love you, Rachel."

Reaching up, she grasped his hand and brought it down to her lips. "I love you!" she cried.

Slowly he removed his hand from hers, and she clutched tightly at the thin air. With tears streaming down her face, she watched him ride away from her.

Barely above a whisper, she said, "I love you, John Reynolds, and I will always love you!"

Rachel was in the nursery sitting in the rocking chair holding her son when the house servant, Juanita, knocked lightly on the door before entering. " 'Excusame' Señora, but Señor Granger, he wishes to see you in the bedchamber."

"Very well, Juanita. Tell him I'll be right there."

Smiling down at her son, she rose from the chair and carried him to the crib. Gently she lay the child in his bed. "You'll be six months old tomorrow, darling. You're getting to be Mama's big boy, aren't you?"

As though he could understand her words, he smiled up at her and murmured soft baby sounds. Laughing lightly, she explained. "I must go see what your father wants, but I'll be back." She leaned over the crib and kissed his forehead.

Rachel left the room and walked swiftly down the hall to the bedroom she shared with her husband. Opening the door, she rushed inside. "Did you want to see me, William?"

Startled, she saw that he was lying across the bed.

Hurrying over to him, she asked, "Are you all right?"

Sitting up, he answered, "I think I've come down with the grippe."

She reached over and touched his brow. "You're burning up with fever. You must get to bed immediately!"

"I will, Señora, but first I must ask a favor."

"What is it?" she asked.

"I am suppose to meet a Malcolm Pritchard at the bank in El Paso. He wants to buy some cattle from me. Will you please go into town and give him my apologies? Tell him if he can stay on a few days, I'll meet with him as soon as I am able."

"Of course. What time were you supposed to meet with him?"

"You'll have to leave now, Señora. It's almost ten, and we planned to meet around noon. You shouldn't have any trouble recognizing him. He's my height, black hair, dark complexion, and around thirty years old."

"He sounds Spanish."

"Yes, but he is a 'gringo,' " he replied.

"Don't worry, I'll find him. Now you lie down and rest. I'll be back this afternoon. I'll stop by the doctor's office and ask him to come see you."

Lying back on the bed, he ordered, "Use the buggy and have one of the men drive you. Take some of the vaqueros with you; it's unsafe for you to travel alone."

She had already turned away from him, so he was unable to see how she raised her defiant chin or the mischievousness in her eyes. Glancing back towards him, she saw that his eyes were closed, so stealthily she went to the cedar chest and removed her favorite garments and the boots.

Quietly but speedily, she left the room. She would ride into town alone, and on her palomino! If only for a few hours, she'd relish her unrestricted freedom!

Entering the nursery, she hastily removed her dress and petticoats, happily slipping into the pants and shirt. After she put on the boots, she walked over to her son's crib. She saw that he had fallen asleep. Quietly she bent over him and placed a light kiss on his rosy cheek.

"Mama will be back home in a few hours, darling. Sweet dreams my precious baby," she whispered.

Taking one last look at her sleeping child, she turned and walked out of the room, never imagining that she had kissed her son for the last time.

As Rachel walked into the bank in El Paso, her thoughts were on buying some yard goods while in town to make her son some new clothes. He was growing so fast, that he was quickly outgrowing everything he had to wear.

It was almost lunch time, and the bank was practically empty. She noticed an elderly man attending to some business with the bank teller. Looking around the room, she saw another man standing beside a table apparently looking over some papers. He was a huge man with a full brown beard, and long unkempt hair. Obviously he wasn't Malcolm Pritchard.

Glancing towards the other side of the room, she could see a man heading for the bank teller with what appeared to be a small bag of money. She observed that he seemed to fit William's description of Malcolm Pritchard.

Quickly she moved over to him, and called, "Excuse me, sir. You must be Mr. Pritchard. I am Mrs. William Granger. My husband asked me to meet you."

The man made no reply, and she looked into his face closely. He had a masculine magnetism about him that caused Rachel to involuntarily catch her breath. He wasn't handsome, or especially good-looking, but Rachel was completely awed by his strong presence. His dark complexion was deeply lined by the many hours he spent in the sun. His eyes were a deep brown, framed by thick black eyebrows. When he smiled at her, the whiteness of his teeth contrasted against the darkness of his skin.

"My husband is ill," she explained, while trying not to be affected by his overt masculinity. "I think it's only the grippe, and I'm sure he'll be well in a few days."

When the man spoke for the first time, his voice sounded deep and slothful. "Ma'am, I'm not Mr. . . . Pritchard? Was that the name?"

"Oh dear," she gasped. "I'm sorry, sir. Please excuse me."

"I kinda wish I were this Pritchard fellow, if it meant becoming better acquainted with you. Did you say you're Mrs. William Granger?"

"Yes. Do you know my husband, Mr. . . . ?"

"The name is Bronson, ma'am. Klu Bronson. No, I don't know your husband, but I've heard of him. He's a very wealthy and powerful man."

"I wonder what happened to Mr. Pritchard. He was supposed to meet with my husband about buying some of our cattle. Oh well, I'm sure he'll be here soon."

Slipping the small money bag into his jacket pocket,

he inquired, "Your husband owns quite a large herd of cattle, doesn't he?"

"Yes, he does. Are you in the cattle business, Mr. Bronson?"

"Yeah, in a roundabout way, I guess you could say I'm sorta in the cattle business."

Looking at him with bafflement, she replied, "I don't understand. Exactly what kind of business are you in, sir?"

While still smiling, he looked intensely into her eyes. "Among other things, Mrs. Granger, I rob banks!"

What he had said barely had time to sink into her consciousness, before he drew his pistol from its holster and the huge man whirled away from the table with his gun pointed at the teller. Roughly the door swung open, and two Mexicans holding rifles rushed into the room.

Frozen with fear, Rachel stood immobile and watched as Klu Bronson approached the bank teller and pushed aside the elderly man who had been depositing his money. Harshly he ordered the frightened teller to put all the money into a bag.

The old man he had shoved, took a step toward him, but was immediately shot through the head by the huge bearded man. As blood gushed out of the man's temple, Rachel began to scream hysterically.

"Goddamn it Jake!" Klu yelled. "There was no reason to kill him!" Shouting to one of the Mexicans, he demanded, "Make her shut up!"

The smaller of the two Mexican bandits moved quickly to Rachel. Grabbing her painfully by the arm, he slapped her severely across the face. "Shut up, Señora, or I will be forced to hit you again!" With her cheek burning from his powerful blow, Rachel controlled her hysteria.

"Hurry up!" Klu ordered the nervous bank teller. "Damn it, Jake, the whole town probably heard that shot. We've got to get out of here fast."

Grabbing the bag of money, Klu walked swiftly across the room. "Let's get the hell out of here!"

"I ain't leavin' no damn witness," Jake said, moving toward the frightened bank teller.

Klu pivoted in his direction, but he was too late. Sneering cruelly, Jake pointed his pistol at the teller's horrified face, and pulled the trigger.

Seeing the man's face reduced to a bloody pulp, before he fell lifelessly to the floor, made Rachel nauseous. Swallowing hard, she fought back the sickening bile that had risen to her throat.

Suddenly, the huge man began walking toward her, and terrified, she felt that she could see her own death reflected in his cold, sadistic eyes.

Alertly Klu reached out for Rachel, and grasped her arm. Jerking her next to him, he informed Jake, "She's going with us!"

"We don't need no damn woman slowin' us down!"

"She's worth a helluva lot more than what we got from this bank. Her husband is William Granger, and he'll pay a high ransom for her."

Jake's eyes traveled hungrily over her feminine curves. "Might not be so bad havin' her along. Yeah, let's take her with us!"

Dragging her roughly behind him, Klu opened the door, pulling her through the doorway. Forcing her to run with him, they quickly reached his horse, and he flung the money bag across the saddle. Then turning around, he propelled Rachel toward the horse.

As gun shots suddenly began exploding all around them, she pushed him away and shouted, "Let me go!" She tried to flee, but tenaciously he held her arm.

"Hold your fire!" she heard someone yell from somewhere close by. Aware of William Granger's power, the sheriff cautioned loudly, "For God's sake, don't shoot! They have Mrs. Granger!"

"Get on the horse!" Klu demanded.

"No!" she yelled.

Tightening his grip cruelly on her arm, he hit her so hard across the face that she was almost knocked unconscious. Her knees buckled, and as she started to fall, he caught her in his arms. Quickly he lifted her onto his horse, hastily swinging himself up behind her. With Jake and the two Mexicans following, they sped down the dusty street and out of town.

Rachel's jaw throbbed painfully, and her whole body was aching from being jolted on the speeding horse for what seemed like endless hours. She wondered where the men were taking her. They had crossed the Rio Grande, and she knew they were now in Mexico. Finally, as dusk fell, they pulled up their horses to camp for the night. Klu rode his horse a short distance from the others. He easily dismounted, then reached up and pulled her roughly to the ground.

"Sure could use a cup of coffee," Jake said, walking toward them. "Hey, woman, make a fire and get me some coffee brewin'!"

"There'll be no fire," Klu objected. "In case there's a possee on our trail."

"It's gonna be mighty cold sleepin' without no fire,

330

and only one thin blanket to keep me warm." Scanning Rachel with his eyes, he added, "I bet you could keep me good and warm, couldn't you?"

"Stay away from me!" she demanded. "If you touch me, I'll kill you!"

For such a big man, he moved with deceptive speed and seized her by the arm. His fingers dug brutally into her skin. "You listen to me, bitch! I'll touch you any time I want to!" His lips curled in a snarl. "And anywhere I want, cause you're gonna sleep with ole Jake tonight."

Rachel's heart was beating rapidly in fear, but her temper exploded at the thought of the barbarous man putting his hands on her intimately. "I'd rather sleep with a filthy pig!"

He pulled back his hand to strike her, but Klu swiftly deflected his arm. "Leave her alone!"

Flinging Klu's hand off his arm, Jake spun his large frame in Klu's direction. "You plannin' on keepin' her for yourself?" he asked savagely.

The way Klu was looking carelessly at the man, reminded Rachel of John Reynolds. He appeared to be perfectly at ease, but Rachel was fully aware that Klu was extremely dangerous. She noticed how he kept his right hand close to the pistol hanging at his hip.

Nervous sweat broke out on Jake's brow, as he contemplated drawing his pistol against Klu. Apparently afraid of the man's fast draw, Jake said gruffly, "Ain't no woman worth gettin' shot for."

As Jake strolled away angrily, he muttered, "Hell, you can have her!"

The Mexican, who had slapped Rachel earlier, walked over to Klu. "Amigo, do not turn your back on him," he advised.

Smiling, Klu answered, "Don't worry, Miguel, I won't."

The Mexican glanced at Rachel and then back at Klu, and with a cunning smile, he sauntered away from them.

Apprehensive and silent, Rachel watched Klu as he moved to his horse and grabbed the money bag and the two rolled-up blankets from behind his saddle. Moving soundlessly, he walked back towards her, and dropped the blankets at her feet. "Unroll 'em!" he ordered sharply.

"No!" she snapped.

Anger flared in his dark eyes. "Damn you, woman! Unroll the blankets and spread them on the ground!"

When she made no move to obey him, he clutched her arm painfully. "Mrs. Granger, you already have one ugly bruise, and if you don't want another one to match it, then you'll do as I tell you!"

Deciding he wasn't bluffing, she pulled away from his grip and knelt beside the blankets. Irritably she unrolled them, and spread out one of the blankets. Holding the other one possessively in her arms, she stood glaring at him with her chin raised arrogantly.

"What in the hell do you think you're doing?" he asked impatiently.

"Am I to sleep without any cover?"

"That blanket happens to be my cover, Mrs. Granger."

"Mr. Bronson, in case you are too ignorant to be aware of the fact, it happens to be the month of February. The nights are quite chilly, even in Mexico!"

"I'm fully aware what month it is, Mrs. Granger."

Jerking it out of her arms he added, "And that's why I intend to keep my blanket!"

Trying to control her temper, she watched as he went over to the blanket she had spread on the ground and lay down. Smiling up at her, he put the other one over him. "Get my saddlebags!"

"Get them yourself!" she scowled.

"Are you one of those women who enjoy getting the hell knocked out of them?"

Angrily, she whirled and strode over to the horse. Swiftly she pulled down the saddlebags, then walked back and dropped them on top of him. "Your saddlebags, Mr. Bronson!"

Reaching inside one, he asked, "Are you hungry?"

"No!" she replied curtly.

"You should eat, Mrs. Granger. Keeps up your strength."

"Why? So I can wait on you?"

Laughing lightly, he held out a strip of jerky. Noticing her distasteful frown, he said, "It isn't so bad."

"I know how it tastes, Mr. Bronson. I've eaten it before."

Looking at her with surprise, he questioned, "William Granger's wife eating jerky?"

"I wasn't always his wife!"

Taking a large bite of the dried venison, he informed her, "Ma'am, if you need some privacy, you can go to the bushes there behind us. But I'll have to insist that you keep talking to me the entire time."

Understanding her look of puzzlement, he explained, "If I can hear you, Mrs. Granger, I'll know you're still close by. So just keep talking to me."

"I have nothing to say to you!" she stated indignantly as she moved toward the bushes.

"I don't give a damn whether you talk, sing, or recite poetry; but if you become silent, I'm comin' after you!"

He stuck the saddlebags under the blanket for a pillow, and lying back leisurely, he listened to Rachel's constant chatter.

"Someday, I will see you behind bars, Mr. Bronson! . . . I hope you rot in prison for what you've done. I hope they put you so far back in the prison that you'll have to live with the rats ! . . . And that goes for your friends too ! . . . Except for Jake ! . . . I hope they hang him ! . . . My husband won't rest until he has caught every last one of you ! . . . You'll pay for this, Mr. Bronson ! . . . I just hope I'm there to see you when you finally get what's coming to you!"

Hearing her return, he replied, "Now that you have relieved yourself . . ." He paused intentionally before adding, ". . . of your bitterness that is, you can shut up!"

Stopping beside him, she questioned, "Where am I supposed to sleep?"

Grinning up at her shrewdly, he pulled back the top blanket. "Right here. Beside me."

"I don't intend to sleep under that blanket with you!"

"Would you rather sleep with Jake?"

"I refuse to sleep with either one of you!" she remarked angrily.

He raised up and glanced across the short span that separated them from the others. "Mrs. Granger, if you don't lie down and stop yapping, I'm going to call Jake and tell him he can have you! I'm tired and I want to get some damned sleep!''

"You wouldn't give me to that . . . that horrible man!'' she exclaimed.

But detecting the seriousness in his eyes, she hurriedly dropped to her knees and squirmed under the cover. Turning her back to him, she ordered, "Just don't touch me!''

"I'm afraid this blanket isn't wide enough to prevent it,'' he answered grinning, as he lay back beside her.

Instantly, she became acutely aware of his hard muscular body next to hers. Feeling a desire that shocked her shamefully, she moved as far from him as she feasibly could, while still remaining under the warmth of the blanket.

In her dream, she was still at Fort Craig and there had never been a William or a marriage. She was contentedly lying beside the man she loved, and he was holding her closely in his strong arms. Halfway between sleep and consciousness, she snuggled next to him, nestling her head on his shoulder.

As her heavy eyelids slowly opened, she murmured to her dream lover, "Good morning, darling.''

Suddenly her eyes flew open, and she bolted upright. It wasn't morning, and she wasn't at Fort Craig! Oh God, she was out in the middle of nowhere!

"Mrs. Granger, you are one hell of a woman to sleep with! First you wake me from a sound sleep by pressing your very desirable body next to mine. Then you call me darling, and as if that isn't enough, you all of a sudden jump up and jerk my cover off with you! Must you go from one extreme to another?''

"Don't be absurd!'' she answered, glaring at him.

"I wasn't calling you darling!"

"Let me guess, you were dreaming about your husband, right?"

Maturity in age hadn't cured Rachel's habit of speaking without thinking first, and she blurted out, "Of course not! I wasn't dreaming about him!" Noticing his obnoxious grin, she embarrassingly realized what she had said.

Grabbing her arm, he pulled her back down beside him. "Maybe I was wrong, and your husband won't pay your ransom. He might be glad to get rid of an unfaithful wife."

"I hope he doesn't pay it! It'd serve you right!" she snapped.

"You'd better hope he does, because your husband's wealth is all that's keeping Jake from killing you."

"And you'd let him, I suppose. Let him! You'd probably help him!"

Leaning over her brazenly, he replied, "That's a hell of a way to talk to someone who saved your pretty neck. Have you no gratitude, Mrs. Granger?"

"You only saved me, so you could get your grubby hands on my husband's money!"

"How do you know I didn't save you for myself?"

Trying unsuccessfully to push him away, she scowled, "I find you detestable!"

"Do you? I don't think so," he answered, moving his body over hers. Before she had a chance to protest, his mouth came down forcefully on hers. For an instant, she involuntarily responded to his demanding kiss, but quickly regaining her composure, she tried to push him away.

Slowly removing his lips from hers, he stared deeply

into her eyes as he said lazily, "By the way, ma'am, bein' that we're sorta livin' together and all . . . and obviously we're attracted to each other. . . . Well, would I be goin' too far . . . if I asked your name?"

Angrily she shoved him away. "I'm Mrs. Granger to you!"

When he laughed, the whiteness of his teeth flashed brightly in the darkness.

Trying to ignore him, she turned her back but he swiftly swatted her on the rear. "It's time to get up, Mrs. Granger."

"It's still dark!" she replied irritably.

Rising, he looked down at her and commented, "Really? I'd never have known it, if you hadn't told me." Reaching down, he grabbed her arm and roughly pulled her to her feet. "Roll up the blankets!"

"Will you stop ordering me to do everything! Don't you know how to ask?"

"Ma'am, I admire your damned spirit, but it's going to get you in a helluva lot of trouble with me! If you're going to be my woman, you need to learn to show some respect."

"Your woman!" she scoffed. "I'd rather be dead!"

Before leaving her to wake the others, he sneered, "Would you, Mrs. Granger? Well, if Jake has his way, that could be a distinct possibility!"

PART THREE

Chapter Nine

For two days Rachel rode on the same horse with Klu and slept beside him at night. Although she missed her baby desperately and was terribly afraid of Jake, she had to continually fight the attraction she felt for Klu. She was totally shocked and abashed by her own feelings. How could she conceivably find a man like Klu Bronson desirable?

Around noon on the third day, Klu abruptly pulled up his horse, causing the others to do the same. He dismounted, then reached up and drew Rachel down beside him.

As he untied the bandanna from around his neck he explained, "I'm going to have to blindfold you, Mrs. Granger."

The vulnerability of being blindfolded frightened her, and as he took a step forward, she yelled, "No! Stay away from me!"

"I'm not going to hurt you, damn it!" he replied irritably.

He gripped her arm firmly, and furious, she kicked at him, striking him sharply in the shin. As Klu hobbled painfully on his leg, the other three laughed uproariously.

"Hey, Juan," Miguel began glancing at the Mexican beside him, "I think Klu has captured himself a wildcat. Si?"

"Si, amigo, but the 'cuestion' is, can he tame her?" Juan chuckled.

"Klu," Jake called. "If you can't control that gal, why don't you give her to a man who can?"

Swiftly Klu swerved in their direction, and the rage in his eyes silenced them instantly. As he turned back toward Rachel, the savage expression on his face caused her to fearfully step away from him. In two easy strides he was beside her, and painfully he clutched her arm. Roughly, he jerked her to him.

Lowering his voice so the others couldn't hear, he sneered, "I ought to knock the hell out of you! You little fool! You're too damned stupid to realize I'm only trying to help you. If I take you to the hideout we're heading for without blindfolding you, they'll never let you leave! Not alive!"

Remembering the story Zeke had once told her about him and John being blindfolded for the same reason, she finally understood what he was trying to tell her. Quietly she apologized, "I'm sorry. I don't know why I panicked. But the thought of not being able to see Jake frightens me! Klu, promise you won't let him near me!"

"You'll be on my horse with me. He won't bother you, Mrs. Granger." Stepping behind her, he tied the bandanna securely over her eyes. Placing his hands gently on her shoulders, he whispered into her ear, "Do you realize you called me Klu?"

"Only a slip of the tongue, I assure you. Don't get

342

any ideas, Mr. Bronson. I still think you're detestable."

Chuckling, he answered, "You have many virtues, Mrs. Granger, but honesty is not one of them." Taking her hand he led her to his horse, helped her into the saddle, and then swung himself up behind her.

Rachel found the darkness under the blindfold terrifying. Images of the bank teller and the elderly man at the bank kept flashing across her mind, and she could envision Jake's pistol pointing directly into her face. She knew he wanted to kill her. It was in his eyes every time he looked at her.

Sensing her uneasiness, Klu slowed his horse until they trailed the others at a distance. "Try to relax. I told you that I won't let Jake bother you."

"He wants to kill me," she whispered frightfully.

"Sometimes I think he wants to kill everyone he sees. But don't worry, I won't let him hurt you."

"You're not like him," she began. "Why do you ride with a man like that?"

"I'll never ride with the sonofabitch again! I swear to you, Mrs. Granger, I didn't know he was going to murder those men."

"How did you get mixed up with him?" she pried.

"That's a long story, but usually Miguel and I ride alone."

"Miguel? Is he a good friend of yours?"

"The best I could have." Hearing her give a deep sigh, he questioned, "Is anything wrong?"

"No. I was only remembering two other men who are very close friends."

"Obviously two men you know very well."

Vividly their images crossed her mind, tearing painfully at her heart. "Two men that I love."

She could feel a sudden stiffness in the arms circling her. "Just how many men do you love, Mrs. Granger? I'd be willing to bet neither of these men are your husband."

For the first time in three days, a smiled curved the corners of her mouth. "You would win the bet, Mr. Bronson."

He remained silent for a moment before informing her, "Somehow, I'm going to get you out of this."

"What do you mean?"

"Mrs. Granger, I never wanted to bring you along in the first place."

"Surely you don't expect me to believe that! It was your idea to kidnap me!"

Drawing his dark eyebrows into a frown, he gritted his teeth. "It was my idea to save your ungrateful neck!"

"If your intentions were to save me, why haven't you told me so before now?" she asked warily.

"I almost wish to hell I hadn't told you. I doubt if I can trust you not to act so damned obvious that Jake will catch on. But I thought if I let you in on my plans, you might stop being so damned hostile."

"Hostile! I haven't forgotten how you hit me, Mr. Bronson!"

"How else was I to get you on my horse?" he asked bitterly.

"You could've let me go!"

"Have you forgotten how much money you're worth? Even if I had let you go, Jake would've grabbed you, and I can assure you, Mrs. Granger, when he finished with you, you'd have had a broken jaw instead of a bruised one!''

''I want to believe you, but how can I possibly trust a man like you?''

''Like me?'' he questioned.

''You're an outlaw, a murderer, and no telling what else!''

''And what makes you think I'm a murderer?''

''Have you never killed a man, Mr. Bronson?''

''Yeah, a few times, but always in self-defense,'' he answered.

''If that poor bank teller had drawn a gun on you, would that have been self-defense?''

''It'd be kill or be killed, wouldn't it?''

''And you would have killed! In my estimation, that makes you a murderer!''

He moved his lips so close to her ear that she could feel his breath against her face. ''If you think I'm detestable and also a murderer, then why are you attracted to me?''

''Don't be preposterous! I don't find you attractive!'' she smirked, while very conscious of how his lips had traveled down to her neck.

''That first night when I kissed you, for an instant you responded. Why?''

Her cheeks blushed scarlet. ''It must've been your imagination!''

Fondling her firm breast, he ran light kisses over her neck and up to her ear. Against her own volition, she felt her passion rising.

''Please don't!'' she pleaded.

''Why? You tell me why you respond to me and I'll stop. Tell me!''

''All right!'' she replied sternly. Pushing his hand

away she confessed, "I'm attracted to you, and it makes me feel ashamed! Do you understand? I'm ashamed!"

She could hear his intake of breath before he asked, "Do you think I'm that far below you?"

"I've never had anything to do with criminals! You and the others are the first outlaws I've ever had the misfortune of knowing. But I've always considered your kind to be the filth of the earth, and from what I witnessed in that bank, I see no reason to change my mind! And to think that I could actually be attracted to someone like you . . ."

"Be quiet!" he demanded. "Just shut up, damn it!"

"You don't like hearing the truth about yourself, do you?"

Quickly he pulled up his horse and swiftly dismounted. Grabbing Rachel by the waist he jerked her off the horse. Her hands flew to the blindfold to remove it, but he seized her arms pinning them behind her.

Roughly he pulled her to him and pressed her body intimately close to his. "I may not like hearing the truth, but you don't like knowing the truth. And the truth, you high and mighty bitch, is that you want me as much as I want you!"

Very aware of his strong masculine nearness, she could feel herself trembling as she protested feebly, "No!"

Tightening his powerful grip, he held her even closer. "You want me!" Admit it!"

"Please leave me alone!" she pleaded. "My God, have you no mercy? I can't even see you!" With the vulnerability of a child she cried, "Oh Klu, I don't like being in the dark! It scares me!"

Touched by her pitiful plea, he released his hold and said gently, "You won't have to be blindfolded much longer. We're almost there, Baby."

He was confused when she suddenly yelled, "Don't call me that! Please, don't call me that! I can't stand it!"

Tenderly he gathered her back into his embrace, and holding her closely, he replied, "All right, Mrs. Granger, I won't."

"Oh God," she moaned. "I want to go home!" Pushing out of his arms, she thrust her fists into the darkness, hitting him on his chest as she cried with hysteria, "I want my baby! I want my baby!"

Grabbing her small fists, he held them tightly in his strong grip. "Calm down, Mrs. Granger!" Releasing her hands, he clutched her shoulders, and shaking her he ordered, "Damn it! Don't get hysterical!"

He could suddenly feel her body become limp, and he watched her with pity, but Rachel's courage and spirit had been born into her, and with determination she forced herself to stand tall. Straightening her slim shoulders, she raised her chin bravely.

Rachel missed her baby so deeply that her arms actually ached from not holding him, and she needed John Reynolds so desperately that her heart felt like it was breaking; but, somehow she would be strong and survive her ordeal. She would push the thoughts of her child and John Reynolds to the far recesses of her mind, because if she didn't, Rachel feared she'd start crying for them and never stop.

"I'm all right!" she insisted firmly. Suddenly she could hear a horse coming toward them and then Miguel's voice, "Is anything wrong, amigo?"

"No," Klu replied as he reached for Rachel. Carefully he helped her onto his horse and swung himself behind her.

"Miguel," Klu began as they started riding in the direction of the others. "Mrs. Granger doesn't believe we're going to help her."

"Señora," Miguel said. "Klu and I, we have done many things but we do not steal another man's wife for money." Glancing at Klu he chuckled, "We may steal her for love, si amigo?"

Pressing his lips close to Rachel's ear, Klu told her, "Don't worry, Mrs. Granger, I don't want your husband's money, and I've never loved a woman."

If Rachel had been able to observe their travels, she'd have seen steep sheer cliffs towering on each side of them, and a passageway so narrow that they were forced to ride single file.

Startled, she jumped slightly when a male voice from somewhere far above called out, " 'Alto,' Señor Bronson! The 'patron' and some of his vaqueros are on their way down to meet you. We have been aware of your arrival for the past mile, Señor."

"Where are we?" Rachel asked nervously.

"Just be quiet, Mrs. Granger. For God's sake try to keep your mouth shut. If I can't convice the 'patron' to let you stay, you may not have much longer to live!" Klu answered bluntly.

With her heart beating rapidly in fear, she waited silently. When at last, she heard the sound of multiple horses advancing upon them steadily, she unconsciously gripped Klu's arm as though it were her life line.

"Klu!" she heard a voice call cheerfully.

"How have you been?" Klu asked.

Pulling his large white stallion up beside them, the 'patron' answered, "Just fine, amigo." Glancing toward the others he asked with apparent surprise, "Why are you riding with Jake?"

Klu grinned bitterly. "We all make mistakes."

"Who is the señorita?" the 'patron' inquired.

"Señora," Klu corrected. "Señora Granger."

"William Granger's 'esposa'?" Rachel could distinctly hear astonishment in the man's voice.

"None other," Klu answered.

"Ah . . . I see, amigo. Ransom for the beautiful Señora!"

"I'll see that you get a large share of the ransom, if you let us keep her here for a while."

The 'patron' seemed to seriously consider what Klu had told him. He was a large man in his early fifties. He easily weighed over two hundred pounds but it was all muscle. His thick mustache curled at the corners of his mouth as he smiled. "William Granger is a very powerful man, amigo. This time you may have, as you gringos say, bit off more than you can chew. Si?"

"Don't worry, I won't make contact with Granger until we're gone from here."

"Why do you need to hide?" he asked.

"We just pulled a bank robbery in El Paso and that stupid sonofabitch, Jake, killed two men. That's also where we grabbed Mrs. Granger. We need to lie low for awhile until we can be sure they've stopped looking for us."

The 'patron' watched him closely for a moment as he studied the situation. "If it were anyone but you, Klu,

I'd say no. Señora Granger, she is more dangerous than lit dynamite. Her husband will not rest, amigo, until he sees you hanging from a rope! But it is your neck. Si?''

"That's right. It's my neck," he replied.

"You are welcome to stay, Señor," the large man decided. Turning his horse, he galloped ahead of them.

Before following the 'patron,' Klu whispered to Rachel, "I wonder, Mrs. Granger, if by trying to save your life, I haven't gone and stuck my neck into a noose."

When they reached the hideout, Rachel hoped her blindfold would be removed. She wished Klu would take it off so that she could see where they were. As he helped her down from the horse, she concentrated deeply trying to identify the many sounds drifting around her. She heard the barking of dogs, the clucking of chickens, and the braying of a donkey. She could hear many different voices, even those of children. Mostly it was Spanish, so she had no conception of what was being said.

Klu held her arm firmly as he guided her up a flight of steps and then through a doorway. When he closed the door behind them, he removed the bandanna from her eyes.

After being in total darkness for hours, Rachel had to blink a few times before she could focus her eyes. Looking at her surroundings she saw that she was in a small and sparsely furnished bedroom. There was a bed in the center of the room spread up neatly with a bright colorful quilt. The floor was bare, except for one small throw rug. Next to the bed was a table with a basin, water pitcher, and a small lamp. One large chair was placed beside the far wall next to a window that was framed with white plain curtains.

"I'm sure it's not as elegant as the bedroom you share with William Granger at the hacienda. Or do you share a bed with your husband?" Klu asked teasingly.

Glaring at him, Rachel lifted her chin haughtily as she snapped, "How do you think I got my son!"

Klu's laughter had a pleasant ring to it, and against her will Rachel found herself smiling at him; but her smile quickly vanished as he continued, "I'm looking forward to sleeping with you in the privacy of a bed instead of on the hard ground."

"What!" she exclaimed. "Mr. Bronson, you are not going to share this bed with me!"

Pulling his eyebrows into a deep frown he asked sternly, "When in the hell are you going to learn that you don't tell me what to do?"

With her Irish temper consuming her, she placed her hands on her hips and shouted, "I refuse to sleep with you! Out on the plains I had no other choice! But this is entirely different! How dare you be so audacious and rude as to think for one moment that I would allow you to . . . to . . . !" At a loss for words she did the only thing she could think to put emphasis on her point. Angrily she stomped her foot.

Meeting her anger head on with his own he raged, "I'm not going to leave you alone at night unprotected! How long do you think it would take Jake to find a way to get in here? Damn it woman! Why do you have to be so hard-headed and so damned ignorant?"

Realizing his threat concerning Jake could very well be true, she suppressed her anger as she insisted, "We won't share that bed!''

"Then Mrs. Granger, you will sleep on the floor!''

"You are the most ill-mannered man I've ever known!''

"Just what do you expect from a man who is the filth of the earth ? . . . I'll have someone bring you up some dinner and after you've eaten, I'll have a tub and water sent up so you can bathe.''

As he walked to the door she called to him, "Klu, will you get me a brush and a mirror?''

Opening the door, he replied politely, "I'll see what I can do.'' But before leaving the room he turned back toward her and grinned slyly as he reminded, "By the way, ma'am, the name is Mr. Bronson.''

As Klu locked the door securely behind him, Rachel walked to the window, pulled back the curtains, and looked out. Obviously the window was situated at the rear of the building for she could see nothing but dry barren land surrounded by sheer cliffs. Disappointed, she moved away and walked to the bed. Feeling fatigued she lay back across the soft quilt and closed her eyes. Within minutes she was asleep.

Rachel was awakened by a key turning in the lock. When the door opened she sat up on the bed expecting it to be Klu. She was surprised to see a Mexican woman entering the room with a tray of food balanced in one hand while she closed the door with the other. "I have brought your dinner, Señora Granger,'' she explained in a soft voice.

Rachel studied the woman closely as she began walking gracefully toward her. Although she seemed much too thin, Rachel was amazed by her beauty.

Placing the tray on the bed beside her, the woman

352

said, "After you have eaten, I will see to your bath."

"Thank you," Rachel answered. As the woman turned to leave she quickly called to her, "Please, don't go. It would be nice to have someone to talk to."

"I'm sorry, Señora, but Klu, he would not approve." Seeing Rachel's obvious disappointment, the woman added tenderly, "But if you need anything, I will try to help you."

"Could you possibly find me some clean clothes?"

Smiling, she answered, "Si, Señora. I will send them to you when you have your bath."

She walked toward the door but Rachel stopped her by saying, "Thank you . . . Miss . . . ? May I ask your name?"

"Of course, Señora Granger. My name is Carmelita."

Rachel rose from the bed so abruptly she almost overturned the tray of food. All the color drained from her face as she stared at the woman.

"Señora, are you all right?" she asked.

"Your father," Rachel declared breathlessly. "He's Manuel! And his last name is Villano. He's Manuel Villano!"

Hastily Carmelita moved toward her as she questioned, "How do you know this?"

"You're John's wife!" she gasped.

Carmelita's dark eyes opened wide with astonishment, and her hand flew to her mouth as she caught her breath. "What do you know of John? Is he alive? Is he well?"

For a moment the two women studied one another as the tension between them hung suspended in the air. Breaking the silence, Carmelita pleaded, "Have you seen him? Please answer me!"

"I saw him two months ago."

"Was he well?" Carmelita asked again.

"Yes," Rachel answered simply.

"Señora, what do you know about John, my father, and myself?"

Slowly Rachel sat on the edge of the bed. "I know that once John and Zeke were brought here to your father's land." Glancing up at her, she continued, "You and John were married and lived on a ranch in southern Texas."

Nervously Carmelita clasped her hands together tightly. "Do you know about our son?"

"I know everything," Rachel acknowledged.

She watched Carmelita as the woman clutched at the cross hanging from a gold chain around her neck. Rachel was surprised when Carmelita hung her head, and her narrow shoulders went limp as sobs tore from deep in her throat. Feeling a surge of compassion Rachel never dreamed she could feel for Carmelita, she moved to her and consolingly held the pathetically thin woman in her arms.

Between heartbroken sobs, Carmelita asked, "Does he still hate me?"

Rachel wondered if she should tell Carmelita the truth. She had no desire to intentionally hurt the woman, but she realized it would be unfair not to be honest with her. "Yes, he does. . . . I'm sorry," she answered.

Regaining control of her emotions, Carmelita walked slowly to the bed and while sitting down, she unconsciously caressed the small cross between her fingers. "For John to have told you so much about his personal life, he must know you very well.''

Raising her chin slightly, Rachel remarked, ''I love him, Carmelita, and he loves me.''

''But you are married to Señor Granger!''

''I loved John before I met my husband,'' Rachel explained.

''But Señora, you said that you love him, not that you once loved him.''

''It's a long story, Carmelita, and one I'm sure you wouldn't be interested in.''

''But you are wrong!'' she responded quickly.

Remembering all Zeke had told her about Carmelita, Rachel regarded the woman with suspicion. ''Why are you here? Why would the 'patron's' daughter bring a tray of food up to my room instead of a servant?''

''I heard Klu and my father discussing you, and my heart went out to you, Señora. You have suffered such a terrible ordeal. I wanted to be sure that you were all right.''

Shaking her head, Rachel protested, ''No, the Carmelita I have heard about wouldn't care!''

Rising from the bed, she sighed, ''I do not blame you for not believing me, Señora. Eat your dinner before it gets cold. I will see that a tub and water are brought up for your bath. And a change of clothes. Perhaps, I will see you tomorrow. 'Buenas noches,' Señora.''

Bewildered, Rachel watched her as she moved gracefully across the floor and out of the room. Carmelita was as beautiful as Zeke had said, but Rachel thought she had detected a tenderness in her eyes that was definitely at variance with her reputation.

* * *

Rachel immersed herself in the tub of water and leisurely enjoyed the hot bath. She had two servant girls to help her bathe and to help wash her long, thick hair. Neither of them spoke English, and she tried to make them understand by using hand gestures that she needed a brush. She wasn't sure if she was able to convey her message.

Carmelita had sent her three changes of clothes and also a dressing gown. As soon as she dried off she slipped into the sheer white silk gown. It felt smooth and cool next to her skin.

One of the girls quickly went to the door and opened it. Embarrassed by the transparency of the dressing gown, Rachel stepped hastily to the corner of the room as two men came in to remove the tub. Thankfully she noticed that neither one of them so much as glanced in her direction. After they had carried out the tub, the young Mexican girls hurried to follow them out of the room. As they were leaving, Rachel tried one last time to make them understand that she wanted a brush for her hair.

When the door closed behind them, she despondently walked to the side of the bed and sat down. Angrily she mumbled, "Let it dry in a hundred tangles! I don't care!"

Rachel jumped slightly as the door was roughly swung open. She felt her nerves grow taut when she looked up to see Klu standing in the doorway. Suddenly becoming conscious of how she was dressed, her cheeks flamed red as she asked, "Will you please leave?"

Slamming the door closed behind him, Klu sauntered into the room. It was then she noticed that he carried a brush and a hand mirror. When he reached the bed, he dropped them into her lap. "Your brush and mirror, Mrs. Granger."

"Get out!" she hissed.

Leaning over her brazenly he ordered, "Stop telling me what to do! I swear to God, woman, I'm goin' to lose my patience with you!"

She could distinctly smell the odor of whiskey, and feeling perturbed by his insolence and condition, she commanded angrily, "Get away from me!"

He stared intensely into her eyes for a moment as she unflinchingly stared back at him. Then with a smile that puzzled her, he turned and walked to the chair beside the window. "Brush your hair. It's a damned mess."

"Mr. Bronson, I would like to get dressed!"

"Why? It's time to go to bed," he replied lazily.

Realizing he was determined to be contrary, she began brushing vigorously at her tangled locks. He watched as she tried in vain to smooth out her thick auburn hair. Taking her completely by surprise, he moved to her and took the brush from her hand. Sitting beside her, he began brushing her hair.

Trying to keep her mind from concentrating on his comforting and sensual gesture, she asked, "How well do you know Carmelita?"

"Carmelita? Did she come in here?"

"She brought up my dinner tray." When he remained silent, she impatiently asked again, "How well do you know her?"

"I don't actually know her as a woman. To me, she's more like a saint."

Trying to keep the shock out of her voice, Rachel inquired, "What do you mean?"

"She's so gentle and kind. And a very religious woman."

"Has she always been this way?" Rachel asked, hoping she sounded casual.

"No. I don't know that much about her life. I know when she was seventeen she got married and moved to a ranch close to El Paso. I'm not sure of the exact location. You may have heard of it. It's owned by her husband, a man named Reynolds. From what her father has told me there was some kind of tragedy concerning their son and she moved back here. About a year later, she started becoming the way she is now. A woman very close and very devoted to her God." Placing the brush on the table, he continued, "Tonight her father told me that she is ill. He's taken her to doctors, but they say there's nothing they can do for her."

Turning toward him, she asked, "You mean, she's dying?"

"Yeah," he answered so quietly that she could barely hear his reply.

Rachel wondered why the knowledge of Carmelita's illness made her feel so sad. She barely knew the woman, but there had been something about the tenderness in Carmelita's eyes that had acutely touched her heart.

Rachel was startled out of her thoughts when all at once Klu rose from the bed and started removing his holster. Apprehensively she watched him. She wanted desperately to move as far away from him as she possibly could, but the sheerness of the dressing gown prevented her from rising.

Placing the gun belt on the table, he sat back on the

bed reaching down toward his boots.

"What do you think you're doing?" Rachel exclaimed.

While tugging at one of the boots, he mocked, "What in the hell does it look like I'm doing?"

She started at him in astonishment. "You really do intend to sleep in this bed, don't you?"

Taking off the other boot, he specified, "I ain't sleepin' on the floor!" He glanced towards her and smiled. "Don't worry, Mrs. Granger, I've never raped a woman, and I don't plan to start tonight."

"If you were any kind of gentleman . . ." she started.

Throwing back his head he laughed loudly. "A gentleman! I don't even know the meaning of the word. Besides I'm the filth of the earth, remember?"

Completely forgetting the sheer gown she was wearing, Rachel rose from the bed and vented her outrage, "This is all nothing but a game to you! My life is in danger, my husband must be half out of his mind with worry, and my baby needs his mother! But you find the whole situation comical!"

Suddenly she became frightfully aware of the expression of desire on his face, and embarrassingly she realized how the gown temptingly revealed the contours of her body. With an astute sense of foreboding, she tried anxiously to gather the garment's folds protectively around her; but instantly he was on his feet, and in one swift movement he had her in his embrace.

While trying to push out of his arms, she pleaded, "Please leave me alone!"

"Damn it, I want you!" he confessed fervently, pulling her closer.

359

"You said you've never forced a woman!" she reminded him.

"I'm not going to rape you, you little fool! I'm going to seduce you!" he responded as his lips came down demandingly on hers.

Rachel was determined not to respond to him, but easily, he pried her mouth open under his as he pressed her so intimately close that she could feel the mold of his hard body against hers.

Quickly he lifted her onto the bed, and leaning over her, he gasped, "I've never wanted a woman more than I want you! I've slept beside you without touching you, but not tonight!" She tried to turn her face away, but he was too quick, and his mouth found hers again.

Rachel could feel the weight of his body being lowered on hers. Unwillingly she arched her hips and her arms circled him. She accepted his kiss with a burning desire of her own as she abandoned her resolution and returned his passion.

He ran light kisses over her neck as he whispered, "Baby! . . . You want me as much as I want you."

Because he was taken totally by surprise, she was able to push him away and leap from the bed. Covering her face with her hands, she cried, "What am I doing?"

Instantly he was standing beside her grabbing her by the shoulders as he jerked her toward him. "It's because I called you Baby, isn't it?" he demanded.

When she gave no reply, he shook her roughly yelling savagely, "Answer me, damn you! Answer me!"

With her hair flying wildly over her face from his violent reaction, she shouted, "Yes!"

His fingers dug into her deeply and she winced in

pain. "Who in the hell calls you, Baby? Is it the same man you call 'Darling'?"

As her shame turned into rage, she blurted out angrily, "It's none of your damned business!"

Without lessening his powerful grip he warned, "Don't ever tease me again! If you do, I swear to God, you'll pay for it!"

Cruelly he shoved her with such force that she lost her balance and fell roughly to the floor. Without even glancing in her direction, he picked up his boots and gun belt and strode over to the door, slamming it shut behind him.

Slowly Rachel stood and walked to the bed and fell across it, struggling to hold back her tears. Oh John, she thought. How can I desire another man when it's you I love? Determined not to cry she pushed John from her thoughts. She closed her eyes and the face of her son appeared vividly. Firmly she also cleared his image from her tormented mind.

Restlessly she rose from the bed and paced nervously around the room. There was a part of her that actually longed for Klu to come back and take her into his arms. Rachel couldn't begin to understand the conflicting battle raging within her.

Unexpectedly she heard a sound outside the door, and quickly she ran to investigate. "Who's there?" she asked fearfully.

"It is Miguel, Señora. Klu, he asked me to stand guard in front of your room," she heard Miguel reply from beyond the door.

"Is he coming back tonight?" she asked, though uncertain what she wanted his answer to be.

"I do not know, Señora." he replied.

Ashamed by her confusion she moved away from the door and returned to the bed. Turning down the kerosene lamp, she pulled back the covers and lay down. She had feared that her inner turmoil would keep her awake, but exhaustion from the past two days caused her to fall asleep almost immediately.

The swirling mist surrounded her, and deliriously Rachel tried to escape the heavy fog. The distant sound of a horse's hoofbeats echoed through the dense fog, with each pounding beat growing louder and louder as it steadily approached her. Suddenly the fog vanished and Rachel felt as though she were somewhere far above. She looked down upon the earth and saw herself riding a horse speedily across the plains. Then again the heavy fog fell over the scene. The terrifying pain penetrated her heart!

The mist dissolved again, and Rachel could see herself standing with one fist raised towards the sky. Vividly she could see the look of agony on her tear-stained face. The thick fog drifted down from the heavens . . . The aching pain returned and it was so acute that she wanted to scream!

When the fog once again disappeared, she was lying face down in the grass with her head resting across her arms, and she could hear her own heartbroken sobs. The gray mist crept silently over her. The pain became horrifying! Desperately she tried to escape, but the heavy fog enveloped her in its suffocating mist. Frantically she fought her way out from under the blinding fog!

With tears streaming down her face, Rachel tossed her head from side to side on the pillow as she half-consciously cried, "The pain! Oh God, I can't stand the pain!"

Feeling his strong comforting arms reaching for her she flung herself into his embrace. With her head on his shoulder, she sobbed, "Hold me! Oh, please hold me!"

"Sh . . . shh. . . . Don't cry. It was only a dream," he murmured soothingly, gathering her into his arms.

Opening her eyes, Rachel gently pushed away from him and vacantly glanced at her surroundings. As awareness returned to her she could see the small bedroom dimmed by the low burning lamp. Slowly she looked into the face of the man sitting beside her. His dark eyes studied her with concern as she lingeringly regarded this man she was so strongly attracted to. He wasn't handsome, his eyes were too small, and his face too heavily lined. But there was a masculine ruggedness about Klu that set him apart from others and made him desirable.

"It must've been quite a dream," Klu said, breaking the silence.

"It wasn't a dream," she whispered.

"What do you mean?"

"It's a premonition. This wasn't the first time it's happened to me, and it won't be the last. I will continue having this terrible premonition until it finally comes true. I know that now."

"Do you want to tell me about it?" he asked gently.

Looking deeply into his sympathetic eyes she found herself telling him about the recurring dream. When she had finished, she asked, "Do you think it's a premonition?"

363

"I don't know, but for your sake I hope it isn't. I'd hate to think of you ever suffering that much heartache." He looked warmly into her eyes, and Rachel could acutely feel her passion beginning to stir. She glanced away, but he placed his hand under her chin, turning her face to his.

"Look at me," he ordered. Fighting her desire for him, she raised her eyes to his. "I can't share this room with you and not make love to you. Woman, you'll eventually drive me to rape."

"Then why don't you stay somewhere else?" she suggested, hoping she sounded uncaring.

"Is that what you really want?" he whispered as he took her hand in his. Dropping her gaze, Rachel looked at the hand holding hers. Klu's hand was strong, yet his touch was gentle; so much like John's.

Slowly he leaned closer to her, and Rachel knew this would be her last chance to stop him. If she allowed him to take her into his arms, it would then be too late. There would be no stopping him, even if she were to fight.

Her better judgement screamed at her to turn away, to order him to leave! But that other part of her, the part she couldn't understand, sent such strong signals to him that he actually caught his breath with the palpable desire, before pulling her into his embrace.

"Rachel!" he said passionately, his voice deep and authoritative; so similar to John's.

Wrapping her arms around his neck, Rachel brought his lips down to hers, and releasing all inhibitions, she matched his passion. His kiss was demanding, stimulating, and yet tender, bringing to Rachel's mind all the kisses she had shared with John.

Hastily, Klu rose from the bed and began impatiently to remove his clothes. Hurriedly Rachel pushed back the covers, before slipping off her dressing gown.

As he returned to her side, she gathered him back into her arms. With uncontrollable yearning she kept her lips locked to his as his hand traveled over her body, her unexpected response making him moan with desire.

"Now!" she pleaded. "Please come to me now! Oh Klu . . . Klu I want you!" Rachel could not understand why she felt an overwhelming need to have him make love to her, she only knew that she wanted him.

Frightened and lonely, Rachel instinctively reached out to Klu's compassion and strength, unaware that it was these simlarities between Klu and John that made her want Klu so desperately.

Although Rachel was sincerely drawn to Klu, both physically and emotionally, it was still John's image that came to her mind. As she continued to respond to the man making love to her, tears came to Rachel's eyes, because it was thoughts of John Reynolds that were controlling her heart and arousing her deepest passion.

Klu left early the next morning, before Rachel had even risen, leaving word that he would return later. He'd been gone a few minutes when the door was unlocked, and Carmelita entered the room, once again carrying a tray of food.

"I have brought your breakfast, Señora," she said, walking toward the bed.

Conscious of her nudity, Rachel pulled the covers up under her chin. "Put the tray on the table, please."

Doing as Rachel requested, Carmelita asked, "May we talk?"

"Later," Rachel answered shortly. She wondered why she didn't want Carmelita to suspect that she and Klu had been lovers.

Carmelita understood Rachel's aloofness. "Do not be embarrassed, Señora. Klu is a very sensual man. You should feel no shame that you were unable to refuse him. Very few women have the willpower to turn away from Klu Bronson."

Hoping that Carmelita could help her, Rachel impulsively cried out to her, "But I love John! He's the only man I'll ever love! How can I love him, but still want Klu?"

Smiling at her as if she were a child, Carmelita approached the bed and sat down. "You honestly don't know, do you, Señora?"

Looking at her in complete confusion Rachel sighed disconsolately, "No, I don't."

"You are attracted to Klu because he reminds you so much of John."

"But that's ridiculous!" Rachel exclaimed. "They look nothing alike."

"Señora, their similiarity goes much deeper than a physical resemblance."

"You're wrong, Carmelita! John's not anything like Klu. He'd never rob banks or any of the other underhanded things that Klu does. He probably also rustles cattle, holds up stagecoaches, and God only knows what else!"

"What you say is true, but you must remember that Klu did not have John's, as you say, upbringing. If he had, he would be a man very much like John Rey-

366

nolds.''

"If Klu does subconsciously remind me of John, that may explain why I find him attractive, but that's no excuse . . ." Lowering her voice, she confessed, "For what I did last night."

"Do you feel so guilty that you must find an excuse?''

Sighing deeply into her pillow, Rachel answered forlornly, "Yes."

Standing, Carmelita reached down and picked up the dressing gown from the foot of the bed. Caressing the garment she said dreamily, "It's very beautiful . . . yes? My father gave it to me last year for my birthday. I have never worn it. I have no need anymore for sheer dressing gowns." Handing it to Rachel, she told her, "Put it on and I will get your breakfast."

Quickly Rachel slipped into the garmet, and as Carmelita returned to the bed with the tray, Rachel fluffed up the pillows and leaned back on them.

Placing the tray on her lap, Carmelita coaxed, "Señora Granger, why don't you tell me about yourself. Perhaps if I know you better, I can help you find the excuse you want so desperately."

Rachel watched the woman closely as she sat beside her. She wondered if she could trust her. Was she truly all Klu had said? Had she really undergone such a drastic change? But as she detected the tenderness in Carmelita's dark eyes, she intuitively sensed that she could trust her.

While eating her breakfast, Rachel began to recall her life at the Knolls. Her memory of her parents and her brothers tore at her heart as she spoke of them to Carmelita. She relived her recollections of the war, and once again she could envision their magnificent home crumbling to the ground in flames. She explained why her father had decided to move to California after the war, and how the wagons were to meet in St. Joseph, Missouri. The wagon train, she informed Carmelita, would be led by a man named John Reynolds.

When Rachel suddenly became silent, Carmelita reached for her tray and carefully placed it on the table. "Go on, Señora," she encouraged.

As she spoke, Rachel's adoration and worship for John Reynolds shone clearly in her eyes. "I was in my hotel room with my sister. I had gone to the window, and as I looked down to the street below, he was tying up his horse in front of the hotel. The sight of him took my breath away. I had never in my life seen a man so masculine. I couldn't see his face because it was hidden by the shadow of his hat. Then, as though he somehow sensed he was being watched, he glanced up in my direction. Our eyes met . . . and I think I have loved him from that moment!"

Rachel found it easy to tell Carmelita about her first encounter with John Reynolds. The mysterious way he had looked at her during the dance, and how she had foolishly hidden in the wardrobe in his hotel room. Carmelita laughed with her when she revealed that she had impulsively called him a bastard.

As the minutes steadily ticked away the morning hours, Rachel told Carmelita about her life with John Reynolds. She spoke of their journey to California, her life in San Francisco without him, and her move to Fort Craig. She left out nothing! She did not even spare Carmelita's feelings, but truthfully explained the circumstances that had brought about the night that he had first made love to her. She didn't cease until she had told her everything that had eventually led to her present situation.

When she had finished, Carmelita gently placed her thin hand over Rachel's. "I am sorry, Señora, that I stood between John and the woman he loves. It seems John is still paying for my mistake." Rachel could see a look of heavenly contentment in Carmelita's eyes as she added, "Soon, he will be free of me."

Suddenly remembering what Klu had told her about Carmelita's illness, Rachel tightened her hand on Carmelita's. "What do you mean?"

"I am dying," she stated simply. Noting the concern on Rachel's face, she smiled as she told her, "I have made my peace with God. I am not afraid to die. I only wish . . ."

"What Carmelita? What do you wish?"

"I wish for John's forgiveness," she said so softly that Rachel barely heard her reply.

Quickly she glanced away from Carmelita to hide her sudden tears. John would never forgive her. He was too bitter and too full of hate.

"I know I will never have his forgiveness, Señora. He will never try to find me, and I could never send for him."

Rising from the bed, Carmelita walked to the window, and vacantly looking out she explained, "I have lived with that day every minute of my life. But, with God's help I have learned how to live with it. I had hoped that by now, John would have learned to live with it too."

Turning back toward Rachel she smiled as she abruptly changed the subject. "Now that I know you better, I think I can tell you why you have such a strong desire for Klu.'' Walking slowly to the bed, she continued, ''You are a very daring woman, Señora, and most men are going to find you a challenge they cannot refuse.'' Pausing beside her, Carmelita proceeded, ''From what you have told me about the men in San Francisco and the soldiers at Fort Craig, you, Señora, are a flirt, but a very charming one. If a man is the least attractive, he does not go unnoticed by you, si? Josh, Edward, John, Major Hartly, William, and Klu. You have felt a certain attraction for all of them. You lost interest in Josh because he is too meek, Edward became too much like a brother, and Major Hartly you only gave a passing glance because you were too happy with John. William Granger leaves you cold because his powerful ego you cannot understand. If you weren't already in love with John, I think perhaps, you would fall in love with Klu. But from what you have said, and I believe you, even men like Klu are overshadowed by John Reynolds.'' Sitting on the edge of the bed, she gently touched Rachel's hand as she continued. ''Do not be ashamed of what you feel for Klu. For you to reach out to a man like Klu is most natural. You are alone and frightened. You need someone who is strong, yet gentle. Basically Klu is a good man, Señora. He has told me that he plans to help you escape. Be thankful that you have him, and take what he has to offer you. You will not regret it, Señora. It is not impossible, my friend, to feel love for more than one man.''

''Love!'' Rachel exclaimed. ''But I only love John!''

Carmelita smiled. ''I know you love John. I can see it in your eyes. But, Señora, at this time in your life, do not turn away from Klu Bronson. You need him. You need his protection, as well as the comfort of his arms."

A family residing on a small ranch a few miles from Fort Craig had been massacred by Apaches. The father, mother, six children, and seven ranch hands had been mercilessly tortured and killed. Captain Godwin and his company had been the first to come upon the scene. The family and the ranch hands had been dead for three days. As his men were digging the graves that would cover the grotesque bodies, Captain Godwin had sworn that he would get even with all Apaches!

On the same day that Rachel had the private discussion with Carmelita, John Reynolds and Zeke were riding across the dusty plains of New Mexico at the front of the colonel's troops. It had been Colonel Reynolds' responsibility to locate and seize the band of warriors that had murdered the white family and the men who had worked for them. Earlier that morning the small band of braves responsible had been apprehended by the colonel and his troops, but Captain Godwin and his men were as yet unaware of the capture, and were still out searching for the Indians. Colonel Reynolds and Zeke were attempting to find the captain so that he and his soldiers might return to the fort. Having found the tracks made by Captain Godwin's troops, Colonel Reynolds and his men were tracking them at an unhurried pace.

Glancing at the man beside him, Zeke asked the question that had been on his mind for days. "John, them thar reenlistment papers are still on yur desk at yur office. They been just a-settin' thar for a week. Are ya goin' to sign 'em or not?''

"I don't know. What do you want to do Zeke?"

"Tell ya the truth John, I'm a-gitten' too damned old to do much of anythin'." Watching his friend closely to observe his reaction, he continued, "I think I'd like to settle down fur a change. Just set around and take it easy fur the rest of my days."

"Settle down!" John exclaimed.

"That what I said, ain't it? Hell, don't ya ever git tard of ramblin'?" Zeke asked, agitated.

Smiling fondly at the old man, John inquired, "Where would you like to settle down?"

"Well, I was sorta thinkin' 'bout your ranch."

"No!" the Colonel refused sternly.

"It's 'cause of Miss Rachel, ain't it?"

Disregarding his question, John told him, "If you want to live on my ranch, feel free to do so, but don't expect me to join you!"

"All right then, damn it! We'll settle somewhar else!"

"Zeke, I really don't think I'm ready to settle down."

"You've always been too restless fur yur own good."

Laughing lightly, John replied, "You have a lot of room to talk, you old coot! You'd been ramblin' for twenty years before I met you."

Chuckling good-humoredly, Zeke agreed, "Yep, reckon I had at that, but now I'm a-gittin' too damned old."

"Zeke, you just tell me where you want to settle, and I'll see that you get there. If you want a ranch of your own, I'll buy you one, or perhaps you'd rather own

372

some land in the mountains. Just tell me what you want and you'll have it.''

Looking at the Colonel with love and gratitude written all over his aged face, Zeke's voice broke with emotion as he asked, ''You'd do that fur me?''

Studying the old man with obvious puzzlement, he replied, ''Hell, yes! I don't see why it should surprise you.''

''Well you ain't one fur expressin' yur feelins to people who care 'bout ya. If'n ya was, ya'd never have lost Miss Rachel.''

''Must you always bring up her name?'' he asked, trying to sound nothing more than slightly perturbed, although his emotions were much deeper. The sound of her name was a sharp pain severing his very soul!

''Bein' that her name has been brung up, I reckon this is as good a time as any to tell ya what I've been a thinkin' 'bout doin'.''

''What's that?'' John asked.

''I think I'll go visit Miss Rachel fur a few days. I miss that little gal a powerful lot, and I'm sorta hankerin' to see that thar baby of hers.''

''I tell you what Zeke, why don't you take some time off and go to the ranch and while you're gone decide what you want to do.''

''You're plannin' to stay in the Army, ain't ya?''

''Maybe,'' he replied.

Suddenly acutely aware of how lonely his life would be if he weren't sharing it with the man he loved as a son, Zeke decided, ''Well, don't make no never mind. I'm a-goin' wherever you go.''

''I thought you were getting too old,'' John reminded.

"I reckon I ain't as old as I thought I was. Besides, when I set around a lot, my rheumatiz starts a-actin' up." As their eyes met, the unspoken understanding between the two men was unquestionable.

They rode in silence for a few minutes before the colonel asked, "Zeke, by the direction of these tracks, where do you think Captain Godwin is heading?"

"I'd say the stupid jackass is a-headin' straight fur Chief Lone Eagle's village."

"So would I. Zeke, maybe you'd better ride on ahead and see if you can catch up with him. If he's already at the village, tell him I said to get the hell out of there and leave the chief and his people alone!"

"Ya want me to wait fur ya at Lone Eagle's village?"

"Yeah, I haven't seen the old chief in quite a while. But tell Godwin to return to the fort."

Zeke started to leave, but pausing momentarily, he said, "John, reckon I'll leave tomorrow and go see how Miss Rachel is doin'. I worry 'bout her."

Nodding his head in agreement, the colonel admitted, "I worry about her too, and God, I think about her all the time!" Finding himself unable to hide his true feelings, he confessed, "Sometimes, Zeke, I miss her and want her so damned much that it's like a continuous pain that keeps eating away inside of me."

Deciding it was best not to say anything, because there was really nothing that he could say that would help, Zeke encouraged his horse into a gallop and quickly rode away.

Pulling his horse up beside the colonel's, Major Hartly asked, "Where is Zeke going?"

"It looks like Captain Godwin is heading for Chief Lone Eagle's village. Zeke is trying to catch up to him before he gets there.''

"Chief Lone Eagle?" the Major repeated vaguely. "I can't remember ever hearing his name.''

"He's an old chief and his village is quite small. He refused to unite with the other Apaches and declare war against the white man. But soon he'll have no choice but to unite with the others. Our own kind have lied to him too many times. But most of his braves considered him to be as weak as an old woman, so they packed up their families and moved. A few of the braves remained with him so there are some children and young squaws still in his village, but mostly old men and old women are all that's left.''

"You know, Colonel, sometimes I wonder just what in the hell you are doing in the cavalry. You don't sound like a man who wants to fight Indians.''

Laughing, John answered, "You've got a good point there, Major. What in the hell am I doing in the cavalry!''

"How far away is the village?'' he asked.

"We should be there by late afternoon,'' the colonel replied.

Smiling to himself, John wondered how Zeke would react when he told him that they were leaving the cavalry. And by God, they'd buy a piece of land somewhere, and settle down!

Chief Lone Eagle's village was located in a secluded valley enclosed by small rolling hills. As Colonel Reynolds and his soldiers drew nearer they spotted thick smoldering smoke, billowing into the air and drifting over the extending hills. Feeling a frightful sense of foreboding, John broke his horse into a gallop, followed closely by his troops.

The colonel was fully aware of the awful possibilities awaiting him on the other side, but he never imagined that he'd be forced to witness a massacre and holocaust so dreadful that the horrifying and shocking scene would haunt him for the rest of his life!

As the pungent odor of burned flesh assailed the horses' nostrils, they neighed excitedly and trembled nervously beneath the colonel and his soldiers. Masterfully retaining control of the frightened animals, the cavalry rode slowly down the hill and into what had become a village of death!

Captain Godwin's troops were standing at a distance from the burned and massacred Indian camp. The colonel could vaguely detect the sorrowful groans of some of the soldiers as their temporary insanity had passed, and they were being suddenly confronted with what they had done.

Forgetting to give his men permission to dismount, the colonel slowly swung down from his saddle as though he were in some kind of trance. Following his lead, the major and the stunned troopers quietly dismounted their horses.

As one of the young soldiers surveyed the gruesome slaughter of the Indians he had to turn away, and he violently vomited onto the ground. Another soldier leaned against his horse for needed support and agonizingly moaned, "Oh dear God! . . . My God!" The others could only stand immobile as they incredulously stared at the horribly murdered and burned bodies lying before them.

Hearing a loud and constant flapping coming from above him, Major Hartly glanced up into the sky and saw that the buzzards had already congregated over the once peaceful Indian village. When the carnivorous birds opened their beaks their shrill squawking resembled ear-splitting screams, descending eerily down toward the earth. Losing his usually controlled composure, the major put his hands tightly over his ears to try to muffle the high-pitched shrieking and cold-blooded screams of the vultures.

Shocked, the colonel walked across the village, carefully stepping over and around the dead bodies. He groaned aloud and looked away in horror when he came upon an infant with a sword thrust completely through his tiny body. Lying next to the baby was the mother who had probably been partially decapitated with the same sword that had also taken her child's life.

As the shock he was experiencing began to slowly fade, John cried out in alarm, "Zeke! Oh God, Zeke, where are you?"

Suddenly panic-stricken, perspiration sprung out heavily on his brow as his strong voice rose loudly above the shrieking of the vultures, "Zeke ! . . . Oh damn ! . . . Zeke ! . . . My God, answer me ! . . . Zeke!"

Frantically he maneuvered around the bodies of the Indians as his eyes searched wildly for a glimpse of the old mountaineer. Brusquely he wiped the nervous sweat from his brow as his inner fear increased to a climactic crescendo. "Zeke ! . . . Where are you ! . . . Oh God, please let him answer me!"

John Reynolds had seen many gruesome sights during his years in the war, but nothing had ever affected him so violently as the body of the squaw that he had blindly approached. Her eyes were wide open and staring vacantly up at the sky. The terror and pain she had suffered was frozen on her lifeless face. The sour taste of bile rose in the colonel's throat as he saw how her womb had been ruthlessly slashed open, and the small fetus removed, stabbed, and then thrown carelessly across her legs.

Trying desperately to remain steady, the colonel quickly swerved away and resumed his search for Zeke. While looking for his friend, he came upon the remains of old Chief Lone Eagle, who had so many gun wounds that he was drenched in his own blood.

As John's eyes frantically scanned the village he suddenly spotted the familiar sight of buckskins. His heart was accelerating with fear and dread as he hurried to the still form lying a few feet away.

Zeke was face down on the ground. Kneeling beside him, the colonel gently turned him over. When the old man's eyes fluttered open he gave a sigh of hopeful relief as he called loudly, "Major! Major, it's Zeke! He's been wounded!"

"Get my bag!" he could hear the doctor shout to one of the troopers.

"John . . ." Zeke whispered faintly.

Holding him tenderly in his arms the colonel pleaded, "Don't talk. Save your strength."

"I tried to stop 'em," he began weakly, "but they all . . . went berserk."

"Who shot you?" he asked.

"Ain't gonna tell ya. Don't want ya a-goin' after 'im and gittin' yurself courtmartialed. . . . He was chasin' a little girl . . . was goin' to shoot her. I tried to save the child. . . . I ran fur her and I reckon I got in the line of fire. Did any of em' survive, John? The child

. . . is she dead? She's such a tiny little thing, 'bout three years old.''

Noticing the body of a small Indian girl lying nearby, John compassionately refused to answer his question. ''The major is coming, Zeke. Please just be quiet and save your strength.'' Hearing Major Hartly approaching the colonel called, ''Hurry!''

Hastily the doctor knelt and quickly examined the ghastly wound in Zeke's back. He had lost so much blood that the major was astounded that he could still be alive. Looking over at Colonel Reynolds he shook his head sadly.

''John . . .'' Zeke called feebly.

Unconsciously John brushed the dirt from the old mountaineer's face. ''I'm right here, Zeke.''

''Tell . . . Miss Rachel. . . .'' he began.

''Tell her what?'' John asked.

Coughing weakly, he whispered, ''Don't reckon . . . ya need to tell her. . . . That little gal . . . knows how I feel 'bout her.'' Feebly, Zeke clutched at the colonel's hand. ''John,'' he groaned before slowly closing his eyes.

As the vultures were screeching overhead, and the black smoke from the destroyed teepees was drifting up into the clouds, Zeke died in the arms of John Reynolds.

Gathering the old man lovingly into his embrace, the colonel held his face against the top of Zeke's head, and his voice quivered with grief as he moaned, ''Oh no! No! Oh God! No!'' Holding Zeke's body tightly to him, hard sobs tore deeply from his throat.

Sympathetically Major Hartly watched as John reluctantly released the old mountaineer and gently laid him back on the ground. As the colonel glanced in his direction, the major was startled by the burning rage that shone hysterically in the colonel's eyes. Stunned into temporary muteness, the major silently looked on as Colonel Reynolds stood and abruptly walked away. Fearing an act of uncontrolled violence on the colonel's part, the major hurried after him.

As John paused beside the infant that had been brutally murdered, the major easily caught up to him. With his hands shaking, Colonel Reynolds reached out and grasped the handle of the sword that was lodged into the child. Tears of compassion and anger filled his eyes as he pulled out the sharp-edged blade from the baby's bloody torso.

"What in the hell are you doing?" Major Hartly demanded.

The eyes that looked over at him were full of hate and madness. "Only officers carry swords!"

Swiftly the colonel swerved and with the sword held securely in his hand, he strode briskly past the sprawled bodies. Steadily he stalked towards Captain Godwin's troops, as the major followed him.

"Where is he?" the colonel bellowed angrily.

With their shame and regret showing plainly on their faces, not one man had the courage to look him in the eye.

"Where's Godwin?" he shouted savagely.

Finding his courage, one of the soldiers replied meekly, "I don't know for sure, sir, but right before you rode up . . ." While pointing in the correct direction, he continued, "I saw him walking over that hill."

Major Hartly stood with his gaze fixed steadfastly on the colonel as he turned and headed quickly toward the hill overlooking the village.

Wasting no time, the major ran to the colonel's troopers as he called, "Corporal!"

Stepping forward the young man replied, "Yes, sir!"

"Come with me and for God's sake, hurry!"

Captain Godwin was completely satisfied. He couldn't have felt more fulfilled or more content if he'd just sexually climaxed with a woman. He'd never before realized how thrilling and how pleasurable it could be to kill an uncivilized savage! There's one thing for sure, he thought, those damned Apaches will never kill a white person!

Smiling cleverly, he lay back and stared up at the sky that was shadowed by the black vultures. "You buzzards will feast today," he told them. Suspecting the Indians he had attacked were not the ones guilty of the massacre on the white family didn't bother him in the least. They were Apaches, and all Apaches should be dead!

Suddenly hearing a sound coming from behind him, he hastily got to his feet, and turning, he was surprised to see the colonel. He'd been so wrapped up in his blissful satisfaction that he had not been aware of the troop's arrival. He caught his breath in fear when he saw that the colonel was carrying his sword.

Trying to compose himself, Captain Godwin called, "I suppose you want an explanation, sir."

The man didn't answer, but steadily approached him with long determined strides. As he drew nearer the captain could see the hard expression on his face. "I was only planning to question the chief," he explained, while fearfully backing away from the huge man's approach. "But when we rode up they started shooting at us. I had no other choice but to order my men to attack."

Easily Colonel Reynolds' long strides caught up to the captain's, and with his eyes glaring, he yelled, "You lying sonofabitch!"

"If you don't believe me, sir, you can ask my men."

"Why? You've got them so goddamned brainwashed they'll lie for you!" Raising the sword, he continued, "I found something that belongs to you, Godwin! Do you know where I found it?" His voice broke with compassion as he raged, "In a baby! You goddamned murdering bastard!"

His blow came so fast that Captain Godwin never had a chance to deflect the sword. The flat side of the blade struck him powerfully across the side of his head knocking him to the ground. Throwing down the sword, Colonel Reynolds pulled the captain roughly to his feet. Before the major and the corporal could reach him, his large fist caught Godwin sharply across the jaw, and then flatly it struck against the captain's nose, causing fresh blood to spew down his uniform mingling with the dried blood of the Apaches he had murdered.

As they grabbed for him, it took all the strength the two men possessed to pin the colonel's arms and pull him away from the captain.

"I'll see that you are court-martialed for this!" Captain Godwin shouted with his courage returning now that Reynolds had been restrained.

Forcefully the colonel jerked loose from the hands holding him, and stepping forward, he swung his powerful fist. It landed above the captain's eye and, losing sensibility, he was knocked backwards. His knees buck-

382

led and he fell clumsily to the ground.

Once again Colonel Reynolds' arms were seized by the major and the corporal. "Let me go!" he ordered, trying to pull away.

"Good God man!" Major Hartly shouted. "He's not worth killing! If you kill him the army will hang you!" Noticing his words went unheeded, the major said firmly, "Zeke wouldn't want it to be that way! For his sake, let it be!"

Hearing Zeke's name brought his sanity back to him and he relaxed in their strong grip. Cautiously they released him, and the colonel said quietly but commandingly, "Get him out of here!" With no further words he walked away from them.

"Major," the corporal began, "Captain Godwin isn't going to get by with what he did, is he? He murdered those people!"

"You heard what he told the colonel. They fired on him first and his men will swear to it. They have no other choice."

"You didn't believe him, did you?"

Shrugging his shoulders he answered, "No, but what I believe doesn't matter. So some Indians were killed. Do you think the army will give a damn?"

"But what about the other Apaches?"

"They, Corporal, will most assuredly give a damn! And they will seek their revenge!"

Slowly Major Hartly moved over to the captain and knelt beside him. Consciousness had returned to him, and while sitting up unsteadily he said angrily, "Major, you and the corporal are my witnesses! You saw the colonel strike another officer!"

"I don't know what in the hell you're talking

about," the major denied. "I saw you climb that hill over there and then lose your footing on the way down. You really took a hard fall. Those jagged rocks cut your face up pretty badly."

Captain Godwin stared at the major in disbelief and then quickly he looked at the corporal. "You saw what really happened!"

"Yes, sir!" he confirmed.

Captain Godwin reverted his gaze to Major Hartly and smiled smugly, but the smile faded as the corporal added, "Next time, sir, you should be more careful. You could break your neck falling down those steep hills."

Helping Godwin to his feet, Major Hartly ordered, "Corporal, take him back to the village." Looking at the captain he warned, "If you have any instinct for survival you'll get on your horse, and get the hell out of here before Colonel Reynolds decides to kill you after all!"

As the corporal and Captain Godwin were leaving, one of the colonel's soldiers unexpectedly appeared over the rise of the hill hurrying toward the major.

As he drew closer, the major questioned, "What do you want, Private?"

"Excuse me, sir, but there was an Indian boy in the village. I grabbed him, but he pulled loose, and got to his horse. Do you want us to go after him?"

Shaking his head, the major answered, "No, let him go."

"Sir . . . ?" the man began. "I think the kid was a half-breed because he could speak English. Sounded like a Mexican accent."

"What did he say?"

"He asked for the colonel's name," he replied.

"Go on back to the village. I'll report this incident to the colonel," the major said as he turned and began walking in the direction John had taken. The major wondered where he had gone and if there was any way he could help him with his grief. Then from a distance he spotted the colonel. He had climbed one of the small hills and was leaning against a tall boulder while looking down on the burned village. He watched as John Reynolds unexpectedly struck the large rock with his bare fist. With blood dripping from the cut and bruised hand, he yelled across the valley that even the vultures had finally left in deathly silence. "RACHEL! RACHEL!" Her name echoed over the quiet plains from off the surrounding hills.

The major had always wondered which soldier Miss O'Brian had so obviously loved, and now at last he knew.

Rachel was asleep when Klu entered their room, so he went quietly to the chair by the window and sat down. Reaching into his shirt pocket, he took out a cigar and match.

An instant after Rachel's name had echoed miles away across the plains of New Mexico, she sat straight up in the bed and screamed, "John! John!"

Dropping the cigar and match, Klu hurried to her and gathered her into his arms. "Did you have a nightmare?" he asked.

Gently pushing out of his embrace, she looked at him in confusion. "Wh . . . what happened?"

"You just screamed out a name. Don't you remember?"

"No," she replied, muddled. "Who did I call?"

"John," he answered.

At the mention of his name Klu could easily see the disturbance and fear on her face. "Oh, my God! Why? Why would I scream for John? I don't remember dreaming about him. Maybe there's something wrong! Maybe he needs me!" Clutching his arm frantically she groaned, "Oh God, what if he's hurt?"

Thinking such grave concern could only be for her child, Klu tried to reassure her, "I'm sure your son is just fine."

"My son!" she exclaimed. "His name is William!"

Feeling a resentment that was strange to him, he rose from the bed and while staring down at her he asked angrily, "He's the man that calls you 'Baby,' isn't he?"

Perturbed by his unreasonable jealousy, she stood abruptly as she replied sternly, "My personal life is none of your business!" Pushing past him, she strode to the window and turned her back to him as she looked out at the barren land. "You have no right to be jealous!"

Hastily he crossed the room and moved to the door, but instead of opening it, he turned towards her and said bitterly, "Why should I be jealous? I'm the one who has you!"

"Against my will!" she stated as she turned and faced him.

He grinned cleverly. "We both know only part of what you say is true, don't we, Mrs. Granger?" Wrinkling his brow into a frown that almost caused Rachel to laugh aloud, he asked, "What in the hell is your name?"

"Rachel," she answered. "Before I was married, it

was Rachel O'Brian.''

"So you're Irish. Now I know why you have such a temper and why you're so damned stubborn. But I like the name. Rachel. Somehow it seems to fit you.'' Caressing the name, he repeated, "Rachel.''

Crossing the room, she walked over to him. Gently she touched his cheek. "I won't deny there isn't a part of me that wants you. For some unknown reason, I find myself reaching out to you.'' Stepping away from him, she confessed, "There is a part of me that belongs to you, but Klu, my heart always has and always will belong to only one man!'' Her eyes shone with the truth as she proceeded, "I love John and I will love him until the day I die!''

Detecting her unmistakable expression of love, he swerved swiftly and opened the door.

"Where are you going?'' she asked.

"I need a drink!'' Glancing towards her he said determinedly, "But I'll be back!'' He strode out of the room slamming the door behind him.

Wondering why he should so obviously be jealous, Rachel walked back to the window and stared at the dry desolate land stretching out before her. Forgetting about Klu, her thoughts returned to John. She couldn't shake the gnawing feeling that something was terribly wrong. Leaning her head against the pane, she sighed, "Oh darling, what is it? What has happened to you?'' Tears welled up in her eyes and rolled down her cheeks. Barely above a whisper, she said, "I love you, John Reynolds, and I will always love you!''

While Rachel was crying for John Reynolds, he was still standing alone on the hill in New Mexico, staring down at the massacred village below him. He was shocked and grieved by what had happened to Chief Lone Eagle and his people, but the sharp, endless pain that tore at him was caused by Zeke's death. He had loved the old man for over twenty years. With every fiber of his being he longed for the one person who could comfort him, because she alone could share his grief for the old mountaineer.

Leaning against the tall boulder beside him, he whispered hoarsely, "Rachel, you loved him too! Oh God, Baby, I need you! Rachel . . . !"

Chapter Ten

Rachel remained a prisoner inside the small, unadorned room for two long and nerve-wracking months. She had to continuously fight back a rising feeling of claustrophobia. Except for the two servant girls, she was not allowed to see anyone but Klu and Carmelita. During the secluded weeks Rachel spent locked inside the tiny room she and Carmelita became close friends. For hours Carmelita would sit patiently, listening attentively as Rachel elaborated on her love for John Reynolds.

Unknown to Rachel, Carmelita was also in love with John, although she hadn't loved him when she married him. She'd been too selfish and too immature to love anyone, even her own child. But years before, when she made her peace with God and with herself, her heart had filled with love for the man she had married. Although Carmelita envied Rachel and John's love, she wished the best for them, and she believed that John Reynolds and Rachel belonged together. But she realized the chance of the two of them ever sharing a future was very unlikely, if not altogether hopeless.

Rachel not only loved John Reynolds but virtually

worshipped him, yet she had absolutely no control over her desire for Klu Bronson. The weeks they spent together were often spent making love. Rachel was fully aware that she felt something special for Klu. Perhaps Carmelita had been correct, and if she weren't already in love with John, she would have fallen in love with Klu. But the guilt she had experienced at the onset of this new relationship was now gone, so she consumed very little of her time analyzing her feelings for Klu. Rachel believed what she and Klu felt for one another was only temporary. Compared to her love for John Reynolds, she thought, it was all inconsequential.

Rachel had always possessed a complete and total lack of insight. Not only was she unaware that Carmelita loved John, but also had not realized that Klu had fallen in love with her.

Klu Bronson had never loved a woman, he had never loved anyone. It wasn't because he was incapable of love, for Klu had been born with the capacity to love and to care, but from the moment of his birth his will to love had been taken away from him. It was as Carmelita had said: if he'd been born into John Reynolds' circumstances he'd have become a man very similar to John. But Klu hadn't been born into that kind of life.

Klu was born the bastard of an aging prostitute named Jewel Bronson. When she had first realized that she was pregnant, she tried to get rid of the unwanted child, but Jewel failed at her attempt at abortion the same as she had failed miserably at everything else in her life. When the madam discovered that Jewel was pregnant, she threw her out of the cheap and shabby house of prostitution in San Franciso, which had been Jewel's only residence for years.

Klu's mother was saved from vagrancy and starvation by a huge sadistic man who owned a run-down saloon on the Barbary Coast. He immediately put her to work waiting on tables, and it was understood that after the birth of her child, she would also prostitute for him.

Klu came into the world in the middle of the night as the heavy fog from the ocean crept in from the sea. Except for the owner of the saloon, there was no one to help with the delivery.

On hearing her child's first cry, Klu's mother had asked, "Abner, is it a girl?"

"Nope, it's a boy, and his damned cryin' is already gettin' on my nerves!"

Carelessly Abner dropped the newborn infant onto the bed beside his mother. Jewel took one look at her child and hated him on sight. If the baby had been a girl, perhaps she could've felt something for him, but Jewel hated the whole male population. They had been the cause of all her hardships.

More than likely, Klu would have died of starvation if Jewel's breasts hadn't ached when they filled with milk. The only relief was to nurse her child, so reluctantly she would feed the baby, a baby who had never known so much as one moment of love.

Klu learned early in life that if it wasn't his mother finding some reason to unjustly harass him, it would be Abner gladly handing out his own merciless and cruel punishments. By the time Klu was five years old he'd been beaten with belts, razor straps, and a homemade paddle. He had been locked in a narrow dark closet for as long as a week at a time with nothing to eat but bread and only water to drink. When Klu turned six, Abner decided that he was old enough to start earning his own keep. The chores that he piled on the small child kept him laboring from dawn until night. Klu was seven years old when Jewel deserted him to run off to the gold fields with two men. Klu felt no remorse over losing his mother, he was only thankful that now there would be only Abner to torture and punish him.

During the next six years Klu worked and lived with the huge ruthless man that he hated with every fiber of his being. At the end of that time, Klu realized he'd soon be old enough to venture out on his own. He had no idea where he'd go or what he'd do, but at the young age of thirteen he could see no further than getting away from Abner.

But his escape would come much sooner than he had anticipated. One week before his fourteenth birthday, he was helping Abner close up the tavern. The man had been drinking heavily and in his drunken stupor he mistakenly thought his money box was short twenty dollars. Immediately he accused Klu. As he approached him, the boy fearfully backed away from the monstrous man, trying to convince him of his innocence. But Abner had no intention of listening to his pleas. Savagely he removed his belt, and Klu realized the cruel man would again beat him mercilessly. In his fear Klu had backed himself behind the bar where Abner kept his loaded pistol. As he reached over and his hand tightened around the handle of the gun, Klu knew that Abner would never beat him again. He pointed the pistol into the huge man's shocked face and pulled the trigger. Before the age of fourteen, Klu Bronson had killed his first man.

He took the cash from the money box, stole Abner's horse, and in the early hours of dawn he rode out of San

Francisco, never to return. With luck and fortitude the young boy arrived safely in a small town in Texas. He was offered a job in a saloon as a cleaning boy in return for room and board plus a meager salary. Across the street from the saloon was the general store. It was owned by Tom Burks, who had at one time been a teacher. He took pity on Klu's ignorance and charitably decided to tutor the boy. Klu was thirsty for knowledge, and he greedily absorbed all Tom had the time to teach him. Klu lived in this quiet town for two years. For the first time in his young life he found a certain degree of happiness and contentment, but it would be only temporary because life would once again deal him a bitter hand of injustice.

During the middle of the night, Tom Burks' store was broken into and burglarized while he slept peacefully in his bedroom at the back of the store. The thief planted some of the stolen merchandise inside Klu's room to frame the boy and then informed the sheriff that he'd seen Klu sneaking out of the general store. On that same night Klu had gathered up his books and slipped off to the quietness of the stables to concentrate deeply on the books Tom had loaned him; thus he had no alibi. He was immediately accused of the crime and quickly found guilty. When the state marshal came through town he took the boy with him to the penitentiary.

At the vulnerable age of sixteen Klu was locked behind cold stone walls with men who were not only ruthless but also cold-blooded murderers. Klu had to learn how to fight for his very survival.

Before Klu was released his cellmate told him how to contact his brother, Luther, who had his own gang, and who was certain to need a young man like Klu. At eighteen Klu left the prison a hard, bitter man. Not knowing what else to do, he headed straight for Luther Wells.

Luther promptly took a liking to Klu and taught him everything he thought he should know. Willingly he instructed him on how to rob banks, rustle cattle, stay alive on the trail, cover up his tracks, draw a gun swiftly, and shoot accurately. Although Luther tried diligently, he continually failed in his effort to teach Klu to forget the compassion that had been born in him. Sometimes it would seem to lie dorment, but it was always there deep inside, just waiting to suddenly leap to the surface. Often Luther warned Klu that someday his compassion could very likely be the cause of his death. Despite this flaw, Luther successfully turned Klu into a criminal, but a ruthless criminal he would never be.

For six years Klu rode with the Wells gang, but when Luther was killed during a bank robbery, Klu left the gang to strike out on his own. Soon after that he met Miguel, and they had been riding together for ten years when they joined Jake and Juan to rob the bank in El Paso.

And now, at the age of thirty-four, Klu Bronson had fallen in love. He loved her spirited green eyes, her smile that could be so sweet yet so enticing, her uninhibited passion that gave as much as it received; but most of all, he loved the fact that she was so unsophisticated and natural. With all his heart, Klu Bronson loved Rachel O'Brian Granger, but dolefully he believed that she would never return his love. Once again life had dealt him a losing hand.

* * *

Klu hurried up the flight of steps, unlocked the door, and rushed into the room. Closing the door behind him, he said, "We're leaving tonight."

Rising from the chair, Rachel stared at him in astonishment. Then suddenly she smiled as she exclaimed, "My baby! Soon I'll be seeing my baby! Oh Klu, I've missed him so much!"

Moving toward her, he replied, "I know it's been difficult for you."

"Difficult!" she cried. "That's putting it mildly! But, of course, being a man, you couldn't possibly understand how a mother would miss her child!"

He looked deeply into her eyes as he answered. "No, I wouldn't understand."

Incapable of detecting his tone of sadness, or the sorrow in his eyes, she scoffed, "If your mother is still alive, the next time you see her, that is if you ever bother to visit her, ask her how it would feel to be separated from her baby. I'm sure she could tell you!"

Rachel was startled when all at once he threw back his head and laughed uproariously but bitterly. "My God, you've got to be the most dense woman I've ever met. But I suppose your ignorance excuses your insensitive outburst. Do you honestly believe that all mothers are like you? Are you really so ignorant of life?"

Suddenly Rachel's mind flashed back to a hotel room in San Francisco. She could once again see Edward's handsome face as he had asked her the very same question. She could feel a moisture in her eyes as she wondered where Edward was and if he were well.

"What are you thinking about?" Klu asked, puzzled by the sadness which had come to her face.

Disheartened, she sighed, "I was thinking about Edward Phillips."

Fighting the sudden impulse to laugh aloud, she watched Klu as he stalked across the room and then swerved in her direction, yelling, "Damn! How many men are involved in your life? Granger, John, two close friends, and now someone named Phillips? Are you in love with him too?"

"In a very special way, I love Edward. But Klu, those two close friends you mentioned, one of them is John."

"And the other?" he asked.

"Zeke." Unable to restrain her laughter, she giggled merrily. "But Zeke is old enough to be my grandfather."

"And these men," Klu began, "I'm sure they all love you." His love for Rachel was revealed on his face and could be heard in his voice as he added, "You're an easy woman to love, Rachel."

With her usual lack of perception, Klu's remark escaped her notice. "Klu what is your plan? How do you intend to help me get away?"

"I don't have a definite plan," he answered. "Jake has ten men riding with him. It's going to be hard as hell for Miguel and me to get you out of this."

"Klu, maybe you shouldn't try. Why don't we just let William pay the ransom. Then Jake will let me go, and you won't need to risk your life."

"When he gets the money, he still won't let you go," he commented.

"What!" she cried.

"You heard me, damn it!" Klu shouted. "He won't let you go! He'll kill you, and he'll try to kill me in the

396

process because he knows I'll make an attempt to stop him!''

"But why should he kill me if he has the ransom?''

"Because you know too much and you've heard too much. He realizes Granger will try to track down every man responsible for your abduction. He's scared of your husband's power and reputation. He'll kill you to silence you! The less Granger knows, the less chance he has of finding him.''

"What did you mean, by my husband's reputation?''

She could distinctly hear the sarcasm in his voice as he explained, "William Granger has a reputation for hanging a man and asking questions later!''

"But that's not true!'' she protested. "William would never hang someone!''

He looked at her keenly as he answered, "It would seem you're as ignorant of your husband as you are of life.''

"I refuse to believe that William would unjustly accuse a man, let alone hang him!''

Smiling cunningly he taunted, "Why Mrs. Granger, if I didn't know better, I'd think you were a loyal and faithful wife.''

Placing her hands on her hips, she stated angrily, "I'm perfectly aware that my husband is arrogant and imperious, but he isn't an executioner!''

"An executioner? A murderer? Call it what you want, but it all comes down to the same damned thing! Your husband has killed and more than once!''

"That's not true!'' she insisted.

"How can you be so damned sure it's not true?''
Swiftly he moved to her and grabbed her roughly by the

shoulders. Staring down into her eyes, he repeated, "How can you be so damned sure?"

She could feel a foreboding chill running through her as she answered, "Dear God, I don't know if it's true or not!"

As though he suddenly found her role as William Granger's wife revolting, he disgustedly shoved her aside. "When you return home, I suggest you have a long conversation with your husband. Obviously you aren't very well acquainted with him."

"But Klu . . ." she began.

But rudely he whirled from her and vented his outrage. "I have no use for his kind! Your husband thinks of himself as a god, and he relishes handing out unjust punishments to his inferiors!"

"Why are you so bitter?" she asked.

Facing her he replied, "Because the William Grangers of this world have always looked down on me as though, to borrow a quote, I were the filth of the earth!"

"But only because you're an outlaw, Klu!"

She was taken aback by the fury in his dark eyes as he said violently, "He unjustly accuses people and then finds them guilty!" Angrily he reached for her, pulling her harshly towards him. "But what could you possibly know about being unjustly accused! You've been pampered and spoiled all your life!"

Pushing his hands away she replied furiously, "Pampered and spoiled! Do you call staying locked up in this room for two months being pampered and spoiled?"

"It's kept you alive!"

"Oh Klu, do you have any idea what it's like to be kept a prisoner? It's as though you have no will of your own. You don't even live, you only exist!''

Immediately sympathetic to her cry of despair, he gently took her into his arms. Holding his cheek against the top of her head he told her soothingly, ''I understand how you feel. I understand more than you know. But soon, Rachel, it'll all be over. You'll be back home and reunited with your son.'' Tenderly he released her as he explained, ''We're going to a small town called Arido. It's close to the Mexican border, and Jake plans to make contact with your husband from there.''

''But if we're going into a town, surely there will be a sheriff there to help us.''

''The sheriff is the town drunk. We'll get no help from him or from anyone else. Why do you think Jake chose that particular town?''

Noting the worry and fear she was trying to conceal, he drew her back into his arms. ''I won't let Jake or anyone else hurt you. Somehow, I promise you, I'll get you away safely.'' He tightened his hold on her, and her slim body relaxed within his comforting embrace. Suddenly he longed to whisper the three words to her that he'd never spoken to anyone in his entire life.

But before he had the chance to confess to Rachel that he loved her, she gave a deep sigh and unintentionally disheartened him by saying, ''I wonder if John has heard about my abduction.''

Rachel was startled and confused when abruptly he stepped away from her. She couldn't understand the anger glaring in his eyes as he asked, ''He's always uppermost in your mind, isn't he? Damn you, Rachel! Damn you for making men want you when you only want one man!''

He reached for her, but the rage on his face didn't

frighten her, and she slipped out of his grasp. "How dare you insinuate that I made you or anyone else want me!"

As she carefully backed away from his steady advance, he replied angrily, "You send out signals to a man, Rachel, that tear him to pieces! You challenge him and you taunt him, and just when he thinks you really care, you remind him of how much you love another man!" Grabbing her arm he roughly pulled her toward him and swiftly lifted her into his arms. Carrying her to the bed, he said sharply, "You're a teasing little bitch! But by God, I'm going to have you one last time!"

Roughly he dropped her on the bed, and blinded by his fury he ripped her blouse, removing it by force. As he reached for her skirt he suddenly recalled to Rachel's mind the two men who had almost raped her, and frantically she cried, "No! Please! No!"

Detecting the torment on the face of the woman he loved, Klu subdued his anger. As the truth of what he'd almost done began to register, he slumped on the bed, leaning his head in the palms of his hands. "I'm sorry . . . I'm sorry, Rachel," he moaned.

Shielding herself with the torn blouse, she sat up on the bed watching him warily as he explained, "I'm not mad at you, Rachel, but I took my anger out on you. I'm sorry."

"Why are you so angry?" she asked.

He raised his head from his hands and looked at her pathetically. "I've been angry all my life. You know why I stay so damned angry? Because sometimes, in the middle of the night, even after all these years, I can still remember being locked in that dark closet!" For

400

the first time in his life, Klu opened up the old but still painful memories as he ranted, "My God, I can still hear those damned rats crawling in the walls. The beatings I could take; but, that small, confining black closet! I was horrified of it!" Reaching over and clutching her hand, he asked pleadingly, "How could they do that to such a little boy? How in the hell could they do it?"

"Klu, what are you talking about? My God, what happened to you as a child?"

Regaining control of his emotions because he'd never learned how to share them, he said firmly, "Forget it! Forget everything I've told you!"

"But Klu . . ." she started.

"No!" he yelled. "Forget it!" Brusquely he drew her into his arms, and before pressing his lips to hers, he whispered with the pleading of an unloved child, "I need you! Make love to me, Rachel. Please make love to me!"

Responding to his passionate kiss, she pulled him down on the bed beside her and willingly granted his request.

Klu had informed her that they would leave shortly after dusk. Restlessly Rachel walked to the small window and glanced up at the darkening sky. The setting sun cast a peaceful glow across the barren plains. Soon now she would be free from the restricting room that had been her prison for two months.

Hearing a key turning in the lock, Rachel drew her gaze from the window and anxiously watched the door. She expected to see Klu, but instead, Carmelita rushed into the room.

Noticing that Rachel was dressed in the same clothes she had worn when she had first arrived, Carmelita said, "Then it is true, Señora. You are leaving tonight."

Smiling happily, Rachel answered, "Yes! Oh Carmelita, I'll soon be home with my baby!"

Quickly Carmelita moved over to Rachel and hugged her tightly. "I will be praying for your safety. And for Klu's."

Realizing how much she would miss her new-found friend, Rachel replied, "You've been a good friend to me." Studying the woman's pale and thin face, she began, "Carmelita, if I should see John . . ."

Interrupting, Carmelita said forcefully, "No, Señora! Do not mention my name to him! Promise me that you won't!"

"But why?" she asked.

"He may decide it would be best to come see me, and I could not bear seeing the hate that would still be in his eyes. He will never forgive me, Rachel. And I think perhaps, he will always hate me."

"But if I tell him how you have changed and how kind you were to me, then maybe his feelings toward you would be different."

Smiling fondly at Rachel's naive and simple solution to her problem, Carmelita replied, "No, Señora."

Deciding not to argue the point because she was too afraid that Carmelita was right, Rachel brusquely changed the topic of conversation. "Obviously Klu has spoken to you about his childhood because you once said that he didn't have John's upbringing. What kind of childhood did he have?"

"He told me once that it had been very unhappy. He

402

said that his mother never wanted him and never loved him. Unlike John, he was not born into wealth and respectability."

"Did he ever mention his father?"

"No, Señora," she answered.

Apparently talking more to herself than to Carmelita, she said vaguely, "Then I wonder who he meant when he said how could . . . they . . . do that to such a little boy. They? Was he speaking about his mother and father?" Looking at Carmelita, she questioned "Did he tell you anything else?"

"Si, Señora. Once I told him that I would pray for him. I can still remember the bitterness on his face as he told me, 'Don't bother to pray for my soul. It was lost in Hell the night I was born.' "

Wrinkling her brow into a worried frown, Rachel replied, "I wonder what he meant."

"I do not know, but obviously Klu's childhood was very tragic, and perhaps very cruel."

Sighing with a disappointment she felt toward herself, Rachel walked across the room, then turning back to Carmelita she said, "I'll soon be twenty-one years old, but I'm still as ignorant of life as I was when I was a girl living under Papa's protection."

Laughing lightly at Rachel's look of desperation, Carmelita told her gently, "Do not be so hard on yourself, Señora. You cannot visualize Klu's childhood because you have always been protected from the harsh cruelties of life. First you had your father's protection, then John's, Edward Phillips', William Granger's, and now Klu's. Oh, Señora, with your lovely and innocent charms you will always have a man's protection. Consider yourself fortunate."

403

"I'm not sure that William would try to protect me from cruelty."

"Why?" she asked.

"Because, I'm afraid that the man I married . . ."

"Yes, Señora?" Carmelita coaxed.

"I'm afraid that he is cruel, himself." Trying to shake off her unpleasant intuition, she continued, "No! . . . No, I'm wrong. I just let something Klu told me influence me."

"What did Klu tell you?" Carmelita questioned.

"That William has unjustly hanged men." When Carmelita quickly glanced away, Rachel caught her breath apprehensively as she gasped, "Dear God, it isn't true, is it?"

"I do not know, Señora. I only know what I have heard. Please do not question me about your husband."

"Very well, Carmelita. I won't question you, but when I return home, I have a lot of questions for my husband. And damn him, he's going to tell me the truth!"

Noticing the clothes that she had loaned Rachel folded neatly on the bed, Carmelita walked over and gathered them into her arms.

"I'm sorry, but you will find one blouse torn beyond repair," Rachel apologized.

Smiling, Carmelita answered dreamily, "That is all right, my friend. I can still remember how a man can become overanxious."

Suddenly Rachel was struck with acute jealously as she wondered if perhaps Carmelita was remembering a special moment with John. But as the door opened unexpectedly their thoughts fled as Klu hurried into the room.

"We'll be leaving in a few minutes. Are you ready?" he asked while untying his bandanna.

"Must I be blindfolded? It'll soon be night. What could I possibly see?"

"I'm sorry, but when we're about an hour's ride from here I'll remove it."

Realizing that their departure was near, Carmelita took a step toward Rachel but then halted as she said, "Goodbye, my friend."

"Goodbye," Rachel replied.

Carmelita crossed over to the door. Opening it she looked back at Rachel and before leaving she said, *'Vaya con Dios.'* Quietly she pulled the door shut behind her.

Rachel stared forlornly at the closed door. "I wonder if I'll ever see her again." Turning to Klu she asked, "Did the doctors ever say how long she has?"

"I don't think they know. Try not to feel sad, Rachel. Carmelita doesn't want you to grieve for her. Think about your son, and how you'll soon be home with him."

"If . . . I ever get home," she replied.

Intentionally letting her remark pass, he explained, "You'll be hearing a lot of different voices because Jake's men are riding with us."

With the heartrending pleading of a child she cried, "Oh Klu, how can you and Miguel possibly protect me from Jake and ten of his men?"

"If you're worried about being raped, they won't bother you. No man will volunteer to make the first move because he knows he'll be the first sorry bastard I'll kill. And you don't have to worry about Jake. He wants to keep you alive until the ransom is paid.''

Holding the bandanna in his hand, he moved towards her. He started to step behind her, but she stopped him by asking, ''Klu, why did you want to hurt me?''

''I didn't want to hurt you. I've already told you, damn it, that I wasn't mad at you! I was angry at life in general!'' He moved away, then with undisguised anger in his voice he pivoted towards her as he raged, ''Life has never given me an even break! I was doomed from the night I was born over a cheap saloon on the Barbary Coast. Until you came into my life I was able to live with it because I didn't give a damn; but now, Rachel, when I see you I see all that I'll never have. You know you don't miss what you've never had. I never had a goddamned thing, so I had nothing to miss! But now, Rachel, for once in my life, I actually had something. For two months I had you!''

Once again Rachel was incapable of comprehending what he was trying to tell her. Instead of saying what he longed to hear, she replied, ''Klu, perhaps it'd help if you were to talk about it. Obviously your deep resentment goes back to your childhood.''

Swiftly and angrily he reached out, turning her around roughly. Placing the bandanna over her eyes and tying it securely he told her, ''My mother was a cold-hearted bitch! And that says it all! Talking about it won't change a damned thing!'' Putting his hands on her shoulders, he placed his lips close to her ear as he said barely above a whisper, ''Twice now I have tried to tell you how I feel but neither time have you heard me.''

Taking her hand he led her to the door, opened it,

and guided her out of the room. Because of her anxiety at leaving the safety she had found in the small room, Rachel spent no time wondering what he had meant.

Two days later they arrived at the town of Arido, and once again Rachel was locked inside a plain, bare bedroom. The refreshing and stimulating hours she had experienced outdoors once again made the room seem unbearably confining. But this time she hadn't been blindfolded, and as they had ridden into town she'd been able to see the shabby hotel that would be her next temporary prison.

Nervously Rachel paced continuously across the bare wooden floor. She had crossed the room so many times that she memorized how few steps it took to cover the limited space. It had been three hours since Klu and Jake brought her up to the room and then left her alone. Immediately she had contemplated escape, but one of Jake's men was standing guard under the window, and another was stationed at her door. Escape would be impossible.

Hearing the doorknob turning, Rachel backed across the room. Dear God, she thought, what if it's Jake and Klu isn't with him? Maybe he's killed him and now he's coming after me!

She let out a sigh of relief as Klu strode energetically into the room. Grateful for his presence, she hurried to him and threw herself into his arms. ''Thank God, it's you!''

Holding her tenderly, he asked, ''Were you afraid it would be Jake?''

Clinging to him tightly, she answered, ''Yes! He frightens me, Klu!''

Moving her gently so that he could see her face, he smiled lovingly at her irresistible vulnerability. "I won't let him hurt you. I'm going to get you out of this. I promise you."

"When does Jake intend to make contact with William?"

"He's sending a messenger to Granger in the morning." Releasing her, he said lightly. "Now smile for me, and look pretty because I'm taking you to dinner."

"To dinner?" she asked with enthusiasm.

"Well actually we won't be going any farther than downstairs to the dining room, and believe me, to call the crummy place a dining room is to stretch the imagination."

"Oh, I don't care what it looks like! I'm just glad to be leaving this room."

Laughing warmly at her obvious exhilaration, he studied the face gazing up at him with open joy. "You are not only the most naive woman I've ever met, but the most natural. Rachel, you're a lovely woman, but it's not your beauty that makes a man love you. The country is full of lovely women. Your power over men lies behind those beautiful green eyes. You're just so damned enticing." Understanding her look of confusion, he laughed again as he added, "And you're completely unaware of where your charms lie. Perhaps that's why they are so irresistible."

Klu took her hand into his and opening the door, he led her into the hallway. For a moment she tried to analyze what he had said, but it all went beyond her conception of herself. Rachel would forever lack the knowledge to understand why a man could love her so deeply, but she wasted no time trying to figure it out. She was being freed from that confining room and going downstairs, and at the moment, that was much more important.

When they entered the dining room, Rachel saw what Klu had meant. The unclean and greasy-smelling room was relatively small, with five tables placed randomly in the restricting area in front of the bar.

Klu led her to a table in the corner of the room. As he pulled out a chair for her, she looked in the direction of the bar, meeting Jake's sadistic eyes staring at her.

Following her gaze, Klu warned, "He's going to be watching your every move, so don't try anything foolish. Just make yourself as inconspicuous as possible."

Sitting in the chair, Rachel fleetingly surveyed the room. Besides Jake, the rest of his men were also standing at the bar. She noticed two men at a table greedily devouring their food as though they hadn't eaten in days. She could see a man sitting alone at the far table, but he was in the shadows, and she was unable to see his face.

Trying not to draw attention to herself, she stared down at the table. Distastefully she discovered that the tablecloth was dirty and stained.

"I'm sorry, Rachel. Perhaps you'd rather eat in your room," Klu apologized, as he sat in the chair across from her.

The man sitting alone in the shadows, rose from his chair and slowly sauntered toward them. Rachel detected the man's movement, but intentionally she kept her gaze lowered. She knew Jake would be watching her like a hawk.

"Are you Klu Bronson?" she heard a voice ask. A strange, mysterious feeling set her pulse racing.

409

"Why do you want to know?" Klu questioned.

"I was talking to Jake a few minutes ago and we're getting up a poker game. We thought you might be interested in joining us."

It all happened in a matter of seconds, but Rachel felt as if she and the whole world had suddenly slid into slow motion as she recognized that once-familiar voice and raised her eyes anxiously to look up into his handsome face.

Fortunately for Rachel the man was blocking Jake's view, and he was unable to see her reaction, but Klu was immediately aware of her undisguised astonishment.

"Rachel!" he whispered strongly. "My God woman, must you be so damned obvious!" As she glanced back at the unclean tablecloth, Klu continued, "Well, it's quite apparent that you two know each other."

Rachel had to force herself not to rise and fling herself into the man's embrace. While choking back a sob, she whispered, "Edward!"

Keeping his voice low, Edward Phillips asked, "Are you all right, sweetheart?"

Nodding her head, she answered, "Yes, I'm fine."

Glancing at Klu, he said casually, "I thought the lady would be wise enough to pretend that she didn't know me, but I thought wrong, didn't I?"

Watching him skeptically, Klu asked, "Who in the hell are you?"

Answering the question herself, Rachel told him, "This is Edward Phillips. I mentioned him to you a couple days ago."

"Tell me, Bronson. Do you intend to shoot me now or later?" Edward asked as though it were only incidental.

Cautiously Rachel raised her eyes and looked up at Edward. He was more handsome than she had remembered. His black curly hair perfectly matched the black hat he wore pushed back from his forehead. Edward's dark brown eyes, shadowed by his long thick lashes, were staring unflinchingly into Klu's. His sensual, pouting lips were curved very slightly with the beginning of a sly grin. He wore a pale blue shirt, and it fit snugly under a black gold trimmed vest. As her eyes traveled lower, she was surprised to see that he was wearing a holster and gun strapped around his hips. His tight black pants outlined his long muscular legs. Edward Phillips had grown more handsome and more masculine during the two years that had separated them. Suddenly she remembered the last words he had spoken to her that night in San Francisco. Feeling a flush rise to her cheeks, she looked away from him, reverting her eyes to the table. . . . I wonder if he still loves me?

"We don't have much time, Phillips," Klu began. "Jake will be over here any minute, but during the game tonight we have to find the opportunity to speak alone."

Drawing his dark eyebrows together into a puzzled frown Edward asked, "Why?"

"With your help, maybe I can get Rachel out of here."

Edward started to question him, but hearing Jake's approach, he said clearly, "After you and the lady have dinner, we'll start the game."

As Jake's huge frame neared their table Rachel hastily glanced up, and for an instant her eyes met Ed-

411

ward's; and in that fleeting instant the familiarity in his loving gaze brought back memories of the past. In a matter of seconds she could once again see the wagon train rolling endlessly beside the Platte River. She could envision her father walking proudly beside his wagon, snapping the whip over the heads of the oxen. She heard her mother's soft and gentle voice. She could see Zeke as he teasingly told her his outlandish tale about Scotts Bluff. She heard the breeze whispering through the tranquil night as she stood with John beside the Platte River. She remembered how he had taken her hand into his, and she had mysteriously sensed that when she was with him she was where she belonged.

When Klu entered the dimly lit room he could see Rachel lying on the bed. He approached the bed and lovingly observed her sleeping face. In sleep she appeared to be even more vulnerable. He reached down and caressed the long auburn hair that radiantly framed the young woman's beauty. Gently he sat beside her, and as the bed gave under his weight, she restlessly tossed her head as consciousness slowly returned.

Leaning over, he placed a kiss on her forehead as he whispered, "Rachel."

Instantly her eyes flew open. "Klu! I didn't mean to fall asleep! What time is it? Where is Edward? Did you two have a chance to talk privately?"

Laughing lightly, he replied, "It's a little past midnight. Phillips will be here shortly and, yes, we had a chance to talk. You're leaving tonight, Rachel."

Startled, she bolted straight up on the bed and clutched his arm. "Tonight! But how?"

"About an hour ago we finally got rid of Jake. He drew to an inside straight once too often. He was broke so he went on to bed. The others that had been playing had already quit, so Phillips and I were left alone. A few of Jake's men were still up at the bar, but they couldn't overhear us, so while we played cards we planned your escape."

"How do I escape?" she asked breathlessly.

"Phillips has been here for a few weeks and he has this . . . lady friend . . . who will willingly do anything he should ask her. He and the woman will be here in a few minutes. Jake has two men guarding the door, but Phillips and I talked so loud and carried on so much that they all know Phillips owes me two hundred dollars. He'll pretend to be bringing me the money, and his girlfriend will be with him, which shouldn't cause any suspicion because he loudly informed me that he'd have to borrow the money from his woman. She's about your size, but she has darker hair, so she'll be wearing a scarf. You'll change into her clothes, and then you'll leave with Phillips. The hallway is pretty dark, with the scarf covering your hair, it just might work.

"But what will Jake do to you when he finds out I'm gone?"

Placing his hand over hers, he asked, "You care, don't you, Rachel? You really care what happens to me."

"Of course I do!" she replied honestly.

"Phillips will tie and gag me, and the woman also. We're going to make it look as if he took me by surprise, and that he had it all planned. Jake isn't too bright, and he may be dumb enough to fall for it. I

413

talked to Miguel before I came up here. He'll have two horses saddled and waiting for you behind the hotel. There will be food in the saddlebags, and the canteens will be filled with water."

She spoke so softly that he barely heard her. "Klu, I'm so afraid."

"Try not to be. I'm sure Phillips will get you away from here safely."

Grasping the hand that was placed over hers, she cried, "I'm not afraid for myself! I'm afraid of what Jake may do to you! Oh Klu, you're risking your life to save mine! If Jake doesn't believe you weren't involved, he'll kill you!"

Seeing Rachel's unselfish concern for him on her worried face, he had the impulse to confess how much he loved her, but at that moment Edward's voice suddenly announced his arrival at their door.

"Wh . . . where can I find Klu Bronson?" they heard Edward ask one of Jake's men.

"What do you want with 'em?"

"I owe the lucky bastard two hundred dollars and I want to pay off m . . . my debt."

Rachel realized Edward was intentionally slurring his words as though he were drunk. She glanced at Klu and smiled knowingly. She had no inkling how her enticing smile sharply penetrated him. Sending the woman that he loved back to her husband was the hardest thing he'd ever done in his life.

"Sugar," Rachel heard a woman's voice begin, "you better not be lyin' to me about owin' some man two hundred dollars. If I find out you want my money for some woman, I'll kill you! I swear it!"

"N . . . now, Mary, don't get all riled up sweetheart. It's not for another woman. It's for Bronson. But I can't seem to find the lucky sonofabitch!"

Klu rose from the bed and hastened to the door. Swinging it open roughly, he raged, "Who in the hell are you calling a sonofabitch?"

The light from the room was shining through the open door, and Rachel could see into the hallway. Edward was standing casually with one arm over the woman's shoulders as though he were in need of her support to stay on his feet. She noticed that he carried a bottle of whiskey carelessly at his side.

"Aw . . . come on, Bronson! Didn't mean no offense. I've come to br . . . bring you your money. I always pay my debts."

"You mean, I always pay your debts!" the woman remarked sarcastically.

"Just to prove there's no hard feelin's . . . let's all have a little drink," Edward said drunkenly.

"I only want my damned money!" Klu stated.

Pushing past him, Edward and the woman walked unsteadily into the room. "You'll get your money, but first we'll have a drink."

Looking at the two men standing in the open doorway, Klu ordered, "If he and his friend aren't out of here in five minutes, come and drag them out!"

Smiling cheerfully, one of them replied, "You might as well have a drink with him. He ain't gonna shut up until you do."

"Yeah? Well, I was just gettin' ready to get myself somethin' a lot better than a drink."

Observing Rachel sitting on the edge of the bed, the man answered, "She sure looks better than a drink to me."

"You got any glasses?" Edward asked loudly.

Slamming the door, Klu said clearly, "Just give me the damned money, then get the hell out of here!"

Immediately Edward unbuttoned his vest pulling out the strips of rope that he had concealed. Hastily Mary began removing her red dress, and glancing at Rachel's shocked expression, she said, "This is no time to be bashful, dearie." Standing unembarrassed in her sheer petticoat, she threw the gaudy dress towards Rachel. "We ain't got much time, so you'd better remove your modesty along with your clothes."

Slowly Rachel picked up the garment, and vacantly, she stared down at the dress. "Put it on, damn it!" Klu ordered harshly.

She had never undressed in front of two men, and she could feel a flush burning her cheeks. She glanced at Klu and then at Edward. They were watching her closely, but Rachel could read their concern for her in their eyes, and reprimanding herself for being so foolish, she quickly removed her clothes.

Walking to Rachel, Mary paused beside her and slipped off her shoes, as she said, "I hope they fit."

Smiling timidly, Rachel replied, "Thank you for your help."

Rachel put on the dress, then stepped into the shoes. Removing the scarf, Mary handed it to Rachel, and quickly she tied it over her auburn hair.

"On the bed!" Edward ordered.

Rachel looked on silently as Mary and Klu obeyed Edward's order. She watched as Edward grabbed Mary's arms and pulled them over her head. Using the strips of rope, he began tying her wrists to the bedpost. He then tied her feet to the post at the foot of the bed.

"Rachel," Klu whispered. "Honey, I'll never forget you."

She knelt beside him, and reaching for his hand, she guided it to her lips. "Thank you, Klu. Thank you for everything you've done for me."

Edward moved to their side of the bed, and quickly, Rachel stood and watched as he tied Klu in the same fashion that he had tied Mary.

"Don't forget the gags," Klu reminded him.

Reaching into his pocket, Edward brought out two handkerchiefs. Handing one to Rachel, he said, "Use this to gag Mary."

As she began walking to the other side of the bed she could hear Klu saying, "This isn't good enough. Jake knows no man could ever tie me down like this, not if I was awake." She halted her steps, and understanding what he meant, she looked fearfully over at Klu. "You'll have to knock me out, Phillips," he continued.

"No!" Rachel gasped.

Ignoring her protest, Klu warned, "Just be sure that you don't hit me hard enough to kill me."

"Oh Klu! No! He could accidentally kill you!"

Looking at Rachel, he said impatiently, "We don't have time to argue, damn it! Do as Phillips told you and gag her!"

Extremely worried about Klu's welfare, she moved to Mary and with trembling hands tied the handkerchief over the woman's mouth.

Rachel looked over at Edward and held her breath in fear when she saw him removing his pistol from its holster. Grabbing it by the barrel, he lifted it over Klu. As the handle of the gun came down, making contact against the side of Klu's head, Rachel unconsciously bit into her bottom lip so hard that she drew blood.

"Will he be all right?" she cried.

"God . . . I hope so," Edward groaned, but noting the deep anxiety on Rachel's face, he said encouragingly, "He'll be out for a couple of hours and have a bad headache for a while, but otherwise, he should be okay."

He returned his gun to its holster. Then he removed Klu's pistol and concealed it under his shirt. Taking the handkerchief, he tied it over Klu's mouth. Glancing at Mary, he told her, "Thanks a lot, Baby." Turning from the bed, he headed towards the door as he said, "Let's go Rachel, and remember to keep your face down."

She began following Edward, but impulsively she ran back to the bed. Lovingly she placed a kiss on Klu's forehead. Looking down at the unconscious man, she pleaded, "Please God . . . please keep him safe!"

Edward and Rachel traveled continuously during the remainder of the night and the following day. They didn't stop to eat, but ate while still on horseback. The only rest their horses received was when the riders would dismount and walk beside them.

Once Rachel tried to question Edward, but he abruptly cut her short, informing her that they would talk later. Rachel wondered if Edward had known of the circumstances surrounding her abduction when he had walked brazenly over to her and Klu in the hotel dining room, or had he only suspected something was wrong when he saw her with a man like Klu Bronson? Had he somehow known she was married to William Granger? Had he perhaps seen Deborah and Josh?

And if so, how had he known where to find them? Had someone told him where Deborah and Josh were living? Was it possible that he could've learned of their whereabouts from John?

Rachel was relieved when at last Edward decided to stop for the night and make camp. The sun had set hours before, and though there was a full moon the sky was overcast, causing the still night to be extremely dark.

Edward started a small fire and feeling comforted by its light and warmth, Rachel settled herself close to the flickering flames. She tucked the folds of the dress under her legs. She wished that she were wearing trousers instead of being bothered with the nuisance of a dress. Distastefully, Rachel glanced down at the bright red skirt. She had never worn such an unbecoming garment. Rachel wasn't ungrateful to Mary for her help, but she wished the woman had worn something without such a revealing neckline and such a loud color.

Taking a blanket from one of the horses, Edward unrolled it and placed it over Rachel's bare shoulders. Sitting beside her, he asked, "Are you hungry?"

Gathering the blanket around her, she answered, "No, not really. Edward, I have so many questions to ask you."

Smiling at her tenderly, he replied, "I know, sweetheart, and I already know all the questions you need to ask, so why don't I just tell you how I found out about your abduction."

"Then you did know!" she exclaimed.

Taking her hand, he held it gently in his. For a moment he stared at the small hand that was enclosed within his. "It was about two weeks after your abduc-

419

tion that I arrived at the ranch. At the time I knew nothing about what had happened to you. I was merely planning on visiting with Deborah and Josh.''

"How are they?" she asked.

"They're both very concerned."

"Poor Deb, she must be half out of her mind with worry."

"William Granger stopped by the ranch while Deborah and Josh were telling me what had happened to you." When she made no comment, he asked, "Don't you want to know how your husband is doing?"

He could easily detect the irritation in her voice as she answered, "Oh, I'm sure he's just fine!"

"He looked pretty worried to me, Rachel, and like a man who hadn't slept or eaten in days."

"I honestly didn't think he cared," she replied softly.

"Well, obviously he does."

Regaining her irritation, she replied, "Of course he cares! I am one of his possessions!"

Edward wondered if he should tell her that while William was at the ranch, one of his vaqueros had arrived from the hacienda with a message that the 'patron's' son had taken ill, but he decided it would be best not to tell her. By now the child was probably well, and he would only be worrying her needlessly.

"I left the ranch the next morning. I headed straight for Arido. I knew that men like the ones that captured you usually end up in towns like Arido. I was gambling on a long shot by hoping that I might hear some inside information concerning your whereabouts, but I never dreamed that I'd actually see you!" Chuckling, he continued, "When you so transparently let on that you knew me, I thought for sure you had signed my death warrant. Lucky for me, Bronson was on our side."

She looked at him, and the shimmering glow of the fire was reflected in her eyes, making them dance with wild excitement. "Who told you where to find Deborah and Josh?" she asked breathlessly.

Edward studied her closely. He had seen that expression before, and he knew she could be thinking of only one person. My God, he thought, she still loves him!

Slowly he released her hand as he reached into his shirt pocket for a cigar and match. He appeared to be in deep thought as he sat quietly rolling the cigar back and forth between his fingers. Leisurely he struck the match across a nearby rock, and placing the cigar between his lips, he lit it. Then he took a long drag from the cigar before blowing out the burning match. "I was in New Mexico," he began, "and I remembered that Kendall and Reynolds were stationed at Fort Craig."

"So you went to Fort Craig?" she questioned.

Nodding his head, he answered, "Yeah, I went to the fort."

Clutching his arm, she asked anxiously, "Did you see John?"

He moved his hand over hers and held it securely. "He isn't there, Rachel."

"What do you mean, he isn't there? Where is he?"

"I don't know," he replied.

"Why didn't you find out? Didn't you ask someone where he had gone?"

She could detect the seriousness in his voice as he said, "I don't know where he is, but I do know why he left."

The warmth from the glowing fire was unable to prevent the cold chill that ran through her fleetingly. "What happened? What happened to him?"

"When I arrived at the fort I met Major Hartly, and I told him that I was looking for Kendall and Reynolds. We had a long conversation, and he told me about Josh being wounded and where he had moved. I asked him if you were still living with your sister. He spoke very highly of you, Rachel. He seems to think a lot of you. He said that you had been living with Deborah, but Zeke told him you had married."

"And John? Did he tell you about John?"

Edward looked away from the pleading in her eyes as he continued, "Captain Godwin, and I understand you're acquainted with him, attacked a small Indian village. Reynolds and his troops got there shortly after the massacre." Looking back at Rachel he could see the horror and repulsion materialize on her face as he told her in detail what John Reynolds and his soldiers had witnessed.

"Reynolds had sent Zeke on ahead to tell Godwin to stay away from the village, but by the time Zeke arrived, the massacre had already started."

"Zeke!" she said lovingly. "Did he leave Fort Craig too? But of course, he did. He'll always stay with John."

Hearing the affection in her voice, he asked carefully, "Rachel, how close are you to that old man?"

"I couldn't love Zeke any more if he was my own grandfather." Suddenly she felt Edward's hand tightening painfully over hers. Feeling a dreadful sense of foreboding, she held her breath in fear as she inquired, "Why?"

"Zeke was killed during the massacre," he replied.

Edward wasn't sure what he had expected from her. Hysterics maybe, tears definitely, but instead she simply pulled her hand free of his. He saw how her whole body seemed to stiffen as she stared into the flames. Her voice was strained as she said, "Tell me about his death."

As the fire continually burned lower and the many sounds of night could be heard off in the distance, Edward told her how John had found Zeke, and how the old mountaineer had spoken Rachel's name before he died in John's arms. Silently she listened as Edward talked about John's reaction to Zeke's death and the way he had attacked Captain Godwin.

Placing a few branches on the dying fire, Edward continued, "Major Hartly walked away from Godwin and the corporal to search for Reynolds. He finally found him. He was standing on top of a hill leaning against a boulder. The major said he saw Reynolds swerve and strike his fist against the rock and then he . . . he . . ."

Rachel turned to Edward, and he noticed how her lips trembled as she asked, "He what?"

"He called for you."

Although she didn't say a word, her heartstricken anguish could be seen on her face, and heard in the low mournful moan that escaped from deep in her throat.

They both remained silent for a long moment and vacantly watched the small fire as darting sparks snapped and crackled from the dry burning branches.

"Zeke was buried in the military cemetery at the fort, and the next day Reynolds left for Fort Stanton to file a complaint against Godwin and to turn in his resignation. Major Hartly asked Reynolds how he could get in touch with him, but he told him that he didn't know where he would be. But Rachel, I'm sure he'll eventually return to his ranch. He probably just needs some time alone.''

While staring into the fire, she asked, ''Did the army prosecute Captain Godwin?''

''I don't know, but the major was quite certain that Godwin would never come to trial. The charges against him would simply be dropped and forgotten.''

Rachel turned to him and he was startled by the cold rage in her eyes. ''If there is any justice in this world, someday Captain Godwin will pay for what he did! And I hope he pays with his life!''

He saw how her rage unexpectedly vanished as once again she looked down into the glowing fire. Reaching over and patting her shoulder gently, he got to his feet. Realizing she would need time alone, he walked over to tend to the horses.

There were no tears in Rachel's eyes as she stared at the darting flames flickering over and above the branches that Edward had placed on the fire. Her mind began drifting back over the months, until finally, she found herself recalling the day that Zeke had come to the hacienda, traveling all the way from Fort Craig just to be with her.

Rachel remembered how she had been in her bedchamber sitting in the large chair in front of the fireplace, when hearing a firm knock on her door, she had called weakly, ''Come in.''

Rachel's eyes had widened with surprise and joy when Zeke walked briskly into the room. With enthusiasm she hadn't displayed in months, she had jumped from the chair, rushing into Zeke's outstretched arms.

Hugging her vigorously, he said, "Miss Rachel, ya always feel good to these old arms of mine."

Tenderly she looked up into his eyes as she smiled, "Oh Zeke, it's so good to see you again!" Taking his hand, she led him over to one of the chairs. "Sit down, Zeke, and tell me what you're doing here. Why did you leave the fort?"

"Thanks, Miss Rachel, but I reckon I'll just stand. What I got to say to ya, I ain't gonna say a-settin' down."

"What's wrong?" she asked, confused.

"Miss Deborah and yur husband sent me a wire askin' me to come to the hacienda. The wire said that ya was ill, so I high-tailed it here as fast as I could. And what do I find when I finally git here? That ya ain't sick at all! That yur just bein' ornery, stubborn, and a dadblasted fool!"

Indignant, she raised her chin, glaring at him. "And don't go a raisin' that thar stubborn chin of yurs! Miss Rachel, just whar do ya git off a-worryin' yur sister and yur husband this a way? And just who in the hell do ya think ya are to take a chance with the life of that thar baby God's a givin' ya!"

He could see a trace of tears in her eyes as she cried unbelievingly, "Zeke, how can you talk to me this way?"

Angrily he strode across the room and then back toward her. "Ya can just dry up them tears, cause this is one time yur cryin' ain't gonna make no nevermind with me! Ya know, Miss Rachel, thar's been more than one time when I thought a good spankin' wouldn't do ya no harm, and if it weren't fur that thar baby yur a carryin' that's exactly what ya'd git from me!"

Placing her hands on her hips, Rachel started to reply, but he stopped her as he quickly continued, "Little gal, I've felt a lot of things fur ya. Thar's been times when I've been mighty proud of ya, like that time ya fought the Apaches with me, and when ya risked yur own life to stay with Lieutenant Kendall in the infirmary. And thar's been times when my old heart has ached fur ya. When ya lost ya parents, and when John rode out of the fort knowin' ya'd be leavin' fur Texas. Thar's been times when I've been downright angry with ya, like when ya told me ya married up with Granger. And, Miss Rachel, thar has also been times when ya made me realize how much I loved ya. But I never thought I would dislike ya!"

"Dislike me!" she exclaimed.

"Yep, that's what I said. I just got through havin' a long talk with Miss Deborah and Granger, and, Miss Rachel, I just ain't got no use fur the woman you've done become! I ain't got no use fur her at all!"

Anger flashed in her eyes as she shouted, "How dare you come in here and talk to me this way! If you don't like me, then get out of my room, and out of my life!"

Shouting right back at her he replied, "I ain't a-goin' nowhar 'til I've had my say. I didn't ride all them thar miles fur nothin'!"

"Then have your say and then get out!" she yelled.

"Ya might as well control that thar Irish temper of yur's little gal, 'cause I still got a lot more to tell ya!"

"Indeed! Well, I'm not interested!"

He moved over and stood in front of her, looking down into the green eyes staring steadily into his. "All yur life, Miss Rachel, if ya didn't git what ya was a-wantin', ya cried and carried on 'til ya got it.

426

Whether it was somethin' ya was a wantin' from yur Mama or yur Pappy, or anyone else who loved ya. And if'n they didn't give it to ya willingly, ya found some other way to git what ya was a wantin'. Even if it meant a-sneakin' out of yur hotel room to go to a dance. Did ya ever wonder, little gal, what might have happened to ya if'n ya'd a-hid in some man's room besides John's? At Fort Craig, ya cried and carried on enough that ya finally got John to go against his principles and make love to ya. Did ya think just 'cause he took ya to bed, he'd be yurs just fur the askin'? Didn't ya realize he'd eventually have to send ya away from that thar fort? And damn it, Miss Rachel, didn't ya know marryin' a man ya didn't love weren't the answer? Now little gal, you've made yur bed, and ya don't wanna lie in it! Ya figger if ya cry and carry on enough someone will make everythin' all right again. Well, ya ain't got no parents to make things right fur ya, and John ain't gonna come a-ridin' down here and steal another man's wife and child away from 'im! This time, Miss Rachel, ya ain't got no choice but to reap what ya done went and sowed!"

"But Zeke, I love John," she cried.

"Yes'm, I know ya do, but ya done lost 'im. Ya got to face up to it and then go on from thar."

"I don't want to live without him," she stated stubbornly.

"Yes, ya do, Miss Rachel! Ya wanna live, if'n ya didn't ya'd have kilt yurself long 'fore now! Ya just wanna set up here and sulk and be all weepy 'til someone makes everythin' right fur ya. Well, that ain't gonna happen! Thar ain't gonna be no miracles, Miss Rachel! John ain't gonna come fur ya! So if ya want yur life to be right again, yur goin' to have to do it fur yurself.''

Pouting childishly, she replied, ''But Zeke, I feel as though I have nothing to live for!''

''What do ya mean, ya ain't got nothin' to live fur!'' he yelled. ''Ya got everythin' to live fur. Ya got yur whole life ahead of ya, and ya got people who love ya and need ya!''

''No one needs me!'' she cried despairingly.

Placing his hands firmly on her shoulders, he replied gently, ''I cain't speak fur no one else, Miss Rachel, but I need ya.''

''Oh Zeke, how could you possibly need me!''

'' 'Cause I ain't got no one but you and John, and I need ya both, but in a way I think I sorta need you more. I need someone I can hold in these old arms, and someone who'll hug me the way you do. It makes me feel loved and even an old coot, like myself, wants to be loved. Yes'm, Miss Rachel, I reckon I need ya, and ya know I wouldn't be a-tellin' ya this if it weren't true.''

''I love you, Zeke!'' she cried impulsively.

''And I love you, little gal. No matter what happens, we got each other. Just remember that, Miss Rachel.''

Tenderly she took one of his hands and held it lovingly in hers. She had never noticed before how aged and wrinkled his hands were. With love she brought it up to her face and rubbed the callused hand gently across her cheek. ''You're right, Zeke. I've been sulking because I didn't want to face what I had done. And secretly I was hoping that somehow William would let me go, and I'd be free in case John ever came back to his ranch. But he isn't coming back, is he?''

''If'n he did come back, Miss Rachel, wouldn't matter none how he felt 'bout ya, he'd leave ya again. He ain't gonna stay at his ranch and you a-married to Granger. But I sorta wish he would, I got a hankerin' to settle down on that thar ranch of his.''

"Oh Zeke, if only I could see him again!"

"Miss Rachel, you're a woman full growed now, and ya got to stop that foolish thinkin'. Ya got a baby to consider. Don't ya realize, little gal, that if'n ya don't start a-takin' care of yurself, ya could cost that thar baby's life!" Raising his voice angrily, he added, "Yur that baby's Mama, and it's high time ya started a actin' like it!''

Feeling ashamed, Rachel had started crying uncontrollably, but Zeke had taken her into his arms, and he had held her tenderly as she cried.

Her thoughts returning to the present, Rachel stared silently into the flames. She could not yet find release in an outpouring of grief; instead her tears came to her slowly and achingly, tracing tiny rivulets down her cheeks. Pulling the blanket around her securely, she drew up her knees, folding her arms across her legs. She raised her gaze toward the sky, and her voice quavered as she cried piteously, "Oh Zeke! I love you! Zeke! God bless you! You wonderful, sweet old man!''

Rushing over to her, Edward pulled Rachel to her feet. As the blanket fell from her shoulders, he tried to gather her into his arms, but she pushed free of his embrace, and as she whirled away from him, her hair flew wildly across her tormented face. Her tears were at last overflowing, and they obscured her vision as she ran from the glowing campfire. With deep sobs now tearing painfully from her throat, she halted her fleeing steps to lean against a small boulder. Dispiritedly she fell across the rock, placing her head on her arms. The rock's surface felt smooth and cool against her flushed cheek.

"John!" she cried. "I know why you called for me! We both love him and we both need him! Oh God, how much we need him!"

She felt a hand touching her shoulder and instantly she turned, throwing herself into Edward's waiting arms. Placing her head on his shoulder, she sobbed, "I'm going to miss him so much! I loved him! Oh Zeke . . . Zeke!"

He held her tightly in his embrace as she heartbrokenly cried for the old mountaineer she would never see again.

Major Hartly was walking leisurely towards his quarters when a young soldier hurried over to him. "Sir," he began, "I just spotted someone at the cemetery, and I think . . . I . . ."

"You think what?" the major asked impatiently.

"'Sir, I think it's Colonel Reynolds," he replied.

Quickly the major strode across the courtyard, and as he neared the gates he ordered them opened. Hastily he ran from the fort and in the darkness of the night he headed for the small cemetery that was located behind the fort.

Even in the blackness of night there was no mistaking the powerful physique. Clearing his voice before speaking, the major said quietly, "Colonel?"

John had heard his approach, so there was no look of surprise on his face as he turned his large frame toward the major. "It's not colonel any longer; I resigned."

Slowly Major Hartly walked to the man, and

430

pausing beside him, he glanced down at the tombstone. As the moon appeared from behind a cloud it shone down on the simple epitaph. The marker was engraved with the name "Zeke" and the date of death.

"Why do you suppose he never told you or anyone else his last name?" Major Hartly asked.

"I don't know," John began. "But Zeke was in his late forties or early fifties when I first met him. He'd already lived another life."

"A life he never spoke about?" the Major asked.

"He was from back in the mountains somewhere in Tennessee. He left his home and never returned. That's all I know, but whatever happened to him in that other life, I think it happened while he was still a young man."

"But why did he refuse to tell anyone his last name?"

"Hell, Zeke probably wasn't even his real name," John replied.

"I wonder just who in the hell he really was and why he changed his identity. If we knew, it'd probably be quite a story."

Kneeling beside the tombstone, John brushed his fingers across the letters that spelled the name "Zeke." "His secret died with him. So be it!"

"Colonel, I mean John, would you care to join me in a drink?"

He took one last look at the simple gravestone, then rising he answered, "No, thanks. I'm only passing through."

"The day after you left for Fort Stanton, a friend of yours and Lieutenant Kendall's was here looking for you," the major continued.

"A friend?" John asked.

"Edward Phillips. I told him that Josh was living on your ranch."

"Phillips! I didn't think we'd ever hear from him again."

"Are you heading for your ranch?" the major asked.

"No," he answered shortly.

"Then where are you going?"

Heavily John walked to his horse and swung himself into the saddle. Looking down at the major, he answered, "I don't know, but I guess I'll know when I get there. So long, Major."

He turned his horse and rode off into the quiet night. Major Hartly watched him until he was out of sight and then he strode back to the fort.

The moon disappeared slowly behind an approaching cloud, and the simple tombstone that represented Zeke's life on this earth was once again left in darkness. But the man who was riding steadily away from the lonely grave could still feel acutely the loss of his friend, and many miles from the cemetery a young woman was humbly crying for the old man she had so dearly loved.

Chapter Eleven

The journey from Arido to Granger's hacienda could have been completed in a day's ride. But Edward was fully aware that if Jake decided to come after them he would be expecting them to take the fastest way. Trying to avoid a possible confrontation with Jake and his men, Edward and Rachel were taking a longer circuitous route.

After setting up camp for the second time since leaving Arido, Edward relaxed beside the fire as he informed Rachel, "Tomorrow, by midday at the latest, we should be on Granger property."

Handing him a cup of coffee, she replied, "It'll be so wonderful to see my baby again!" She glanced down critically at the offensive gown. "And it'll be so nice to take a bath and to get out of this horrible dress."

"The dress isn't exactly to your taste, but your figure does wonders for it."

Becoming conscious of the low neckline, Rachel could feel a blush in her cheeks. Changing the subject, she asked, "Why did Mary help me? Why would she do that for a perfect stranger?"

"Because she's a woman with a heart, and I also paid

her quite a tidy little sum."

Rachel smiled slyly, "She's probably in love with you." Studying his handsome features, she admitted, "I can understand why a woman would fall in love with you."

Night had fallen, but the glow from the fire shone on his face. It illuminated the softness in his brown eyes. His pouting lips were curved very slightly with a small grin. He removed his hat and she noticed how his black hair touched the collar of his shirt. He had let his sideburns grow long, giving him an appearance of maturity that had been lacking when she'd first met him. When he turned his head to look at her, she realized that she had never seen a man more handsome than Edward Phillips.

"If I'm so easy to love, then why didn't you fall in love with me?"

"But I do love you."

"As a brother?"

"Yes," she answered.

"You really know how to hurt a guy," he replied with a forced laugh.

"Besides, even if I had fallen in love with you, I'd only have received a broken heart for my effort. You'll never settle down with one woman."

She noticed how his face became serious as he replied, "We both know why I can never marry."

Rachel remained silent for a moment before she asked curiously, "Edward, how did Deborah react when she saw you again?"

"Very cold and aloof. But the morning I left she walked to the hitching post with me. As I was getting on my horse, she seemed to be studying me intensely.

434

Then all of a sudden she turned away and hurried over to Josh. I always remembered your sister as being a beautiful young woman, but she's gone to an awful lot of trouble to hide her beauty. I also sensed quite a strain between Josh and Deborah. I don't think she's made him very happy. I feel sorry for Josh, he deserves more than Deborah has given.''

"Were you surprised to learn they were married?'' Rachel asked.

"No, not really. I knew they were writing to each other when you two were living in San Francisco.''

"Hearing the truth about you came as quite a shock to Deborah. She married Josh because she knew she could never have you.''

"What about you, Rachel? Why did you marry Granger? What happened between you and Reynolds? I thought for sure I'd find you two happily married.''

"John's married. He has been for years.''

"Well, I'll be damned! So that's why he tried to avoid you. It must've been hell for Reynolds having you on the same fort with him. You had to be quite a temptation to him.''

"Please, I don't want to discuss it.'' Talking about John made her think about Zeke, and losing the old mountaineer was still too new and painful to bear.

"All right, sweetheart, besides we need to turn in. I want to get an early start in the morning.''

"Goodnight, Edward.'' Rachel stood and walked to where her blanket was spread on the ground. Her grief over Zeke had kept her awake the night before, but tonight pure exhaustion caused her to fall asleep almost as soon as she lay down.

* * *

435

Rachel was awakened abruptly by a sharp pain in her side. As her eyes flew open she became aware that it was early dawn. She winced and moaned achingly when the boot once again kicked cruelly in her ribs. Panic-stricken, she rolled over onto her back and looked up into the bearded face of one of Jake's men.

"Get up, bitch!" he ordered harshly.

Awkwardly she got to her feet. Glancing across the burned-out campfire, she saw Edward held captive by two armed men.

"Ole Jake is gonna be mighty happy to get you back," the bearded man said while scanning her hungrily with his eyes. "He said to bring you back alive, but he didn't say nothin' 'bout what kind of condition he wanted you in. You ain't got Bronson to protect you no more, so I'm gonna help myself to what you got. But first I'm gonna let you watch while I kill your boyfriend."

"Please!" she begged. "Let us go, and I promise you my husband will pay you twice what you'll get from Jake."

"Ain't no way I'd trust Granger," he replied.

"I give you my word!" she swore.

"Your word ain't worth shit! That sonofabitch you're married to would repay us by hanging us from a rope!"

"No! I promise you that he won't kill you!"

"Shut up, goddamn it!" he yelled, slapping her across the face. The powerful blow knocked her backwards, causing her to lose her footing. Stumbling, she regained her balance.

"You damned bastard!" Edward shouted.

The heavyset man standing beside Edward placed

his pistol in its holster, and doubling his fist, he gave Edward a jab to the stomach. He fell forward grabbing at his middle, but as he did the man swung his fist again. It landed sharply against Edward's jaw, knocking him to the ground. Taking a step towards him, the man pulled back his leg, kicking him viciously in the side, and as he rolled over from the severe blow the man's boot caught him in the head.

"Stop him!" Rachel screamed. "He's going to kill him!"

"That's enough!" the bearded man bellowed. "Get him to his feet. I know a better way to kill the sonofabitch!" Reaching for his side he pulled a knife from the sheath on his belt. "I'm gonna slit his throat, and see if he'll squeal like a pig!"

The other man slipped his pistol into its holster and helped pull Edward off the ground. Dazed, Edward was unsteady and between the two of them they held him in an upright position.

Desperately Rachel surveyed the campground. She saw Edward's rifle beside his blanket, a few feet away. As the man held his knife and slowly approached his helpless victim, Rachel pretended hysterics.

"Dear God!" she cried deliriously. "Please . . . please help him!" She looked up at the sky and began praying as she cautiously neared the rifle. Realizing she was close enough to reach the weapon, she cried out feebly, "Oh God, I feel faint . . . I . . . feel . . ." Allowing her whole body to go limp, she fell heavily to the hard ground.

"The dumb bitch done went and fainted," the bearded man said, laughing cruelly. Looking back at Edward he continued, "Reckon you'll be as lucky,

437

Gambler, and faint from fear before I slit your throat?''

As he advanced steadily toward his prey, Rachel sat up swiftly, reached for the rifle, and before he was aware that she had made a move she shot him in the back of the head. The force of the bullet knocked him off his feet, up into the air, and when he hit the ground Rachel could actually hear the breath gushing from his lungs.

Before she had time to cock the gun and aim at the other two, they had their pistols drawn. For a split second she could sense her own death. Then as two shots suddenly burst forth both men fell lifelessly to the ground.

Frightened, Rachel scanned her surroundings, trying to detect from which direction the shots had come. Unexpectedly, she heard her name being called from up in the rocks behind her. With relief she saw Miguel and Klu leading their horses around and down the steep boulders.

"Klu!" she cried, running to meet him. Taking him by surprise, she flung herself into his arms.

Glancing at Miguel, Klu said, "Check on Phillips."

"Oh Klu . . . thank God!" she sobbed against his shoulder.

Tenderly he moved her so that he could see into her face. "I didn't know you were such a good shot. And to think of all those weeks when I left my gun lying within your reach. I'm glad you never got mad enough to want to kill me."

Her eyes flashed wildly as she cried incoherently, "I never wanted it to be like this! I never wanted to kill anyone! He's not the first man I've killed . . . I shot two Apaches . . . and . . . and I've been forced to witness violent deaths! . . . I never wanted any of this! I never wanted to live this way! All I ever wanted from life was simply to be with John!''

At the mention of his name, Klu stiffened, stepping back from her. ''Get a hold on yourself, Rachel! You shoot like a man, but you have damned hysterics like a woman!''

Angered by his callus attitude, she shouted, ''I should've known I'd get no sympathy from you because I had to kill a man! Killing is second nature to you! In your estimation a person's life probably means nothing!''

''If you're referring to those three bastards, then you're right. Their lives meant nothing! Don't you think you should see how Phillips is doing instead of carrying on like a crazy female!''

Klu watched as she whirled angrily and hurried over to Edward. He fought the impulse to call out to her. He wanted her back in his arms. Klu admired her bravery, and he totally understood her compassion; but unintentionally she had hurt him again. The only protection he had was to pretend an aloofness he was far from feeling.

Kneeling beside Edward, Rachel asked, ''Will he be all right?''

''Si, Señora,'' Miguel replied.

Sitting up unstably, Edward grimaced with pain. ''I'm sorry, sweetheart. I was a fool to let them slip up on us.'' Detecting Klu's approach, he asked, ''What in the hell are you two doing here?''

''You took something that belongs to me, Phillips, and I'd appreciate it kindly if you'd return it.''

''What was that?'' he questioned.

''My gun,'' Klu replied.

439

"Hell, Bronson, you don't expect me to believe that you followed us for a damned gun."

"Si, Señor," Miguel began. "Klu, he sets a great store by that pistol."

"How many notches does it have?" Rachel asked sarcastically.

"No notches, Señora," Miguel answered.

"I'm used to the feel and the balance of the pistol," Klu explained. "And I don't care to take the time to get used to another one."

Standing, Rachel replied bitterly, "But of course, gunslingers would have a certain fondness for their weapon."

Disregarding her remark, Klu inquired, "Are you up to traveling, Phillips?"

"Yeah, sure. I'm okay," he answered, getting to his feet unsteadily.

"We'll ride along with you for a while," Klu offered.

As Edward and Miguel headed toward the horses, Rachel stared at Klu. "But what about these dead men? Aren't you going to bury them?"

"Hell, let the damned buzzards have 'em," he answered harshly.

"You can't do that!" she exclaimed.

"What in the hell is wrong with you, woman? Do you expect me to bury them and then say a prayer over their graves?"

She lifted her chin stubbornly. "Well, it would be the Christian way of doing it."

Throwing back his head he laughed loudly. "My God, I don't believe you! First we kill the bastards, and then we pray for their rotten souls. Somehow, Rachel, I don't think that is Christianity." Suddenly, he placed

440

his hands on her shoulders as he said irritably, "You may find this a little hard to believe, but I don't carry a shovel around with me, and I sure as hell don't intend to dig three graves with my bare hands!"

"It just seems inhumane to leave them this way," she answered softly.

"I'm sure some of their friends will find them." He didn't bother to inform her that even if they were discovered by their comrades, they would still most likely remain unburied.

Taking her hand, he began leading her toward Edward and Miguel as he said, "We'll unsaddle their horses and turn them loose." Noting her worried expression, he continued with annoyance, "Damn it, Rachel! They'll roam free and have one hell of a good life!"

Finding his irritation toward her amusing, Rachel smiled up at him, and when she did, he was once again reminded of how much he loved her.

Klu was riding ahead of the others, and encouraging his horse into a gallop, Edward rode up beside him. Smiling, he remarked, "She's quite a girl, isn't she?" When Klu offered no comment, Edward told him, "I almost fell in love with her, but I knew she'd always love another man, and I hate to lose."

"I'm not interested in your love life, Phillips," he answered ill-temperedly.

Edward was quite certain that Klu was in love with Rachel, and he watched him closely as he said, "If you could ever see the way she looks at Reynolds, you'd understand what I mean."

"Reynolds?" he asked.

"John Reynolds. I find it hard to believe that Rachel hasn't told you about him. She usually doesn't give a damn or else is too dense to realize . . ."

Interrupting, Klu questioned, "Does this Reynolds own a ranch close to El Paso?"

"Yeah, he does. Do you know him?"

"Carmelita's husband! No, I don't know him, but I sure as hell know his wife, and so does Rachel!" There was a strange expression in his eyes, as he said vaguely, "I wonder if she only pretended to be friends with Carmelita, when all the time she was in love with Carmelita's husband?"

Looking at him with confusion, Edward asked, "What are you talking about?"

Klu started to answer when Miguel rode up to them. "Amigo, I think it best that we turn around. This is dangerous territory for us."

"You're right, Miguel." Glancing at Edward, he said, "Maybe we'll meet again, Phillips."

"Maybe. Thanks, Bronson, for all your help," he replied.

Touching the brim of his hat, Klu nodded to him slightly before riding over to Rachel. "Goodbye, Mrs. Granger."

"Goodbye, Klu," she whispered, holding back a desire to cry.

He found himself unable to leave without knowing if she'd been honest with Carmelita. "Rachel, did you tell Carmelita that you're in love with her husband?"

"Of course! She knows all about John and me. But how did you learn that John is Carmelita's husband?"

"That doesn't matter. I'm only glad that you're all I'd hoped you'd be." He leaned over his horse and

442

kissed her lightly on the lips. Fighting back the compulsion to tell her that he loved her, he turned his horse and rode away.

Rachel watched Klu and Miguel ride steadily into the distance. She wondered if she'd ever see Klu again. Bewildered, Rachel also wondered why the thought of not seeing him again made her feel sad. Shaking off her feeling of melancholy, she looked at Edward and smiled, "I'm almost home."

Returning her smile, he replied, "Let's go. You must be anxious to see your son."

Rachel never saw the coiled rattlesnake at rest behind the small rock. As her horse's hoofs pounded against the dirt beside the waiting snake, it struck quickly. The poisonous fangs missed their deadly entrance into the animal's leg, but panicked by the dangerous reptile, the horse's eyes rolled back in fright and he bucked wildly. Rachel screamed with terror as she was thrown over the horse's head. She could feel her whole body jarred painfully as she landed solidly on the hard ground. Swiftly Edward drew his pistol and shot the snake as it began to recoil.

Klu heard Rachel's frightening scream followed by the shot from Edward's pistol. He and Miguel had ridden to the top of a ridge where, even from a remote distance, he could see Rachel lying motionlessly on the ground. Turning his horse, he started to ride back to her when Miguel warned, "Amigo, do not go down there! We may not be the only ones who have heard the scream and the shot."

For only a moment Klu considered his friend's warning, but his love for Rachel overcame his better judgement. "Wait here for me!" he hollered to Miguel, breaking his horse into a fast run.

Kneeling beside Rachel, Edward turned her over, lifting her head gently as he brushed the dirt from her face. Slowly her eyes fluttered open, and smiling with relief, he said, "Just lie still, sweetheart. You took quite a fall."

"I'm all right. At least I think I am. Nothing seems to be broken."

"All the same, I want you to rest for a moment."

"What happened?" she asked.

"Your horse was startled by a rattlesnake."

"A snake!" she exclaimed.

"It's all right. I killed it."

"Did my horse run away?"

"Took off like a streak of lightning. If we don't find him on the way to the hacienda, then Granger can send some men out to search for him."

Hearing a rider approaching, Edward turned and saw Klu heading toward them. "He shouldn't have come back. If any of Granger's vaqueros are close by I'm sure they heard the shot."

Before his horse had the chance to fully stop, Klu was leaping from the saddle, and noticing the dead snake, he rushed to Rachel's side. Kneeling, he pulled her from Edward's embrace encircling her within his arms. "Thank God, you're not hurt!"

Moving back a little so that she could see into his face, Rachel concentrated deeply on the man holding her, and for the first time she understood the expression in his eyes. Only then did she become aware that Klu Bronson was in love with her.

"Now that you know she's all right, why don't you

get the hell out of here!'' Edward said sternly.

Looking intently into Rachel's eyes Klu told her quickly, ''One of your husband's vaqueros is a cousin to Miguel. His name is Ricardo. Rachel, if you ever need me he can find a way to get a message to me.''

''Oh Klu, please leave! Someone may have heard that shot!'' she pleaded.

He started to rise, but abruptly he pulled her into his arms, meeting his lips passionately to hers. Realizing how very much he meant to her, she wrapped her arms around his neck, and with all her heart she returned his farewell kiss.

As he suddenly and dramatically appeared from around the bend, William Granger saw his wife in the arms of another man!

Breaking their embrace, Rachel and Klu looked toward the advancing riders. They were still a distance away, and Rachel pleaded with mounting fear, ''Hurry Klu! Hurry!''

Swiftly he ran for his horse and leaped into the saddle. He turned the animal and headed for the nearby boulders. The horse had taken only a few strides when a group of Granger's vaqueros seemed to appear from nowhere, blocking Klu's retreat. Roughly, he pulled up his horse. He was trapped and he knew it. As though it were all of little importance he tugged gently on the reins and walked his horse over to Edward and Rachel. Appearing perfectly at ease, Klu sat on his horse, waiting for William Granger.

William approached with his vaqueros as his other men advanced from the rear. When William halted his horse beside Rachel, her heart was pounding rapidly with fear and dread. Lifting her head courageously, she looked her husband steadfastly in the eyes. Examining her vulgar dress and mussed hair, his lips curled in a sneer of disgust.

"Señora," he said. The coldness in his voice sent chills up her spine. "I see you are still alive. Perhaps it would have been better if you had been killed. I could have felt grief for my wife, instead of shame!"

William Granger had cared about his wife's safety and had hoped that she'd be returned to him alive, and untouched! But now it was obvious she not only had been violated but had enjoyed it! Uncontrollable anger consumed him as he thought of the many sleepless nights he had suffered wondering if his beautiful wife was being raped by scum. He had actually pictured their dirty hands on her soft and slim body. He had finally even prayed for her safe return, and to see her again, only to find her in the arms of another man! She was no better than a whore!

Slowly William got down from his horse. Taking a step toward Rachel, he drew back his arm, slapping her with the back of his hand so powerfully that she was knocked completely off her feet.

Instantly Klu and Edward made a move but were stopped immediately by the vaqueros' guns pointing at them from every direction. The slap Rachel had received earlier had bruised her cheek, and there was an ugly cut on her forehead caused by the fall she had taken. William's blow had split her lip and blood flowed from the corner of her mouth. Looking down on the woman he loved, Klu's heart went out to her. He wondered how much more she could take.

"Who do I have to thank for my wife's return?" Glancing at Edward, he asked, "You, Señor Phillips?"

Swerving quickly, he added, "Or do I have you to thank, Señor Bronson?"

"So you know who I am," Klu answered calmly.

"Si, amigo. Did you think I would not learn the names and the descriptions of the men who dared to abduct my wife? I will see to it that all four of you are hanged!"

Clumsily getting to her knees, Rachel exclaimed, "William, no! You don't understand! Klu didn't kidnap me! He saved my life!"

"Shut up, Rachel, before I decide to hang you beside your lover!"

Hastily she rose to her feet and rushed over to him. "Klu only pretended to kidnap me to keep Jake from killing me! He never intended to collect any ransom."

"What she says is true," Edward began. "Bronson helped her escape at the risk of his own life."

"Where have you been all this time?" William asked her.

Loyalty to Carmelita prevented her from revealing the name of Manuel Villano. "I don't know. I was kept blindfolded until they took me to a room somewhere. I was kept a prisoner inside the room and never allowed to see anyone."

"Jake decided to take her to Arido," Edward explained. "That's where I found her. With Bronson's help we managed to escape. This morning three of Jake's men slipped up on us, and if it hadn't been for Bronson, Rachel and I would both be dead."

"Next you are going to tell me that Klu Bronson did not rob the bank in El Paso, and did not cause the death of two men."

"But he didn't shoot them!" Rachel cried. "Jake

447

did!"

William appeared to be seriously considering what they had told him. Then the memory of Rachel in Klu's arms crossed his mind. Violently he shoved her aside and angrily walked away. "Take his guns!" he ordered.

One of his men promptly dismounted. Hurrying over to Klu, he took his pistol and rifle.

Glancing at another of his vaqueros, William demanded harshly, "Put a rope on that tree, then hang the bastard!"

"NO!" Rachel screamed. With her skirt flying around her legs, she ran toward her husband. Reaching him, she clutched frantically at his arm. "NO! Please don't hang him! Oh William, please!"

The eyes staring into hers were ice-cold. Rachel held her breath with shock when suddenly she was confronted with the truth. What she had always sensed lacking in her husband but had never rationalized, had been simple mercy!

Although she knew it was futile, she dropped to her knees in front of him, clasping her hands together tightly. "I'm begging you to spare his life! I'm begging you!"

"Rachel!" Klu yelled. "Don't beg him for my life!"

Too distraught to hear Klu's words, she looked up to her husband pleading, "Please William! Don't kill him!"

"Rachel!" Klu shouted. "Don't beg the sonofabitch! Damn it, woman, leave me my pride!"

This time what Klu said penetrated, and her shoulders slumped as she bowed her head. Tears mingled with the dirt and blood on her face while sobs tore painfully from deep in her throat.

Edward helped her to her feet, but she brusquely pushed away from him and fled to Klu. Reaching his horse, she leaned her face against Klu's leg and cried, "Oh Klu! I'm sorry! I'm so sorry!"

Tenderly he touched her hair, caressing her auburn locks between his fingers. "Go home, Rachel," he said softly.

Watching Klu, Edward detected the open look of love on his face, and it became quite apparent to him that Klu hadn't followed them for a pistol. It had been his concern for Rachel's safety. And now his love for Rachel would cost him his life!

Looking at Edward, Klu called, "Get her out of here!"

"Hang him!" William hollered. With hate and madness in his eyes he watched his wife cling to another man. He was tempted to hang her also, but her punishment would be the torture of remembering this day and the moment that her lover was hanged! When she asked for her child, she would find that God had his own punishment for her to bear! No, her punishment would not be so fast in coming, or so mercifully over!

As the vaquero reached for the reins to his horse, Klu pleaded, "Start for home and don't look back. Promise me, Rachel, that you won't look back! Regardless of what you may hear or what I may say, don't look back!"

Grabbing his hand, she held it next to her cheek as she sobbed, "I promise."

His voice broke with emotion when he explained, "I don't want you to see me like that . . . God, I don't want you to see!"

Edward put his arm around her shoulders, trying to urge her away. Fighting him, Rachel clutched desperately at Klu's hand. I don't want you to die! Oh Klu . . . Klu!''

As the vaquero began leading the horse away, Klu's hand slipped free of hers. ''NO! . . . Oh Klu! . . . I'm sorry! . . . I'm so sorry!'' Rachel shrieked pathetically.

When they reached the tree, and Klu's hands were tied behind him, he could still feel her tears clinging to the back of his hand. The rope was swung over a limb, and the noose placed around his neck. Slowly, with his pistol drawn, William advanced steadily toward Klu.

Deliriously Rachel screamed, ''No! William, no! Oh God, please! This is a nightmare! Oh God, it must be a nightmare!''

''Phillips, will you get her out of here!'' Klu yelled frantically.

Firmly Edward took hold of Rachel's arm and forcefully turned her away. Fighting against him furiously she screamed repeatedly for Klu. Pulling her to his horse, Edward warned, ''Do as he said, Rachel, and don't look back! Oh God, sweetheart, whatever you do, don't look back!''

There was a sudden ringing in Rachel's ears, and the ground tilted under her feet. As her knees weakened, Edward had to support her to keep her from collapsing.

Vaguely she heard Klu's voice and it sounded to her as though it came from somewhere far away. ''Rachel . . . I love you!'' For the first time in thirty-four years, Klu Bronson had at last said the three words that all his life had been denied him.

The blast from William's pistol seemed to carry for

an eternity across the dry, open plains. As Klu's horse ran past, with an empty saddle, Rachel's scream of agony cut piercingly into the still air.

Edward grabbed the reins to his horse, who had been startled by the shot. Then swiftly he lifted Rachel in his arms, and placed her on the saddle. He pulled himself up behind her, and while holding on to her securely, he coaxed his horse into a run.

As the rhythmic sound of the horse's hoofbeats faded in the distance, William and his vaqueros watched the hanging man. The creaking of the swaying rope was all that could be heard over the eerie quiet of the plains.

Carrying Rachel into the parlor, Edward placed her carefully on the large sofa. She hadn't spoken a word since Klu's hanging. Her face was deathly pale, and her expressionless eyes seemed to be staring at nothing.

Hearing their entrance, Juanita rushed into the room. With astonishment she exclaimed, "Señora Granger! You are alive! Thank God! The 'patron,' he will be so happy!"

Moving in a trance, Rachel rose from the sofa and demanded in a strained voice, "Bring me my baby!"

The servant's eyes widened, and she clasped her hands together nervously. "Señora, please lie down and rest until the 'patron' returns. Si?"

"Bring me my baby!" she shouted.

Juanita glanced hesitantly at Edward, then back to Rachel. "Please, Señora, wait for the 'patron.'"

Rachel acted like a woman who had gone insane. Her hair was falling wildly around her face. The bruised cheek made her face appear distorted and dried blood was caked in the corner of her mouth. The fright-

451

ened servant backed away from the 'patron's' demented wife, and chills ran through her very soul when the woman shrieked, "Where is my baby? My God! My baby!"

Edward reached for Rachel, trying to capture her in his grasp, but violently she shoved him aside. Juanita had never seen a mad woman, but as she watched Rachel walking toward her, she made the sign of the cross over her breasts. The servant was certain that Señora Granger had gone completely mad.

"My baby!" Rachel screamed. "Where is he? Answer me! Why won't you answer me?"

The front door suddenly slammed shut, and footsteps could be heard crossing the bare floor of the foyer. Pausing, William Granger stood arrogantly in the entrance to the spacious parlor.

Rachel looked up into his hostile stare. "Where is my baby?"

He didn't answer but continued staring with hatred at the woman he had married. When finally he spoke, his voice held no warmth or compassion. "Our son is dead."

Rachel didn't cry and she didn't scream. The only reaction Granger received from his words was to see his wife's entire body jerk awkwardly, her eyes continuing to roll wildly.

"He died of pneumonia, two weeks after his mother ran off with her lover!"

"You cold-hearted bastard!" she hissed. Rachel turned so swiftly that William was too astounded to move. Nearing Edward's side, she drew his pistol from its holster, and as she aimed it at her husband madness shone in her eyes. "I'm going to kill you!"

452

William could foresee his death in his wife's eyes. Shocked, he realized that in her temporary delirium she was capable of pulling the trigger. But roughly Edward grabbed at Rachel's arm, knocking the pistol from her hand.

Edward knew he would never forget the look of betrayal in her upturned face when she cried to him, "Why did you stop me? He deserves to die! He should die!" Drawing her into his arms, he could feel her tears wetting his shirt as her shoulders began to shake. "Oh Edward, my little baby! I want my baby!"

He felt her growing weak and he lifted her in his arms. For a moment he held his cheek against her flushed forehead, then looking down into her face, he saw that mercifully she had fainted.

Watching the stranger with a full, unkempt beard sitting alone at the rear table, the bartender noticed how the man's blurred eyes seemed to be staring vacantly. When he clumsily overturned his glass of whiskey, the huge Mexican walked over to him. "Get out, Señor!" he ordered. "I do not want any loco drunks in my cantina. Go somewhere else, amigo, and sleep it off."

When he made no move to obey him, the bartender grabbed him by the arms, pulling him from the chair. The stranger leaned against him for support, as he was hastened to the swinging doors and shoved through them. Falling awkwardly, he hit the wooden planks, then rolled down the steps and into the dusty street.

Carmelita and her servant, Rosa, were walking away from the church when they witnessed the man being pushed brutally out of the cantina.

"We must help him out of the road. He could be run

over!'' Carmelita exclaimed.

Clutching her arm, Rosa protested, ''No, Carmelita! He is only a drunk. Let him be!''

Brushing her hand away, Carmelita hurried to the man. Cautiously, she knelt beside the still form. He was lying face down, and it took all the strength the frail woman possessed to turn the man onto his back. In spite of the heavy beard that almost covered his face, and the thirteen years that had separated them, Carmelita recognized him instantly. ''John!'' she cried.

Hearing his name, he tossed his head from side to side and moaned. Lovingly, she reached over and touched his brow, only to feel that he was burning with fever. As Rosa walked up behind them, Carmelita cried out to her in alarm, ''Go find the driver and tell him to bring the buckboard!''

''We cannot take a stranger to the hacienda!'' Rosa declared.

''He is no stranger!'' Carmelita shouted. ''He is my husband!''

Quickly Rosa ran to fetch the driver and Carmelita moved closer to John. Tenderly, she placed his head on her lap, and brushed the unruly hair back from his feverish brow.

''Rachel,'' John called feebly.

Carmelita realized that his high fever was making him delirious, and with her lips trembling, she replied, ''Yes, John. I'm right here, my darling.''

''Rachel . . . we lost him . . . Zeke. We lost him. He's dead.''

''Sh . . . ssh . . . you must save your strength. You are very ill.''

''Baby, don't leave me.'' Carmelita was startled

when, all at once, his voice rose loudly. "Don't leave me, Rachel!" Then once again, he drifted back into the depths of unconsciousness.

Hanging her head, Carmelita wept.

It took seventy-two hours for John's fever to finally break. For three days and nights, Carmelita remained at her husband's bedside praying faithfully and working diligently to save his life.

Carmelita was sitting in the chair, dozing fretfully, when she was awakened by John's weak plea for water. Immediately she rose and reached for the pitcher. After pouring the water into a glass, she lifted his head, and held the glass to his dry lips. His parched mouth made him try to tilt it greedily.

"Only a little," Carmelita said softly. She placed the glass on the table next to the bed. She watched as her husband slowly opened his eyes. The recognition he was experiencing was evident in the eyes that were now lucid. He stared at her coldly. "Carmelita! Where am I?"

"At my father's hacienda," she answered.

"How did I get here? What in the hell happened to me?"

"You were very ill, John. Rosa and I found you in town. You had been thrown out of the cantina, and you were lying in the street."

He studied the woman standing beside his bed. He hadn't seen her in such a long time. She was still as beautiful as he had remembered, but he noticed how her complexion was too pale, and she was much thinner than she had been in her youth. His brow wrinkled with confusion. He sensed there was something very different about her.

"When I rode into town, I was feeling sick. I stopped at the saloon for a drink, and hell, that's the last I remember . . . My horse, where is he?"

"We brought him with us. I knew he was yours because the words U.S. Cavalry were on the saddle blanket." Clasping her hands, she continued hesitantly, "Why did you come to town? Were you planning to get in touch with my father or me?"

John could see how she seemed to be waiting breathlessly for his answer. "I don't know," he replied truthfully. "Maybe, but I may have just ridden out of town."

"John, you have not been taking care of yourself, have you?"

Rubbing his hand across the full beard, he replied, "I've been doing a lot of traveling."

"And much drinking, si?"

"Yeah, I've done my share of that too. If you'll give me my clothes, I'll get the hell out of here."

"No!" she cried. "You are too weak to go anywhere!"

"Damn it! I don't want to feel obligated to you!" he replied angrily. He sat up on the bed, but fell back on the pillows, exhausted.

"You are not going anywhere, John Reynolds. You were very ill, and your strength will be slow in returning. And you owe me nothing, Señor. You owe your life to God."

Carmelita held her head proudly. Gracefully she turned her slim frame, walked across the floor, and out of the room. It wasn't until Carmelita had left that John suddenly wondered how she had known that he'd been in the cavalry.

John was awakened by the door opening, and a voice calling, "Amigo, I was glad to hear that you will recover."

Sitting up, John leaned back against the large headboard. Smiling, he replied, "Hello, Manuel. It seems I once again owe my life to you and your daughter."

The man drew his bushy eyebrows together into a frown. "My daughter, si, but your wife, Señor." He walked further into the room, and reaching for the chair he proceeded, "Twice she has saved your life." Lowering his huge frame onto the narrow chair, he asked, "Has she not repaid you, Señor, for a young girl's foolishness?"

"Foolishness!" John cried vehemently. "My God, Manuel! Her foolishness, as you lightly put it, caused the death of our son!"

"No!" he protested. "Your son's death was an accident! She was guilty of adultery, not murder!"

The tenseness left John as he replied, "It all happened a long time ago. Let's leave it where it belongs, in the past."

"Si, amigo, I agree, but have you been able to forget that day?"

"Of course not!" he answered.

"My daughter, she does not forget either, Señor, but she has learned to live with it. You, too, must learn, amigo."

"It took years, but I finally learned how to live with it." Suddenly thinking of Rachel, he closed his eyes as he rubbed his hand across his brow.

"Señor," Manuel began, "on my way to see you, I

passed my daughter's room, and I could hear her crying. Do you know why she weeps?''

''I don't know. Hell, earlier I was a little short with her. Maybe she's crying because I hurt her feelings.''

Rising quickly, Manuel angrily knocked the chair backwards. ''Señor, I must insist that you do nothing to make her cry! She does not deserve to be hurt!''

''I can't pretend something I don't feel. I don't hate her, but damn it, Manuel, I'm going to get a divorce!''

As he tried to control his violent temper, a nerve in the corner of Manuel's mouth twitched repeatedly. ''You will not have to 'divorce' her! She will soon die!''

Looking at him with shock, John asked, ''What do you mean?''

Slowly Manuel picked up the chair, and moving it closer to the bed he once again sat down. ''She is ill. She has been for a long time. The doctors, they cannot help her.'' His shoulders sagged as he continued, ''Each day, I watch my daughter grow weaker and weaker, and with each passing day, my heart, it breaks a little more.''

Remembering how much Manuel had always loved his beautiful daughter, John replied sympathetically, ''I'm sorry.''

''Are you, Señor? I do not believe you. Have you not many times wished my daughter dead?''

''You aren't being fair, Manuel! You see Carmelita through a father's eyes, but I saw her as an unfaithful wife and a damned poor mother to my child!''

''Si, what you say is true, Señor. But when a man is angry he is not always fair, and I am angry because I do not want to lose her.''

"What do you want from me, Manuel? Surely you don't expect me to resume our marriage!"

"No, amigo. I do not expect such charity. My daughter, she does not need or want your charity. I only ask that you be kind."

When he didn't answer, Manuel questioned, "Is what I ask more than you can give?"

"I already told you that I don't hate her; and, of course, I'll be kind."

"There is something else I think you should know about Carmelita."

"What's that?" John asked.

"Señor, I realize that Carmelita showed no love for her child, but that was my fault, not hers. With all my heart, I loved Carmelita's mother. When I lost her Carmelita was only a baby. Back then, Señor, no bandidos were welcomed in my little village. My people and I lived as my good wife wished us to live. But after she died, I returned to my old ways and my old habits, si? Many bandidos have come to me and have never left. They are now my trusted vaqueros and they guard my land. I make much money, amigo, from men who come here to hide from the law. Even the law does not try to enter my land. It is guarded too well, si? But, I always felt guilt because my wife, she never wanted that kind of life for our child. So to ease my guilt, I pampered Carmelita, and I spoiled her. I am to blame for my daughter's behavior in your marriage. I never taught her to be responsible or to even care about another's feelings. I made her believe that she was more special and more important than anyone on this earth."

"Why are you telling me all this? I always knew Carmelita's selfishness was caused by the way she was raised.''

"Please, amigo, let me finish. Shortly after Carmelita returned home, she began making frequent trips into town. One afternoon I followed her. Rosa had told me where Carmelita spent her hours when she was in town, but I could not believe it, Señor! I had to see with my own eyes! Do you know where she was spending her time, Señor?''

"How in the hell would I know," he answered shortly.

"In church, amigo! She would spend hours talking with the priest and praying to God.''

John looked at him with surprise but said nothing.

"Carmelita found her peace through God. She is now a very religious woman, Señor, and she has been for many years. At first, I was afraid that she would move away because of her father's way of life, but she has never left me, although I know she disapproves of many things that I do. No, amigo, she is not the same Carmelita that you once knew. There is no woman more gentle or more kind than my beloved Carmelita.''

Although the day was growing late, and the shadows from the dismal afternoon crept into the study, Rachel did not light the kerosene lamp. Instead, tucking her legs under her, she settled herself comfortably against the soft leather upholstery. The huge chair, behind John Reynolds' desk, was too large for Rachel's delicate frame, giving her the appearance of a small and lonely child.

Since returning to her sister's home, Rachel had spent many hours sitting alone in the study. Four weeks had passed since that fateful day when Klu was hanged and she had learned that her baby was dead. Rachel had immediately left the hacienda and had not seen her husband since. She wished that she would never see him again. Rachel had never known real hatred, but now she hated William Granger! Her hatred for him and her love for John Reynolds were all she had left. Continuously she fed her will to survive by mentally nourishing both emotions.

Rachel stared at the unopened bottle of brandy on the desk. Carefully she picked it up, and caressed the bottle soothingly. When she leaned forward to look down at the bottle of brandy, the rays from the setting sun shone through the patio doors. The brightness fell across her face, making her lose the child-like appearance. Rachel was a woman who had known suffering and grief. The results showed plainly on her strained face. The hollowness of her pale cheeks and the tightness around her mouth were prominent. The flashing green eyes that had captured many a man's heart were now hard and bitter.

Angrily, she opened the bottle and poured brandy into a glass. Taking a deep breath, she put the glass to her lips and emptied it. The warm liquid went down smoothly, and Rachel welcomed its soothing presence. Unexpectedly, the door opened, and she looked up guiltily to see Edward standing in the doorway.

"Damn it, Rachel! That's no answer!" Closing the door behind him, he walked briskly into the room. Going straight to the desk, he jerked the bottle from her hand, capped it and set it down sharply.

"No? Well, what is the answer, Edward?" she asked irritably.

"Brandy isn't the answer, Rachel!"

"It helps me to sleep. If I drink enough it keeps
. . ." Her voice trembled as she continued, "It keeps
away the nightmares. Without it, I wake up screaming!"

Edward made a move towards her, but she rose
abruptly from the chair and walked to the patio doors.
Silently she stared at the open plains. When at last she
spoke, her voice was so soft that Edward could barely
hear her words. "When I first moved to William's hacienda, I thought the trees that his grandfather had
planted abundantly over his land were beautiful. I foolishly believed that his grandfather had been a man who
appreciated nature's beauty." Turning to face him,
she raised her voice, "But he didn't plant them for
beauty or for needed shade, did he? He planted them so
that his future heirs could own their private gallows!"

"Rachel, stop torturing yourself! You must try to
learn to forget."

Near hysteria, she cried, "Forget! Never! I'll always
remember that day! It will haunt me until the day I
die!" Her lips trembled pathetically, "Oh Klu! . . .
Klu! . . . Edward, I felt if I could just reach my baby,
and hold him in my arms, then somehow I would survive what had happened!"

Hurrying to her side, he held her shoulders firmly.
"Stop it, Rachel! For God's sake, stop punishing yourself!"

Before she could reply, a knock sounded on the study
door. Moving away, Edward walked to the door and
opened it.

" 'Excusame,' Señor," Maria began. "There is a
gentleman caller, and he insists that he speak with

someone, but not to Señora Kendall.''

"Very well, Maria. Show him in.'' As she left to fetch the visitor, Edwards surmised, "He probably wants to see Josh, but he's out on the range somewhere.''

Maria returned promptly and showed the caller into the study, quietly closing the door behind her. Instantly Rachel recognized the visitor. "Mr. Dutton, how are you?''

The man looked anxiously at Rachel. He was in his early fifties, and his hair had already turned completely gray. With mounting apprehension, he rubbed his hands through the full head of hair as he replied, "I'm fine, Mrs. Granger.''

Walking to Edward, she explained, "Mr. Dutton is a neighbor. He owns a small ranch north of here.'' Forcing herself to smile, she paused beside Edward and continued politely, "Mr. Dutton, this is Mr. Phillips, a close friend of the family.''

"How do you do, sir.'' Hesitantly Mr. Dutton exchanged his hat from one hand to the other. "Mrs. Granger, I have bad news for you, ma'am.''

"What is it?'' she asked.

"It's about Mr. Kendall,'' he answered solemnly.

Frightened, Rachel clutched Edward's arm tightly. "Is he hurt?''

"I'm really sorry, Mrs. Granger, but Mr. Kendall has been killed.''

"My God!'' Edward gasped. "What happened?''

"Well, sir, I was on my way here to visit with Mr. Kendall. He's on the town committee you know, and we're havin' a meetin' next Thursday. I was comin' here to tell him. About a mile from here I seen Mr.

463

Kendall out on the range ridin' his horse. I was quite a distance away from him, but I knew it was him 'cause he was ridin' that black stallion of his. I've always admired that horse. I was gettin' ready to call out to him, when all at once this Mexican comes ridin' out of nowhere. He rode straight up to Mr. Kendall, pulled his pistol, and shot him. Mr. Kendall fell from his horse. Then this Mexican, he got down and put his pistol back in its holster. He reached up to his horse and removed his rifle. Dear God, I reckon poor Mr. Kendall was still alive 'cause he put the barrel of that rifle right into Mr. Kendall's face and pulled the trigger. Killin' a man, that's bad enough, but to kill him like that . . .''

Falling against Edward, Rachel moaned, ''Oh my God! Josh!''

''By this time that Mexican seen that I was watchin'. I figured he'd be comin' after me so I got my rifle to protect myself, but he just got back on that pinto of his and rode away.''

''Pinto?'' Rachel questioned.

''Yes, ma'am, he was ridin' a pinto. He was dressed in Mexican clothes, so that's why I reckon he was a Mexican, but I never was close enough to get a good look at him.''

''Edward!'' Rachel exclaimed. ''Miguel has a pinto!''

''But why would he want to kill Josh? No Rachel, I'm sure it wasn't Miguel.''

''Ma'am,'' Mr. Dutton began, ''I was in my buckboard, so I wrapped Mr. Kendall up in a blanket and brought him home.''

She made a move for the door, but instantly the man touched her arm. ''Mrs. Granger, you don't want to see him. Ma'am, there ain't nothin' left of his face."

"Rachel," Edward said gently, "do you want me to tell Deborah?"

"Deborah!" she cried. "I hadn't even thought about Deborah! No . . . no, I'll tell her."

When Rachel entered her sister's bedroom and told her that Josh was dead, Deborah's screams carried throughout every room in the house. Standing motionless, Rachel could only stare at her sister as she fell across the bed. Suddenly Rachel's temporary numbness passed and she hurried to Deborah's side. She tried to gather her sister into her arms, but roughly, Deborah pushed her away.

Looking at Rachel with desperation, Deborah cried pitifully, "But I never told him that I loved him!"

"But you do love him, don't you?" Rachel asked.

"Yes!" Deborah shrieked. "Oh yes!"

"Oh Deb," Rachel sighed sympathetically.

"I don't know when I started loving Josh. Oh, I don't love him the way I loved Edward! But, Rachel, in my own way I do love him. But I've never told a man that I love him." Her lips quivered as she continued, "I never knew how to say the words. I wanted to, but as time passed it only became more difficult for me."

Awkwardly, she rose from the bed and began pacing back and forth across the room. "I always wished I could be like you. I've always envied you, Rachel! I didn't approve of your relationship with Colonel Reynolds, but God, how I envied you! You loved him, and you were never afraid to tell him! You've always been able to express your feelings, but Mama told me that a lady should always be reserved!"

Rising from the bed, Rachel exclaimed, "Mama said a lot of things that were wrong. Maybe they were right for her world, but not for our world!"

There was a wildness in Deborah's eyes as she cried, "I never responded to my husband, but Rachel, lately there were times when I wanted to!"

"Then why didn't you?"

"Because Mama always said . . ."

Interrupting, Rachel yelled, "She was wrong! Do you understand? She was wrong!"

Rushing to Deborah, Rachel pulled her into her arms. Sobbing heavily, she cried, "Oh Rachel, why? Why would anyone want to kill him? He was such a kind man. I never told him how much I appreciated him, and now it's too late! I'll never forgive myself!"

Maria knocked lightly on the door before opening it. Walking quietly into the room, she asked, "Señora Granger, is there anything I can do? Señor Phillips, he told me what happened."

Suddenly Rachel could feel her legs weakening, and the floor seemed to be rocking under her feet. The enclosure of the room began closing in around her. She knew she had to get away, if only for a few minutes.

"Yes, you can stay with my sister. I need some fresh air." Rachel patted Deborah's shoulder tenderly, then without glancing back, she darted out of the room.

As Rachel hurried down the hall, she could hear Edward and Mr. Dutton still talking in the study. Roughly, she swung the front door open, rushing out onto the veranda. The coolness from the early evening air brushed tranquilly against her flushed cheeks. But the soothing feeling was gone the moment she spotted Mr. Dutton's buckboard next to the hitching post. She could distinguish the form of the wrapped body that was placed in the rear of the flat wagon.

Josh's horse was standing beside the buckboard. He neighed with excitement when his nostrils suddenly picked up a scent, and his ears alertly detected a faraway sound, but unaware of the horse's warning, Rachel moved steadily closer to the buckboard.

Before reaching the wagon, she halted abruptly, and with tears in her eyes she looked up at the darkening sky. "Why?" she pleaded. "Why? Zeke, my baby, Klu, and now Josh! I can bear no more! Do you hear me, God? I can bear no more!"

Rachel hung her head, and her narrow shoulders sagged in defeat. At first, the plodding sound of the horse's hoofs didn't register in her anguished mind. As the distant sound slowly penetrated, Rachel raised her tear-filled eyes and peered down the long driveway. The darkness of night was descending over the plains, and she could barely make out the lone horse and the man leading it down the dusty lane.

Rachel's hand flew over her heart, and she caught her breath with astonishment. Was she only hallucinating? Had her grief driven her mad? . . . No! . . . No! . . . It was no hallucination! The man was limping. He was actually limping!

"Josh!" she cried.

Lifting the cumbersome skirt to free the movement of her legs, she raced down the long driveway. She ran head-on into the night air, causing it to blow the tears from her face. When she neared Josh, she threw her arms open wide, smiling joyfully. Puzzled by her greeting, Josh halted, and watched dumbfounded as she flung herself into his arms. Involuntarily, he held her

467

close to keep from losing his balance.

"Josh!" she cried happily. "Josh!"

He made an effort to move her out of his embrace, but her arms clung around his neck with a determination that made it impossible for him to push her away gently.

"Rachel!" he said firmly. "Honey, you're going to break my neck if you don't loosen up a little."

"I'm sorry, Josh," she answered while still clinging to him. "But you're alive! You're actually alive!"

Laughing, he replied, "I won't be for long if you don't stop choking me."

Reluctantly, Rachel removed her arms and stepped away from him. "We thought you'd been killed!"

"Killed!" he exclaimed. "Rachel, what in the hell are you talking about?"

It was only then that she took notice of the horse Josh had been leading. Her eyes opened wide with recognition. "What are you doing with William's horse?"

"I was on the range heading for home," Josh explained, "and I saw William cutting across Reynolds' land on his way to town. His horse stumbled and pulled up lame. I rode over to him, and he asked me if he could borrow my horse. He'd been drinking pretty heavily. Oh hell, Rachel, he was downright drunk."

"William riding alone? But where were his vaqueros?"

"I don't know. If he hadn't been drunk, I'm sure he would've had them with him. Anyway, I loaned him my horse, and he took off for town. That's why I'm late. It takes a lame horse and a lame man quite a while to walk home."

Rachel's whole body stiffened. She whirled brusquely and looked down the dark driveway toward the buck-board. A deep groan escaped from her throat. Once again she lifted her long skirt and rushed off into the darkness.

"Rachel!" Josh called after her.

Quickly she left him behind, running wildly down the dirt lane. When she reached the buckboard her breathing was deep and labored. Her heart was pounding from exhaustion and apprehension as she clutched at the side of the wagon. Staring down at the covered body, Rachel's eyes widened with expectation of horror. Trembling, she reached over to pull back the blanket. Suddenly, Mr. Dutton's words crossed her mind . . . "Ma'am, there ain't nothin' left of his face!" Shaking with fear, she placed her hand over her mouth, trying desperately to hold down a rising feeling of repulsion.

"The ring!" she cried. Rachel remembered that William always wore the ruby ring that had belonged to his grandfather. Ironically Rachel became stable as she reasoned that his left hand would be on the side nearer to her. Slowly she reached toward the blanket. Tightly she grasped the cover, and in one swift motion she pushed the blanket aside. Without flinching, she looked down at the exposed arm. Her eyes traveled to the still hand. Even in the dark the large red ruby sparkled its brilliance.

"William!" The expression on Rachel's face was un-feeling as she stared down at the partially covered body of her husband. "Then it was Miguel!" Her voice rose to a shrill pitch: "Revenge, William! You murdered his friend, and for revenge he killed you!"

Violently she pulled the blanket back over his arm.

"I wish I could care! But I don't! God help me! You're dead, and I don't even care!"

Carmelita strolled languidly past her prized flower garden. She took no notice of the radiant variety of colors, nor did she pause to take in their sweet aroma. Her eyes were still red and swollen from the tears she had shed, and she folded her hands tightly to prevent their trembling.

The group of men who had ridden in that morning had said that Klu Bronson was dead. A month had passed since Klu's hanging before the news reached Manuel Villano's hacienda.

"Klu," Carmelita whispered. "I have prayed for your soul. May God in his mercy forgive you your sins." Carmelita had always believed that basically Klu had been a good person. She was sure that his childhood had been the source of the kind of life Klu had chosen to live.

Slowly Carmelita opened the front door and walked quietly into her home. The sluggish steps she took down the long hallway were caused not only by her grief, but also by her deteriorating health. She grew steadily weaker with each passing day.

Composing herself, she approached the door and knocked lightly. "Come in," she heard John call.

She compelled herself to smile as she entered the room. John was expecting her and had dressed for the first time since his illness. He was sitting up in bed, waiting impatiently. As Carmelita regarded her husband she thought him to be a very handsome man. He had shaved his beard but had decided to let the moustache remain. The recent streaks of gray at his temples added a distinguished air to his good looks.

"Where have you been?" he asked. Following his talk with Manuel, John had given Carmelita the benefit of the doubt and accepted her without prejudice. While he slowly convalesced, Carmelita spent many hours beside his bed, conversing with him quietly and maturely. Her gentleness he found soothing, and her kindness was like a sedative that eased her inner turmoil. But their son, and the tragic day that had brought about his death was never mentioned.

John heard her sigh of exhaustion as she sat in the chair beside his bed. "I am sorry to be late, but I was in the chapel."

"Chapel?" he questioned.

"Si, Papá had it built for me. Oh John, it is so beautiful! When you are better, I must show it to you."

Observing her swollen eyes, he asked, "Have you been crying?"

"Si. I learned earlier today that a friend of mine died."

"A close friend?"

"No, I don't suppose you could say we were close friends, but there was something about him that I always found so appealing. Sometimes, he reminded me of an unloved and unwanted child. I often longed to hold him in my arms and comfort him. I wanted to take away all his hurt, as one would do for a little boy. But Klu, he would not allow anyone to get close to him, and he never wanted to love anyone, not until . . ." Catching herself, Carmelita became silent.

"Not until when?" John asked.

Carmelita looked away from his questioning stare. She knew that her husband was still in love with

Rachel. During his delirium he had called her name repeatedly.

From the beginning, Carmelita had decided not to tell John of Rachel's abduction. How could she possibly explain what had happened without telling him everything? How would he react if he were to find out that Rachel had shared a room with Klu Bronson for over two months? He would demand to know if Klu had raped and violated her. What would it do to him when he learned that Rachel had welcomed Klu into her bed? Could a man like John Reynolds understand how Rachel could willingly make love with an outlaw? An outlaw, who had previously been involved in a bank robbery where two men were murdered in cold blood? A murder Rachel had witnessed!

"Not until when?" he repeated.

"He fell in love," she replied softly.

"Did she love him?"

Carmelita raised her eyes and with sadness she looked deeply into his. "Si, I think she did. But for various reasons, Klu's love for her was lost before he even found it, and her love for him was overshadowed by a much greater love."

"It sounds like quite a tragic love story." Smiling his boyish grin, he added teasingly, "Or perhaps you're just being overly romantic."

Thankful for the excuse to make light of a conversation that was much more serious than John imagined, Carmelita answered, "Perhaps, Señor. Maybe I am only a foolish romantic."

Remembering what he had wanted to ask her, he replied, "Not to change the subject of love, but, Carmelita, the day when my fever broke you said something that puzzled me.''

"What was that?''

"I'd completely forgotten about it, but today it suddenly came back to me. You told me that you knew which horse was mine because the saddle blanket was cavalry issue. How did you learn that I was in the cavalry?''

John easily detected the look of surprise on her face. He noticed how the hands in her lap were clasped together with apprehension.

"I cannot tell you!'' she gasped.

"But why?'' he asked, confused.

Bolting from the chair and standing rigidly beside his bed, she pleaded, "Please do not ask me! Please!''

Carmelita's apparent distress concerned him, and reaching for her slim hand, he held it tightly as he questioned, "Why can't you tell me? Who told you I was in the cavalry?''

"I beg you to please let it be! Do not insist that I tell you!''

"But Carmelita, there's no reason to be afraid. If you're trying to protect someone, there's no need.''

"No!'' she cried loudly. "I will discuss it no more!''

Carmelita's outburst sapped her limited strength and, weakened, she fell forward. Instantly John rose from the bed and gathered her into his arms. "I won't question you anymore, Carmelita.''

She relaxed in his comforting embrace. Hesitantly she wrapped her arms around her husband, leaning her frail body against his strong frame.

John Reynolds was not in love with his wife. He would never be in love with her, but much to his own surprise, he suddenly became aware of how much she had come to mean to him. Tightening his embrace, he whispered, "Carmelita."

Rachel refused to wear the traditional black to her husband's funeral. Deborah had pleaded and argued with her sister that she must show proper respect for her husband, but she had failed in her attempts to change Rachel's strong convictions. Under no circumstances would she pretend a grief that she was far from feeling. But Rachel did compromise, however, and reluctantly decided on a simple unadorned gray dress.

Josh was hitching up the buggy to take them to the hacienda for William's funeral, when Maria found Rachel sitting alone in the study.

"Señora," Maria began, "Mr. Andrews is here to see you."

"William's lawyer!" she exclaimed. "Very well. Show him in."

Rachel rose from the chair and walked across the room. Impatiently she waited for Maria to return with the unexpected visitor.

The elderly man strode into the room with long demanding strides. "Mrs. Granger."

"Mr. Andrews," Rachel replied softly. Looking at the servant, she told her, "That will be all, Maria."

"Si, Señora," she answered as she left the study, closing the door behind her.

Mr. Andrews scruntinized Rachel intensely, making her feel quite uncomfortable. "Mrs. Granger, it is important that I speak with you."

"Very well. May I fix you a drink?"

"No, thank you," he replied briskly. "Mrs. Granger, are you aware that only a few days before your husband was murdered, he changed his will?''

Looking at him with surprise, she answered, ''No, I didn't know.''

''He left his entire estate to a cousin in Mexico.''

Rachel's shoulders drooped slightly as she replied, ''I see. But my jewelry!''

''I'm sorry, Mrs. Granger, but the jewelry is a part of the estate.''

She raised her chin proudly. ''It doesn't matter. I want nothing that belonged to my husband.''

Taking a step toward her, he said hesitantly, ''I realize there are two sides to every story.''

Interrupting, she asked brusquely, ''What are you trying to say?''

''Mrs. Granger, I am only familiar with one side. But when you were abducted, your husband was very upset. For days he barely slept or ate. Then when his son became seriously ill, well, losing his son almost destroyed him. He was devastated!''

''Why are you telling me this?'' she asked short-temperedly.

''Young lady, do you have any idea what it did to William to find you in a lovers' embrace with an outlaw? A man like Klu Bronson?''

Her eyes flashed anger. ''Oh yes, I know exactly what it did to him! To punish me, he murdered an innocent man!''

''Innocent? Surely you don't expect me to believe that!''

''I really don't give a damn what you believe!''

''Mrs. Granger, do you know who murdered William?''

Cutting her eyes at him sharply, she answered, ''I'll

475

tell you exactly what I told the sheriff. I have no idea! If you have finished your business with me, I'd appreciate your leaving!''

''I will leave, Mrs. Granger, but first a word of warning. William's vaqueros and their families are very hostile toward you. They blame you for the death of their 'patron,' and they will be present at his funeral today.''

''But why should they blame me?''

''They believe that it was William's grief over you that caused him to ride without his vaqueros. Of course, he had been drinking heavily, but they also blame you for that. If you insist on attending your husband's services, then be very cautious Mrs. Granger!''

''He is being laid to rest beside our son! Of course I'll be there!''

''Then for your own safety, exchange that dress for respectable black!''

''What can they do to me? William held the power in this territory, not his vaqueros. I have no fear of his people.'' Standing straight and holding her slim frame stiffly, she added in a voice that was cold and brittle, ''I have no fear of anyone or anything! Not even of Hell itself! I've already been there!''

Mr. Andrews could see the strain and bitterness in Rachel's face. He had always thought Mrs. Granger a lovely, vivacious woman. He had found her dancing green eyes captivating and her smile enticing. More than once he had succumbed to her alluring charms, causing him to harshly chasten himself for acting like an old fool. But now the merriment was gone from her eyes, and there was a hardness around the corners of her mouth. ''You are a woman who knows no fear be-

476

cause she has already known the worst. And that, my dear, is very tragic in one so young.''

The priest and the people from town were mostly kind to Rachel, and they expressed their sympathy. Politely she had accepted their condolences. But she'd received no sympathy from William's vaqueros and their families. Through the entire service they had stared openly at her with hatred and hostility.

William's coffin had been lowered into the ground and two men with shovels in hand stood in the distance. When the mourners were gone, they would place the dirt over their beloved 'patron.'

As everyone moved slowly from the family cemetery, Rachel remained beside William's open grave.

Deborah made a move to return to her sister's side, but Josh touched her arm. "Let her have some time alone."

She looked up at her husband, and placing her hand in his, Deborah cried, "Oh Josh, she looks so forlorn!"

He gazed up at Rachel standing alone on top of the small hill. "I wish I knew how to find Reynolds."

"I'm not so sure that even John Reynolds could help Rachel."

"She still loves him," he replied firmly.

"Yes, I know she does, but Josh . . .''

"What?" he coaxed.

Inhaling deeply, Deborah quickly stated what she feared to be the truth. "I think Rachel loved that outlaw!" She glanced up at her sister and then looked back at Josh. "She not only grieves for her baby, she also grieves for Klu Bronson."

"That's ridiculous! I'm sure she was grateful to him

477

for saving her life, but Rachel could never love a man like Klu Bronson!'' Josh exclaimed.

"How can you be so sure? After all, she spent two months with the man. She came to know him very well. And to be honest, what do we really know of Klu Bronson?'' Deborah insisted.

"We know he robbed a bank where two men were murdered! I think it was wrong of Granger to hang him, but if he hadn't, the law would've hung him anyway.''

Taking one last look at her sister, Deborah suggested, "Let's wait for her in the carriage.''

Rachel turned quickly from her husband's grave and descended the hill in long strides. The vaqueros and their families were still gathered at the bottom of the small incline, and as the 'patron's' widow neared them, they stared at her with undisguised hostility.

Pausing in front of them, Rachel spoke in a voice that was strong and clear, "Which one of you is named Ricardo?''

Reluctantly, a young man stepped forward. "I am Ricardo, Señora.''

Looking him steadily in the eyes, she asked, "Where is Klu Bronson buried?''

"In the cemetery behind the church in town,'' he stammered.

"Does his grave have a tombstone?'' When he didn't answer instantly, she asked loudly, "Does it have a tombstone?''

"No, Señora,'' he answered quickly.

"I own a palomino and a very expensive saddle. They are not a part of William's estate. I want you to take the horse and the saddle into town and sell them. Use the money to buy a large tombstone. It is to be engraved with Klu's name and date of death.''

''Si, Señora,'' he replied.

''Tell the engraver that I want Psalms 25: verse 7 engraved on the tombstone. And it is to be written clearly and in large print. Can you remember? Psalms 25: verse 7!''

Hesitantly he answered, ''Si, Señora, I can remember. But Señora, what are the words?''

''I'm sure the engraver has a Bible, Ricardo.'' She made a move to walk away, but abruptly, she turned toward him. Tears filled her eyes and her lips trembled, but her voice remained strong. ''Remember not the sins of my youth, nor my transgressions: according to thy mercy remember me for thy goodness' sake.''

Rachel looked away from Ricardo as her eyes unflinchingly scanned the group of people watching her silently. Holding her head high and her narrow shoulders straight, Rachel began walking toward the crowd. With inborn bravery, she strode courageously through the very center of the congregation. Awed by her courage, they quickly stepped aside. The gallantry of Rachel's Irish ancestors was flowing proudly through her veins.

Chapter Twelve

Studying Rachel as she sat quietly in the buggy beside him, Edward noticed that her face was drawn and pale. She appeared to be making very little progress in recovering from the trauma she had suffered. Hoping to lift her spirits, Edward had taken her on a picnic, but now the day had grown late, and the sun was descending over the horizon.

"Edward," Rachel began, "you've been living in El Paso for four months. How long do you intend to stay? You told me once that a gambler never remains in one place for any length of time."

"What would you say if I told you that I'm seriously considering staying here?"

Rachel looked at him with surprise. "I'd say that I don't believe you!"

Laughing, he replied, "The owner of the saloon in town wants to sell, and I'm thinking of buying."

"Oh, Edward!" she exclaimed. "That would be wonderful!"

He was taken aback by her unexpected enthusiasm. "Do you really like having me around that much?"

"Of course I do! Surely you must know how much I

love you."

"As a brother?"

Edward could see the pleading in her eyes as she asked, "Is that so wrong?"

He moved his hand over hers. "I've always wanted you to love me like a woman loves a man, but I guess I'll try to love you as a sister, if that's what you want. But it won't be easy."

Avoiding a topic she didn't want to discuss, she held his hand firmly and changed the subject. "Buy the saloon, Edward. Please!"

"All right, Rachel, I think I will! Besides, owning a saloon is much safer than being a gambler."

An idea began to materialize in Rachel's mind, and watching him carefully, she began, "Edward, do you realize how degrading it is to live off the charity of others?" Not giving him the opportunity to reply, she continued hastily, "It steals one of one's pride, and, Edward, I'm left with no pride because I'm forced to be wholly dependent on Josh. I know there are no jobs to be found in town because I've already tried to find one. But Edward," she said very sweetly, "if you buy that saloon, you can give me a job."

"WHAT!" His bellow was so loud that it startled the horses, and he was forced to pull back on the reins sharply. "Whoa there, boys. . . . Whoa. . . ." he called gently. As the buggy rocked to a stop, he turned to Rachel and repeated, "What?"

"You can give me a job."

"Oh no I can't!" he shouted strongly.

"Yes you can!" she insisted.

"My God, Rachel! Have you decided to take up prostitution?"

"No, of course not!" she replied, blushing.

"Then just what kind of work do you plan to do in a saloon?"

Rachel knew precisely what kind of work she wanted, but with the feminine intuition that had been implanted in woman since the beginning of time, she realized there was only one way of achieving her goal. Somehow, she must shrewdly make Edward believe it had been his idea.

"Surely there must be something I could do besides . . . besides what you said." Composing her face into an expression of pure innocence, she asked, "The large saloons in places like St. Louis and San Francisco, don't they hire women? Women who aren't . . . well, you know what I mean."

"Sure," he answered. "They're entertainers."

"Entertainers?" she questioned, while trying not to smile victoriously.

"Dancers and singers," he clarified.

"Singing!" she exclaimed. "Oh Edward, what a marvelous idea! I'd never have thought of it! I love to sing, and I've always been told that I have a nice voice." He made an attempt to speak, but she quickly proceeded. "Of course, I can't be riding back and forth every day from the ranch to town. Are there rooms above the saloon?"

"Yeah, but Rachel . . ."

Refusing to allow him to state his disapproval, she decided promptly, "Then I'll move into one of the rooms!" Her brow suddenly wrinkled into a worried frown. "I'll need an accompanist. Does the saloon have a piano and a piano player?"

"Yeah, but Rachel . . ."

"Oh good!" she interrupted. "I'll sing while standing next to the piano."

"Damn it, Rachel!" he raged. "You can't work in a saloon!"

"Why not?" she asked stubbornly.

"Well . . . because you're a lady," he commented firmly, as though that should explain everything.

"Great guns and little switches!" she cried with exasperation. "What has being a lady got to do with it? Are you trying to tell me there are no ladies among entertainers?"

"No, of course not," he replied, feeling flustered. "But Rachel, have you stopped to think what people will say? Women who are friends with Deborah? And just how in the hell do you think your sister will react?"

"Poor Deb, she'll probably swoon. But Edward, I don't care what people will say! After what I have seen and have lived through, public opinion is of no importance to me!" With anguish in her voice, she continued, "Oh Edward, if I'm forced to go on living on the ranch with Deborah and Josh, I'm afraid I may go out of my mind! I have nothing to do but remember . . . and remember! I'll never get any better if I continue living this way!"

"All right, sweetheart," he compromised soothingly, "I'll let you work for me under one condition."

"What is that?" she asked.

"If I can find some way to be sure no man will bother you."

Disheartened, Rachel sighed, "How can you possibly find that kind of assurance?"

Startled, she jumped slightly when he bellowed, "George!"

"George?" she questioned. "Who is he?"

"He works for the blacksmith. I think he's a distant relative. Have you ever seen him?"

"No, I don't think so."

"Rachel, that man must weigh close to three hundred pounds, but it's all muscle. He isn't very bright, but he's a fairly genial fellow until he gets mad, then he's meaner than a mama bear protecting her cub. And I'm going to offer him a job protecting you!"

With her enthusiasm returning she questioned, "Do you think he'll take it?"

"Why not? I'll just offer him more than he makes working for the blacksmith."

She studied him with puzzlement. "Edward, where did you get the money to buy a saloon, and money to so freely offer someone a higher paying job?"

"Sweetheart, there's a lot of money to be made in gambling if you're good at it, and I'm good at it!" He smiled cheerfully, "But a gambler's life is dangerous, and I've got this hankerin' to live to a ripe old age."

"When are you going to ask George?"

"I'll tend to everything tomorrow, then ride out to the ranch and let you know how it all went. Now, I'm taking you home. It's grown so dark that I can barely see two feet in front of me."

As his hand tightened on the reins, Edward spotted a horse and rider approaching very slowly. The darkness prevented him from being able to make out who he was, and carefully Edward drew his pistol from its holster. Suddenly, the rider pulled his horse to an abrupt stop. He was still too far away for Edward to recognize him, and cautiously, Edward pried back the hammer on his pistol.

The gentle breeze blew a small cloud toward the west, and the exposed moon shone down on the lone rider. The man's face was shadowed by his hat, and Edward still couldn't see him, but Rachel's entire body stiffened.

Rachel inhaled so deeply that it caused Edward to look away from the rider and turn to her with instant concern. He placed his hand on her arm, but pushing it aside brusquely, she leaped from the carriage. The rough pebbles dug sharply into her fragile slippers as she began running carelessly across the darkened plains.

It was reasonable for Rachel to recognize the rider by the shape of his frame, or in the familiar way he sat on his horse, but her recognition did not come by either possibility. Rachel instinctively knew it was him; because she loved him, and she would know him anywhere!

As Rachel hurried toward him, he hastily dismounted his horse, and using long strides he ran to meet the woman he loved.

He opened his arms and she flung herself into his embrace. Placing his hands on her waist, he easily lifted her off the ground, and joyously swung her around and around. Her rejoicing laughter was music to his ears. While still clinging to her he very slowly lowered Rachel to her feet. He held her so close that she would've found his embrace painful if not for her exhilaration. "Rachel! Rachel! I love you!"

Suddenly sobs tore painfully from deep within her. She tried to speak to him, but her emotions were too overpowering, and leaning her face against his shoulder, Rachel wept.

Holding the trembling woman tenderly but securely,

he looked behind her and saw Edward stop in his tracks. Smiling, Edward promptly returned his pistol to its holster.

Gently moving Rachel and looking down into her face, he whispered, ''Rachel, honey, are you going to be all right?''

With unrestrained tears still streaming down her face she looked up into his familiar eyes, and with love she placed her shaking hand against his cheek. Finding her voice at last, she cried, ''Klu! Dear God! Klu!''

With the initial shock passing, Rachel's knees weakened and she fell forward. Catching her, Klu lifted her into his arms. Carrying her to a nearby boulder he sat down and cuddled her in his lap as though she were a child.

Rachel slipped her arms around his neck and with her tears unabated, she asked, ''How can you be alive? Oh God, Klu! How can you be alive?''

Slowly Edward moved closer to them, and at his approach Klu spoke, ''Hello, Phillips.''

''I'll be damned!'' Edward exclaimed. ''Hell, I know Granger hanged you because as Rachel and I were riding away I looked behind me. You were hanging from a rope!''

When Klu spoke again they noticed that his voice was hoarse and scratchy, ''The bastard did hang me, but the fall I took wasn't a far enough drop to break my neck, and I was slowly choking to death. It didn't take long until I mercifully blacked out. I was later informed that Granger and his vaqueros had ridden off soon after you two left. Granger ordered Ricardo to stand guard over me until he was certain that I was dead, but the moment Granger was out of sight Ricardo cut me down. By that time, Miguel had reached us. They took me to the priest in town. He not only gave me sanctuary, but he nursed me back from the depths of hell. It was days before he knew if I'd live or die.''

"Did Miguel kill Granger?" Edward asked.

Clearing his throat, Klu answered, ''Yeah, he killed him. I didn't know he was planning to shoot him, but when he told me what he had done it didn't surprise me. After he shot Granger he came to the church and slipped me out of town. He took me to some friends of his that live close to Arido. I stayed with them until I recovered.''

"Why did you come back here?" Edward questioned. "If the sheriff finds out you're still alive, he'll arrest you for that bank robbery."

"I felt I had to come back. When Miguel took me from the church he never gave me a chance to thank the priest for saving my life; he didn't even know that Miguel was taking me away."

Nodding his head, Edward replied, "Well, I guess I can understand why you'd want to thank the man who saved your life." Realizing they would need time alone, he offered, "Bronson, I'll let you take Rachel home."

Tenderly Klu moved Rachel in his arms so that he could see her face. "Do you want to stay with me or leave with Phillips?"

Clinging to him possessively, she sobbed, "I want to stay with you!"

Smiling, Edward said, "Goodbye, Bronson, and I'm glad to have the unexpected pleasure of seeing you again."

"Goodbye, Phillips. Maybe we'll meet again,

friend.''

Silently Klu and Rachel listened as the sound of the carriage wheels faded into the distance. Then Klu reached over and brushed the tears from Rachel's face. ''Last night, the priest took me to the cemetery behind the church. Miguel had already told me about the empty grave, a precaution Miguel took against Granger asking to see where I'd been buried.'' His arms tightened around her. ''Remember not the sins of my youth, nor my transgressions: according to thy mercy, remember me for thy goodness' sake.''

Moving out of his embrace, she stood in front of him and studying his face lovingly, she spoke, ''Psalms 25 verse 7. My grandmother had the words engraved on my grandfather's tombstone. I don't know that much about him, but I do know that he was fleeing from the law when he brought his bride from Ireland to America. Apparently, my grandmother believed he needed God's merciful forgiveness for his past sins and transgressions.''

''And you believed the same about me?''

Lowering her eyes from his gaze, she answered, ''We all need forgiveness for our sins, but some more than others.''

Laughing softly, he replied, ''And I fall in the latter category.'' His laughter ceased, and in the darkness Rachel was unable to see the barest trace of tears in his eyes, as he added, ''But honey, what you did for me was very sweet, and I was deeply moved.''

''Why didn't Ricardo tell me that you were alive?''

''Miguel had warned him not to tell anyone. Rachel, I wasn't even planning to take the chance of coming out here to see you. Then last night, when I saw what you had done, I knew I couldn't leave without seeing you once more."

"Klu! Where are you going?" she asked.

"Miguel is waiting for me in Arido, and from there we'll go to Manuel's hacienda. I'm sure he and Carmelita have heard about the hanging. I want to let them know that I'm alive."

"And then?" she questioned.

"For some reason, Rachel, God has given me a second chance at life. I don't know, maybe He figured He owed me one. Well, let's just say I'm through with my old ways. I guess Miguel and I will go our separate ways, and I'll see if I can hire on somewhere with a cattle drive."

She knelt in front of him and clasped his hands tightly in hers. "I'm so glad!" Smiling with happiness, she teased, "You didn't make a very good outlaw anyhow."

Looking into Rachel's upturned face he was struck anew with how much he loved her. Rising, he drew Rachel to her feet, gathering her into his arms. "Honey," he whispered, "Ricardo told me about your son. I'm sorry."

She leaned her head against his shoulder. "Oh Klu, that day . . . that horrible day! I was already in shock because of what happened to you, and then to find out that my baby had died! I don't know how I lived through it without losing my mind!"

"You're a very strong woman," he answered.

Stepping back so that she could look up into his face, she asked distastefully, "A survivor?"

Hearing the unmistakable bitterness in her voice, he replied, "You speak as though it were a curse."

Despondently, she walked a short way from him. "Sometimes, Klu, I wonder if perhaps it isn't a curse."

He moved to her and placed his hands gently on her shoulders. "Losing a child must be a hard cross to bear."

Rachel went gratefully into his consoling arms. "My baby, my parents, Zeke, and I thought I had lost you too."

"Zeke?" he questioned. "Isn't he the old man you said was good friends with Reynolds?"

"Yes, he was killed during an Indian massacre."

"And Reynolds? Have you seen him?" he asked stiffly.

"No, I haven't." She held him closely as she cried, "Oh Klu, no one knows where he is!"

Carefully, Klu moved her out of his embrace. "Damn it, Rachel! Do you have any idea what it does to me when you're in my arms but you're wanting him?" Klu could see the blank expression in her eyes. Impatient with her total lack of comprehension, he drew his lips tightly over his teeth. "What must I say or do to make you understand that I love you!"

"But Klu, I told you from the very beginning that I would always love John Reynolds!"

With anger he turned away but then swerved back toward her. "No woman would beg for a man's life the way you begged for mine unless she loved him! I can still remember your cries and your pleas. The last I heard before I blacked out was your scream. Damn it, Rachel, that scream was the scream of a woman who had lost the man she loved! And what about that tombstone? You arrogantly stood right in front of Granger's people and ordered it for my grave! Would a woman do that for a man she didn't love?'' He reached for her, roughly pulling her toward him. ''Can you look me in the eyes and tell me that you don't love me?'' His hands tightened painfully on her arms, and the hoarseness in his voice increased, ''Can you? Tell me that you don't love me! Tell me, Rachel!''

Looking him straight in the eyes she tried to tell him that she didn't love him, but the words couldn't be said. Suddenly, Rachel realized that she had always loved Klu, but until that moment she had been unaware of the simple truth.

''Oh Klu,'' she sighed. ''I can't tell you that I don't love you because I do love you.'' The knowledge brought her no happiness, and with heartache she cried out to him, ''I love you the way a woman loves a man! I want to be in your arms, I want to kiss you, and I want to make love to you. I need you in all the ways a woman needs the man she loves!''

He clutched her arm firmly. ''Then marry me, Rachel! Ricardo told me that Granger cut you out of his will, so you have nothing to keep you here. Come with me, Rachel! I need you! Does Reynolds need you? Has he ever needed you?''

''Yes!'' she shouted. ''He needs me!''

''Then why isn't he here with you?'' Klu asked angrily. ''Why hasn't he come by to check on you? To see if you're all right!''

Rachel's shoulders bent as she bowed her head. ''I don't know,'' she whispered. Klu could hear the anguish in her voice. Raising her head, she brought her eyes to his. ''But he needs me, and I need him!''

''You say you need him, but by God is he here? I'm the one who is once again risking his neck to be with you!''

"He doesn't know about William and my baby. If he knew he'd be here!''

"How can you be so damned sure?'' he asked.

"Because he loves me, and I love him!'' she cried.

"You tell me that you love him, and yet you also say that you love me. My God, Rachel, how can you love us both?''

Slowly she walked a few steps, then turning to face him, she cried, "I don't want to hurt you. It would break my heart to make you unhappy, but Klu, you must listen to me. I was only sixteen when I first saw John, and from the moment I set eyes on him, no man has been able to replace him. I was seventeen when I realized that I loved him. Not only did I know that I loved him, but I also knew that I'd love him until the day I died! I once believed that our love had been pre-destined. Now, I'm not so sure it was destiny, but I am sure that I'll always love John Reynolds. You ask how can I love you both? I don't know how, Klu. But I do know that I belong with John. I lost him once before because I married William Granger. I'll not lose him that way again.''

"So you're going to wait for him, even though you know he may never come back.''

"The hope that someday he will come to me is the only hope I have left.''

"It's not the only hope left, Rachel, it's the only hope you want.''

She raised her chin and answered firmly, "John is all I've ever wanted.''

"To be loved the way you love him! Does he know, Rachel? Does he have any idea how much you love him?"

"John is aware that I love him, but I don't think he fully realizes how much."

"Why not? He'd have to be blind not to see it."

"Because I was so young when I first fell in love with him, and he was so much older. He believed it was only an infatuation. When he finally realized that what I felt was love, I don't think he really had any conception of its depth."

Klu coughed to try and clear some of the hoarseness from his throat. "You're the only woman I've ever loved. . . . Woman, hell: you're the only person I've ever loved, and I've lost you. But I never really had you to lose, did I?"

Rachel moved closer to him and brushed her hand tenderly across his cheek. "Klu, your voice, will it always be like this?"

He reached over and took her hand into his. "I don't know. I hope it'll get better in time."

"Oh Klu!" she cried, "I'm so sorry! I'll never understand how William could've been so cruel and cold-blooded."

"I can understand William Granger and his kind, Rachel. They're raised to believe that where their inferiors are concerned, they hold the power over life and death. But I think his primary motive for killing me was to punish you." Suddenly his eyes hardened. "And if Miguel hadn't shot him, I'd have killed him! I don't know if my voice will ever be normal again, but I do know that I'll carry this reminder for the rest of my life!" In one swift move he removed the bandanna from around his neck.

Rachel's eyes widened with shock, and she placed

494

her hand over her mouth to smother the gasp that had escaped from her throat.

With unhidden bitterness, Klu spoke, "It's an ugly scar, isn't it? Shaped just like the noose that was around my neck!"

Rachel lifted her gaze from the scar and looked up into his face. In the moonlight she could easily see his features. His hat was pushed back from his forehead, and his dark hair was falling over his brow. His eyebrows were drawn together into a frown, making his eyes appear even smaller. There was a tenseness around his mouth, and the horror he had suffered was depicted vividly on his face, but Rachel did not see a man full of anger and hate; to her, Klu was just a young boy who had been hurt unjustly. Tenderly her eyes once again took in his features. Klu wasn't handsome, but he possessed a sensuality that few women could resist.

Placing her arms around him and putting one hand on the back of his neck she pressed his lips down to hers. Moaning with passion, he smoothly pulled her body against his.

"Rachel!" As Klu whispered her name she could acutely hear his love and his heartache. Carefully he stepped away from her. "I don't want to say goodbye. I want to make love to you. Your passion and your need cry out to me." Gently he took her hand into his. "But I love you too much to take you and still be able to ride out of your life." The husky sound in his voice penetrated her heart. "Losing you is tearing me to pieces! I love you, Rachel!"

Tears filled her eyes and her lips trembled. "Oh Klu, I never wanted to hurt you!"

Speaking brusquely he told her, "I'm taking you home. I have to, Rachel!" Compelling himself to smile he added, "If I don't, I just may repeat history and abduct you again."

Klu led Rachel to his horse. He helped her into the saddle and then easily lifted himself up behind her. Encircling Rachel within his arms, he picked up the reins. "Seems familiar, doesn't it?"

Laughing lightly, she replied, "Obviously we rode together to Manuel Villano's hacienda because we were short one horse, but, Klu, why did we share a horse on the ride to Arido? Why didn't you ask Manuel for an extra one?"

Placing his lips close to her ear, he whispered, "For purely selfish reasons, I assure you. There's nothing I like better than having you in my arms the way you are now. But Rachel, I wish you'd forget the name Manuel Villano."

"Why?" she asked.

"If Manuel knew you were aware of his name he wouldn't like it, and he might decide to rectify the situation."

"Surely he wouldn't have me killed!" she exclaimed.

"Just forget the damned name, okay?"

"I haven't revealed his name to anyone, but not to protect him. I've kept silent for Carmelita's sake. Klu, when you see Carmelita, tell her she's often in my thoughts."

"I'm looking forward to seeing her again. I wonder if perhaps it wasn't Carmelita's prayers for my lost soul that convinced God to give me a second chance." Chuckling, he added, "You know, I wouldn't doubt it.

I wouldn't doubt it at all!''

When Rachel informed Deborah in no uncertain terms that she planned to work in Edward's saloon, Deborah had indeed swooned! Josh pressed a damp cloth to his wife's brow, and Rachel had repeatedly patted her hand until she regained consciousness. But no amount of pleading on Deborah's part had been able to change Rachel's mind. Work in a saloon she most assuredly would; and if people were appalled and shocked then that was their problem, not hers!

Edward moved Rachel into the largest room above the saloon. He had already warned her that she would be sharing the upstairs with the three saloon girls who worked for him. He'd tried to explain to her that she'd be hearing different men in the hallway on their way to visit the girls, but Rachel had only laughed at his obvious frustration and embarrassment as she declared, ''Great guns and little switches, Edward! Stop treating me like an innocent babe. I know how prostitutes make a living!''

More than once Edward reprimanded himself severely for allowing Rachel to talk him into such an outlandish scheme. He often wondered just how in the hell she had managed it. George was his only assurance of Rachel's safety, and with each passing day he became more grateful for George's presence.

When he first heard Rachel sing, Edward realized that she had been putting it mildly when she told him that she had a nice voice. Rachel's voice was beautiful, and her Irish ballads would often put tears in the eyes of the coarsest of men. Immediately Rachel became a big attraction, and Edward's customers loved her with a passion. Word soon spread like wildfire. The cattle drives would set up camp close to town, and other travelers would journey out of their way, just to come to Edward's saloon to hear the lovely Irish lass with a voice like an angel. Rachel's sentimental ballads caused the hardest of men to drift back to their long-ago childhoods and recollect the mother's love that they hadn't remembered in years. Her ballads of love made the younger men dream of the woman that would someday share their lives, or remember the girl they had left far behind. Rachel soon acquired many fervent admirers, but none more so than George Putnam.

When George Putnam moved into town, all the women actively shunned him. They found his huge gawky frame and homely features repulsive, and his simplemindedness frightening. George knew he intimidated the ladies, so he tried walking with his broad shoulders slumped to camouflage his big frame, and his head lowered so the delicate ladies wouldn't be forced to view his homely face. But much to his bewilderment, they would still hurry to the other side of the street to avoid crossing his path. The jeers and the cruel teasing from the children were even worse; he would have liked to have been friends with them. It would have been so much fun to play games with them, the way his father had once played games with him.

George's father had been a widower who owned a small farm in Illinois. To protect his simple-minded son from the cruelty of people, George had been isolated from the public. Living on his father's farm, George had grown up wild and free as a deer. The animals in the woods were his companions and the outdoors was his haven. George had been a young man of twenty, with the mind of a child, when his father unexpectedly died. The only relative the authorities could locate was a cousin to George's father, Ben Putnam, a blacksmith in El Paso. Ben offered to take care of George in return for the money from the sale of the farm, thus George came to live in El Paso with his only remaining kin.

George had been living with Ben for six months when one day he spotted two men mercilessly teasing a stray dog. George loved all animals. They were the only friends he'd ever had. They never shunned him and they were never frightened of him. Edward had been a witness to George's violent reaction. After seeing how easily George had handled two grown men as if they were no stronger than children, Edward became aware of the man's monstrous strength and kind-hearted nature.

George had been shocked speechless when Edward offered him the important position of actually protecting a lady. But George had bowed his head, bashfully shuffled his feet and refused to answer. Edward had demanded a reply, but George had been too ashamed to tell the gentleman that the lady would hate him because he was ugly and stupid. Ben, hoping to be rid of his burdensome relative, had insisted that George accept Mr. Phillips' generous offer. So a few days later, George reluctantly packed his meager belongings and followed Edward to the closed saloon. Edward had immediately led George up the flight of stairs, but as he was climbing the steps George quickly surveyed the main level. The one room was large with tables and chairs placed randomly over the floor space. He noticed a piano in the corner of the room. He loved music. He hoped that Mr. Phillips would let him listen to the piano sometimes. His large feet had come to an abrupt stop when he spotted the picture hanging behind the bar. The portrait of a nude woman.

The look of astonishment on George's face caused Edward to laugh out loud. "Women are beautiful, aren't they?" he'd asked.

George couldn't understand why Mr. Phillips had insisted on continually speaking to him as though he weren't the idiot that Ben had repeatedly called him. He wanted very much to somehow impress the man who would be paying his salary, and he'd never been paid a salary! So George bravely looked the gentleman in the eye, as if he were the man's equal, and trying hard to sound intelligent, he stated, "You know, Mr. Phillips, I've noticed that some ladies are prettier than others."

Smiling cheerfully, Edward answered, "That's very perceptive, George."

George wished that he knew what the word "perceptive" meant, but Mr. Phillips had said it as though it were something good. Experiencing a strange feeling of pride, he followed Edward to the top of the stairs.

The moment that Edward knocked on Rachel's door, George instinctively drooped his powerful shoulders and lowered his head. When the door was opened, he wanted to glance up at the lady he was sure would find him repulsive, but staring down at his feet he trailed Edward into the room. As Edward introduced him to the lady he kept his gaze lowered. The sound of the lady's voice had been so soft and gentle that George felt his huge frame trembling with dreaded expectation. He hated it when women looked at him as if he were detestable. Why, he wondered, had God made him so

500

ugly?

George was totally shocked when the woman actually reached for his hand. He watched with disbelief as her small hand became concealed within his huge one. At last, finding the courage to raise his head, George looked straight into a pair of sparkling green eyes. When the beautiful young woman smiled and spoke his name with kindness instead of repulsion, she instantly won George's complete and undying devotion.

Edward had explained patiently to George that his job would consist entirely of protecting Miss Rachel. He was to stay protectively close to her downstairs when she was performing, and then he would stand guard in front of her door until the saloon closed.

Standing very straight and holding his massive frame proudly, George promised Edward that he'd protect Miss Rachel with his own life. And never had George said anything that he'd meant more!

George stifled a yawn as he waited impatiently for Rachel to finish her song. The room was packed with men of all sizes and shapes, but the saloon was extremely quiet as everyone listened attentively. The poker players called their bets in lowered voices. The crowded room, heavy with smoke from all the cigars and cigarettes, caused George to rub at his irritated eyes. He wished Miss Rachel would hurry up and finish. He loved to hear her sing, and up until tonight he had always been disappointed when she'd end her performance. But he had a present for Miss Rachel, and he could hardly wait to give it to her.

Rachel finished her song, and George joined the clamorous applause as he loudly clapped his large hands. Promptly Rachel moved over and stood beside her protector. When she looked up into his face and smiled enchantingly, George firmly believed that even the angels in heaven couldn't be more beautiful or sweeter than his Miss Rachel.

Making sure that he remained protectively close to her, he escorted Rachel across the crowded room and to the stairway. As they began to climb the steps, she glanced down at the rifle that he was carrying by his side. When Edward had first told Rachel that he was going to teach George how to shoot, she'd been highly skeptical. She had feared it would be like putting a gun in the hands of a child. But George had learned quickly to respect and to properly handle the dangerous weapon.

"How are your lessons coming along?" she inquired.

"Today, I hit the center of the target three times! And Miss Rachel, I only shot at it five times!"

"Three times out of five! That's very good!"

They neared the door to Rachel's room and George hesitantly touched her arm. "Ma'am, I have a surprise for you."

Smiling, Rachel asked, "A surprise?"

"It's a present," he answered bashfully.

"George, how sweet! I love presents!"

Grinning timidly, he replied, "It's in your room."

Before he could grasp the opportunity to warn her, she hurriedly turned the knob and swung open the door. The huge fangs were long and the snarling growl was ferocious, as the large animal leaped savagely toward the doorway. Rachel was frightened so unexpectedly, that her scream was only a feeble shriek, and her eyes opened wide with terror. Moving with unbelievable speed, Rachel pulled the door shut at the same instant that the beast struck powerfully against it.

"Miss Rachel," George began with excitement, "you didn't give me a chance to explain. That's your present! That's my dog!"

Placing her hand over her pounding heart, Rachel tried to control her labored breathing. In a shaking voice, she answered, "I don't think he likes me!"

"That's because he don't know you're his friend."

"George," Rachel commented, "he may be right. I don't think I am his friend."

"Sure you are!" he insisted.

Trying to substitute humor for fear, she asked, "If I'm his friend, then will you please pass the information on to him?"

"He's been mistreated, Miss Rachel, and he don't trust people he don't know. Once I seen these two men bein' real mean to 'im. I made 'em leave 'im alone, and since then he's been my dog."

"But why are you giving him to me?"

"Ma'am, even after the saloon is closed, I don't get much sleep 'cause I'm worryin' about you. I'm afraid some man will break into your room."

"I understand, George. With that monster in my room, no one would dare."

"Yes'm, Miss Rachel. Don't you think it's a good idea?" he asked proudly.

"It's a marvelous idea." Glancing cautiously at the closed door, she added, "But I'm not so sure that the dog agrees with us."

"Will you let me go in first, Miss Rachel?"

Quickly she stepped aside as she answered, "I

wouldn't dream of trying to stop you."

Opening the door, he called, "It's me, boy!"

Standing in the hall, Rachel watched as the monstrous dog wagged his tail and joyfully welcomed his master. Walking into the room, George told her, "Come on in, Miss Rachel. He ain't gonna hurt you."

Rachel had to force her feet to move as she warily entered the room. Trying desperately to conceal her fright, she looked down at the huge animal that watched her every move.

"Speak to him," George suggested.

Clearing her throat, she said in a feeble and shaking voice, "Hi there, fellow." With his bushy tail wagging, he moved to Rachel and gentle licked the back of her hand.

"See there!" George declared. "He likes you! I knew he would. He's a good judge of people!"

Carefully, Rachel patted the top of his head. He was an enormous long-haired and solid-black dog. Turning his large head sideways, he peered up at her with a pair of very sad-looking brown eyes. One ear was held up straight, but the other remained stubbornly at half mast.

Laughing, Rachel asked, "Does he always hold his ears this way?"

"Not always. Sometimes they both droop."

"What's his name?"

"I ain't never really given 'im a name. But Ben always called 'im that mean ole dog with the lopsided ears. So I sorta started callin' 'im Lopsided. But he answers to it, Miss Rachel. Watch and I'll show you."

Quickly, George crossed the room and stood in front of the window. "Lopsided, come here." Immediately

504

the dog ran to his side and playfully jumped up on him.

"Lopsided!" Rachel giggled. "Oh George, what a name for a dog!"

"You don't like it?" he asked seriously.

Observing George's somber expression, she replied generously, "As a matter of fact, I do like it! It's not only different, but it positively suits him."

"Miss Rachel, call 'im, and see if he'll come to you."

Kneeling down, she called gently, "Come here, Lopsided."

In one long and clumsy stride the dog bounded toward her. His huge paws struck her shoulders so powerfully that she was knocked backwards. Her full skirt and multiple petticoats floundered around her legs, as Lopsided affectionately covered her face with his wet tongue and cold nose.

Laughing, Rachel sat up and while trying to push the large dog aside, she hastily straightened her skirts. "I think he wants to be my friend."

"Do you like your present?" George asked with hopeful enthusiasm.

"Yes, I do! I like my present very much! Thank you, George. And from here on out, you and I both will sleep better knowing that Lopsided is guarding my room."

The sudden knock on Rachel's door was firm and loud. Swinging it open, Edward called cheerfully, "Rachel, are you decent?"

With his hair bristling on his back, Lopsided snarled savagely at the intruder. Making his departure with due speed, Edward backed straight into the hallway and promptly slammed the door.

Rachel and George laughed so hard that they lost their breaths, when they heard Edward bellow from the other side of the door, "Well, I'll be damned!"

Carefully, John plucked a rose from the full and blooming bush. Turning to Carmelita and pushing aside her long hair, he placed the flower behind her ear. Looking up into his steel gray eyes, she was once again acutely aware of how much she loved him. John had recuperated from his illness weeks ago, but he still lingered at her father's hacienda. Many times Carmelita had wanted to ask him when he planned to leave, but she was too afraid to bring up the dreaded subject. She hoped he would stay with her for the remainder of her days. Carmelita had no fear of death, but since John had come back into her life, she didn't want to die. And it was with a mixture of sorrow and happiness that she lived through each passing day.

Although John had not resumed his role as a husband to Carmelita, he felt a deep and sincere fondness for the woman that was his wife. Looking down into her drawn face he became aware of her fatigue.

Placing his hand on her arm, he began leading her through the abundant flower garden. "I want you to get some rest, and I'll see you later at dinner."

"I am tired. I seem to tire so easily," she sighed.

With sympathy and concern his hand tightened on her arm securely. "Carmelita, I want to take you to the doctors back East. Perhaps to Boston."

"My father has already taken me to the finest of doctors." Feeling a shortness of breath, she inhaled deeply before continuing. "Besides, I am not well enough to undertake a long journey."

Slowly they climbed the short flight of steps leading up to the veranda. In long strides John walked over and opened the front door. He stepped aside for Carmelita to enter. As he closed the front door behind them, he heard Manuel yell with excitement. "Carmelita! Come here! I have good news!"

Hastening their footsteps they crossed the foyer and entered the spacious parlor. Grinning expansively, Manuel hurried to greet them. He took both of Carmelita's hands into his and exclaimed, "Señor Bronson, he is alive!"

John observed Carmelita's reaction, and alertly, he caught her in his arms as she fell against him. "Oh Papá! How can he be alive?" she cried. 'Papá, how do you know this to be true?"

"He is here, Carmelita!" he said eagerly. "He has gone to the stable to see to his horse, but he will soon return. Klu, he wants very much to see you!"

Remaining in John's arms, she rubbed her hand across her brow in a gesture of confusion. "But I do not understand. Was he not hanged?"

"Si, he was! But Señor Granger, he and his vaqueros rode away before Klu was dead. Miguel's cousin Ricardo, he cut him down. Miguel and Ricardo, they took him to the priest in town, and he gave Klu sanctuary."

Immediately, Carmelita became aware of how John's arm stiffened, when her father spoke the name, Señor Granger.

"Why would Granger hang Bronson?" John asked urgently.

"But of course, you do knot know, do you amigo?" Manuel replied.

"Papá . . . no." Carmelita's pitiful plea was so feeble that it went unheeded by her father.

"Klu Bronson, he abducted Señor Granger's wife."

Carmelita was taken aback by the shock and anger materializing on her husband's face. Releasing her, he took a step toward Manuel and demanded, "Did he hurt her? My God man, what happened to her? Is she alive?"

Puzzled by John's apparent concern and rage, he answered hesitantly, "Si . . . si, she was not harmed. Señor Bronson, he was involved in a bank robbery in El Paso. Señora Granger and two men were in the bank. Klu, he kidnapped the Señora for the ransom, but the two men, they were killed. He brought her here, and for two months he kept her locked in one of the rooms at my boarding house. He allowed no one to enter except for two servant girls and Carmelita."

"And Bronson? Where in the hell did he stay?" John asked furiously.

"With the Señora, of course. She is a very beautiful woman!"

The choked pain in her husband's voice tore at Carmelita's heart. "You mean she had to submit to that bastard for two months?" He turned away to hide his anguish, but hastily regaining control of his emotions, he pivoted back toward Manuel. "Did he collect the ransom?"

"No, amigo. He and the others, they took the Señora to the town of Arido to make contact with her husband. But Señora Granger, she escaped with a man named Edward Phillips."

"Phillips!" John exclaimed with surprise.

"Si, amigo, and Klu, he caught up to them. But so

did Señor Granger and his vaqueros.''

John swerved and stalked out of the room so quickly that Carmelita never had the chance to stop him. Her fear grew as she listened to his heavy footsteps hurrying down the hallway. Carmelita heard him entering his room, but within seconds she could hear him returning down the corridor.

Swiftly she ran to meet him, and as he approached the foyer, Carmelita gasped in fright. Startled, she watched him buckle on his gun and holster.

"John, where are you going?" she asked breathlessly.

"To the stable!" he answered harshly.

She clutched frantically at his arm. "Why?"

Brusquely he pushed her hand aside. "I'm going to finish the job Granger started."

As his long strides neared the front door, she cried out to him, "No! You do not understand!"

But ignoring her pleas, he swung the door open and rushed out of the house.

Klu's acute instinct had sensed the man's presence, and turning cautiously from his horse, he looked behind him. Seeing the stranger's hostility, Klu knew instantly that the man had come to kill him.

"Are you Klu Bronson?" he asked.

Holding his right hand close to his pistol, Klu answered, "Yeah, I'm Bronson. Who in the hell are you?"

"The name's Reynolds."

"Aw . . . goddamn!" Klu shouted angrily. Jerking his hand from his gun, Klu's rasping voice became strained with emotion. "Don't ask me to draw against

509

you! I can't kill you! Damn it . . . I can't!''

John was confused by Klu's strange behavior. He started to question him, when suddenly, he heard Carmelita calling him. Leaning on her father for support, she hurried into the stable.

"Papá," she pleaded, "leave the three of us alone, please."

Looking at her with grave concern, he asked, "Will you be all right?"

"Si, Papá, but I must talk to John."

Nodding his head absently, Manuel walked slowly away from his daughter and out of the stable. Moving to John, Carmelita placed her hand on his arm. With tears in her eyes she told him, "You cannot kill Klu!"

Inwardly, he sensed that Carmelita had somehow learned of his love for Rachel, and angrily, he shouted, "He raped her!"

"No!" she opposed. "He did not rape her!" Carmelita's voice rose, and heartbroken, she revealed the truth, "They were lovers!"

"NO!" John shouted with tremendous rage. "NO!" His powerful hands grasped her shoulders cruelly. "Rachel wouldn't be the lover of a damned murderer!"

In a trembling voice she cried, "Klu is not a murderer! I know what Papá said but it wasn't Klu who . . ."

Interrupting, Klu yelled gruffly, "Let it be! Just let it be Carmelita!" Staring at John with an expression of indifference, he said calmly, "If you want to shoot me, Reynolds, then go ahead and get it over with. But I won't draw against you. It's not because I'm afraid I can't beat you. I think I can. But there ain't no way in hell that I'm goin' to be the one who kills the man Rachel loves.''

John's piercing eyes stared unflinchingly into Klu's. The heavy tension between them hung suspended in the still air. Carmelita's gaze darted from one man to the other, and she could literally feel the powerful force from their male magnetism. It was no wonder that Rachel loved them both. They were so different, yet so similar. John's masculine physique seemed to tower over Klu's slimness. John's handsome features were strong, whereas Klu's were rugged. But, with uncanny similarity both men stood in the same fashion. The expression in their eyes was reflected from one to the other, as if they were looking into a mirror.

Recognizing the truth in Klu's face, John swerved swiftly and began walking away as Klu yelled, ''Granger is dead!'' John's back was to him and Klu couldn't see his facial expression, but he noticed how Reynolds' long strides slowed. Klu continued, ''Rachel lost her son. He died of pneumonia.'' John's steps came to an abrupt stop, and Klu detected the sudden rigidness in his large frame. The groan that came from John's throat was soft but painful. Trying to clear the hoarseness from his voice, Klu said with compassion, ''She needs you. Damn it, Reynolds, it's you she needs!'' John didn't turn around to acknowledge him, but continuing his departure, he left the stable.

Instantly Klu crossed over to Carmelita and tenderly drew the frail woman into his arms.

''Klu,'' she sighed, ''I am so happy that you are alive.''

''I'm sorry,'' he apologized, ''if I caused trouble between you and Reynolds.''

Reluctantly, she stepped free from his solacing embrace. "I have always known that John would react this way."

"He had Rachel up on a pedestal, didn't he?" Klu asked.

Carmelita remained silent for a moment before answering. "John is a realist. No, I do not think he had her on a pedestal."

He frowned bitterly. "Then it's not what she did, but who she did it with!"

Distressed, she cried, "Oh Klu, you were involved in a bank robbery! Two men were murdered and Rachel witnessed the brutal killing! John does not understand how she could willingly turn to a man . . ."

Interrupting, he asked bitterly, "A man who is the filth of the earth?"

"But Klu, you are not! And if John knew you, he would know this to be true."

"Maybe he doesn't know me, but damn it, he knows Rachel! Doesn't he have any faith in her integrity?"

"I do not know. John and I, we have never discussed Rachel."

"Well it's about time someone set him straight!"

He swerved to move away from her, but she grabbed at his arm. "Klu! You and John should not speak together! It is too dangerous!"

"Oh yeah?" he asked with a sneer. "What's the worst that could happen? He'd kill me? Hell, I'm already dead, remember?"

"No, Klu!" she begged. "Please, do not go to him! He has a violent temper!"

Observing her concern for his safety, Klu told her gently, "Reynolds isn't the type to shoot an unarmed man." He pulled his pistol from its holster and handed it to her. "Where can I find him?"

Accepting the pistol, she answered, "I will leave your gun in your saddlebags." Touching his arm, she said, "There is a large tree to the west of my flower garden. It is secluded. Many times he has gone there when he wishes to be by himself. I believe maybe he goes there now to be alone with his thoughts."

The day was growing late, and the setting sun cast long shadows over Manuel's hacienda when Klu spotted John leaning against the trunk of a huge tree. He was looking in the opposite direction from Klu's approach, but John's sense of hearing easily detected the man's footsteps.

Cautiously, he turned away from the tree, and with a hard expression in his eyes, he watched Klu saunter closer to him. "What in the hell do you want, Bronson?"

Moving to the tree and appearing relaxed, Klu propped himself against it. Reaching into his pocket, he removed a pouch of tobacco and paper. "I don't want a damned thing."

"I find it hard to believe that you followed me just for the pleasure of my company."

Klu grinned slightly. "No . . . we both know there could never be pleasantries between us." He finished rolling the cigarette and offered it to John.

"A peace pipe?" he asked, taking the cigarette.

Beginning to roll one for himself, Klu responded, "So to speak."

"Why did you follow me Bronson?"

"There's only one reason why I'm here, Reynolds

. . . Rachel.''

John reached into his pocket and brought out a match. Striking it against the tree, he lit his cigarette, then offered a light to Klu. ''Is she in love with you?''

Klu took a long drag off the cigarette. ''Yeah, but because of you, it doesn't mean a damned thing!''

''Well, don't let me stand in the way!'' John replied angrily.

''Believe me, Reynolds, if there was any way I could get you out of the way, I would gladly do so.''

''Damn it, Bronson! What in the hell are you trying to say?''

''I ain't trying to say anything. I just want to know what in the hell you intend to do about Rachel.''

''I don't see where it's any of your business!''

Anger flared in Klu's eyes. ''I'm making it my business!''

A strained silence remained between them for a moment, before John inquired, ''When did you last see her?''

''A few nights ago.''

''How was she?''

''Considering what she has gone through, she was doing extraordinarily well.''

A small smile curved the corners of John's mouth. ''Rachel has a lot of character.''

Once more silence fell between them. This time Klu spoke first, and clearing his throat, he asked, ''You can't understand how she could've turned to someone like me, can you?''

Studying Klu closely, John answered, ''All I know about you is what I've heard, but Bronson, I don't think you're a murderer.''

"Why not?" he questioned.

"Because Rachel obviously cares about you."

"Then you do have faith in her integrity?"

John dropped his cigarette, then ground it out with the heel of his boot. "In some ways, Rachel will always remain naive, immature, and impetuous. But she'll always have integrity."

"I'm not one for telling long stories, but I'm goin' to tell you everything that happened to Rachel from the moment she walked into the bank at El Paso."

The long shadows disappeared and were replaced by darkness as Klu recalled all that Rachel had seen and endured. When he finished he looked at John and asked, "What are you goin' to do about her?"

"What in the hell do you want me to do?" John asked impatiently. "Do you want me to ride out of here and go to Rachel? And just what would it do to Carmelita? How can I do that to a dying woman?"

"Carmelita," Klu said softly.

"Had you forgotten about her?" John asked crossly.

"Yeah, for a moment I forgot." He paused then added, "But Carmelita will understand how you feel."

Klu could see the glint of hope in John's eyes. "You're right, Bronson. She'll understand."

Stepping away from him, Klu replied, "We may never meet again so . . . good luck, Reynolds."

"Are you leaving?"

"I'm ridin' out tonight."

"Bronson!" John called. Klu turned and looked back at him. "More than once you saved Rachel's life, For that I'm grateful to you."

The smile on Klu's face was disagreeable. "Saved her life? Hell, Reynolds, Rachel is my life! And now

515

it's goin' to be hell learning to live without her. Goodbye, Reynolds.''

"So long, Bronson." John watched him, until he vanished into the darkness.

In long vigorous strides John crossed the foyer, as he headed for Carmelita's bedroom. Unexpectedly, Manuel hurried from the parlor and called to him, "Amigo!"

Halting his steps, John asked, "Is Carmelita resting?"

"Si, but before you go to her, we need to talk. Please Señor!"

Impatiently, he followed Manuel into the parlor. Pausing in the center of the room, he watched Carmelita's father pacing nervously across the highly polished floor.

"Manuel, what do you . . ." he began, but the huge man waved away his words.

"Amigo, I know everything."

"What are you talking about?"

Manuel ceased his pacing and looked at John. "Carmelita, she told me of this great love that you have for Señora Granger." Using strong, demanding strides he moved to John. "Do you plan to leave my daughter? Are you returning to the Señora, who is now a widow?"

"Damn it, Manuel! You talk as if Carmelita and I had reconciled our marriage."

Manuel's rage turned his face red as he shouted, "Then it is true! You will leave her! You have no compassion for her and no pity!"

John raised his voice in anger. "I have compassion

516

for Carmelita, but I'm not in love with her!''

"You cannot love your own wife, but you can love another man's wife."

"It's not quite that cut and dried."

He could hear the pain in Manuel's voice, "But my daughter, she loves you."

Sighing sympathetically, John replied, "Yes, I know she does."

"But you cannot love her?"

"I care very deeply. Believe me, I do care about Carmelita."

"Then do not break her gentle heart, Señor!" he pleaded.

"Break her heart?" he questioned. "But Manuel, she knows how I feel about Rachel."

"Nonetheless, amigo. If you leave, it will break her heart. She has not much longer to live. Can you not wait?"

Sensing defeat, John turned away from the man's pleading stare, but Manuel clutched at his arm, forcing John to face him again. "For many years, I have seen Carmelita live with peace and contentment but with no happiness. But now, amigo, once more she is happy. She knows that soon she will die, but still I see the joy in her eyes. The joy that you have put there. If you leave, Señor, you will take her happiness with you." Tears filled the man's eyes, and without shame he allowed them to roll unhindered down his face. "Must I beg you, amigo?"

John placed his hand on Manuel's shoulder. "No, my friend. There's no need to beg for your daughter's happiness. I will stay."

* * *

John knocked lightly on the door. "Come in," he heard Carmelita call. Opening the door, he strode into the room. Carmelita was standing beside the window. Her hands were clasped tightly with worry.

"John!" she cried as she hurried to him. "Is Klu all right? Did you fight with him?"

She was looking up into his face, and John could detect the fear in her eyes. "No, we didn't fight. I have no quarrel with the man. He never raped Rachel. I knew the truth before I left the stable."

"Klu would never hurt Rachel. He loves her!"

Gently he placed his hands on her shoulders. "Why didn't you tell me?"

"I wanted to protect Rachel. I was afraid you would not understand her need for Klu. But John, I did not know Señor Granger was dead. If I had known, I would have told you. Now, she is free to be with you, and soon my husband, you shall also be free."

Watching her face closely, he asked, "Is that what you want, Carmelita? Do you want me to leave here and go to Rachel?"

Carmelita's torment shone in her eyes. "No! I do not want you to leave! You are my husband, and I hold our marriage vows sacred. God has forgiven my one act of adultery, and all these years I have been faithful to our vows. If only . . ."

"What?" he encouraged.

"If only you could forgive me."

"If forgiveness is what you want from me, then you have it. You were a young spoiled girl and it was an impetuous act of youth. Nothing more."

Carmelita started to bring up the subject of their son, but decided against it. He could forgive adultery, but she feared he'd never forgive her neglect of their child.

"When will you be leaving?" Carmelita waited breathlessly in dread to hear his answer.

"I'm staying," he answered.

"But John . . ." she began.

"I said I'm staying!"

"I do not understand. You love her! Why . . ."

"Damn it, Carmelita!" he shouted. "Don't ask for explanations!"

"But John . . ."

"No!" he roared angrily. "Don't ask questions! Just accept my decision!" Detecting her hurt caused by his unfair outburst, he reached over and softly touched her cheek. "You should rest."

"Si, it has been a strenuous day for me."

With ease he lifted her in his arms and carried her to the bed. Laying her down gently, he replied, "I'll see you later."

She clutched his hand and brought it to her lips. "Oh John . . ."

He leaned over and placed a kiss on her forehead. "Rest well, Carmelita. When you awaken, I'll be here."

Tenderly, he smiled down at her with his boyish grin, then turned and walked out of the room. Carmelita's tears fell on her pillow. "Oh Rachel, please forgive me! You will have him for years and years. I only ask for days!"

It was with a mixture of anger and compassion that John walked steadily into the parlor. He headed straight for the bottle of bourbon on the cart behind the sofa. Swiftly he wrenched it open and poured a large portion of the liquid into a glass. In one swallow he emptied the full contents. Looking across the room, he saw Manuel watching him. Glaring at the man, he furiously threw the glass against the far wall. As it shattered into little pieces, John raged, "What kind of a sorry sonofabitch have you asked me to become?" He grabbed the bottle by the neck, and helped himself to another drink. "What in the hell am I doing? Am I waiting for my wife to die so that I can be free to marry another woman? What kind of man does that make me?" Again he tilted the bottle up for a drink. "I don't want her to die! Oh God! I want her to live!"

Slowly, Manuel moved toward him. "Amigo, if you continue to feel this way, her death will not set you free. Your guilt will imprison you."

"The cost of Carmelita's life for my happiness! It isn't worth the price!" His eyes glared with madness. "My God, Manuel, how can I ever be sure that somewhere deep inside of me, I won't be relieved when Carmelita dies. Only through her death can I marry Rachel!"

John watched as Manuel bowed his head, and let his shoulders grow limp. Sighing deeply, he lowered his large frame into a chair. Although he knew it could cost his daughter's happiness, he said, "John, my friend, I cannot let you punish yourself with such guilt and self hate. I hold you in high esteem, amigo, and I owe you the truth. I must be honest with you. My conscience will haunt me until my dying day if I allow you to feel this great guilt. Señor, you are free to go to the woman that you love. No one stands in your way."

"Manuel, I'm not staying here because I'm biding my time until Carmelita dies! Damn it, I'm staying with my wife because she needs me! And I can't bear to hurt her! I only wish to hell that Rachel and I weren't dependent on her death for our future!"

"But you are not," he mumbled.

Looking at the older man with confusion, John asked, "What do you mean?"

Manuel leaned over and placed his head in the palms of his hands. "Amigo, I have betrayed you and Carmelita. I have also sinned against God."

In haste John crossed over to him and paused stiffly in front of his chair. "How did you betray us?"

Manuel raised his head and looked up at him. "John, please try to understand, I beg of you, please do not tell Carmelita my confession." He leaned back in the chair and wiped the perspiration from his brow. "All I wanted, Señor, was my daughter's happiness. There was no happiness for her here and no future. Not until you came. You were not an outlaw. You were an honest and wealthy man. I wanted you to be my daughter's future."

"I know all this, Manuel. But I wanted to marry her."

"Amigo, you do not know what lengths I took to ensure my daughter's future. I was afraid if too much time passed, your friend Zeke would talk you out of marrying Carmelita. So at the time, I believed I had no other choice. Remember, Señor? Back then, there was no priest in town. But I told you and Carmelita that I was able to locate a priest who was passing through."

John could feel his nerves growing taut, and his large hands doubled into fists. "I remember."

Manuel's hands were wet from nervous sweat as he folded them together. "But I was not able to locate one.

I paid the man to impersonate a priest. You and Carmelita were never married."

John's fury was so severe that it distorted his face as he grabbed Manuel and pulled him to his feet. "Damn you! Damn you!" Abruptly, he turned him loose and the man fell back into the chair. "My God, how could you do that to your own daughter?"

"When she returned home, many times I wanted to tell her the truth. But when she became religious, I was too ashamed to let her know how her father had sinned against her."

"How could you let us go all these years believing we were married? And to think you had the damned gall to stand in this room only moments before and speak to me about my obligations to love my wife! Damn you, Manuel! All these years! All these wasted years! My God, why didn't you tell me before now?"

"I did not know how to find you."

"Did you even try?"

"If you had known, Señor, would your life have been different?"

Whirling away from him, the image of Rachel flashed into John's mind. Would I have married her, he wondered. After taking her virginity, would I have married her? That day in my office, could I have left for Fort Stanton, without marrying her first? . . . Aw Rachel, I would have married you! Regardless of our ages, I'd have married you!

"Yes!" he yelled. "My life would have been different!"

"Amigo, I have released your guilt. You need no longer wait for a wife to die, so that you can marry another woman. Go to the woman that you love. My

522

daughter and I do not stand in your way.''

John swerved back around and faced Manuel. "I still can't leave Carmelita.''

"Si, Señor, I knew you would not forsake my daughter. But now, amigo, you are merely being kind to someone who needs you. And you will continue to be kind, until she needs you no longer. Señor, I ask you, where is your guilt?'' When John didn't reply, Manuel asked, "It is gone, is it not, amigo? Do you not 'comprender'? The guilt, it is mine!''

The twirling mist was so dense that it obstructed her vision, and deliriously Rachel tried to escape the thick, smothering fog. The sound of a horse's hoofbeats returned. The mist magically vanished. From somewhere remote and high above, Rachel looked down and saw herself riding a horse across the plains. Then mysteriously, the swirling fog covered the scene. . . . The terrifying pain penetrated her heart!

The fog dissipated again and Rachel could see herself standing with one fist raised toward the sky. Everything around her was blurred and hazy, concealing from view all but the look of torment on her face. The gray mist fell from the heavens. . . . The pain was so unbearable that Rachel felt she was losing her mind!

When the fog dissolved once more, she was lying face-down on the grass. Rachel could hear her own woeful cry of heartbreak. The recurring fog crept over her soundlessly. The pain became so acute that she wanted to scream! Rachel tried desperately to waken but the heavy fog captured her in its eerie depths. Frantically, she fought her way out of the blinding mist!

* * *

Rachel's eyes flew open as she bolted straight up on the bed. Her hair, wet from perspiration and tears, clung to her face. "No! No!" she cried. Wildly her eyes searched the darkened bedroom, but as her stability returned, she fell dispiritedly back against the pillows. There were no strong arms to comfort her, and trembling from fear of the unknown, hard sobs tore from her throat.

She felt a cold nose touch her hand, and turning, Rachel looked down at the huge black dog. Moving over, she patted the side of the bed, and instantly he jumped up next to her. Rachel wrapped her arms around his furry neck and buried her face in his thick coat. Releasing her tears, she cried. Whining softly, Lopsided nestled protectively closer to his mistress.

John's strong physique was bent under the weight of his sorrow, as he lit the kerosene lamp beside Carmelita's bed. Sadness was in his eyes when he looked down on the woman, whose illness had made her so frail and exhausted.

"John," Carmelita whispered.

With extreme gentleness, he sat on the bed beside her, gathering her thin hand tenderly into his. Carmelita had been confined to bed for days. The small amount of strength that had sustained Carmelita for weeks had at last deserted her. John studied her pallid but still beautiful face. Not even the black hand of approaching death could rob Carmelita of her beauty.

"John," Carmelita whispered again in a voice that was weak, "we must talk. We can avoid our son no longer."

"No, Carmelita, don't think about it," he pleaded.

John was surprised at the strength left in the hand that suddenly clutched his tightly. "I must have your forgiveness! Oh John, please tell me you forgive me! Please!"

"His death was an accident," he replied.

"But it was my fault! Oh John, I let our little baby die!"

He brought her hand up to his lips and kissed the feverished palm. Holding her hand against his cheek, he answered, "Carmelita, don't torture yourself. You were so young and so immature. As a girl you were selfish and inconsiderate, but Carmelita, you have grown into a beautiful and compassionate woman." Gripping her hand tightly, he continued, "I forgive you, Carmelita. From the bottom of my heart, I forgive you." He placed his other hand over hers, and holding her slim hand between his, he asked, "Will you please forgive me?"

"Why do you want my forgiveness? You have done nothing wrong, my husband."

"For years, I unjustly hated you. You never deserved my hate. Carmelita, I'm sorry. At the time, I should've had more compassion and understanding. I shouldn't have hated you and turned on you the way I did."

Slowly she raised her other hand, and smiling, she brushed the unruly lock back from his forehead. "I want to thank you for these past months that you have shared with me. I was always afraid that I'd never see anything in your eyes for me but hate. But, my husband, I see in your eyes that you care. But John, you must go to Rachel!" A glow shone brightly on her face. "She loves you so! Always, I have known that you and

Rachel belong together. Dearest husband, it is with my blessings that I now send you back to her. Return to her, John. Life is too short to waste one precious moment." Tears filled her eyes. "Be happy! Please be happy!"

John wanted to find the right words to say, but his sorrow was too strong, forcing him to turn away to conceal his sadness.

"Hold me!" Carmelita pleaded. "Before you leave, hold me in your arms!"

Lying beside her, he drew her into his embrace. As she placed her head on his shoulder, he whispered, "Carmelita, I'm not leaving you."

PART FOUR

Chapter Thirteen

Rachel's employment in a saloon made Deborah's trips into town extremely embarrassing. When Rachel took up company with the simple George and a monstrous dog, Deborah's shame prevented her from going into town except to church on Sundays. But when Rachel was seen walking brazenly down the streets of town in the company of the three harlots employed by Edward, Deborah refused altogether to show her face in public; she remained home and hid in disgrace!

Rachel learned to live each day as it came, and her new way of life advanced into weeks and then into months. Rachel grew to love George and Lopsided. She had never had a closer friend than Edward, and she found a certain degree of companionship with the saloon girls. But Rachel was not happy. The recurring dream haunted her sleep frequently. Deep in her heart she grieved for her child, and not a moment passed that Rachel didn't long for John Reynolds.

On Sundays Edward would drive Rachel out to the ranch, where her weekly visits with her sister were always strained and uncomfortable. Often Rachel was tempted to terminate them entirely, but every Sunday

Rachel would consistently return. And with eternal hope glistening in her eyes, she'd ask Josh if he had heard from John. Sympathetic to her plea, he'd sadly shake his head, but Rachel would again refuse to abandon her hope.

One Sunday, on their way back to town, Edward became aware of Rachel's depression. Pulling the reins, he turned the buggy off the main road.

"Where are we going?" she asked.

"There's a cool spot a short way from here. I thought we'd stop for a while. Maybe you'll feel like telling me what's bothering you."

Maintaining her silence, Rachel stayed buried in her dismal thoughts as Edward guided the horses to the secluded glade. Jumping down from the carriage, he walked around and helped Rachel to the ground. Placing his arm over her shoulders, he led her to a large tree. Pausing beside it, he questioned, "Your visit with Deborah, was it that bad?"

"No different than usual," she answered.

"Then why the depression?"

"Oh Edward!" she sighed. "It's been over a year!"

"What has been over a year?"

He could hear her heartbreak when she cried, "Since I last saw John!"

"Sweetheart, I wish I knew where he was. I'd go after him and if necessary bring him back at gunpoint."

Smiling at him, she answered, "Now you're beginning to sound like a big brother."

"Just remember, Rachel. That's the way you wanted it. It wasn't what I wanted."

Wishing to avoid the course their conversation had

taken, Rachel walked away from him as she absent-mindedly surveyed her surroundings. The day was warm, but there was a pleasant breeze rippling the tree-tops. Grass was sparse in southern Texas, but it grew abundantly in the fertile glade. Suddenly, an inexplicable chill ran over her fleetingly. She could feel a nervous perspiration gathering on her brow.

Observing her distress, Edward hurried over to her. Clutching at his arm, Rachel cried, "I don't like it here!"

"What do you mean, you don't like it here? Rachel, what's wrong with you?" he asked confused.

"I don't know, but Edward, I want to leave!" He was touched by her heartrending plea, "Oh Edward, take me out of here! . . . Please!"

Taking her hand, he led her to the buggy. Not waiting for his assistance, she stepped up into the carriage.

Standing beside her, he asked, "Can't you tell me what it is about this place that frightens you?"

Tears came to her eyes as she looked around her. "I don't know, but I feel as if I've been here before."

"Maybe you were once in an area similar to this one, and something frightening happened. Perhaps when you were a child."

"No!" she began with excitement. "I've been here before, but I wasn't frightened."

Edward was startled when she cried hysterically, "The dream! This is where I am in my dream! Oh God, Edward, take me away! It's not fear that is waiting here for me! It's my sorrow!"

Hastily he climbed up into the carriage and grabbed her shoulders firmly. "That damned dream! Rachel, if you'd stop believing in the crazy nightmare, it'd probably go away!''

''It isn't crazy! Someday, it'll come true!''

Impatiently Edward picked up the reins and slapped them sharply against the horses. As the buggy lurched forward, he replied angrily, ''Dreams aren't premonitions! Damn it, Rachel, you're becoming obsessed by that dream!''

She clasped her hands together tightly, trying desperately to regain control of her emotions. Although Rachel was not capable of understanding her premonition; she now knew where it awaited her!

Edward's saloon was extremely crowded, and protectively, George escorted Rachel down the stairway for her afternoon performance. Keeping his large hand on her elbow, he led her to the piano. In his other hand, he carried his rifle.

Carl, the piano player, was waiting for Rachel, and appraising her beauty, he smiled admiringly. Carl was a small man, his hair beginning to thin.

Rachel liked Carl, but she had to force herself to return his smile. She was feeling terribly depressed. She had been feeling dispirited for days, but yesterday when Edward had taken her to the glade, her apathy had grown even stronger.

George propped his rifle against the piano. Putting his hands around Rachel's small waist, he lifted her with apparent ease and placed her on top of the piano.

Rachel made a pretty picture, causing many of the customers to eye her with desire and admiration. Her dress was pastel green and cut to reveal the fullness of her breasts. Her auburn hair fell seductively over her bare shoulders as she straightened the folds of her skirt, settling herself comfortably.

Once again, she had to compel herself to smile. The saloon became quiet as the patrons waited for Rachel to speak. "Carl," she began, her voice soft, with an undertone of sadness, "has written a very beautiful song. I would like to sing it for you."

Rachel hoped she could get through the song without crying. She had practiced it often with Carl, but it always brought tears to her eyes. It was as if the song had been written just for her and John. Oh John, she thought, my love waits for you!

Carl's agile fingers moved across the keys, and the slow, sentimental melody floated through the silent room. In her sweet, lovely voice, Rachel sang the words to Carl's song.

> Before the storm, with hearts unyielding,
> Our love awaits the wind.
> Like troubled, dark clouds gath'ring,
> Restless 'til the storm begins.
> Now we're caught up in its fury,
> The wind has reached the sky,
> Our love is in its glory . . .
> Lo . . . the storm passes by.
> In the stillness, all is over,
> Whis'pring breezes closing in.
> My love has gone forever,
> Drifting in the dying wind.

Rachel was unable to stop the tears that rolled down her cheeks as she continued:

* * *

Weeping willows bow in sorrow,
Crying raindrops, as they bend.
Though I know there's no tomorrow,
Still my love awaits the wind.

The applause was clamorous and the cheers rambunctious. Usually, Rachel gloried in her popularity, but tonight, she had to make herself appear as if she were enjoying the customer's praises. Oh why, she wondered, do I feel so depressed?

But suddenly, Rachel's false smile vanished as she spotted a tall man in buckskins pushing aside the swinging doors, leaving the saloon so quickly that she had barely caught a glimpse of him. She had only seen him from the back, but the man had been extremely tall, with powerful shoulders, and he had been wearing buckskins. She hadn't seen the color of his hair, because he had worn a hat. It could only be one man! John! It had to be John!

Gasping, Rachel leaped from the piano so swiftly that her full skirt and multiple petticoats flew upwards, giving the customers a quick and tantalizing glimpse of her long, shapely legs.

Worried, George grabbed hold of her arm. "Miss Rachel, what's wrong?"

Flinging his hand from her arm, she cried shrilly, "John! John!"

Wildly, Rachel began pushing her way through the jammed crowd. Puzzled by her irrational behavior, they stepped aside as she rushed madly toward the doors. Shoving the doors open, she heard Edward calling her name as she ran out to the sidewalk. Looking to the right, she once again caught the sight of a tall man in buckskins as he disappeared into the livery stable.

Lifting her cumbersome skirt, Rachel began fleeing toward the stable. Her heart was pounding so rapidly that her chest ached. Oh John, why? Why are you leaving me? Rachel's plea seemed to scream across her mind, making her head actually hurt from the piercing cry exploding through her heart, body, and soul.

Rachel was so overwrought that she didn't even hear Edward and George running behind her. She could hear nothing except her own heart crying out to the man she loved.

Reaching the stable, Rachel turned toward the entrance so sharply that she lost her balance. She fell to her knees, before catching herself by throwing her hands palms down on the ground. Near hysteria, tears streamed from her eyes, and using her hand she wiped at them to clear her vision. The dirt that clung to her hand mingled with Rachel's tears, leaving streaks across her face.

The tall man in buckskins was saddling his horse, and his back was turned to Rachel. He was at the far end of the stable, and getting to her feet, Rachel flew past the stalls. Oh John, don't leave me! Please don't leave me!, her heart begged as desperately she hurried to the tall man.

Panicking, Rachel grasped the man's arm, whirling him in her direction. Rachel's knees weakened, and she would have fallen if the man hadn't alertly grabbed her by the shoulders to steady her.

Looking up into a face she had never seen before in her life, Rachel became hysterical. Insensible, her fist pounded on the man's powerful chest. "No!" she screamed. "No! You're supposed to be John! No!

Damn you! Damn you!''

Shocked and annoyed by the woman's erratic behavior, the stranger was relieved to spot the two men rushing into the stable. He hoped they were coming after the woman. He didn't want to hurt the lady, but if she continued hitting him, he would be forced to restrain her physically. He had heard her perform at the saloon, and she certainly hadn't appeared to be so irrational.

Edward was the first one to reach them, and strongly he pulled Rachel away from the stranger. Rachel's hysteria was climbing to its peak, and insanely she fought against Edward's tenacious hold. "Let me go!" she shrieked. "Let me go!" Blindly, she struck out at Edward, but easily he avoided her careless blows.

Grabbing her by the shoulders, Edward shook her roughly. He continued to shake her, until finally, her hysteria faded, replaced by soft, pitiful whimpers. Tenderly, he drew her into his arms, hugging her close.

"Oh Edward," Rachel cried piteously. "I thought he was John."

"I know, sweetheart. I know," he crooned soothingly. He held her for a moment, then releasing her, he coaxed gently, "Let's go, honey." Taking Rachel's hand, Edward began leading her toward the entrance to the stable, as George apologized to the stranger for Rachel's peculiar behavior.

Abruptly Rachel paused, and looking at Edward, she stated calmly, "John isn't coming back." Her chin quivered, but bravely, Rachel controlled her emotions as she continued, "Oh God, Edward, I lost him! I lost the only man I'll ever truly love!"

"Rachel, you don't know that," Edward tried to reassure her.

Slowly, Rachel shook her head. "No, it's over."

"You only feel this way because of what happened. It was such a traumatic disappointment . . ."

Interrupting, Rachel replied, "But this incident has made me face the truth. John isn't coming back to me." Rachel shrugged casually, and her quiet composure worried Edward. "Maybe, he never really loved me." Removing her hand from Edward's, she continued dispassionately, "I want to be alone. Please, Edward, let me be alone."

Quickly Rachel left the stable, but she knew she would be returning. Her destiny was lurking, waiting for her; it had been waiting for years.

Edward and George were in the saloon, standing at the bar discussing Rachel, when suddenly, she appeared at the top of the stairs. She had exchanged her dress for trousers and a plaid shirt. Her long hair was falling loosely around her face. They watched her as she quickly descended the stairs.

Completely oblivious to the usual hubbub in the saloon, Rachel headed straight for the front doors. Before departing, she whirled sharply, her gaze meeting Edward's. For a brief moment, their thoughts were telepathically communicated from one to the other. Edward knew exactly where she was going and why, and Rachel sensed he whole-heartedly approved.

Rachel smiled at Edward, but her smile was so weak that it barely curled the corners of her mouth. Turning swiftly, she darted out of the saloon, but Rachel's tiny smile had touched Edward's heart more than anything she could have said.

"Where is she goin', Mr. Edward?" George asked.

Edward filled his shot glass with whiskey, then downed it in one drink. Sitting the glass down heavily, he mumbled, more to himself than to George, "She's going to tell John Reynolds 'goodbye.' "

When Rachel returned to the stable to get Edward's horse, she put his bridle reins on him, but she didn't bother to saddle him. After all, in her dream, the horse was never saddled, was he?

Rachel gave the stallion free rein, and powerfully the animal sped across the plains. Riding at a breakneck speed, Rachel's hair was blown back from her face, the long tresses streaming in the wind.

She would live her dream! And then . . . and then it would miraculously go away! Her pain and heartache would be gone forever!

Rachel's thoughts tore severely at her heart. . . . I must tell John "goodbye"! . . . He's never coming back to me! . . . Never! . . . Never! . . . Never! . . . The word screamed through her heart. Never be held in his strong arms! Never hear his robust laughter! Never see his boyish crooked grin!

Rachel's pain grew so acute that it penetrated cruelly into her mind, body, heart, and soul. She had lost her love! She had lost John Reynolds!

Abruptly she slowed the stallion's pace, and changing course, she headed the horse toward the fertile glade where Edward had taken her. When they reached the green meadow, the horse halted, and leisurely began nibbling at the tall grass.

Sliding from the horse's back, Rachel despondently walked a few paces before pausing. She bowed her head as a southern wind to emerged. It whipped at her hair, spreading it across her tormented face.

As her emotional pain grew unbearable, she slowly looked up toward the sky that was beginning to grow dark with the approaching night. Shaking her fist at the heavens, she cried, "Why? Why was I destined to love John, only to lose him? I don't want to live without him! He's my life! My very reason for living!"

The wind whispered forlornly through the treetops, and Rachel fell to her knees. Hanging her head, her small shoulders grew limp. "I have to tell him 'good-bye' ", she moaned. "I can't go on this way. I can't keep waiting for a man who is never coming back to me."

Doubling her hands into fists, she cried so loudly that her voice carried over the silent meadow and across the surrounding plains. "John!" she yelled. "I love you! I love you, John Reynolds! I love you!"

Falling down in the grass, she pillowed her head across her arms, and heartbroken, Rachel wept.

Sitting at the desk in his study, John Reynolds asked, "You wanted to speak with me, Mrs. Kendall?"

Feeling uneasy, Deborah stood next to the chair across from his desk. The man's strong masculinity still awed her and made her quite uncomfortable.

John had arrived unexpectedly at his ranch only moments before. He had asked immediately about Rachel, but Josh had simply informed him that she was living in town.

"I must speak to you concerning my sister," she said softly.

Instantly his eyebrows were raised, and a tension could be seen on his face. "Rachel? Is she all right?"

"Yes, she's fine. But, Mr. Reynolds, you have always had a lot of influence with her. Will you please tell her that she must move back home?''

"Why should I?" he questioned.

"Because Rachel doesn't belong in a saloon!"

"A saloon!" he shouted. "What in the hell is she doing in a saloon?"

"Not only does she work in the place, but she lives there!"

"What!" he bellowed. While trying to suppress his rage, John suggested, "Mrs. Kendall, why don't you sit down and tell me just what in the hell is going on."

Nervously she sat on the very edge of the chair. "Mr. Reynolds, so much had happened since you last saw Rachel."

"I'm already aware of her past abduction and William Granger's death. I also know that she lost her son."

Looking at him with surprise, she asked, "But how . . . ?"

"It's not important," he replied briskly.

"When Rachel returned home from her horrible ordeal, she came here to live with us. Soon after, her husband was murdered. Then about four months later, Edward purchased that saloon in town."

"Phillips?" he questioned.

"Yes, and . . . and he actually had the bad taste to give Rachel a job."

"Doing what?" he demanded.

A flush appeared in Deborah's cheeks as she explained, "She certainly isn't a . . . a . . . a loose woman! She sings!"

"Sings!" he repeated.

"Yes, but that is all!" she stated with finality.

"Mrs. Kendall, I never thought she had been hired as a prostitute."

Deborah had never been more embarrassed. Must he be so blunt?, she wondered. Quickly changing the subject, she informed him, "There are rooms above the saloon. And that is where she lives."

"It's extremely dangerous for Rachel to be living above a saloon. Anyone could force his way into her room. I should think Edward would have better sense then to put her safety in jeopardy."

Deborah's lips tightened angrily over her teeth. "Oh, she's protected! By a monstrous simpleton named George. Plus a ferocious dog, that actually sleeps in her room!" Rising from the chair, she leaned across the desk, and her eyes were blazing wildly. "Sometimes, I'm almost glad that Mama and Papa are not alive to see how their daughter has fallen!"

"Tell me about this George and the dog," John said calmly.

Returning to her chair, she answered, "Edward hired the man to protect Rachel. He stays with her when she's performing and stands outside her door, until the saloon is closed. And then, she is protected by that huge animal!"

"You say George is a simpleton?"

"He's a grown man, but he has the mentality of a child. I'm afraid that someday he may turn on Rachel and . . . and attack her!"

Because of her anger and overwrought nerves, the look of disgust on John's face went unnoticed by Deborah. "Mrs. Kendall, obviously the man is mentally retarded, not insane. And where did this dog come from?"

"He was a stray, but George started taking care of him. Then he gave the dog to Rachel, because he was losing sleep worrying about someone breaking into her room."

"And that's the kind of man that you're afraid will turn on Rachel?"

"Well, with his type you never can tell!" Not detecting the coldness in the steel-gray eyes staring at her, she continued breathlessly, "It's gotten so bad that I'm ashamed to show my face in public! When Rachel first went to work in a saloon, I was almost too embarrassed to go into town. Then when she became bosom friends with that simpleton, I almost died of disgrace. But, Mr. Reynolds, she has been seen on the streets with those . . . women . . . who work for Edward! Well, needless to say, after that I discontinued my trips to town!"

Deborah was taken totally by surprise when John unexpectedly threw back his head and laughed uproariously. Leaping from her chair, she shouted, "Mr. Reynolds, this situation is not humorous!"

His laughter ceased, but he was still grinning widely as he replied, "Rachel and the town misfits!"

Feeling greatly perturbed, Deborah said severely, "You sound as if you were proud of her!" Irritated with him, she sat back down.

John rose from his chair and walked around the desk. Due to his towering height, Deborah was forced to lift her head at an uncomfortable angle to see into his face.

"Proud of her?" his strong voice roared. "You're damned right, I'm proud of her!"

"Well, it's quite obvious that I'll receive no help from you!" she huffed.

Sitting on the edge of his desk, he studied the young

woman closely. He noticed she no longer wore her hair pulled back into a severe bun. She still wore it up, but it was fashioned to hang becomingly loose around her face. Her dress was a floral print of multiple and flattering colors. He wondered if Deborah was aware of how beautiful she could be, if she were to soften the hardness in her eyes and the sternness at her mouth.

"It's hard to believe that you and Rachel are sisters. Rachel is a very warm and compassionate woman."

Holding her small frame stiffly, she inquired, "And I?"

"Mrs. Kendall, you are very cold and totally uncharitable!"

Her dark eyes glared with resentment. "How dare you!" she hissed.

Raising his eyebrows, and wrinkling his brow, he replied, "How dare I, Mrs. Kendall? How dare you, to belittle the woman I love!"

"But I love her too!" she cried.

"Do you? And your husband, do you love him?"

Becoming ill at ease, she answered hesitantly, "Yes . . . yes . . . of course I do!"

"Do you ever bother to tell him?"

Swiftly she got to her feet, but in doing so, she found herself in such close contact with the large man that she caught her breath in dismay. Awkwardly, she turned to move away, but instantly he grabbed her arm. The strength in his powerful grasp held her motionless.

He was so near that Deborah could feel his breath against her face. "Tell me, Mrs. Kendall, do you invite Edward Phillips to sit at your table for dinner?"

"Of course!" she replied sternly.

"You tell me that you're glad your parents aren't

alive to see how Rachel has fallen." His grip on her arm tightened painfully. "What would your father have said about you dining with a man who was once a slave?"

For an instant Edward's handsome face crossed her mind, as she tried desperately to ignore the unforgotten love that could still tug at her heart. Tears filled her eyes, and her chin quivered. Controlling her distress, she answered, "He would have disowned me!"

Dropping into the chair and wiping at her tears, Deborah admitted, "You made your point, Mr. Reynolds. I was wrong to judge George because he . . . he . . . isn't as fortunate as others."

Leaning his tall frame against the desk, he inquired teasingly, "And the women who work for Edward?"

Deborah raised her eyes and looked up into his face. He was smiling down at her, and blushing, she replied, "Mr. Reynolds . . . please!"

Suppressing the urge to laugh, he turned and walked behind his desk. Returning to his chair, he said, "When you allow your heart to guide you, instead of your father's teachings, you're a warm and charitable young lady."

"Like my sister?" she asked.

His crooked boyish grin appeared on his face. "I doubt if Rachel ever practiced what your parents preached."

Laughing lightly, Deborah replied, "When we were girls at home, she used to do the most outrageous things! She embarrassed poor Mama continually. Why, she'd wear trousers, ride astraddle, and tag along behind our brothers. Much to Mama's embarrassment, and Papa's concern, Rachel was determined to be a tomboy. She climbed trees like a boy, learned to shoot a rifle, and never once suffered the vapors, as all young ladies were expected to suffer on occasion. But gracefully, of course.'' Deborah puckered her face, unaware that the expression made her appear delightfully cute. ''Rachel could even put a worm on a fishing hook without feeling squeamish. Our brothers teased Rachel a lot, but they were so proud of her! And actually, I think they were thrilled to have their little sister following them around. Oh, Mr. Reynolds, they loved her so much!'' With a questioning look in her eyes, she continued, ''So many have loved Rachel. Not only her own family but . . . Edward, Zeke, George, and I think maybe . . . another man loved her also.''

''Klu Bronson?'' he inquired.

''But how did you know?'' she asked with surprise.

''It doesn't matter, but you're right. He loves her, and so did my wife.''

''Your wife!'' she exclaimed.

''Rachel hasn't spoken to you about Carmelita?''

''No!'' she answered.

''Obviously, you are not Rachel's confidante.'' He rose from the chair and moving toward her, he said, ''Mrs. Kendall, many have loved Rachel, but none more so than I.'' Pausing in front of her, he leaned over and placed his hands on the arms of her chair. She was taken aback by his nearness, and her eyes opened wide in astonishment. His smile curled the corners of his moustache. ''You can rest easy, madam. Rachel will not be working in a saloon much longer.''

Flustered by his closeness, she replied breathlessly, ''Thank you, Mr. Reynolds.''

Deborah thought he would stop being so brazen and

step back, but he only continued smiling, as he replied, "I think we should call one another by our Christian names."

Barely able to find her voice, she asked, "Why?"

"I hope to become your brother-in-law. When I see Rachel, I plan to ask her to marry me."

"But you're already married!"

"No, ma'am. I'm not married," he answered softly, stepping away from her chair.

Rising quickly, Deborah asked, "Your wife, did she . . . ?"

Cutting her off rudely, he replied, "I'd rather not discuss it!"

"But," she began, "I always thought the difference in your ages would prevent you from marrying Rachel."

"Our ages scare me. I'm forty-five years old, and Rachel is not yet twenty-two. I fear that someday she will look at me and see an old man. If her love should ever turn into pity . . ." In long strides, he crossed over to the door. Placing his hand on the doorknob, he turned back to look at Deborah. "Are you against our marriage?"

Deborah's smile was so bright it lit up her face. "Against your marriage? I thank God you have returned. Rachel loves you so much! I couldn't be happier, Mister . . . I mean, John!"

Opening the door, he called, "Josh!" When he wasn't answered immediately, he roared, "Lieutenant Kendall! Report in here on the double! I have business to discuss with you!"

Hurrying from the back of the house, Josh answered from habit, "Yes, sir! Right away, sir!"

* * *

Edward was seated at a rear table when John Reynolds stepped into the saloon. Out of the corner of his eye, Edward caught a quick glimpse of a man dressed in buckskins, but thinking it was the same man who had been in the stable, Edward gave him little thought. He continued to stare at the whiskey bottle sitting on the table in front of him, his thoughts returning unequivocally to Rachel.

Pausing in the middle of the room, John tried to find Rachel or Edward. The saloon was quite crowded, but glancing toward the rear of the room, he spotted Edward. Maneuvering his way past the customers, most of them rowdy with drink, John hurried over to where Edward was sitting.

Standing beside Edward's chair, he said strongly, "Hello, Phillips."

Edward had been in the process of taking a drink, but recognizing the man's voice, Edward dropped his glass, and hitting the table it rolled off, spilling the contents.

Springing to his feet, Edward grabbed John's hand, shaking it vigorously. Grinning from ear to ear, he exclaimed, "Man, are you ever a sight for sore eyes! I can't believe it! You're actually here!"

John hadn't expected Edward to be quite so happy to see him. Edward continued to pump John's hand vibrantly, and grinning, he replied, "I only hope Rachel is as happy to see me as you are."

"Rachel," Edward repeated vaguely, still in shock that John Reynolds had actually returned.

"I just came from the ranch, and Deborah has told me everything." Finding Edward's continual handshake a little embarrassing, John pulled his hand free from Edward's firm grip. "Deborah and Josh will be here shortly!" Looking around, he asked, "Where is Rachel?"

Pulling out one of the chairs at the table, Edward said, "Sit down. Before you see Rachel, I have something to tell you."

Obliging, John sat down as Edward returned to his own chair. Hastily Edward told John about Rachel mistaking the man in the stable to be him. He told John about her hysterical behavior, and the eerie calmness that had followed.

"Where is she?" John asked.

"She's gone to live that damned recurring dream," Edward replied.

Confused, John answered, "I don't understand."

"She believes that dream is a premonition."

"I know," John replied impatiently.

There were no glasses on the table, so Edward took a drink out of the bottle. Handing it to John, he explained, "A premonition she has lost you forever."

Accepting the bottle, John helped himself to a generous drink. Setting it back on the table, he asked calmly, "Where do I find her?"

Night had fallen, but the moon was full, casting a soft glow over the secluded glade. Rachel had no idea how much time had passed since she had first arrived. She seemed to have lost all track of time. She had fallen into her recurring dream as one would plunge into a bottomless pit. She had no place to go, except farther and farther down into a vast emptiness.

Rachel was still lying in the grass. She had cried and

cried, until at last, there were no tears left to shed.

Slowly, she pushed herself up to a sitting position. Her hair was mussed, falling wildly across her cheeks. Unconsciously, she pushed the heavy tresses back from her face.

Edward's horse whinnied, as his ears picked up a sound and his nose detected a strange scent. But Rachel was unmindful of everything, except her own sorrow.

Once again, Rachel clenched her hands into fists, as suddenly, a raging anger consumed her. Looking up at the sky, she cried from the bottom of her heart, "I've always known this day would come to pass! Oh John, deep down inside I knew, I always knew my dream meant that someday you would break my heart!"

"No, my love."

As she looked behind her, Rachel's hand flew to her mouth to hold back a scream. My God, her grief was driving her mad! John's voice! Was it really John's voice she had heard?

Stepping out of the dark shadows, John continued, "Rachel, your dream only represented all the pain and heartache you had to endure, before I could finally come to you to surrender my heart."

Rachel wanted to jump to her feet and run to the man approaching, but her shock rendered her incapable of moving. This was no fantasy, no illusion! John Reynolds had come back to her! She longed to cry his name, but her voice was only a hoarse whisper, "John! . . . John!"

Rachel thought she had no tears left to shed, but sudden tears filled her eyes. Overflowing, they streamed down her face as she watched John Reynolds coming closer and closer to her.

The full moon shone down on the man she loved, making it possible for Rachel to see him clearly. Oh, how could she have mistaken the man in the saloon to be John? He hadn't been nearly as tall, or his shoulders nearly so powerful!

John wasn't wearing a hat, and as he drew even closer, Rachel noticed the gray at his temples, mingling attractively with his golden brown hair. She was surprised to see he had grown a moustache, but she approved. It made him even more handsome, if that were possible.

He paused at her side, and because she was sitting, she had to arch her head to look up into his face. Although her tears were flowing down her cheeks, Rachel had to smile at the way John's unruly locks still fell haphazardly across his forehead.

Gazing down at Rachel, John could see her love for him written all over her beautiful face. In that moment, John knew beyond a doubt that the difference in their ages would never stop Rachel from loving him. Their ages only made their love more precious. So precious that they must never waste one minute of it.

Leaning over, he took her hands, drawing her to her feet. Rachel looked up into his face, and smiling his boyish crooked grin, he said lovingly, "Hello, my beautiful little hypocrite."

Rachel's deep sobs came to her all at once, and crying heavily, she could only say his name over and over, "John! John! John!"

Cupping her face in his hands, John kissed her forehead, then her cheeks, tasting the salt from her tears. Slowly, he moved his lips to hers. At first, their kiss was tender, both of them content just to feel the other's touch. But suddenly, John drew her into his arms so strongly, that Rachel actually gasped while her lips were still under his.

Placing his hand on the back of her head, he pressed her mouth to his, their kiss becoming so passionate that Rachel felt as if she were drowning in a pool of ecstasy, and she hoped she never came up for air.

John held her slim frame against his so tightly that they seemed to become an inseparable part of each other.

Slowly, almost reluctantly, John removed his lips from hers. Keeping her in his arms, he whispered, "Rachel . . . I love you, Rachel. Baby, I love you so much."

"Oh John!" she cried. "I thought you were never coming back! Why did you wait so long? How did you know where to find me? I have so many things to tell you! I'm not married! Oh, John, I'm free! Free to be with you!"

He stepped back from her, so that he could see into her face. As the gray eyes she loved so much gazed into her own eyes, Rachel knew she could never have told this man "goodbye." Her heart belonged only to him, for now and always.

Tenderly, John brushed his fingers across her cheeks, wiping away the last traces of her tears. "We have a lot to discuss, Rachel, but it will have to wait." His deep voice broke with passion, as he confessed, "I want you so badly, it's driving me mad!"

His confession aroused her physical need for him more than any caress could have, and flinging herself into his arms, Rachel cried, "Oh yes! Yes, my darling! I want you too! Please, please make love to me!"

Instantly, his mouth was possessing hers, and his kiss made her feel so weak that she felt as if she were melting in his arms.

Releasing her, he said hastily, "I have two blankets on my horse."

Her face glowing with love, Rachel never took her eyes off him as he hurried to fetch the blankets. As he returned, she marveled at the way he always moved with such grace and strength.

Quickly, he spread one of the blankets on the grass, placing the other one beside it. Then he stood at her side, without touching her. She wanted him to take her back into his arms, and puzzled, she looked deeply into his eyes, trying to read his thoughts. But his expression was indiscernible.

"John, what's wrong?" she asked, worried.

He smiled, and as always, his smile touched her heart. "Nothing is wrong," he answered. "I only wanted to look at you."

She also smiled. Barely above a whisper, she said, "I love you, John Reynolds, and I will always love you."

Easily, he lifted her in his arms, and kneeling, he placed her on the blanket. Leaning over her, his lips came down on hers. She opened her mouth beneath his, and their kiss grew intense, sending an exciting thrill through Rachel's entire being.

He removed his lips from hers long enough to whisper her name, then once again his mouth was ravishing hers. Rachel could taste a salty tang as she returned his demanding kiss, but she wasn't sure if the salt had come from her tears, or if he was also shedding tears.

Their love-making didn't come to them gently; instead their passions exploded. Their restricting clothes were removed quickly, flung to the side in disorderly heaps.

When, at last, they lay close with nothing but flesh touching flesh, John ran light kisses over Rachel's neck, and down to the hollow of her throat. Tenderly, his hand caressed her breast. Moaning with desire, Rachel familiarized herself with the touch and feel of his hard, masculine body. Moving her hand across his chest, she could feel the strength in the strong muscles rippling beneath her fingertips. Lowering her hand, she found his male hardness. She could feel John tremble as her fingers closed around him.

"Rachel, my love," he groaned, before taking her hand and bringing it to his lips. "There's magic in your fingers, a magic that drives me wild."

Crushing her against him, he pried her lips open beneath his, and as his tongue entered to explore her mouth intimately, Rachel thrust her thighs upward against his.

Using his lips and hands, John brought Rachel to such great heights of passion that she thought she would die if he didn't hurry and take her.

"Now!" she pleaded. "Oh John, I want you!"

Moving over her, he parted her legs with his knee, and locking his lips to hers, he penetrated her swiftly. Clinging to him tightly, she arched her hips, accepting his manhood completely. Rachel's nails dug into John's bare skin, and wrapping her legs around his back, she drew him into her so deeply that the thrill of him being inside her made her bite into her bottom lip. Their passion mounted as they thrust against each other powerfully, reaching for that wonderful fulfillment that had been denied them for so long. Wildly, their love built to a mutual and exciting climax, causing Rachel to cry out loud in total ecstasy.

He kissed her tenderly, before moving to lie at her side. Taking the other blanket, he spread it over them. She went into his arms, nestling her head on his shoulder. Brushing his lips across her flushed brow, he whispered, "I love you, Rachel. And I've come to believe that you were right all along. Our love was predestined."

"Oh John, it's so beautiful, isn't it?" she cried.

"Our love?" he asked.

"Yes," she answered.

Pulling her even closer, he replied, "My sentiments exactly."

She snuggled against him intimately, and with their passion momentarily satisfied, Rachel and John brought one another up to date on what had been happening in their lives. Rachel spoke of her baby, and as she did, John kissed away her tears as she grieved for her son. They talked about Zeke, as they shared their special memories of him. John told her that Carmelita had died. She was sad to hear that her friend was gone, but she was grateful that it hadn't taken Carmelita's death to set John free. Although he didn't tell her, Rachel knew he had stayed away so long because of Carmelita. But Rachel wasn't angry or bitter, she only loved John all the more for not forsaking the gentle Carmelita. But she felt a strong resentment toward Manuel. If he hadn't kept his deceit a secret, she and John could have married years before. She would never have married William Granger, and all that came, would never have been. John said very little about Klu Bronson, and wisely, Rachel didn't press him to say more.

"Before going to town, I stopped at the ranch to talk to Josh and Deborah," John told her.

"Did you have a special reason?" she asked.

"Yes, I'm selling Josh a good portion of grazing land, and fifty head of cattle. There's also a cabin on the land. It's small, but they can build on to it."

Tilting her head, she looked at him questioningly. Understanding her expression, he chuckled pleasantly, before kissing the tip of her nose. "After we are married, they will need a place to live."

Rachel actually gleamed. "Married! Oh John, at last we are going to be married! It's almost too wonderful to be true!"

"Believe it, my love. You are going to be Mrs. John Reynolds, until death do us part." Suddenly Rachel frowned touchingly, and concerned, he asked quickly, "What is it?"

"George," she sighed sadly. "What will happen to George? He'll have to go back working at the black-smith's, and Ben treats him cruelly."

John smiled, loving her kindness. "Pedro is getting old, and I'm sure he'd appreciate an assistant. We'll offer George the job, and he can live in the bunkhouse."

"He'll be so happy!" Rachel exclaimed. "George is totally dedicated to me! And I'm so fond of him." Once again, Rachel frowned, but John already knew what she was going to say.

Laughing good-humoredly, he added, "And George can bring the dog with him."

Wrapping her arms around him, she cried, "I am so happy! So very happy!" Becoming serious, she asked, "John, do you think my dream will return?"

"No, my love. Now, that all your heartache is behind you, there is no reason for your dream to recur." Swatting her on the rear, he said playfully, "It's time to get up."

Snuggling closer to him, she murmured, "No, I want to stay just like this forever."

"Well, if you insist, my passionate little hypocrite, we can stay here all night and make love. But, of course, we'll miss our own wedding."

Bolting straight up, she exclaimed, "Wedding!"

Grinning, he replied, "Don't you think it's about time I made you an honest woman?"

"Do you mean, we're getting married tonight?" she asked breathlessly.

Rachel was unaware of how sweet and vulnerable he found her at that moment. John himself was amazed by how much he loved the enticing Rachel O'Brian. "Why should we wait to get married?" he asked. "Haven't we already waited long enough?"

"I'll get dressed immediately!" she decided.

Chuckling, he grabbed her arm, pulling her to his side. "Don't you want to hear about our wedding plans?"

"What do you mean?" she asked.

"Deborah and Josh are in town making arrangements with the priest."

"Deborah!" Rachel exclaimed. "But John, I thought Deborah disapproved of our love."

"You have her approval and her blessings. Your sister loves you very much." He laughed lightly, recalling his earlier conversation with Deborah. "But she finds it a little difficult to understand you."

"You can say that again!" Rachel agreed. "But I

know she loves me, and I love her too."

"By the time we get back to town, everyone will be at the church waiting."

"Everyone?" she asked.

"Deborah, Josh, Edward, and George," he answered. "Oh yes, I almost forgot. Deborah is bringing you a dress. It seems she made it for your birthday, but now she wants it to be your wedding dress. I already bought you a wedding band, but Josh has it. He'll be my best man."

Perturbed, Rachel sat up, her green eyes flashing indignantly. "John Reynolds, how dare you!"

Trying not to laugh, he asked innocently, "How dare I what?"

"How dare you go to my sister's home and make my wedding plans without consulting me first!"

"Do you want to call it off?" he asked, jokingly.

"Not on your life!" she answered promptly. "By the way, John Reynolds, haven't you ever heard of asking a lady to marry you, instead of just taking it for granted?"

Incapable of suppressing his laughter, he told her between chuckles, "I thought we agreed a long time ago that you are no lady. Besides, Rachel, we both know you've been trying to get me to propose matrimony ever since we shared the Oregon Trail."

"You are the most conceited, ill-mannered, and egotistical man I've ever known!"

Still laughing, he teased, "But you love me, don't you?"

Smiling, she knelt beside him, punching him playfully. While trying to avoid her blows, he grabbed her around the waist and pulled her down beside him. Rolling over, he pinned her small frame beneath him. "Tell me you love me!" he ordered.

Looking up into his face, her eyes shone with adoration. "John Reynolds, I love you, and I will love you until the day I die!"

THE BEST IN HISTORICAL ROMANCE

PASSION'S RAPTURE   (912, $3.50)
by Penelope Neri
Through a series of misfortunes, an English beauty becomes the captive of the very man who ruined her life. By day she rages against her imprisonment—but by night, she's in passion's thrall!

JASMINE PARADISE   (1170, $3.75)
by Penelope Neri
When Heath sets his eyes on the lovely Sarah, the beauty of the tropics pales in comparison. And he's soon intoxicated with the honeyed nectar of her full lips. Together, they explore the paradise . . . of love.

SILKEN RAPTURE   (1172, $3.50)
by Cassie Edwards
Young, sultry Glenda was innocent of love when she met handsome Read deBaulieu. For two days they revelled in fiery desire only to part—and then learn they were hopelessly bound in a web of SILKEN RAPTURE.

FORBIDDEN EMBRACE   (1105, $3.50)
by Cassie Edwards
Serena was a Yankee nurse and Wesley was a Confederate soldier. And Serena knew it was wrong—but Wesley was a master of temptation. Tomorrow he would be gone and she would be left with only memories of their FORBIDDEN EMBRACE.

PORTRAIT OF DESIRE   (1003, $3.50)
by Cassie Edwards
As Nicholas's brush stroked the lines of Jennifer's full, sensuous mouth and the curves of her soft, feminine shape, he came to feel that he was touching every part of her that he painted. Soon, lips sought lips, heart sought heart, and they came together in a wild storm of passion. . . .

Available wherever paperbacks are sold, or order direct from the Publisher. Send cover price plus 50¢ per copy for mailing and handling to Zebra Books, 475 Park Avenue South, New York, N.Y. 10016. DO NOT SEND CASH.